The Watchman's Son

R.J. Stachofsky

This book is dedicated to my family.

To my beautiful and lovely wife Lori; with her ever-present smile and continual joy in her heart, she managed to remain steadfast, always helping me to adjust my moral compass, which allowed me to navigate through this journey. She is my partner in all things, work, play, successes, and failures.

To my son Patrick, by experiencing his birth into this life, I was able to instantly know what unconditional Love truly meant and with that how much my parents must have loved each one of their children.

To my beautiful daughters, Rebecca and Leanne, they taught me that God had not given up on me and blessed me with a second and third chance. I have walked this earth and met many people, but these four and now my grandchildren have given me a gift that cannot be purchased with any amount of money, gold or silver. They have given me the gift of Listening: Listening and Hearing My VOICE.

Acknowledgments

I give a very special thank you to my daughters, Becky and Leanne for their detailed assistance in the editing of this book.

I would like to thank my brother-in-law, Mike for the advice he gave to me when I asked him, "How do I turn this rough draft into a finished book?" He told me in the only way I could understand, "Treat it like a wood working project, sand it until it is polished."

A very special thank you goes to Danielle DeMarco for her detailed illustrations. Danielle listened to my descriptions, deciphered some of my own sketches and photos and with her talent was able to bring them to life to be inserted into the pages of this book. Danielle is currently enrolled at Northern Arizona University.

A brief introduction

Jacob Sparks is a wanderer in his mid thirties. He has spent half his life traveling the back roads of Western Oregon looking for answers to his seemingly endless walk. It is close to the turn of the century as America is about to change from the war torn civil war years into the mightiest industrialized nation on earth.

Jacob's journey led him to learn a trade as a carpenter; a skill that has allowed him to never be a free loader. He has worked in the largest city in the state. He has been welcomed by Native Americans and taught the necessary skills that helped him to survive his nomadic life.

Jacob stumbles upon a place to rest his weary body in hopes of rejuvenation. Unbeknownst to him, he is about to retrace the steps from his earlier years that started him on this path of restless meandering.

Jacob is tired; tired of walking, tired of wandering, tired of searching. He is finally ready to live a simpler way of life.

Part One

Fletcher's Crossing

Chapter 1

As I round the bend of another dusty road, I once again fumble in my money pouch confirming what I have known for the past week; I have very little coinage. I've got just a few coppers and one silver half dollar. Tucked away safe is "Lady Liberty". I should have enough to pay the fee to cross the Rogue River by ferry, but before I cross, I need to rest a couple of days first. These past few weeks of walking have been long and hard. I'm tired, dusty and hungry. Maybe the salmon will be running? If so, I can catch one for a fresh meal and fill my belly while I rest. Yeah, that's what I need most; fill my belly and rest a bit before heading down the road again.

With the river not yet in sight, I turn my good ear to the muffled sound of fast moving water or, could it be the breeze swirling through the tree tops? My nose catches a faint whiff of smoke. That's always a relief, that'll mean some folks could be living close by. If I'm lucky and they are friendly to strangers, maybe they won't mind if I rest a few days. God knows I need it.

I'd be able to wash these clothes out, work for a couple of home cooked meals and catch up on the local news. Hell, I don't even recall what the date is.

With each foot fall, I grow excited. I am anxious to rest at the river's edge but nervous for what lies ahead. Walking the back roads can be an adventure but I can't deny the weariness that overcomes me with being alone. With only myself to talk to, I let my mind drift back to the memory of passing this way one time before.

As I recall, there wasn't much to Fletcher's Crossing, just a rickety, old ferry and a small cabin. The ferry wasn't much bigger than a raft, just big enough for a wagon and its team to fit on. I shared the ferry with a wagon, its driver, and team of horses. With no room to move about I had to stand between the wheels of the wagon in order to stay out of the way of the three men that worked the ferry.

There were two long sagging ropes that stretched from river bank to river bank. The ropes were attached to two of the largest Douglas fir trees I had ever seen. Those trees seemed to be perfectly set on each side of the river just for the purpose of being the anchor points for the ferry. While two of the men used long poles to push the ferry across, the third man pulled on the two ropes that kept us from floating down stream and into a jagged set of rapids.

I remember praying, as I stood between those wagon wheels, praying that a couple of ropes and a rickety old raft would hold together long enough to cross a cold, fast moving river. I remember being anxious for the other side and scared for the unknown life that I had thrust myself in to.

The ferry had cost me two coppers back then and I didn't mind paying it. Using the ferry at Fletcher's Crossing had saved me a twenty mile walk farther east to cross the bridge at Waters.

It wasn't just the extra twenty mile walk that worried me, it was the need to get as far away from these parts and as fast as possible. Crossing on the ferry got me headed north in hopes of finding the refuge I was in need of.

That was a long time ago. I can't remember the exact year.

I tell myself it was around 1880 but that can't be right. It seems like just yesterday; my body tells me it's been a lifetime of yesterdays. It doesn't matter, all I know is, I was a lot younger when I crossed the Rogue headed anyplace *north*.

My past quickly flees my mind as I top the last rise in the road. I clearly see Fletcher's Crossing laid out in front of me with the Rogue River running fast, free, and full from winter's runoff. It's a lot busier than that first time I crossed. There's a new ferry; it looks to be three times the size and it is powered by what looks like a steam engine. I can see white smoke coming out of a boiler chimney as it blows off steam. Faintly, I hear the ferryman yelling at someone to tend to the firebox, he needs more wood stoked and some water in the holding tank. He's a wild one, yelling and pointing and gesturing, all the while looking at his watch.

There's a wagon on the other side of the river that looks like it is ready to cross.

I see men, standing on the banks of the river with long poles in their hands. The salmon must be running. Yep, a guy has got one on his line, his pole is bent, and he is yelling for the others standing on the bank to get out of his way as he tries to control his fish from moving out into the middle of the river and the faster current. I chuckle to myself as he slips on the steep bank and slides into the shallow water. He held on to his pole, I'll give him that. A couple of guys make a quick grab for him and steady him to his feet. All is good; he is able to work his fish into shore.

Nice silver salmon looks to be about an eight pounder, I

bet it'll be good eating. My mouth waters up just thinking about it. Kids that have been playing up in the tree line run excitedly down to the water's edge. The boys are laughing and wanting to touch the fish, while the girls are screaming and acting squeamish. There looks to be about half a dozen kids or so, which means there are a few families around. The guy who caught the fish holds it up and yells back across the river to his wife, "Keep the fire going, dinner is coming."

There is a boat in the water with a couple of men in it. The boat looks like a dory. It has a curved bow at both ends. The guy in front is rowing backwards to hold the boat into the current while the guy in back handles the rod. The boat drifts ever so slowly in the deeper and faster current. To my recollection I believe they call that drift fishing. It seems like it is more work than just fishing off the bank. I've never owned a boat so I wouldn't know. What I do know is that I'm tired of walking and I could really use a hot meal. I wonder what it will take for me to borrow a fishing pole?

As I take my gaze away from the action on the river, I notice a large log cabin built farther up the hill away from the river. It has two chimneys out the roof, one made of stone for a fireplace and the other is a metal stove pipe. There is a nice porch, built for sitting that looks out over the river. Further away and past the large cabin is an area with a few tents set up and a couple of cook fires burning. I have found the source of the smoke I smelled earlier and am relieved that this day's walk will be ending shortly. I know it's been many years since I was here last, but I sure don't remember this little ferry crossing being built up like this. Maybe I just hadn't taken notice.

As I get closer to the cabin, I notice some movement from inside one of the windows.

Hopefully, whoever lives here will be friendly enough for me to get something to eat and a hot cup of coffee. From the back of the cabin a curious dog comes bounding up, "What's your name boy? Come here boy, it's Ok." I put my hand down for him to get a good whiff of my scent saying, "Yah, good boy." Good dogs seem to always welcome a rub of the ears.

I can hear someone out back chopping wood. I decide to walk past the front porch and follow the steady sound of ax on wood. As I pass one of the side windows, I notice a woman as she moves about. I am relieved that I hadn't gone up on the front porch and taken a chance of startling her. Turning the corner I stop and hesitate my approach. Standing before me is a shirtless, muscle-hardened, boy.

I wave my hand asking, "Excuse me son, you live here?" There is no response so I ask again, "Hey, pardon me, do you live here?" Turning away I mutter half out loud, "You're either deaf or just not neighborly."

From the back porch comes the woman's voice, "He's neither, he's just quiet. What can I do for you?"

Startled I turn, tip my hat and say, "Excuse me ma'am, just passing through, don't mean to be a bother."

"No bother, what can I do for you?"

"Well ma'am, I'm just passing through, I could sure use a hot meal. I'll gladly work for it, I don't take hand outs."

"I don't have hot food made up yet, that will be later. All I have is some jerky and some biscuits left over from breakfast. I have some fresh coffee and you're welcome to supper once it's ready. It'll be later, when my husband Sam gets up. That's supper time around here."

"Thank you ma'am, I'll gladly wait for a home cooked meal, course, I sure could use those biscuits and coffee while I wait, as long as it's no bother."

"It's no bother. Give me a minute. You can wash off some of that road dust over there by the hand pump. There's a wash basin, a towel, and a piece of soap. Just help yourself."

"Thank you kindly ma'am. I'll do just that, thank you."

As I walk over to the wash basin, I notice that the boy never stopped chopping. He never broke rhythm the whole time, he just kept chopping. I set my bedroll down and it suddenly gets dead calm quiet. It seems the air even turns still. The boy has stopped, he is watching me and I am watching him. He makes a step in my direction and I grab for my bowie knife just like so many times before, it is a reflex, I can't help it. I feel the hilt of the knife and know I'll be safe, but I don't want to hurt the boy. He appears to be a boy, in a man's body! Look at those muscles, my God; he's built like the legendary John Henry! I relax the hold on my knife as he suddenly stops. He's just picking up the split wood and making a stack. As I begin to relax I look around the area and notice that there are more than a couple dozen stacks of wood. If that's what this kid does, is chop wood, then it is no wonder why he is built as big as a man.

It doesn't take but a couple of pumps on the handle for the cold clear well water to come splashing out. Oh man, does that water feel good. If that woman's cooking is anything like this water, then, I'm in for a fine meal. She's not too hard on

....

the eyes neither. As I dry off, my stomach lets me know it is getting impatient.

Just then the woman steps out onto the porch saying, "Here you go, I brought some jerky and I put a dab of jelly with those biscuits. Hope you don't mind the coffee, we don't have any sugar. We ran out last night and it's a day or two until we go to town for supplies."

"Thank you ma'am, this'll be just fine, better than I've had in a while. Ma'am, might I ask your name?"

"Mrs. Judith Harris, I am Sam Harris's wife." she replies, then asks, "Who might you be?"

"Oh, my name is Jacob, Jacob Sparks."

After a lingered pause she says, "Well Mr. Sparks, I'll leave you to your food."

"Ma'am, do you mind if I ask what day and month it might be."

"It's Tuesday, the 7th, May is the month."

"And the year Ma'am?"

"It's 1897."

"Hmm, '97 and the boy's name?"

"That's Nathan, most call him Nate, he's the watchman's son.

Chapter 2

Before Judith turns to go back into the cabin she says, "Nate, that's enough wood for today. You have other chores to do. In the morning, you will be getting ready to take a delivery to town and get supplies." Nate nods his head and stacks up the last pieces of chopped wood.

Judith continues, "It will be supper soon."

"Yes ma'am."

So, the boy does speak.

Hot coffee and some fresh biscuits, can't wait to taste them. I head around the front and sit at the water's edge. The dog catches up to me and tags along, sniffing for a handout. We sit down and I watch the action on the river. It looks like about three families have set up camps.

There's a little corral holding some horses and beside the boat that is on the river there is another boat pulled up and tied to the shore. This is a nice spot, clear moving river, tall timber around, been thinned out some; glad to see that the two big doug firs are still standing.

I've always loved trees. The mightiness of them when they grow wide at the base and tall at the top; the music they make as the wind passes through their branches and the motion of their dance as they sway back and forth in a stronger wind. With the biscuits and coffee gone, I pull my boots and socks off and soak my feet. I exhale a long breath as the cold water jolts my tired feet instantly back to life.

While sitting there, I notice that not very many fish are

being caught. Then it dawns on me, it's only the first part of May, the salmon haven't started their summer run yet. These guys must be catching steelhead. Yeah, that's right, it's too early for salmon, but steelhead are always in the river. Course, they are harder to catch, very elusive and not as plentiful. Catching a steelhead is a challenge and that is what makes it fun. They are mighty good eating, especially when they are smoked.

As my feet change from tired and sore to cold and numb, I realize that it is not just my feet that are tired. It's all of me, I'm tired, tired of walking, tired of wandering, tired of not having a place to call my own. I'm weary from not sleeping in the same bed each night, lonely from not having a woman to love and share the day with. This life of mine seems like it has been one long walk. Have I been walking or running; a little of both I guess?

Realizing how refreshed my feet feel, I am now reminded that I could sure use a bath. Maybe after supper, if there's still enough light, I can find a secluded spot to do just that. Tomorrow, I can wash out these clothes and hang them to dry. I need to rest longer than a night and this feels like a place I have been looking for. This simple ferry crossing, that is guarded by two, towering doug firs, feels alive, peaceful, and rooted in purpose.

The sun is beginning to lower onto the western horizon, highlighting the tops of the trees. In my youth, that was always the time to stop doing whatever I was doing and get home for supper. Course, Ash Fork was more open and flatter than here; this is in a bit of a valley. Being at the river bottom, sunlight leaves sooner then out in the open. My mind is wandering once again and I realize I must be more tired than I thought. I know I'm still hungry; my mouth is watering and I don't even know what Mrs. Harris is cooking. Shaking the rambling thoughts from my head I decide to tempt my senses and head back up towards the cabin.

As I make my way back to the house I see two men sitting on the porch. Well, one man and the boy. I assume the man must be Sam Harris, the watchman. Guess I'll get acquainted.

Before I step up onto the porch I say, "Howdy, 'scuse me, I'm Jacob, Jacob Sparks. I suppose your wife already told you about me. She was kind enough to share some hot coffee and biscuits, she offered me to stay for supper. Hope you don't mind?"

The man answers, "Nah, I don't mind. But we don't have enough for handouts. So, if you're passing through, then just keep right on passing."

"I understand and I don't take handouts. I'll work for whatever is fair."

"Where you from, not from around here I take it?"

"No, I'm not from around here. I grew up in Ash Fork, but I've been gone from these parts a long time."

"How long is a long time?"

"Not quite sure, been doing the numbers in my mind all afternoon, seems like yesterday, but it's close to fifteen years at least, maybe a few more, give or take."

"Humph, that's a longtime. Lot's changed, especially in Ash Fork. It is starting to feel like a big city, with big city problems. Try to stay away as much as possible. We like it here; it's quiet and not much trouble."

As I extend my hand I say, "Excuse me, but I didn't get your name."

The man doesn't move, he just reaches out his hand, "I'm Sam, Sam Harris. I'm the watchman. This is my son, Nate."

"Yeah, we met."

"Good, cause you're gonna be working for him tomorrow; like I said no handouts." Turning towards Nate, Sam says, "Nate, go see what is taking so long with our supper."

Nate turns and says, "Yes sir."

I look up saying, "The boy doesn't talk a whole lot does he?"

"It's just his way. He's a good kid, hard worker. Look at him; he's as big as a damn tree, strong as an ox, works from sun up to sun down."

Returning Nate says, "Supper is in ten minutes. Judith says to make sure your hands are clean, you too, mister."

Judith yells out, "And no mud on your boots, I just cleaned the floors."

Sam gives me a wry smile, "Let's eat, you look like you could use some home cooking, Rusty, you stay." The dog whimpers a bit, but stops at the door.

As I drop my things on the porch I say, "It's been awhile, mighty obliged."

The cabin is bigger than I first thought. If it wasn't for being built out of logs, I guess you could call it a house. There is a big room with a stone fireplace on the one side. It has nice windows, at least one on each side of the house so the sunlight can come through any part of the day or season. It surely has a woman's touch. There is a nice kitchen area with cupboards and a place to wash up dishes and a cook stove on the back wall. The windows have sheer fabric hanging over them; the window in the kitchen has some ruffled curtains tied back. There are two doors towards the back; one probably goes to a bedroom, the other looks to be the back door. There is a stairway, up the side of the main room that leads to a loft, probably where the boy sleeps.

Taking off my hat I ask, "Nice house, did you build it yourself?"

Sam answers, "Yap, my pa started it, I added on to it. Nate's been here long enough to help some. Judith added her touch and we just kept building until we got it where it suits us. It's not much, but then we don't need much. Too big a house means more furniture and more work to keep up."

"I've been sleeping under the stars for awhile now, so, to be inside under a roof, with a warm fire and sitting in a chair at a table is something special. I thank you kindly."

Judith motions for us to sit. The table seems to be set for a special occasion with plates, cups, saucers, silverware and even napkins. As nice as the table is set, the meal is even better. There is fried chicken, potatoes, corn and hot biscuits. There is even a small bouquet of fresh wild flowers.

Judith reaches out to hold Nate's hand while extending her other hand out towards me. Nate reaches over and grabs Sam's hand. I look at Sam and slowly reach for Judith's up turned hand.

She begins to bow her head and then stops. She stares at Sam and me with a look that says no one is going to eat until we pray; we will not pray until the two of you join hands and complete the circle. Once again, Sam gives a wry smile and reaches out his hand. As Judith begins to bless the food, I reflect on how long it has been since I have been in this type of setting, my mind says it has been a good long while, my mouth says, "Amen" in unison with the others.

As we pass the food around, I begin to feel like I am intruding but welcome at the same time. Judith is warm and steady, Sam is firm with an edge, and Nate is obedient and quiet. I ask of any news from around the area. There isn't much to discuss. At least not much from around Fletcher's Crossing. Oh, there is the usual news about poor crops and a cow or someone's prize bull dying off. Confirming what I already figured out, the salmon haven't started their early run yet, so there aren't many fish in the river, just some steelhead moving around. As always, summer and fall are the busy times around here. Ash Fork seems to be growing at a steady pace; the railroad finally got finished through the valley and up the coast to Portland. I ask myself, have I really been gone that long? The railroad brought progress and jobs; jobs brought people, people brought growth. Progress is good, but I can see why Sam likes it here.

I push my chair away from the table saying, "What a meal, the best I've had in a long time."

Sam stands and motions with his head to join him on the porch. Judith and Nate begin to clear the table. It is a nice evening, no wind; the sky is clear as the first stars begin to appear.

Sam lights up a small pipe and asks if I would like to have a smoke. I shake my head no and explain that I just never cared

....

to smoke. Judith comes out of the door and sits down next to Sam. She has brought out a basket of yarn and begins to work the needles.

Sam points out, "She's making me and Nate wool scarves, hats and gloves for next winter." He chuckles to himself and then says, "Spring and summer are long getting here and hopefully long staying."

Judith raises her eyebrows and lets him know that if he's not careful, winter will be here sooner then he thinks. I chuckle at their light heartedness. Yeah, there is something different here, something comfortable, something warm, something special.

I can hear Nate in the house; he's filling the wood box and stoking up the fire in the fireplace. He moves through the house like a shadow; busy with purpose. He comes out on the porch and says he is headed down to the river to watch the moon come up over the mountain tops. It will be a good night for that. Nothing else is said, Judith and Sam nod their approval. Rusty perks his ears and bounds after him.

Sitting there I begin to get a heavy heart. Not heavy like I miss someone, but heavy like I missed out on something. It's not the first time I have felt this, but it is unnerving and distracting. I excuse myself, needing to find a place to bed down. As I get up to leave, Sam mentions that there is a clean, dry barn up the hill behind the house. He says there should be fresh straw and a lantern hanging on a post near the door if I should need some light. I tell him thank you, gather up my belongings and turn away from the river and the house. I am used to sleeping in the open, under the stars, but warm, soft, fresh straw would be the topper to one of the better days I've had in a long time. Walking away from the river, I tell myself that I'll look for a place to take a bath and wash the dust from my clothes in the morning.

I find the lantern and dig a match out of my small pouch. The lit match shares its flame with the lantern and brightens the inside of the barn. With a quick glance I focus on a fresh pile of straw over in one corner and set my pack and bedroll down next to it. I then lean my bow and quiver of arrows up against the wall. I roll out my ground cloth and blanket; undo my belt letting my bowie knife fall to my feet. Before taking off my boots, I reach in and pull out the small throwing knives that are always handy but tucked away. With a yawn and a stretch, I lay down on this soft bed of straw. Turning the lantern down, I lie back and ponder the day's events and that fine meal. I tell myself that I need to quiet my mind and get some sleep.

For some reason I find myself restless. Maybe it is the soft straw, maybe it's being in a closed space, whatever the reason, I just can't let myself relax. I pull my pack close, finger through it and find my harmonica, hoping that a tune or two will soothe me. I don't know any tunes so to speak, but I do know what I like and always seem to make some sort of melody out of just sliding up and down the scale playing old familiar combinations of random notes. After a feeble attempt at that, I determine that I still can't sleep, maybe it's just too quiet.

Thinking that the cool night air might relax me, I stand up and put my pants, shirt and boots back on. I decide to take a walk towards the river. Before passing the house, I can see a few camp fires still glowing. The fires are not big, they look like they are burning down for the night. The air is nice and sweet as it hits my nose. The crickets are singing a better tune then I could come up with tonight. There is no wind, not even a breeze. The river is moving gently, just loud enough to hear the water lap against the shoreline as it makes its way to the west and the rapids that are downstream. I can hear the low rumble of water on rocks that announce the start of the rapids. With the moon fully up, there is enough light for me to make out the tops of the boulders that turn the calm water into churning swirls of white, angry spray and mist. The loudness of the water, rushing over the rocks, muffles the voices coming from the folks that are enjoying the low burning campfires. Evidently, the kids are down for the night and the adults are close to ending their day as well.

Turning my attention upstream away from the rapids and towards the secured ferry, I notice a lantern burning over by the ferry shack. There is someone sitting close to a small fire, I decide to mosey over there and see what is going on. I look up at the moon and am glad it is as bright as it is, it makes walking the unfamiliar river bank a lot easier.

As I approach the ferry shack, Rusty alerts making a half growl, half bark sound, then he comes towards me with his tail wagging and ears lowered. I give Rusty a pat on the head asking, "Sam, is that you sitting there?"

Sam replies, "Who's there, is that you Jacob?"

"Yep, it's me, Jacob. I couldn't sleep, so I thought I'd enjoy a bit of this cool night air."

"Is there something wrong with the barn?"

"No, the barn is clean and dry."

"Did you find some fresh straw?"

"Yeah I did, it's me, I just couldn't get relaxed enough to sleep, that's all."

"Well, suit yourself, but, morning comes early around here, Nate gets started first thing. It's hard work just trying to keep up with him. He is gonna be getting the wagon and team ready to haul a load of firewood into town. There is gonna be plenty to do come sun up." Sam points to a block of wood suggesting that I sit down.

Sitting down closer to the fire, I say, "Fine by me, the earlier the better. I like being awake with the sun, there will be plenty of time to sleep later." Sam lets out a snort and then I continue, "Is there a place close by that I can get in the river? I need to wash up some and clean the dust off these clothes. I've been in 'em a few days. 'Magine I'm a bit ripe."

"Well, wasn't gonna say anything just yet, but yeah, you could use a bath. The misses said if you leave them clothes on the porch, she'll wash 'um up when you and Nate go into town."

"Into town?"

"Yeah, into Ash Fork. Problem?"

"Ah, no problem, just hadn't thought I'd be getting to Ash Fork so soon."

"You'll be going with Nate, helping him with the team and bringing back supplies. The boy is a hard worker, but he can use the help. Since you don't appear to be in any hurry to get on down that road, you gotta earn you're keep. Summer can get busy around here and the work load picks up. You're not the first drifter to come down that road and stay a bit. As long as you help out, earn your keep, you're welcome to bunk in the barn. That's if Nate don't work ya to death first."

"I thank you kindly, but let me think on it."

"What's to think about?"

"I just haven't thought too much past today is all. I'm not shy of hard work. Been working my whole life, lately I just don't seem to work too long in one place. I've never been able to stay put, I'm always wondering what is around the next bend, what the next farm looks like, next town. Ya, know?"

Sam ponders this and then answers, "No, not really. My pa settled this place, cleared the woods and ran the first ferry. He was the ferryman for a while, but he got bored and decided to start cutting timber. He would haul wood to farmers when they got too busy with their crops. Some of them either ran out of their own wood or ran out of time. Pa started to barter with folks cause he didn't like farming. As more people came, more wood for shelter and heating was needed. My pa saw that need and scratched out this place. Cutting wood and hauling it suited me so here I sit."

"So, do you do this all the time?"

"What do you mean, do this all the time?"

"Sit here and watch the fire and look out over that river?"

With a harshness to his voice Sam says, "I do more than just sit here looking out over that river. I own half that ferry, Red owns the other half, he's the ferryman. He likes running it more than I do. I take care of the maintenance and make sure it's ready for the next day's running. When we have folks stay over in our camp, I watch to make sure no one messes with it during the night. As fishing season heats up and the nicer weather comes we get more folks out here. I walk the grounds, make sure no one causes trouble in camp or disturbs their boats, if they bring 'em. Folks with youngins want to come, stay at a safe, friendly place. This is my home, I watch over it. Just sit here and watch the fire, my ass."

"Didn't mean no disrespect, just asking, that's all. You gotta nice place here, it's real peaceful."

"Yea, and it's gonna stay that way. 'S'cuse me, I gotta walk a bit and you best get some sleep, come on Rusty."

Chapter 3

"Hey mister, mister, wake up."

"Humph, what's that?"

"It's gonna be light soon, get up."

Morning to you too, I think to myself. Scratching my head I try to get my brain to clear. I think through my routine, let's see, pants, knives, shirt, money pouch, coin...roll up my bedding.

Since I'm gonna be working all day, I decide to spend one more day in these clothes leaving me my clean set for going in to town. I gotta remember to leave the dirty set on the porch like Sam said. Now, I gotta head to the river. I need to wash up better than just running water over my head at the hand pump. I wish I had some soap. Maybe I can grab the piece that was over by the wash basin yesterday?

A rooster announces the morning. I never get tired of hearing a rooster crow, well, not these days anyway. My mind begins to clear as I walk over to the water pump looking for the piece of soap. It doesn't take me long to find it so I head down to the river's edge. Sam passes me on his way up to the house. He has the boiler fired up and is letting it build steam before the ferryman shows up. As we pass I say, "Morning Sam, how was your night?"

Sam grunts a reply, "Quiet."

"I finally settled in and slept hard. Nate shook me awake just before the rooster announced the sunrise. I'm gonna wash up in the river."

"Make sure you put that soap back where you got it from."

"Sure thing. Hey, I can't remember if you told me last night or not, but, is there good swimming hole close by?"

"Down river about a quarter mile past the rapids; can't miss it. There's a big rope hanging out of a tree. Kids use it come summer. Better get up to the house, the misses will have breakfast ready shortly; better get it before it gets cold."

I bend down at the river edge and splash the cold clear water over my head, neck and arms.

With the cob webs leaving, I begin to lather up, feeling alive and eager for a new day. Dried off and with soap returned, I step up onto the porch. The cabin is lit up, with a fire burning hot in the fireplace. The table is set as nice as last night, even for breakfast.

Before I open the screen door, I knock and enter saying, "Morning ma'am, Sam said to get up here for some breakfast. Hope I'm not intruding?"

"Good morning Mr. Sparks, how did you sleep? Breakfast will be ready in just a few minutes."

"Thank you Ma'am, I slept fine, especially after that home cooked meal last night."

"Well, it's our pleasure." Judith turns and yells out, "Nate, Sam, breakfast. It's hot now!"

"S'cuse me ma'am, but Sam said if I set my dusty road clothes out on the porch that you'd oblige me and have 'em washed by the time Nate and I get back from town. Don't want to be a bother."

"It's no bother, Mr. Sparks. I'd rather have you in clean clothes, than have to smell them."

She turns again and starts to yell, "Sam, Nate...oh, there you are. Now let's sit, it's getting cold."

Once again, we have to hold hands so Judith can say a prayer. It is not as awkward this time.

It still doesn't feel natural but it's just not as awkward. She doesn't say a long prayer just a simple blessing to start the day and give thanks for the food. Let's see, pancakes, eggs, bacon and fresh coffee; I could get used to this. Best do what I'm told and keep my nose clean.

Once the food is passed back and forth I ask, "So, what are we gonna get started at this morning?"

Sam answers, "Just stay close to Nate; he'll let ya know what he needs you to do. Nate, be nice, don't bury him the first day. He's got two meals to work off."

"And clean clothes if he leaves them," adds Judith.

I push my chair back from the table saying, "Great meal and thank you ma'am. Nate, I'll be out back waiting."

Judith looks over, "Nate, I'll clear the table, you get Mr. Sparks started. Sam, sit awhile with me and we'll have another cup."

"Sounds good to me, it's a perfect morning; I'll be on the porch."

Nate's not far behind me as I step off the back porch steps. I follow him up the hill towards the barn. Rusty is tagging along and then runs ahead, acting all excited. He comes running back, Nate reaches down, pats his head, then picks up a split piece of wood and throws it as Rusty bounds after it. Turning the corner at the back of the barn, there sits a large hauling wagon with tall side boards.

Nate says, "Gotta get the wagon ready to haul to town. We'll need the side barrel filled with fresh water, make sure there is enough for us and the horses; three days worth. We need some fresh hay and some oats, the hay can go up front, the firewood will load on the back. Check the axles and wheels, make sure they are greased. It's a long pull, lots of weight." He leaves me and heads into the barn.

"Where are you going?" I ask.

"I'm getting the harness."

"Don't ya need help with that?" Nate doesn't respond, he just lets out a grunt. I start checking the axels and they seem like they have been greased recently. I check the water barrel and pull the bottom plug letting a small stream of water run onto the ground. Rusty comes over, sticks his tongue out and laps up a drink.

Nate sees me and says, "Don't just drain it on the ground, grab a bucket and put it in the horse trough over there. The animals will drink it up."

There is no need to say anything, I just nod, put the plug back in and grab the bucket off the side of the wagon. Can't be more than a bucket left in the barrel, but he's the boss.

With the water barrel filled and the oats stored, I begin to fork fresh hay into the front of the wagon just as Nate sets the harness and tack out in position for the team. He then starts walking away from the wagon, Rusty bounds after him, with the piece of wood hanging out his mouth. Nate tugs it away and throws it. Nate turns and motions me to follow.

"Where we headed now?"

"Up to the meadow."

I think to myself, *meadow, how big is this place?*

As we crest a small rise, there lays a cleared meadow. It is closed in by a split rail fence that keeps a small apple orchard and forest at bay. I can't help but notice a grove of aspen at the far north end; just outside the fence line. There are sloping hills that converge down to the edge of the aspens, forming a gentle draw that continues to rise up to even higher ground beyond.

As Nate unlatches the gate, two big sturdy plow horses come sauntering over to Nate. One is black with white tufted socks, the other is dark brown with a long streak of white down its muzzle. They are bobbing their heads and snorting their greetings. Nate reaches in his pocket and pulls out a small knife, from his back pocket he pulls out a apple. He cuts the apple in two and offers a half to each.

He nuzzles in, rubs their foreheads and ears saying ever so gently, "Good morning girls, ready to go to work?"

They seem to answer him bobbing their heads and scratching the earth in unison with their front hooves. Not soon after, an even bigger horse comes up, fast paced with ears perked.

"Good morning Gus. No, I didn't forget ya."

Nate reaches in his other back pocket and pulls out another apple. Gus gets it whole. He is big and rippled with strength. His coat is gray, with black spots. His long mane and tail seem to match in color and pattern. Mane and tail both start out black and fade to light gray at the tips.

Nate reaches up and whispers in Gus's ear, "Not this time boy, need you to stay here and take it easy. Your day is coming. How's that shin? Let me take a look." Nate reaches down and lifts Gus's right front leg; he rubs it gently but with a sure hand. Gus whimpers a bit, "Still a bit sore? Yeah, you still need to rest up some."

"Mr. Sparks, this here is Gus, he's the log skidder and the team is Molly Brown and Bess. Bess is the black. Better say hello, they might be a bit skittish, let them smell you first."

"Thanks, I've been around horses before." As I reach out towards Molly's muzzle, her eyes get wide, her ears perk, and she starts to back up. Rusty moves in between us, Molly backs up even more and turns her side towards us.

Nate grabs her halter and holds her head, "Molly, behave. We don't have time for this. This is Mr. Sparks."

"Hey Nate, my name is Jacob. You can call me Jacob, or Jake."

Nate reaches in his back pocket and grabs another apple, cuts it in half, hands it to me, and says, "Here, try this."

I reach out the half apple to Molly; she sniffs it and eagerly takes it from my hand. I guess that's all it takes to be friends; she relaxes as the tension releases from her body. Nate gives me the other half apple and I approach Bess. Bess seems more relaxed having witnessed Molly's approval. Bess flares her nostrils, snorts, and takes the apple from my hand. Gus has turned and sauntered away uninterested. I guess we'll make our acquaintances another day. Nate grabs Molly and attaches a lead on to her bridle, he hands me the other lead and I do the same to Bess. We turn 'em around and head through the gate. There are two cows in the meadow and a bull that has stayed up at the north end; both cows beller out, probably needing to get milked. I ask, "Hey Nate, we gotta milk them cows?"

"Nah, not today, Judith will be up here soon to get Bonnie for milking. The other cow is Daisy and she's about to drop her calf any day. We need to get this team harnessed up, check their shoes, clean their hooves and load the wagon. The bull is Brutus and he is as ornery as can be. He stays to himself."

We head down towards the barn, Molly and Bess seem to get excited as they start to prance a bit and perk their ears. Nate tells me to hold Bess, while he backs Molly in to the tongue of the wagon. He lifts the harness up and around Molly's neck saying, "She likes to pull on the right side." As Nate straightens out the right side reins, he gives me a look like, what are you waiting for, get Bess hooked up. He doesn't need to say anything; the day is still young but I already know Nate's look; he's all business. As I watch Nate turn away and walk towards the house he says, "Check their hooves." I need to find the pick, but before I do, I open the water barrel, grab the ladle and take a drink of nice cool well water.

Judith and Nate come back from the house with two buckets. They set the buckets down in the barn and head on up towards the meadow. Rusty is running alongside with a stick in his mouth. It isn't long before Judith and Nate come back with Bonnie. Rusty is barking and keeps Bonnie moving towards the barn.

After Nate helps to get Bonnie settled in a stall, he jumps up on the wagon saying, "Let's go."

Before I can even get settled in the seat, Nate shakes the reins and gives a sharp whistle. The wagon jolts to life as we head away from the barn and away from the stacked up wood piles.

Nate directs the wagon up towards the meadow with me

asking, "Where are we going? I thought we were gonna load the wagon with firewood?"

"We are."

We ride along the meadow's south edge and turn towards the west rolling up a gradual incline. As we ride in silence, I look out over the forest; it has been thinned out, letting the sunlight filter down to the forest floor. The sunlight has helped to create a lush carpet of small grass and spring buttercups that spread out between hundreds of stumps. New pine seedlings have taken root, a new generation of trees, rebirth. I jump down off the wagon and walk alongside as Rusty runs on up ahead. Looking up towards Nate I ask, "How much farther?"

"Not much, we're almost there."

As we round a bend in the worn wagon path, I look out into a clearing that has straight rows of firewood, all chopped and stacked; must be ten rows, forty maybe fifty feet long and all four feet high.

Nate pulls up to the last row and sets the brake saying, "Here's where we start. We load a cord of ponderosa pine first. Then three quarters of a cord of doug fir and fill out the load with cedar."

In amazement I ask, "Where's all this come from? Who's done all this cutting and stacking?"

"Me, mostly, Sam helps when he can."

"Whose land is this?"

"Sam has the lease on eighty acres up here. His pa homesteaded about twenty acres down by the river and we work this."

"What's all the wood stacked down at the house for?"

"That's wood for the ferry, the house, and the people camping out. We have firewood for 'em so they won't be cutting down green timber, tearing things up and all. Let's get busy."

"Hey Nate, I seen two fat rabbits over by that thicket when we pulled up, how's about I set a couple of snares and we take back fresh rabbit for supper, would the misses cook 'em up?"

"Got a .22 under the seat, shooting would be faster."

"Yeah, but it damages more meat. Since we're gonna be here awhile, a snare will work just fine. I'll be right back, Rusty you stay."

Nate calls Rusty back and makes him sit, "I'll keep Rusty here."

Walking through the underbrush, I cut a couple of fresh branches from a nearby bush and peel the leaves off as I walk. I reach in my pouch and pull out a couple pieces of twine and a thin wire and walk ever so quietly to where I saw the rabbits nibbling on some tender shoots of grass. The rabbits have a couple of worn, matted down trails from constant activity, which makes knowing where to set the snares a easy decision. I ready the snares, slightly camouflaging them and walk away as quietly as possible.

Walking back to the work area, I notice a small lean-to built along the edge of the clearing. Looking up the higher mountain side, I notice groves of aspen that divide large stands of doug fir. I can also make out scatterings of tamarack, mixed with large cedar. With it being springtime, all the trees have fresh green leaves of new growth; their colors all blending together into a mosaic of green. I inhale a big breath and realize I haven't felt like this for a long time. There is a peacefulness here that I have failed to feel...ever.

I make my way back to the wagon and I ask Nate about the lean-to. He tells me that it is a tool shed and he keeps Gus's tack and harness up there and out of the weather.

"You bring Gus up here?"

"Yes sir, I use Gus to skid the logs down here so I can buck 'em up into this here cord wood. I keep a cross cut saw, buck saw, ax, splitting maul, and sledge hammer up here."

Shaking my head with approval I say, "Makes sense, no need to be hauling that stuff up here each time, plus it gives you a place to get out of the weather if and when it turns on you."

"Yes sir, it comes in handy."

We settle into a nice pace and get the load close to half on. Nate says to take a break and grabs a gunny sack from under the wagon seat. He pulls out some biscuits, jerky and a couple of apples. I grab the canteen and Nate motions for us to sit on a couple of stumps. Before I do, I get the water bucket and fill it with some fresh water for the horses. Nate nods a thank you towards me and tells Rusty to stop begging. Rusty tucks his ears and breathes out a disgruntled snort. Rusty walks over and sniffs the water bucket, takes a drink, and looks up at Molly as much to say, "It's my water, too." With drool leaking from his mouth and his tail thumping, Rusty looks at Nate, begging. Nate cuts off a strip of jerky and puts it between his teeth, then snaps his fingers. Rusty bounds over and nuzzles into Nate's face and nibbles the jerky away.

Chewing the jerky barely enough to get a taste, Rusty starts to wag his tail expecting more.

Nate arches his eyebrows, Rusty turns his whole body away from the both of us and lies down with a sigh.

We get back to work with the sun past its highest point in the sky; it is as nice of a spring day as I have seen. The shadows show me that it is past mid-day; they have rotated past straight up and down. Nate takes his shirt off to warm his back. The boy is chiseled hard like a statue made of stone. It makes sense, with all the wood he's chopped. I strip down to my long underwear and pants, wet my handkerchief and tie it around my neck.

We finish loading the wagon without much talk. A hawk screeches high above us. We both stop to look and watch just as it catches an updraft. Its mate calls back and comes into view. One is high and one is low, working together, floating on the same slight breeze that helps to cool us. Once again, I realize how comfortable I am to be amongst these new found friends with their hospitality and their ease of life. How lucky I am to not be walking the dusty back roads and always feeling like I'm chasing after someone's shadow. I can't see it, I can't catch it, I just sense it. There's something always just up ahead, just out of my reach, but being here just feels right and special all at the same time.

Nate chases my thoughts away saying, "Hey, mister, I mean Jake, loads on, we need to be getting back."

"Right, I'll go check them snares." This time I take Rusty with me, "Come on Rusty, let's go see if we caught supper."

Sure enough, two snares, two rabbits. I was only expecting to catch one rabbit, but lady luck smiled today. Rusty is as excited as I am and we half jog back to the work area.

Approaching the wagon I say, "Lookie here, two nice fat rabbits, fresh meat for tonight and maybe Judith can turn the rest into stew for the trip into town. I'll get 'em skinned out before I head down to take a bath in that river, can't stand myself another minute."

The trip back to the house doesn't seem to take as long as it took getting to the meadow; it's the same half mile each way, I guess it's the anticipation of another home cooked meal that makes it seem shorter. The shadows are slanted long and the air has cooled. The sky is as blue as can be and with the trees and bushes budding out with spring green, it couldn't be a more pleasant afternoon.

As we pull up to the barn, I ask Nate if he minds if I skin the rabbits and get them to Judith while he tends to the horses. He nods okay and then I ask him if they have a special place for skinning and cleaning fresh game. He points over his shoulder with his thumb. Turning, I spot a stump with brownish red stains. With rabbits dangling from my hand by their ears, I make my way over to the chopping block. Before I start to skin the rabbits out, I pull out my wet stone, moisten it up and begin to draw the blade across the slick face of the stone. Once the rabbits are skinned and cleaned, I wash my hands and take them up to the back porch. Judith is in the kitchen and does not act surprised to see me.

She asks how the day went and I hold up the two rabbits saying, "Not a bad day even if I do say so myself. I got these two rabbits for supper, if you haven't got it started yet?"

"Two rabbits, you boys must be hungry?"

"Yes ma'am, we are and I thought if it wasn't too much trouble we could have enough left over for a rabbit stew for tomorrow's ride in to town."

"No trouble, Mr. Sparks. I haven't started supper. Fried rabbit and a stew sounds just fine."

"Is Sam up yet?"

"No, he got in late. With Nate up loading the wagon, he had to get the steam up in the ferry first thing, haul some water and such."

At that I turn and say, "Ma'am, I'm gonna excuse myself and head down to the swimming hole Sam told me about, I need a bath, *bad*."

"Thank you Mr. Sparks; you'll be doing us all a favor."

"Sorry ma'am, I've been on the road awhile, not normally this rank."

Nodding Judith says, "Here, let me get you fresh soap and a towel, I'll set them here on the step."

Turning I say, "I'll be right back. I need to get a clean shirt and pants from the barn."

Nate and I pass each other as I am headed to the barn and he is headed to the house. I tell him I'm headed down to the swimming hole for a bath. He nods and keeps walking with Rusty at his heels.

After grabbing my fresh set of clothes from the barn, I head back to the house to pick up the soap and towel that Judith set out for me. I turn and spot a path that hopefully leads me to the swimming hole. The path takes me above the campground area and into the thicker forest. The people camped out are sitting around fires and starting to cook evening suppers of their own.

The kids are running around laughing, yelling and having fun. As I pass by everyone takes notice and quiets down. The boys point and the girls giggle. The grown men just watch and stare, not alarmed, just curious. The women don't seem to take notice.

The path is well worn and easy to follow, but doesn't stay true to the river's edge. It passes through thicker forest that rises slightly exposing a view of the rapids and calmer water beyond.

It then turns back towards the river and drops down coming closer to the water's edge. This must be the spot, the area has opened up with a gentle, slopping, beach like, shoreline.

Turning my gaze back up river, I notice the big old willow, mixed in among some cotton woods and other types of trees. The willow has a large branch that hangs out over the river and there's the rope, just like Sam said.

I strip down to my long underwear and test the water. Not wanting to torture myself by slowly getting wet, I dive in all at once. The water is so cold that as my head pops to the surface, I squeal like a young kid and anxiously gulp the air. Returning to the shore, I lather up while still in my long underwear, grab my socks and scrub them up. I gather up my breath and dive back in to rinse off. The water doesn't shock me breathless this time but it is still a jolt to my body. I stand up in the shallow water and there on the bank stands Nate with Rusty. Nate decided to take a bath as well. Not wearing long underwear, he strips down to his skivvies. Like me, he dives in all at once and pops to the surface with a loud yelp.

With a laughing curse, Nate says what I'm thinking, "It takes a while for the spring runoff to get out of the mountains, the river could stay this cold for another month."

He motions for me to throw him the soap. As I get out of the water, my hand naturally goes to the sown in pocket in my underwear. I always check, yap, "Lady Liberty" is there. I don't know what I'd do if I lost her, I've been holding on to her for all these years; never been broke, never will be broke as long as I got that gold piece. As Nate catches his breath I ask, "Feels good don't it?"

"Yes sir."

"It's Jacob or Jake. You can call me Jacob or Jake, it's okay."

Nate nods and jumps back in one more time to rinse the soap off. Rusty is barking and running up and down the river bank; it's not long before Rusty jumps in after Nate. I don't have an extra pair of long underwear, so I strip them off and wring them out best I can. I dry the rest of me off and put on my clean pants and shirt. I'll dry my underwear later, over a fire if needed and warm myself up while doing it. Fresh clothes, clean body and soon a full belly, it's been another good day.

With Nate still in the water I yell, "Gonna head back Nate."

Nate gives me a wave and dives under one more time. Rusty runs to the bank, shakes off the water from his fur then starts twisting and rolling in the grass.

Back at the barn, I decide to get my things together for the trip into Ash Fork, but before I do, I cut a couple of branches off a young willow and tie them into circles. Not wanting to waste any part of the rabbit, I take the hides and stretch them tight over the ringed branches and hang them up to dry out.

The walk back warmed me up and I decide to forego making a fire. I take my underwear and hang them over the rail of the milking stall. Hopefully they will be dry enough to wear in the morning. It will be dark soon, so I finish getting my things gathered for the morning.

As I head down towards the house, I can smell the rabbit cooking. My stomach quivers and my mouth waters up. I turn the corner of the front porch and there is Sam, sitting with a cup of coffee and having a smoke. "Howdy, Sam, have a good sleep?"

"Yeah, how'd the day go? I see you survived."

"It went good. Nate and I got on just fine. He's a hard worker. You taught him well. Nice place you got here. I thought you just had this place, didn't realize you had that meadow and the timbered acreage beyond. More to this old homestead than I first realized."

"Well, like I told ya, my pa liked what he built here, found a way to make a living and we've kept it all working. Without even knowing it, I'll have lived my whole life here."

Judith comes to the screen door, "Cup of coffee, Mr. Sparks?"

"Yes ma'am, thank you."

Rusty comes bounding around the corner and up the porch, wiggling and nipping at Sam.

"Good boy, good boy Rusty. Did you have a good day, boy? How'd Molly and Bess do? Go get a stick, go on, go find a stick."

"Hey, Sam", says Nate through the screen door. "How was last night? No problems? Need me to do anything before supper?"

"Nah, come out and sit."

"I will, I'm just fillin the wood boxes and bringing Judith some fresh water."

I offer to help, but Sam says Nate can handle it, he's young. Judith comes out with my cup and the pot of coffee. She freshens Sam's coffee first and then pours mine saying, "Supper will be ready shortly. We're having fresh rabbit, compliments of Mr. Sparks."

With raised eyebrows Sam looks my way, throws the stick for Rusty and then asks, "Nate showed you the .22?"

"No, I set up a couple of snares when we got to the wood piles and by the time we were loaded up, we had fresh rabbit. Snares come in handy when you're on the road and not wanting to be carrying a gun and ammo."

"No gun? Is that why you pack that bow and those arrows?"

"Yeah, I don't usually have the money for ammo, besides, guns and I never got along that well. I prefer a good sharp knife and my bow and arrows."

Sam says, "I was up to the barn this morning and saw the bow and arrows setting there. I took the liberty of looking them over. Nice leather and bead work. The bow and them arrows look handmade. You any good with 'em?"

"I'm a pretty fare shot. From twenty-five to thirty-five yards, I usually don't miss. Anything much past that makes for a tough shot, especially with wind or thick brush. I bring down deer and small game. I've never had to face anything big like a bear, I've been lucky that way."

Nate comes to the screen door and tells us supper is ready.

Once again, the table is set with care. Before we start, Judith reaches out for our hands to hold. Sam and I don't hesitate, but we do look at each other. It's a good thing that the prayer is a short one, my mouth is watering, stomach is growling, and I can't take my eyes off the fresh rolls, carrots, potatoes, gravy, and rabbit, all cooked to perfection. The food passes quickly around the table and after very little conversation, I wipe gravy from the corner of my mouth. With my smile remaining in place I say, "Ma'am, thank you for cooking this rabbit, it just might be the best I've ever tasted."

"Well, thank you, Mr. Sparks and thank you for the rabbit. You know it cooks up just like chicken. Some folks like it even better than chicken. I have what's left of the other rabbit cooking up in a stew. There will be some for us and the two of you can take the rest on the road. There should be enough for a couple of hot meals once heated up. I'll send some biscuits as well."

"Much obliged ma'am. Much obliged to all of you, for taking me in like you have. I somehow feel like I've known you all for a lot of years, not just for two days."

Sam nods and simply says, "You're welcome, good rabbit Judith, Nate hand me the gravy."

With full bellies and smiles of contentment, Sam and I head out to the porch while Nate helps Judith clear the table. It's another pleasant evening. Sam lights up his pipe with its sweet aroma. There is hardly a breath of wind as the smoke from the pipe drifts up lazily. Rusty comes around the side of the house, licking his muzzle and also looking content. As he passes by me, he sniffs my pant leg and settles down next to Sam.

Sam pats Rusty's head and asks how his dinner was, "Did you get some of that rabbit boy?"

Rusty beats the floor boards with his tail in reply. "Good boy, Rusty."

Nate and Judith come out with three cups and a pot of coffee. Judith asks, "Another cup for you two?"

"Don't mind if I do, thank you ma'am."

"Sam?"

"Please, that would be nice. Thanks hon." Sam motions for Nate to sit down. Nate sits down on the top step of the porch, Rusty moves and settles next to Nate. Sam takes a drag on his pipe and says, "Nate, when you get back from Ash Fork, I'll have a timber order for you. Mr. Winkler, came by today and told Red that he had a order of lumber for a barn that a farmer wants to build. I guess the farmer lives up river a ways. Anyway, I'll find out more of the details by the time you get back. I hope Gus's shin heals up, you'll need him when you get back."

"Sure thing Sam, in fact, I'm gonna go check on Molly and Bess and maybe I'll go on up and check Gus right quick. Come on Rusty, I'll race ya."

I look at Sam and shake my head saying, "The energy of youth. The boy just doesn't stop."

"Nope, he's a good kid; we're blessed to have him."

Judith reaches out and grabs Sam's hand; she pulls it up to her lips and gently kisses it; Sam lets out a contented sigh. Normally I'd feel awkward in a situation like this, but not here, not with these folks.

Feeling tired and satisfied in my own way, I excuse myself

with a yawn and a stretch saying, "I am sure Nate will want to get an early start." I step off the porch and into the night headed to the barn and a good night sleep.

•

I am wakened by a cold nose and a wet tongue licking at my face, "Rusty, good morning boy, that time all ready. I slept clear through the night."

I get up and start to gather my things. I check my knives, coin, money pouch, all this by feel as it is still dark out, not even a sign of light on the horizon. I need to get that lantern, and splash some water on my face. Fumbling around, I manage to put my pants and boots on and then tell Rusty, "Let's go, show me the way boy."

I hear the horses move a bit and whinny; they sense the activity and are a bit anxious. Walking out of the barn I grab the lantern from the post. I finger a match from my side pouch and strike it on the post; first the match, then the lantern comes to life. I go over to the wash basin I used the first day, pump some water into the wash pan and splash the cold, clear water on my face. I stretch with a yawn and notice Nate is up and stoking the fire in the fireplace, the cook stove is already smoking.

I see Sam has a fire going down by the ferry; I head back into the barn, and grab my long underwear. Being surprised at how dry they are, I decide to wear them. I quickly drop my pants and shed my shirt. In my haste, I miss the leg of my underwear, fall off balance and bang into the side board of the milking stall, which thankfully, stops me from falling completely over.

Hunched over with one leg in and one leg out I regain my balance. Molly shakes her mane and lets out a snort. I chuckle to myself as I slip on my pants and shirt without further incident.

Standing alone in this barn, similar to others I have slept in, I somehow feel like I'm younger, I feel energized, I feel like good things are on the verge of happening. I finish gathering my bedroll, pack, and shoulder bag. I grab my hat, give my jacket a shake, pick up my bow and quiver of arrows and head out to the wagon. I run into Nate as he is checking the wagon and the harnesses one last time. With Nate starting to get the team hooked up, I pack my belongings under the seat. Nate notices the pack and bedroll and asks, "You bringing your whole bedroll?"

"Yeah, just never know what today, tomorrow, or the next turn in the road will bring. When you carry all your belongings on your back, you best keep it all with ya." I help Nate with Molly and Bess, and then Nate turns and heads up the path to the meadow. "Where you going now?" I ask.

"To get Bonnie, for Judith."

"Do you want the lantern?"

"Don't need it." Rusty bounds after him, tail wagging.

I pull out my wet stone, put a couple drops of spit on it and drag my knives across the stone while I wait for Nate to get back. I help him secure Bonnie in the stall. Nate moves the team and wagon around from the back of the barn and gets them pointed towards the ferry. I look to the eastern horizon and notice the blush of first light. No longer in need of the lantern, I blow out the flame, return it to the post, and head towards the house.

With the smell of bacon and coffee filling the air; I lift my nose to take in a good whiff. As I do, I notice that the sky is clear; hopefully this nice weather will continue at least for another day or two. With it still being May; the weather could change quicker than a kid trying to make up his mind while standing at a candy counter. I walk down towards the front porch as Sam is coming up to the house from the ferry. Rusty is running around and can't make up his mind who to run to. He's probably been up most the night hanging out with Sam, but he's excited with all the activity none the less. I see Judith moving about the house. She is setting the table and singing a tune that sounds like something you'd hear in church.

"Good morning, Sam. How was the night?" I ask.

"Morning, Jacob. Last night was just fine, quiet. After I tended to the ferry, I was able to get some sleep. You boys about ready to head out?"

"Yeah, think so. Nate's bringing the wagon down now."

Judith yells out that breakfast is in ten minutes. I set my bundle of dirty clothes on the porch. It feels awkward having a married woman do my laundry. Oh well, she offered, I am helping out and working it off.

"Good morning, ma'am, smells great in here, as usual."

Judith looks up with a thank you and says, "Sam, come sit." She walks to the front porch and yells out to Nate, "Hurry up, the food is hot. You men, it's like pulling teeth to get you two to sit down when I call you."

Sam answers, "Now Judith, it's okay, just relax, you always get a bit crazy when Nate goes into town. It'll be fine and he's got company this time."

After securing the wagon and team, next to the ferry shack, Nate finally makes his way in to the house. He is drying his hands on his shirt. With raised eyebrows, Judith says, "You're right, but I'm not crazy, not yet any way. Nate, come sit."

Nate gets in his chair and grace is said, but with a longer prayer. This morning Judith has added a blessing for the trip. It's not a long or dangerous trip, but the extra blessing and one last hot meal will go a long way to ease Judith's anxiousness. She has done her best to make sure both are as good as can be.

Judith gets up and sets out a gunny sack full of food. She starts telling Nate what she has prepared and then goes over the list of supplies that she needs us to bring back. She can sense that Nate is trying to be patient, so she stops talking, puts the list in the sack and gives him a hug. Nate tells her he laid up some firewood under the bath tub. She'll just need to add the water and start the fire. She nods with a smile and a shake of her head. Sam tells Nate to be careful, and to tell Mr. Kimble hello for him. He then flips a silver dollar to him saying, "Don't spend it all in one place."

I head out to the wagon to wait. Both Judith and Sam walk Nate over to the wagon. Judith gives Nate one last hug. Sam shakes my hand and he tells me, "It's been a pleasure, but if you don't come back, I'll understand."

Judith tells us to be safe.

As I climb up the wagon, I look back at Sam and tell him, "I gotta come back; your wife's got my clothes!"

With that, Nate releases the brake, gives the reins a snap, "Up Molly, up Bess, let's go girls."

The ferryman blows the whistle and releases some steam, "Bring 'em on Nate, slow and easy. Boys, help 'em on, keep them horses calm, they got a heavy load. Chock those wheels boys! Good luck Nate, be safe. See ya in a couple days."

"Thanks, Red, we'll be fine."

Red walks the deck one more time and makes sure that the wagon is secure. Red fires off a long whistle as the ferry pushes off from shore and heads up stream. The ferry needs to go upstream a hundred yards or so, the ferryman will then turn her downstream and steer her into the landing on the opposite bank, letting the current do some of the work. The horses seem to be relaxed, they've done this before and know what to expect. I look down and Rusty is pacing up and down the side rail. As we ease into the bank and dock on the south side of the river, Red blows the whistle again. He starts barking orders at the two crewmen. They secure the ferry, once that is done, they lower the off ramp by block and tackle; allowing the ropes to handle the weight and gently lower it onto the flattened out river bank. Nate waits for Red to give him the signal to move the wagon. Red motions for the few folks that rode across to go ahead and walk off the ramp first. He whistles at Nate, waves him forward and Nate releases the brake. Nate snaps the reins, "Up Molly, up Bess, come on girls, nice and easy now. That's it. Good girls, that's it, come on, a little bit more." As the wagon crosses the ramp, the timbers creak from the weight of the load. Rusty is barking and running around all crazy like.

The horses start to jerk back and forth, Nate and Red both

yell, "Rusty, quiet, you're scaring the horses."

Nate smacks the reins sharp on the horses backs and tells Molly and Bess to go hard. He grabs for the whip, but doesn't use it. Molly and Bess arch their backs, lower their heads and dig their hooves into the earth stretching the worn leather harness tight. Nate gives the reins one more hard snap as the wagon's rear set of wheels clear the ramp and we start up the inclined road. Red and crew give a cheer and wave us on our way. Rusty calms down and jogs up the hill ahead of us. Once the wagon gets on level ground, Nate pulls the team up and sets the brake. He jumps down and walks around the wagon checking the load. He stops and turns towards the north shore, waving to Judith and Sam as they wave back.

Climbing back up on the wagon, Nate asks, "You ready?"

"Yep."

He releases the brake, snaps the reins, "Up Molly, up Bess." The wagon lurches forward and Rusty runs ahead to the road crossing. We turn west at the South River Road. With that, Rusty turns and heads back down to the ferry.

Nate doesn't even wait for me to ask, he just says, "Rusty doesn't like town, he likes staying home."

wagon

Chapter 4

Spring is in its full season. The morning is pleasant, the sky is clear and blue. Warblers, finches and sparrows fill the morning air with the sound of their impromptu songs. The budding trees and bushes are fragrant enough to provide the bees an abundant source of pollen. As we ride along I ask, "Hey Nate, a young guy like you, what do you do for fun? You do have some fun don't you?"

Nate doesn't answer right away, and then says, "Fun? Living is fun. Swimming is fun. I don't know, I haven't ever thought about it. I guess I'd have to say that living at the river crossing is fun. Chopping wood is fun. I like stacking up the piles and making long straight rows. At the end of the day I look back at all that wood and it feels like I got something done. When I see smoke drifting out of chimneys in town, I like to think that's my wood burning and making that smoke. That's fun; is that what you mean?"

"No, not really. I mean things like meeting other young folks your own age. Laughing and spending time with girls. I can't imagine that too many young folks hang out at Fletcher's Crossing?"

"No, not many. Once in awhile some fellas come up and fish the big run of summer salmon. But to be honest, there are a lot of places between here and the coast that you can catch salmon. Besides, most folks around here are farmers, there's not much free time, so no, not many."

"Did you go to school out here close by?"

"No, Judith taught me to read and write and taught me numbers and such."

"Humph, sounds kinda lonely for a young kid growing up."

Starring ahead Nate says, "I was never lonely."

"Hey Nate, mind if I ask you something?" He doesn't answer; he just gives a twitch of the reins and makes a click with his voice as Molly and Bess's ears perk up. "So, I notice you don't call Sam and Judith, ma and pa much, why's that?"

After a long silence Nate answers, "Cause they're not."

"What, not your real ma and pa?"

"Nope."

"Not even Sam; he's not your pa?"

"Nope."

"How's that happen?"

"Look Mr. Sparks, I'd rather not talk any more. Can we just enjoy the quiet?"

I give him a shrug and answer, "Sure."

Then he says, "Besides, it's a long story."

"Well, it's a long ride." I settle back in the seat and drop my hat low over my eyes. In a muffled voice I say, "Sorry, I didn't mean to pry."

The steady, rhythmic sound of the horses' hooves on the travel hardened road is interrupted as we come to the first small town of Prospect. Not much here, just a few houses and a building that is the post office and stagecoach stop all in one. There's a small hotel with a sign that says, "Clean Rooms" and "Hot Food". There's a corral in back of the post office with about a half dozen horses. They perk up as they get the scent of Molly and Bess. The smithy comes out and gives a "Good Morning" wave to Nate, then asks, "Headed into Ash Fork?"

"Yes Sir. Do you need anything hauled back?"

"No, not today, Nate. Safe travels."

"Thanks."

There's a small building that is half store and half house selling dry goods and notions. Not much to Prospect. A few kids come out to wave and chase the wagon for a bit. Nate keeps Molly and Bess moving forward, towards the sun. Once out of town I jump down off the wagon to stretch my legs. After days of walking, my legs let me know they need to keep moving. I just can't sit for very long, never have been able to.

After walking for what seems like a mile or two, I yell up to Nate, "You need me to take the reins for a while?" I can tell he thinks about it, but he probably is so used to making this trip by himself, he knows he can do it without a break. I ask again, "Nate, did you hear me? I can drive the team for a while. Give your backside a break."

Again Nate doesn't bother to answer; he just pulls the team up under the shade of a tree, tightens up the reins, sets the brake and jumps down saying, "Good place to water 'em. We're making good time."

Nate reaches in his bag and grabs a couple of apples. He offers one to me, which I gladly take. He takes his up to Molly and cuts it in half; he rubs her muzzle and shares it with her. I guess I should do the same for Bess. She nods her head as if to say, "Yes, please." Hell, it's only a half an apple, I won't starve; I walk over and offer half to Bess. I grab the water bucket and have a drink as I fill it. I ask Nate if he wants a drink. He says he'll get his in a minute. The horses drink but don't seem to be very thirsty. Suddenly they both jerk their heads up quickly and perk their ears, with nostrils twitching.

Nate grabs both halters and holds their heads, "Rider coming."

As he steadies the horses, the dust is visible down the road. We can't see anyone just yet, just the fine trail of dust. I climb up and stand in Nate's seat to get a better look. Nate, still holding the horses gives me a look like I just ate something off his plate. I tell him, "I can drive a team Nate, take a break."

He says, "We'll hold 'em here until whoever is coming passes us by."

"From up here I can see it's a horse and buggy. Looks like a man and woman headed this way."

Just then, the horse and buggy come into full view. They slow as they pass by. We tip our hats and good-days are exchanged. They don't bother to stop, just nod and move on. Nate lets loose of the horses and hangs the bucket back on the side of the wagon. The remaining water may slosh out but he doesn't want to mix the bucket water with the barrel water. I ask if he is going to climb on up and he says he'll walk a bit. I release the brake, give a small whistle and snap the reins, "Up Molly, up Bess, good girls." It's been awhile since I drove a team, but I guess it's something you just don't forget. The smooth, worn leather straps feel familiar as they lay in my hands. Molly and Bess are easy to work. They are sensitive to the reins; they probably even know the way. Hell, I could probably drop the reins and they'd just keep headed towards the west til the road runs out.

As we crest a small rise in the road the view opens up and another small cluster of buildings are in view. Nate decides to climb back up on the wagon. He motions ahead saying, "Unger's Creek, not much here, even less than Prospect, but there's a good place to stop for the night just outside of town and rest the horses."

"You call that a town?"

"I guess. What would you call it?"

"I don't know, but at least Prospect had a hotel and stagecoach stop."

"Yeah, well, they call it Unger's Creek, you can call it what you want."

We pass through almost unnoticed. A few folks come to the windows to look out. A few kids with dogs come out and run along for a ways. Kids will do most anything for a distraction. A few folks wave but show no concern, just a wagon passing through; simple life for simple folks. Nate points up the road and says, "There's a small bridge that crosses the creek, just past the bridge, there's a small trail to the right. We'll turn down the trail and under a stand of trees, there's a place to stop."

As I pull the team up, the scent of the creek and green grass fill my nose. This is a pleasant spot, there's a gentle creek with clean water, good grass and shady tree cover. There's just enough light left to unhitch the horses and gather some wood for the night's fire. I chuckle to myself thinking; we've got a wagon full of wood. Nate tends to the horses and let's them move around free. I ask him if we need to hobble them and he tells me, no hobbles, we'll just long line them to the wagon, they'll be fine for the night. I get a fire going; get the pot of stew on and fresh coffee starting to brew. There's just enough time to meander to the creek's edge. I sit and take my boots and socks off, soak my feet a bit and then dunk my head in. Yeah, it was time to stop. Feeling refreshed, I head back up to camp. Nate is stirring the stew and tells me it will be ready in a few minutes.

I ask, "Don't you want to wash some of that road dust off? That creek is mighty fine."

"Yeah, I'll wash in a bit, let's eat."

We eat in silence, we are either too tired to talk or we both just know it's okay not to talk. A long time ago I learned that trying to talk can wear you out faster than the sometimes awkwardness of silence.

As we finish our meal I say, "I'll clean up, you go down and wash up. It will feel good."

Nate stands up; he checks the horses real quick, gives them each a cup of oats and lays down some fresh hay. The sun is just beginning to set below the tree line. Dusk is settling in. The crickets come alive and the birds are fluttering about before they settle for the night.

Nate returns from the creek and tells me he is going to take the horses back down, let them enjoy the creek as well. I finish my coffee and tell him I'll join them if he doesn't mind. He unties the horses and hands me Bess's lead. Once at the creek and without hesitation, Molly drops her head, takes a drink and steps into the cool water. Bess whinnies a bit and then follows. Nate cares for these horses like Judith cares for Sam and him. There's no effort, he just knows what needs to be done and does it with a gentle touch. He seems to put the horse's needs before his own. We acknowledge how nice the evening is and then he asks, "Ready to head back up?"

I answer, "Sure, morning will come early. I noticed the sunset was less colorful, less orange than usual. I hope the weather holds."

Just as we get back to the wagon, a slight breeze begins to stir the tree tops. The horses give a bit of a snort putting their noses to the breeze. I pat Molly on the flank and tell her she did good today, "You too, Bess." I put a couple logs on the fire and lay out my bedroll. I pull out my harmonica and ask Nate if he minds. He shakes his head no and we settle back.

The stars are starting to speckle the night sky but in the last bit of twilight there seems to be a bit of a filtering haziness. I believe there is rain coming, Nate sees it too. I play some random notes, no song just a melody I like to play. Nate asks me if I know any songs and I tell him that I don't know real songs, I just like to play notes and string them together as they come to me. He nods his head. I explain to him that I wrote a song once; I'll play it for him someday, but not tonight.

Sitting there I suddenly remember that having spent two nights in the barn, I had noticed that the roof could use a repair. It has an area that has some rotten shingles that surround a couple of decent sized holes. I mention this to Nate. He says he knows but he and Sam haven't taken the time to make repairs. I tell him that I'm a pretty good carpenter and if he has some cedar bolts cut and dried, I can split out some shingles and make the repairs. He doesn't say anything, he just nods his head.

I have to ask, "So, is that a yes?"

"Yeah, Sam won't mind."

"Well, I'll need some nails. Can we add them to Judith's list?"

"Sure, I think we have some roofing nails around someplace, but we can get some just in case."

I am curious about what Sam said during breakfast, about the mill needing some timber, so I ask Nate about it and he explains, "The man that has a mill down river from us, Mr. Winkler, has an order for some timbers and wants Sam to supply him."

Surprised I ask, "So, Sam supplies timbers too? How does he get them to the mill?"

"We cut the trees and skid them to a level spot where Mr. Winkler can bring his long trailers in with his heavy horses and he hauls them back to his mill."

"Does Sam make good money doing that?"

"I don't know, you'd have to ask Sam."

"Thanks, I just might do that."

•

Morning comes early, but not before there are a few rumbles of thunder off in the distance that waken us from our sleep. Hearing the thunder and then seeing the gray skies that have moved in overnight, we quicken our pace and start to pick up camp. I stir the embers and throw on a fresh log.

Nate grunts, "We don't have time for breakfast."

"Not even coffee?"

Sternly Nate says, "As long as you're fast. We might get rained on and I want to get to town before the road gets muddy. The horses work hard enough as it is."

Before I put things back in the gunny sack, I grab a couple of biscuits, some jerky and apples. The coffee is good and hot and I give Nate a cup. While I've been doing that, he's been tending the horses and checking the wagon. We're ready to go at the same time. Nate gives a shake of the reins, clicks his teeth and releases the brake. The wagon lurches forward just as the first drops of rain start to fall.

It is more of a mist than a rain but just enough to make us damp. I reach in my pack and pull out my poncho. I ask Nate if he has one. He says it's under the seat, rolled up in an extra blanket. I get it out for him, just in case the sky should open up. We begin to see a few flashes of lightning and hear faint rumblings of thunder. The lighting and thunder appear to be moving to the south of us; apparently, we are on the outer edge of the more intense weather. Eventually, the rain starts to come down a bit harder with bigger drops. We both put our ponchos on as the horses backs start to glisten up. Molly's head seems to hang lower; the road starts to slicken. Just as fast as the heavier rain started, the brief downpour lets up.

It was just a quick shower; just enough to make the road wet and dampen our clothes. As we make our way around a big bend, we can hear a faint train whistle in the distance. Nate says Ash Fork should be about two miles. From the road we

....

can see a stretch of river and some of the outlying houses come into view.

Ash Fork sits in a valley of rolling hills that spread out towards the north. There are not many trees on those hills. They are mostly plowed fields with scattered patches of prairie grass. Farmers have been growing wheat here for years. The railroad came through here while I was growing up. This helped the big wheat farmers to prosper. They could get their grain hauled by boxcar rather than by a wagon load. Like Sam said, "Progress comes, progress brings people." The hills to the south of Ash Fork are tall and steep; they still have trees on them, thick stands of forest, hard to get to timber. No one wants to clear cut the side of those hills. Reality sets in; it's been a long time since I was here last. I reach up and pull my hat down low. Ash Fork!

Chapter 5

We pull through the main street of town and I recall what Sam said, "Ash Fork has grown since the railroad was completed." Looking from beneath the brim of my hat, there are more people on the streets, more shops, a couple of new hotels, saloons and a larger jail. As we pass the street that leads down to the railroad station I ask Nate where we are headed. He says we are going to the general store. I ask him if it's the one on Main Street.

"No, that one burned down. There is a new one; one block away on C Street, Kimble's General and Hardware Store."

As I sit back in the seat I take in as much as possible, all the while not wanting to make eye contact with anyone.

Nate motions towards C Street and says, "We'll take a right there and then a left and go down the alley to Kimble's loading area in the back of the store."

Most of the streets are still compact dirt, but Main Street is paved cobble, with brick sidewalks. The horse troughs and hitching posts have been removed from Main Street, however they still remain on the side streets. The horses are fairly calm with all the commotion that is going on around us. That is until a new machine, an automobile, comes down the street. It is honking a horn and making all kinds of different noises. Horses and people scramble to get out of its way. Nate has his hands full trying to calm Bess down. A couple kids run by, pointing and laughing. One boy comes by on a bicycle. He sticks his tongue out as he pedals past us. The other kids all stop and laugh at him. Nate turns to the right off Main onto C Street. The noise and commotion quickly begins to subside as we turn to the left and into the alley.

As we pull up to a corralled area, Nate stops and motions for me to open the gate. I jump down off the seat with a groan and a stretch. With the gate open, Nate brings the wagon through and makes a circle so the team is facing towards the gate again. He sets the brake and jumps down dusting himself off. Nate then heads into Kimble's back door. While he is in the store I pat Molly and Bess down. I go ahead and grab the water bucket and let them drink telling them, "It will be just a bit, just got to unload and then we'll get you out of them harnesses. We'll give you a good rub down and let you rest, you've earned it."

Nate comes out and introduces Mr. Kimble, the shop owner.

He looks the load over saying, "Load looks good as usual, Nate. Go ahead and stack it all up over there in the corner. Three stacks, keep 'em separate, just like always."

Nate replies, "Sure thing, Mr. Kimble."

Nate gives me a look like, what are you waiting for, get busy. He walks after Mr. Kimble and pulls a piece of paper out of his pocket. They look over the list and I hear Mr. Kimble tell Nate that he'll get started setting the items aside. He lets Nate know that the supplies will be ready whenever Nate wants to load them up. Before Nate comes back I have the back of the wagon open. I start throwing the cedar off over towards the corner, cedar first, doug fir, then the pine.

The day is hot and with that little bit of rain that fell, it is now very humid. The rain knocked the dust down, but made the temperature rise. I take my hat and shirt off, dip my handkerchief in the water bucket and tie it around my neck.

As I climb up into the back of the wagon, a train's whistle sounds off in the distance; the horses perk up and shuffle a bit. The wagon can't go anywhere with the brake on, but the jerking is enough to make me slam up against the side boards of the wagon. Nate lets out a chuckle and continues to stack the wood that I have been throwing to the ground. He has been stacking the wood just as fast as I can toss it.

Needing a drink of water I jump down and dip one of the coffee cups into the barrel. I offer Nate a dipper of water; he takes it gladly and then jumps up into the wagon. The wood starts flying out the back in a blur and clanking around on the ground. I try to stack it up, but it is obvious I can't keep up with his pace. Nate's going so fast he overthrows a couple pieces and one of them bangs into my shin.

Rubbing my leg I say, "Hey, come on, slow down, Nate!"

"Can't keep up? Stay out of the way!" he answers.

"What's the hurry? Aren't we staying the night?"

"Yeah, but the sooner we get done, the sooner I can tend to the horses, get cleaned up and grab a bite to eat."

"Okay, you just don't have to be wild about it."

"You're right, sorry, guess I'm just used to doing this by myself."

We finish unloading in silence, three separate stacks; two full cords of wood. Nate tells me the stock pile is low because of winter, by this fall the yard will be three quarters full of just cord wood, supplied mostly by him.

"That's what, close to fifty cords of wood?" I ask.

"Yeah, give or take. Mr. Kimble takes mostly Sam's wood cause it's the driest and cleanest, but we gotta get it in first, you know, first come first served."

"So, that's what you do all summer; cut cord wood and sell it to Mr. Kimble?"

"Yeah, unless we get an order for some timber, like Sam mentioned yesterday. Sam says if we have a good summer, we can pay off the lease on the eighty acres we are working on now and then we'd be able to get another eighty acres of timber. Work for our future."

Taking another drink of water I say, "Sounds like you'll have a long summer, doesn't sound too exciting."

"Sam says it puts beans on the table."

"That so, that's what Sam says?"

Nate heads into the store saying, "Yeah, or close to it anyway."

Mr. Kimble returns with Nate to check the stacks, he says it looks good, first of many. Nate starts to unharness the horses and I ask him what he is doing. He explains that since we have to load up the supplies in the morning and the yard is closed in, we can leave the horses here for the night. Mr. Kimble's yard is just as good as a stable, just as safe. I give him a hand with the harnesses and then begin to brush the horses down. We water them and strap on their feed bags filled with some oats.

We finish with the horses by putting down fresh hay and I ask, "What's next?"

Nate says, "Suit yourself. I'm headed over to Cindy's Diner

for a hot meal; maybe go down by the river before dark. It'll be time to turn in after that."

"I know; morning comes early. I think I'm gonna get washed up and get a trim and a haircut, then something to eat and mosey around a little myself. Guess I'll see you back here."

As Nate begins to leave, I yell after him, "Where can we put our stuff?"

He answers, "Your things will be okay here, just leave them with the wagon. I've never had a problem before and Mr. Kimble keeps an eye out."

With that I make sure my bedroll, pack, bow and arrows are tucked away. Realizing it has taken me half my life to get back to these streets and alley ways; I head out of Kimble's back area trying to remember where things used to be.

At the end of the alley I turn on C Street and head toward Main Street. I pull my collar up and my hat down, trying to avoid making eye contact. I look up and down Main Street reading the signs of the different shops. Things have changed, but don't feel foreign. I see Bill's Barber Shop and head across the street. Opening the door I disturb two men playing checkers.

They look up and one asks, "Need a shave mister?"

"Sure do, but I'd like to wash up a bit and then have my beard trimmed and get a haircut."

"I can do that, I'm the barber. That's my name on the sign. There are two wash tubs out back, one is for washing and one is for rinsing. There's a towel hanging on a peg, help yourself. I'll be here when you're ready."

"Thank you kindly."

"Don't thank me yet, I haven't done nothing."

As I return from the wash room, Bill asks, "Well, how'd that feel?"

"Mighty fine," I reply.

"Let's get you in the chair, how much we taken off your beard?" Bill asks.

"Oh, just enough to get the shaggy curls off and do the same with the hair. Don't want to be scalped, but if I'm paying for a haircut I want to know I got one."

"Sounds good, you got a name?" he asks.

"Ah yeah, it's Jacob, Jacob Sparks."

Bill turns to his checkers partner saying, "Mr. Sparks? Hey Mack, you ever know any Sparks?"

Mack speaks for the first time, "Only one and he ain't him."

Bill continues asking me, "So, Mr. Sparks, you from around here or just passing through?"

"I'm not just passing through. I'm staying up at Fletcher's Crossing."

"Fletcher's Crossing? Isn't that Sam Harris's place?"

"Yeah, I stopped there a couple of days ago and they were kind enough to take me in and now I'm helping out some, working off their hospitality."

"Did you come into town by yourself?"

"No, I came in with Nate; we hauled in some cord wood and dropped it off at Kimble's General Store."

Bill says, "I know Nate; he's a good kid, hard worker, strong as a bull."

"Yeah, he's my boss, for now anyway."

"Well mister, you could do a lot worse than to be taken in

by the Harris'. They'll treat you fair and give more than they take." He spins me around in the chair, "How's that, enough off?

"Yeah, that will be fine, how much?" I ask.

"That'll be five cents for the beard and ten cents for the haircut, fifteen cents will do it."

"All's I got is a half dollar, make change?"

"Sure."

As I head towards the door, Mack speaks up, "The Sparks I knew worked on the railroad, had a wife and a boy. I heard that Sparks moved on, working the railroad north and the misses stayed put, worked at the dry goods store. Never did hear much about the boy. That the Sparks you knew?"

I let the door shut behind me.

Leaving the barber shop I turn up the street and recognize the old dry goods store. It is still called Cooper's Dry Goods. I am feeling anxious and walk by fast the first time. I cross the street and double back walking a little slower the second time I pass by. From across the street I try to see anybody that might be inside. There are a few folks in the store but I'm too far away to make any one out. I think to myself, she's probably gray by now. I walk down to the end of the block, cross the street again and walk even slower this time as I pass next to the store windows. I make sure my hat is as far down as it can be while still being able to see where I am stepping. Just past the stores' double doors; I stop at a barrel full of brooms that are for sale. I pretend to look one over real good, but I'm really trying to see in the store. While I'm standing there, a woman with two kids in tow comes out the door. In my haste to get a look inside, I brush up against the sleeve of her dress, she pulls back and grabs her kids up close.

Tipping my hat I say, "S'cuse me ma'am, didn't mean to intrude. I just wasn't paying attention and you startled me when you came out the door."

It's then that I notice that there is a man sitting in front of the next shop over. He's watching and listening with more interest than I want.

He leans forward in his chair and says, "Mister, tip your hat to the lady and apologize." Turning my back to the door and windows, I tip my hat and apologize.

Gathering her kids she says, "No harm done Sir, kindly watch where you are going next time."

"Yes, ma'am, I will."

The guy in the chair says, "Hey, you, you going to buy that broom or dance with it?"

Putting the broom back in the barrel I reply, "Look, don't want any trouble." I quickly decide I better move away from this guy. I don't need any attention and especially right here on Main Street.

Without thinking I open the door and step in to Cooper's Dry Goods. I suddenly feel like I have stepped back in time. The place smells the same as it did in my youth. The same dusty light comes through the windows. There are back counters and shelves all down one side of the shop; the counters in front are filled with buttons and spools of thread. The center of the store is laid out with tables stacked with bolts of fabric. In the back, the pigeon-hole bins are filled with kitchen items and on the other wall there are similar type bins filled with lotions and potions and what not. The squeaky floor boards announce my every step.

Out of the back comes a woman's voice, "Hello there, can I help you?"

"Ah, just looking around," I say.

"Looking for what?" she asks.

"Oh, I don't know right off hand, just kinda looking."

The clerk says, "My name is Flora, let me know if you figure it out."

I meander around for another minute and then stop at a counter filled with jars of candy.

" 'S'cuse me ma'am, can I get some of that licorice?"

"Sure, how much would you like?"

"Just give me a penny's worth." She counts out five pieces and I realize that's not much, I ask for five more.

"What else can I get you?"

"Nothing, nothing more today, I'm just visiting."

"Suit yourself, that'll be two cents."

Clearing my throat as I pay I ask, "Ma'am, is there a Mrs. Sparks that works here?"

With hesitation in her voice she says, "Mrs. Sparks, she hasn't worked here for a few years. Who's asking?"

"Me, ma'am. I just wanted to say hello if she was still here."

Then she asks, "What's your name?"

"I was a friend of the families a long time ago."

"A friend of Mrs. Sparks? I have never known Mrs. Sparks to talk of anyone but her husband and her son and they've both been gone a good while."

"I used to live here when I was younger and I knew the

family. Me and my friend used to play after school and we'd come into this store and Mrs. Sparks would let us have a piece of licorice each. Sometimes if we would sweep the walkway or take the trash out she'd let us pick something else out."

"Well, she doesn't work here anymore, stays close to home from what I hear. Ever since her eyes started going bad, she just doesn't get out much. Can I give her a message for you if I see her?"

As I turn towards the door to leave I answer, "Naw, she probably wouldn't remember me anyway. That was a long time ago. I gotta go. Thanks for the licorice."

To my back she says, "You're welcome, come again big spender, maybe next time you'll buy that broom."

I stuff the bag of licorice in my back pocket and look up and down the street looking for a place to get a hot meal. Down the next block, I see a sign hanging up that says, "Midge's Hot Meals" and has a drawing of a steaming cup of coffee. The sign looks inviting so I start to work my way towards it. I walk up the block passing small shops, a bank and a saloon.

The sounds from the saloon waft out over the sidewalk and into the street. There is a honky-tonk piano playing above rowdy voices mixed with laughter; all combined into one loud symphony, similar to ones I've been an instrument in more times then I like to recall. As I pass by I can't resist the urge to look over the sheer curtains and take a look inside. I don't really want a drink as much as I just miss being a part of the crowd. I miss the action, the banter with the folks that I know and those that I may come to know. With a drink in my hand, I was friends with everyone. The front doors are double-swing, café doors and bar patrons are having a great time. The smell of cigars and stale beer hits my nose and suddenly I am relieved that I am on the outside looking in.

I have to think back some, but I realize I've been sober for a few years now and shake my head at the thought that I had spent most of my life in places like this. The working girls are sitting, talking with any man that will buy them a drink. They hope that they'll get a chance to get more of their money by inviting them upstairs. Behind closed doors, that's where the real money is made. Course the girls don't make much, the house takes most of it. The girls don't seem to mind though, each one of us, man or woman has to live with the choices we make that end up coloring our lives.

There's a card game going and for some reason, I stop and take a longer look through the window. One of the card players looks up and makes eye contact with me. The girl sitting on his lap does the same. She gives me a half wave and motions for me to come on in. Suddenly she finds herself pushed off the guys lap. This action makes me a little anxious; I realize that I still have a longing to be in the game, be inside, and be a part of that environment. That life; it was fun, and I was good at it but I just can't, not today, not any day. I don't trust myself. Nervousness takes over my anxiousness and I move quickly down to the café. I want a hot meal more than a drink and a laugh.

With each step that takes me farther from the saloon, I begin to relax and begin to remember some of the funnier times I had and start to laugh to myself. Not realizing that I am laughing out loud, I walk into Midge's. Everyone turns and

....

looks my way as the door clanks a cow bell behind me. I tip my hat and make my way to the counter. The air is heavy with the smell of fresh coffee, bacon, steaks, fresh bread and pies.

From back of the counter a voice says, "Coffee, mister?"

"You bet, thank you."

"Do you need a menu or do you know what you'd like? That is if you are eating and not just having coffee?" the waitress asks as she sets down a cup of steaming coffee.

"Yes please, I'll take a menu. Give me a minute, everything smells so good I need to let my stomach settle."

"Sure thing, just let me know when you're ready, my name is Carol and don't forget to check out the daily special, it's written on that chalk board at the end of the counter."

"Thanks, Carol. Right now the coffee is great."

I settle onto a stool and try to blend in, like I've been here before. Being back in Ash Fork after all these years seems to make my skin crawl, and I can't help but feel like someone is watching me, remembering me. How could they though, it was so many years ago. I was just a kid in my teens. I sure wasn't a grown man, not like I am today.

Carol comes my way asking, "Figured out if you're hungry yet?"

"Yeah, I am. Think I'll have the meat loaf with mashed potatoes and gravy and corn, no, give me the carrots and a piece of corn bread."

"Sure 'nough, good choice." she says.

"And I'll have a piece of that fresh baked pie."

"Which one, apple or cherry?" she asks.

"You pick."

With a wink Carol says, "Sure, thing."

Everyone seems to be enjoying their own meals and take no notice of me. I relax and enjoy my food. As I pay I look out and see Nate across the street headed in the direction of Mr. Kimble's store. By the time I get out the door, I see Nate enter the same barber shop I had gone into. Good for him, the kid could use a haircut and maybe a shave, can't tell if he is trying to grow a beard or just hasn't shaved for awhile. I figure I'll just head on back and check the wagon and horses.

It's starting to get dusk, the sun is going down and the lamplighters are starting to light the street lamps. When I get to the back of Mr. Kimble's, I find the horses are quiet and seem to be relaxed. The wagon is undisturbed. I walk up and let Molly and Bess see me and get my scent. They have gotten used to me; they snort and shift a bit, looking for an apple. I reach up under the wagon seat and grab an apple out of the bag and cut it in half. You'd think they hadn't eaten all day the way they drool and munch the equal portions. I look around and notice they still have water and some hay. I grab the brush out of one of the side cupboards and start to give Bess a brush down. To my surprise, Molly gives Bess a gentle nudge in her ribs trying to move her out of the way. I grab Molly's mane and tell her she will be next. She gives me a snort and stomps one of her hooves while giving her head a shake.

I look at her saying, "You're spoiled, you may lead the team, but right now, Bess is first."

Molly settles just as Nate comes through the gate. He glances at me as he walks past and goes into the store. I finish with Bess and start to brush down Molly. Nate comes out and climbs up into the back of the wagon, he is different and quieter than earlier, he seems almost upset, but I can't tell as he doesn't say anything.

"Everything alright?" I ask. He doesn't say a word he just starts rolling out his bedroll under the wagon. I ask again, "You alright?"

"Better get some sleep; I want to get a real early start."

"Okay, I'll just finish with Molly." There doesn't seem to be enough room for both of us under the wagon so I ask, "Where am I gonna sleep?"

"Any place you want. Suit yourself." he says.

I grab my bedroll and decide the air is a bit heavy to sleep around here. I head across the alley and settle down in a stable behind another shop keeper's place. I just hope Nate doesn't leave without me.

•

After a restless night, I get up and decide to check on Nate. Sure enough he is up already and getting the harnesses' laid out and the horses readied. "Morning Nate, how'd you sleep?"

"Morning, just fine, as soon as the horses are hitched, I'll be loading up the supplies and heading out, if you're coming you best be ready, if not, I'll tell Sam you helped out and your debt was paid."

"Hey, what's up? Did I do something to upset you?"

"Look, I just want to get the wagon loaded and get going."

"Okay, mind if I help?"

Nate replies, "Suit yourself. Mr. Kimble has all the supplies stacked up by the back door; all we have to do is load them up."

Nate starts setting the larger items on the back of the wagon. He then climbs up and starts stacking them towards the front. He is going to load it all by himself if I don't jump in and help, so I grab burlap bags marked with sugar, flour, and coffee beans, and put them on the back of the wagon. At least this way he won't have to jump up and down out of the wagon. There is some fabric, lamp oil, kerosene, a couple of gallons of white wash, wheel grease, all kinds of assorted items.

"Hey, Nate, is Sam trying to open his own dry goods store? There sure is a lot of goods."

"It was a long winter and Judith makes out the supply list, I just do the driving." he says.

"Did you tell Mr. Kimble that I needed some roofing nails?"

"No, I forgot. I'll get him to add some to the list."

"How do you pay for all this stuff?" I ask.

"Credit, Sam supplies firewood and Mr. Kimble gives us credit."

"How do you keep track of the balance?"

"Mr. Kimble sends a tally sheet once a month. Look, can we just load the supplies?"

With that, I decide to stop talking and tell myself, it's sure gonna be a long ride back. The sun is just above the tops of the surrounding buildings as Mr. Kimble comes out with a hot pot of coffee and a couple of cups.

He says to Nate, "Looks like you got all the goods. I trust it was all there?"

"Sure seems like it Mr. Kimble. I didn't really check the list off, always been okay before."

"No problem Nate. Say hello to Sam and Judith. I hope to see them sometime this summer. Either way, I'll have their balance sheet ready when you make your next delivery."

"Sounds good, Mr. Kimble. Thanks for the coffee."

Nate turns to me and says, "We best be gettin' on our way."

I didn't see any nails so I mention it again to Nate.

Nate speaks up, "Hey, Mr. Kimble, can I get a couple pounds of roofing nails? We need to repair our barn roof and I'm not sure if we have enough to do the repair."

"Sure thing Nate, I'll bag 'em up and write 'em in the book, two pounds going to be enough?"

Nate looks at me and I give him a shrug saying, "Two pounds, three pounds, better to have too many than run short. Better to have extra then not have enough to finish."

Mr. Kimble gives a wave of his hand and heads into the store. I grab another cup of coffee and ask, "Hey Nate, we gonna get something to eat before we head out?"

"Should've thought of that sooner, we're ready to go."

"I guess I'll grab a couple of apples, and see what else I can find."

Mr. Kimble comes back out and hands Nate three pounds of roofing nails saying, "Like the man said, better to have extra. You don't want to run short."

"Thanks Mr. Kimble, thanks for everything. I'll see you in a week, gotta get this yard filled up."

Mr. Kimble picks up the empty cups saying, "Have a safe trip, Nate, and what was your name again?"

I answer, "Jacob, Jacob's the name, and I'll be back."

At that Nate releases the brake and gives the reins a snap, "Come on Molly girl, come on Bess, time to go to work. Good girls."

Nate pulls out of the yard, before I climb on I close and latch the gate. Once on board I catch Nate's eye as he gives me a cold stare. I settle into the seat and push my hat back on my head trying to figure out what's got Nate all riled up.

I finally say, "Look Nate, I don't know what I did or what you think I did or if you heard some bad news, but something has got you all upset, it's a long ride back, but if you don't talk to me, I'll just as soon walk back."

Nate says, "Like I said before, suit yourself."

With his jaw set tight, he snaps the reins and turns down Main Street and heads out of town.

I grab a biscuit and bite off a piece of jerky. I offer some to Nate but only get a head shake that says no. I finish the apple as we leave the last few houses, headed east, looking into the early sun. It is a mild morning with a few scattered clouds in the sky, hopefully they won't begin to stack together.

"Nate, I know we have only known each other a few days, but I know a little bit about people and I can sense things about how they feel and all. I know something happened in town to upset you. You might not want to talk to a stranger, but somehow, I don't feel like a stranger. If there is anything, anything at all you would like to talk about, just spit it out. We got a long ride ahead of us and sometimes talking things out helps. Sometimes, just talking out loud to yourself helps. I can sit here and be quiet and you can pretend you're talking to yourself. I won't say a word. " Nate moves in his seat, but his jaw is locked.

I let out a heavy sigh, "Hell, there's no harm in quiet."

The sun is mid-morning high, for some reason I just can't seem to get comfortable in the wagon seat. I've gotten hot starring into the sun so I jump down and get some water. Nate keeps the wagon rolling.

"Hey, Nate, do ya want some water?"

With that, Nate reaches down and grabs his canteen from under the seat.

I stay on the ground trying to sort this all out. I feel all mixed up inside. He's a seventeen year old kid, I'm a grown ass man, yet somehow I feel like all the feelings I've been having these past few days are suddenly all wrong. I haven't spent a lot of time with younger folks but Nate is as close to being a man as I was when I set out on my own. I feel really close to this kid. I climb back up in to the wagon, and try one more time to get him to talk, but to no avail, Nate's jaw is set tight. I reach into my pouch and grab the licorice.

Holding a piece up I ask, "Nate, you want a piece of licorice?"

"Naw."

"Come on, have a piece."

"No thanks."

"Come on, you can have one piece, it's fresh. Well it was when I bought it. Don't tell me you've never had licorice before."

Answering with more than one word he says, "Yeah, I've

had it before."

"Come on, just one, before I have to eat it all myself. Come on." I say as I give him a nudge.

He finally obliges me, "Okay, I guess I can have a taste, thanks."

I settle in my seat a bit and pull my hat down. Out the corner of my eye I see a hint of a smile on Nate's dusty face as he wipes moisture from of his eyes.

As the wagon jerks, so does my head. I realize that I must have dozed off. I quickly sit up straight as Nate brings the wagon to a complete stop and sets the brake. "What's up, why we stopping?" I ask.

Nate speaks for the first time since we had the licorice, "We've been at it for a while, I want to give the horses a bit of a rest and some water."

"Sure thing, I'll grab the bucket, anything else?"

"Nah, just water for now, we'll stop for the night at Unger's Creek again. It won't be long. I just needed to stretch and give my backside a rest."

"Sounds good to me, you want me to drive 'em to the creek, give you a break?"

"Sure."

We change places and settle in for the short haul to the creek. With the sun at our backs and the horses at a steady pace, I say, "Hey, Nate, about earlier, your business is your business. I apologize; it's not my place to press. I was young once myself. There were times when I wished I'd had someone to talk to, that's all. You, Sam and Judith have been real good to me, treated me better than I have been treated in a long time. I guess I was hoping that I had found a place that I could settle into and spend enough time to get to really know some good folks. What you have with Sam and Judith is special and none of it is my business. I over stepped my place." With that I hold out the bag of licorice, "Want another piece of that licorice?"

"Sure."

....

Chapter 6

I set the brake and we both jump down with a grunt and a groan. The horses' nicker and Molly scratches the dirt. Both horses give a good shake of their heads and backs as dust and sweat sift through the air. Nate and I undo the reins and remove harnesses. Molly and Bess both whinny and bob their heads with approval. I grab Molly's bridal and walk her out of the wagon tongue; Nate does the same with Bess. We walk them down to the creek's edge to let them drink and cool their legs.

The late afternoon is pleasant with a gentle breeze that moves through the tree tops whispering a sweet song. There are a few birds chirping and fluttering about, nervous that strangers are here. A pair of squirrels begin chattering back and forth, sounding their alarms and scampering from tree to tree. The shadows, beginning to lengthen, tell us to move the horses back up towards the wagon and get camp set up.

Nate and I remain silent during this time, until finally Nate says he is going to gather up some firewood. I make a comment about maybe next time we should keep a few pieces on the wagon, that way we wouldn't need to gather wood. Nate just shakes his head and responds with a snort.

"Well we should. It wouldn't hurt none to keep a few chunks of firewood for ourselves."

Raising his arms Nate says, "There's plenty of dried wood lying around, it's no bother, need to stretch a bit anyway."

I pull out the gunny sack and sort through what is left for

us to eat. We still have a few apples, some biscuits, and some jerky. Nate comes back with the firewood, I get a fire started and put a pot of coffee on. Nate starts to brush the horses down as the quiet settles in around us.

Before we stretch out our bedrolls, we sit to watch and listen to the fire burn as it sputters and pops. The crickets soon join in with their chirping and there's a couple of frogs croaking down by the creek. The stars are shimmering through a few scattered clouds that seem to be dead still. The moon is bright, but not full, what light it does cast, comes slanted through the trees. I reach in my pack and grab my harmonica and look to Nate to see if he'd mind. He just nods and keeps staring at the fire. As I blow a few notes, Molly and Bess perk their ears and Molly turns, shakes her head and paws at the ground.

Taking my harmonica away from my mouth I say, "I haven't even started yet; let me get my lips warmed up." The crickets go silent and an owl hoots from somewhere out in the tree tops.

Nate says, "Hope you haven't ruined his hunt."

"Well, who knows, maybe someone or something will find my playing a bit soothing? I know it sure has been a friend to me while I have been on the road and alone." Then I ask, "What about you, have you ever played or tried to learn an instrument?"

"Nah, never had much time for it. Judith tried to teach me the fiddle. She played a little bit once in awhile, but nah, I don't have much time or the need to play music. I like to listen though, and I do like the sound of that harmonica you play."

"Well thank you, Nate. I just like to make things up as I go. I find it peaceful and I feel a little better when I lay my head down. There are all kinds of sounds and music filling the air all the time. When I put together a few notes to make a tune, I just feel like I've been a part of one of God's own songs. Just something I feel inside, I guess."

"Well, it's nice and relaxing."

I play a few more notes that I like to string together. Nate gets up and says he is going to make sure Molly and Bess are settled. I throw a couple more pieces of wood on the bed of coals; it doesn't take long before the flames leap up and brighten the camp.

"The horses are fine," says Nate as he settles back down.

The night chill is just starting to creep in around the camp and the crickets have lost their volume. The frogs seemed to have intensified their croaking. Nate shifts around and looks up at the night sky saying, "Hey, Jake?"

"Yeah."

"About today, I don't know how to describe it, but sometimes when I go into Ash Fork, I get a feeling of heaviness in my body that just takes over and I get all sad. Sometimes I get mad and once in a while, I feel both at the same time. I want to run as fast as I can to get away and then I want to hit something, hurt something, make something hurt as much as I hurt. It probably sounds crazy. I know I have to go to Ash Fork for Sam and Judith to get the supplies we need, and I know that they depend on me going, but sometimes, I just hate being there and I can't get away fast enough."

The harmonica twirls through my fingers and I roll on

my back, looking up into the night sky that is filled with a million stars banded together in a stripe that stretches across the heavens. I lay there quiet, wishing, hoping that the next words out of my mouth are the right words.

Without taking my eyes off the stars I ask, "Have you ever talked to Sam about the way Ash Fork makes you feel?"

Nate answers, "I did when I was younger; Sam would take me to town with him when he made the deliveries. I used to be so scared that I wouldn't leave the wagon, sometimes I would just sit under a tarp, rocking back and forth, waiting for Sam to come back. Sometimes I'd be so scared I'd start crying, so he stopped taking me. As time passed, he began to leave it up to me to decide when I wanted to go. I slowly got over my fear, but the mixed up feelings sometimes still get to me. I haven't talked to him about Ash Fork for a long time. I just never wanted to worry him."

We sit quietly for a bit, my mind searching for the right words. Finally I say, "I'd like to tell you I understand, but I don't. What happened that made you scared?"

Nate rolls over and mumbles, "I'm tired, goodnight Jake, morning...."

I interrupt him and say, "I know, morning comes early, goodnight Nate."

•

The early morning dew and dampness creeps into every space of my bedroll. I crack one eye open and it's as dark as it can be. The moon has moved on with just a slight glow that is low in the horizon, leaving only a few bright stars that refuse to fade. No crickets, no frogs, no owl, just early morning quiet. Nate is sleeping deep and has his head buried in his bedroll. I prop myself up on one elbow and take a more observant look around. With a long stick I stir the coals, shake the gray ash off and decide to put a small piece of a tree limb on the now glowing embers. I shimmy out of my bedroll as quietly as possible and see a slight glimmer of light to the northeast. I guess it's not too early to be up, just don't want to make too much noise and wake Nate. Molly and Bess stir a bit, rather than shush them, I walk up to them and rub their muzzles and scratch their ears and foreheads. They are both relaxed and seem undisturbed. I walk down to the creek to splash my head and face. I then decide to strip out of my underwear and take a very quick dip to wash some road grime off. With a muffled shriek, I shake my head knowing that I am now fully awake.

With the early morning sky equally mixed in dark and light colors, I turn my head back to camp; something catches my eye out in the meadow just at the forest line. I can just barely make out what looks like a couple of deer. Damn, I should have brought my bow. Maybe, just maybe I can get my bow and arrows out of the wagon and make my way over to them before they move on.

Nate is still in a deep sleep. He doesn't stir as I fumble around under the wagon seat trying to grab my bow and arrows. Finally free from the quiet of camp, I make my way to the forest edge using the trees and low bushes as camouflage between the deer and myself.

I poke my head up just high enough to see over the tall

meadow grass. Ducking back into the cover of the trees I make my way around the east edge of the meadow in case there is any breeze coming from the west.

My luck has held, none of my movement has spooked the two doe. I still need to get about ten yards closer for a clear shot. My heart is thumping as I slide an arrow out of the quiver. I can't hear anything but the pounding of the blood in my ears. I pull back the arrow as I exhale a deep breath, hold steady, aim small, release. It takes a mere second, with a solid thump, the does' legs buckle and her body slumps to the ground. The second doe bolts away faster than I can blink my eye. The fallen doe lies where she stood, the last spasms of life leaving her body. It was a good clean shot; through her chest, right between her front legs. I bend down and thank her for her life and then slit her throat so she can bleed out quickly. I rise up as the first streaks of sunlight brighten the cloud scattered sky. The pounding in my ears has stopped, replaced with the morning song of unconcerned birds.

With the doe dressed out and on my shoulders I pick up my bow and quiver of arrows and head back to camp. The walk back is shorter as I cut through the meadow. I can see Nate has gotten up and is moving about the camp. I hope he has the coffee on and he likes fresh venison.

I yell out, "Hey Nate, stoke up that fire real good, we got fresh meat for breakfast!" He looks up and waves and then stands there, looking like he's seen a ghost or something. As I lay the deer down I ask, "What you don't like venison, fresh liver, fresh heart?"

With a hint of irritation he says, "No, I love venison, but

we don't have time for that right now."

"Nate, come on, we are just 'bout out of food and a good hot piece of meat would go a long way to getting us through our ride back."

Softening he says, "Yeah, I guess you're right, but we gotta get going, Sam will be needing us back. He's got that new order to fill and there is always more cord wood to take to town. Summer is almost here; it's our busy time to haul."

With insistence I say, "Nate...it's okay, we'll cook up some fresh meat and I'll skin this hide off and we'll be on our way. We will have fresh meat back at the house, Sam will understand. It doesn't take me long to skin a deer. Now, stoke that fire up and get that frying pan out. We got fresh liver to cook."

I grab some rope, loop it over a branch in a tree and tie the deer up by her hind legs with a spreader stick to open her chest up. I draw my knife across my stone a few times and start to skin the hide off the meat. Once the hide is loose, I lay it down. Nate has grabbed some salt out of the back of the wagon. We salt the hide down and roll it up tight. With the carcass hanging in the tree, we settle back and share the fresh liver and hot coffee. We have a couple of biscuits and slice up a couple of apples...not a bad morning's breakfast. Needing to wash up the skillet and plates, Nate pulls out the big kettle and fills it with water and brings the water to boil. In the meantime, I rummage under the seat of the wagon and find a couple of old gunny sacks. I shake them out best I can and head down to the creek to get them good and wet. When I get back to camp, Nate is getting Molly and Bess ready to hitch up to the wagon. I wrap the carcass up tight with the wet gunny sacks and hang the carcass up in the back of the wagon. With the meat wrapped and kept moist, flies shouldn't bother us on the ride back to Fletcher's Crossing.

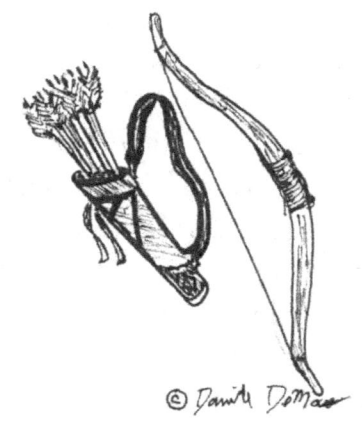

bow and arrow

Chapter 7

We climb up onto the wagon and Nate gives the reins a snap! "Come on girls, let's head home, lighter load going east."

We ride in silence, both staring into the morning sun, hats pulled down low. There is a slight breeze at our backs and there looks to be some clouds building up towards the south. Looking and nodding his head Nate says, "Hope the weather holds off; don't need any rain just yet. Don't need slick and muddy roads."

"Yeah, but we're making good time, already passed Unger's Creek and half way to Prospect."

Nate says, "I know but those clouds are piling up and turning dark; looks like rain."

"Yeah, we'll make it."

Just before Prospect, we pass a farm with fields all plowed and green shoots of spring wheat up about four inches. Set back in a nice grove of trees is a well cared for farm house. At the entry road that leads up to the house there is a red flag tied to a fence post. "Hey Nate, what do you suppose that means?"

"What, that red flag?"

"Yeah, that red flag, someone needs help or something?"

"No, that's the Johnson's place and they must have seen us pass by the other day. They are letting me know that they need a load of firewood next time I head into town."

"That so?"

"Yeah, we trade firewood for their winter hay for the horses and cows, Sam's not a farmer."

We roll through Prospect, a few folks wave and we all exchange "good mornings and good days." Some yell out asking for any news from Ash Fork. There is nothing new to report or share, so we just keep rolling along. A couple of the women yell out to Nate to give their best to Judith, and to remind her that quilting season will start up mid-summer after the fourth. Nate waves and yells back, "Sure will".

Just outside of Prospect we see the first flashes of lightning and hear the report of thunder, none too far off neither. I reach down under the seat, "I'll grab the ponchos, looks like we'll be needing them."

We barely have time to get them on as the sky opens up loud and dark with rain coming down hard. It doesn't take long for the road to slick up and the wagon wheel ruts to fill with water. The horses drop their heads and plod along. No matter how much Nate cajoles them into hurrying up their pace, they know that their pace is what it will be. A muddy and slick road without traction is no time to race on.

With a smack of the reins, Nate yells out, "Come on Molly, pick it up, it ain't that bad. The sooner we get home the sooner we get out of this weather and out of the mud."

Molly shakes her head and pulls herself up. The wagon stops just as a flash of lightning hits off to the left of us and strikes a tall pine. The lightning was so close we could hear it zing through the air and it made the hair on our arms stand up. The crack of thunder that followed was on us quicker then we could cover our ears. Molly and Bess both rear up and want to run; it takes all of Nate's strength to hold 'em in place.

The pine tree exploded into a burst of sparks and split in two; the top is now in two halves, one side burning in a massive fireball, the other half hanging down pointing to the ground, its top branches almost blocking the road.

The horses are agitated and want to bolt. I jump down and grab both sets of reins as Nate sets the brake. We both know that the worst place to be is in the trees, but we can't stay out in the open either. The horses want to run for the cover of the trees, the rain is coming down sideways and hard, there is lightning and thunder all around. We have no choice but to get out of the open. Nate jumps back up and releases the brake, I stay in front holding onto the bridals as we walk Molly and Bess into the cover of a small cluster of trees. Nate sets the brake and we do the best we can to settle the team. Nate thinks it best to grab the hobbles, just in case the horses spook again. We retie the tarp over the load and settle in under the wagon.

I look over at Nate, "That Molly, I think she knew that lightning was gonna hit right next to us; she's some horse."

Nate answers, "Damn straight she is."

Once the storm passes, we pull back out onto the rain soaked road. Nate backs off the earlier pace knowing the next pace will be slower due to the wet and muddy road.

Out of the blue Nate asks, "So Jake, you told Sam that you were from Ash Fork, what made you leave?"

With a half sigh I say, "I was young when I left, things got very complicated really quick and I just had to leave. It's a long story, Nate."

Nate nods his head and looks my way saying, "It's just that you're not like the other drifters we get passing through. You seem different. I noticed you didn't head right to the saloon when we got to town, you don't smoke, don't chew. You're just different. It's like you're looking for something, or maybe found something and don't know what to do with it."

"Nate, you're pretty smart for being so quiet."

Nate continues, "Well, living with Sam and Judith, they're special people and they have let me have my own thoughts, let me observe life, let me listen, and learn things for myself. They are good people. They treat each other with respect and they have a respect for life that they share with all people. They share with those that have a need. They gave me a place to feel safe and showed me a good way to live. For all the traveling you have done and for as long as you've been gone, I see a lot of them in you. You seem to have journeyed a long ways to come to the same place. That's all; I just notice something different about you."

"Well Nate, I thank you for that. Thank you for noticing and you're right, I have journeyed a ways. Actually, it feels like a long, long ways. I have been moving from place to place half of my life, and yes, I was from Ash Fork."

Part Two

Aspen Grove

Chapter 8

"I'll tell you my story Nate, but on one condition, what I tell you stays between you and me. It's my story and I share it with who I decide and when I decide to tell it. I trust you Nate, and I think I can trust Sam and Judith. Just let me tell Sam and Judith in my own time in my own way."

Nate answers, "No problem Jake. Look if it's that big a deal, I don't want to know. I just got a feeling you aren't leaving anytime soon."

I continue, "Well, time will tell, but you're right, and I'm not planning on leaving just yet; that's if Sam is okay with me sticking around. I feel fortunate to have stumbled into Fletcher's Crossing when I did. The road is long and things can get crazy at times. A man, some men are just not meant to be by themselves. Over the years, I think I've come to learn that I'm one of them; I'm one that needs to surround himself with the company of others. For the longest time I felt I wanted to be by myself, be a loner so to speak; that way I didn't have to answer to anybody but myself. As I continued to wander around, I began to realize that I wasn't wandering with a purpose, I was running, running from the voices of my past. During bouts of depression, of which there were many, all I did was hang on to those voices, and run further down the road seeking a place to quiet my mind."

We keep rolling along but occasionally we have to stop to clean the mud build-up from the spoke wheels. It's slow going and the sun is now behind us. The storm passed, but not the cloud cover. The wind is still up, which is good, it is helping to dry out the muddy road, well at least the top layer of mud. The horses and wagon are just heavy enough that their hooves sink in along with the wagon wheels. Nate pulls the team up and we get some water for us and Molly and Bess. Nate seems to have an endless supply of apples and we give one to both. I grab some jerky and we climb back up and continue to slog along while we chew.

"So, you always been by yourself?" asks Nate.

"Oh no, not always; I've had traveling partners; you might call 'em walking partners. Just people like myself, moving from place to place, looking for something or running from something."

"How'd it start?" Nate asks and then continues, "What got you to leave in the first place? Seventeen isn't too young, I mean, I could probably head out on my own, if I wanted to, but, I like my life. I like living at the river's crossing. I have all I need."

"That's good Nate. Some are lucky that way. Most men, have the need to strike out on their own, they have the itch to seek adventure, cut loose from their parents and make their own way. Some like to stay put and grow into their pa's ways. Maybe inherit a farm or take over the blacksmith shop or tend a store in hopes of owning it someday. Some want to go to school and be a doctor or lawyer, maybe be a teacher. Hell, some want to be the sheriff or run the post office. While others run off and get hooked up in the army. I had a few friends run off, catch a steamer up to the Yukon chasing the golden dream. You just never know what makes a man move on or stay put.

We can be as restless as a herd of wild mustangs on the open prairie or settle in with a good woman, scratch out a living and raise up a couple of youngins. Both types of men will be as happy and content as a fat bear crawling into his winter cave to sleep away the cold, you just never know. When I left, I just knew that the life that was being forced on me wasn't for me. I was getting forced into something I wasn't sure that I could handle, not at seventeen anyway."

"Did ya ever get married, have a wife?"

"No, I never married. I've had a couple of women in my life, one wanted to make me stay and tend to her farm. Her husband had taken ill and died, left her with a nice piece of land up in north Oregon. Another woman, she kinda took up my way of life and followed me out of Portland. She is the one I miss the most. She was a real friend, a companion. She always had a smile on her face that would light up a room. She always had a kind word to say to someone or about someone. Her name was Beth. She had the prettiest blonde hair that she would put up top her head and then at night she'd let it down. I just loved her; hard worker too. She wasn't afraid to get her hands dirty, loved to make things grow from seed to harvest, she had that green thumb. Judith reminds me of her. Just the type that when she says she loves you it makes you feel like you're the only man alive. Judith looks at Sam that same way. You just know that Judith is living her life for Sam and also for you. That's a special kind of love, that's what a woman brings to a man's life that he can't find wandering around God's green earth on his own."

"So what happened to her, to your Beth?"

"Well, three winters ago, we were caught out in some real bad weather up north just west of Carver's Pass. We'd been down towards the coast and we were headed up to Carver's Pass to find work. I had gotten word that the railroad had built a lumber and cattle yard up there to load trains and send goods north and east. That meant there would be people looking for jobs and looking for houses to live in. Me being a carpenter, I thought I could make some money working on some houses. Well, we were walking up the pass when a storm blew in hard. It started out with a wind, which brought the rain. Eventually the temperature dropped and rain turned to snow. It turned so quick that we couldn't find our way to any kind of shelter. We couldn't even find a cluster of rocks to shield us. We got off the road and worked our way into the heavy woods but by then our clothes were soaked clean through. I worked at cutting some saplings and made a quick lean-to, but couldn't gather any dry wood for a fire. Poor Beth was shivering something terrible, so I stripped us both naked thinking that our body heat would keep us warmer than being in wet clothes. I threw our rain ponchos over us and then our bedding and then our wet clothes on top and climbed in next to Beth. We tried to settle in but the wind and snow were howling, blowing and shifting so bad that by morning we were under a three foot snow drift. Beth never quit shaking, all night she shivered, her teeth never stopped rattling. I tried to get her warm, keep us both warm, but by morning she had caught a fever. She went from joyful warm one day to pneumonia fever in less than twenty-four hours."

Nate asks, "What'd ya do?"

"There wasn't much I could do. I got up and dug us out of the snow drift that had encircled the lean-to. In the light of day I was able to find some dead limbs up in the trees and was able to get a fire started. I dried out her clothes best I could, got her dressed and rolled her up in the few dry blankets we had. I helped her up to her feet, but she was too weak and dizzy to even walk. I hoisted her up over my shoulder and started carrying her the two miles to Carver's Pass. By the time I got to the doc's place her lips had turned blue, her toes and fingers were blue. The Doc said there wasn't much he could do for her. All he could do was to get her warmed up in a hot tub of water. We'd have to wait and see how strong she was. I sat there all that day and through the night, by the next morning a real bad fever had set in and she was boiling hot. The Doc came in and told his nurse to get some cold water in the tub; he was going to try to cool her down but it was no use. She just seemed to lay there and sleep. She was still burning up, seemed to be burning from the inside out; she had a smile on her face the whole time. She grabbed my hand once and seemed like she wanted to tell me something. I got up to her face real close. She tried but couldn't open her eyes; her breath was weak and shallow. Faintly she whispered, "Thank you." Just like that, she was gone, just gone."

"Sorry, Jake."

"The next day we laid her to rest in the city graveyard, I managed to get a plot that was up on the side of a small sloping hill. The doc said that in the spring the wild flowers would grow and fill the hillside with color. I knew Beth would like that. I walked back out of town, gathered my belongings at the lean-to and just kept on walking."

Nate asks, "You didn't head back to town to find work?"

"No, I didn't see the point. I felt as bad as I had ever felt in my life. There was no way I was going to stay at Carver's Pass. I was now at another crossroad. I could keep walking and searching or I could return to a familiar way of life; at least I would know what to expect. Having had Beth in my life, I knew I could stay strong and not let my old ways creep back in. So, I headed back down the pass to the life I'd just left. You see, I had made a promise to myself and to Beth to live sober. I had been sober long enough to know that each day without a drink felt better than the day before. So, I returned to life as I knew it but stayed sober and felt the pain. Beth was with me a good many years. We had a lot of good times together, her and me. I miss her yet."

"How many years together?"

"Oh, I'd have to say at least seven years...yeah, let's say seven, that's one of my favorite numbers, seemed to be one of hers too."

We talked so long that it is close to being dark and without knowing it we are rounding the curve and are close to the turn off to Fletcher's Crossing. As we draw nearer, good 'ol Rusty comes running and barking up to the wagon. Nate tells me that this is his usual greeting; he's probably been waiting most of the day. I jump down to pet him and let him climb his paws up on my chest. He seems just as happy to see me as he is to see Nate and the horses. Nate tells him to settle down and lead us to the ferry.

"I hope it's still fired up and running," I say to Nate.

"Sam will have kept it running, I am sure he is expecting us, probably was about ready to saddle Gus and come look for us. He knows how long it takes to make this trip, that storm cost us more than a few hours."

"At least it wasn't the deer."

Sam and two of Red's men have the ferry sitting at the south ramp. Rusty runs down ahead of the wagon and lets Sam know that we are coming. With the sun fully set it is now dark at the river bottom. Sam waves a lantern back and forth and yells out to take it easy, the road just before the ramp is muddy. Nate grabs hold of the reins tight and rides the brake down to the ramp area. Sam tells him to get the wagon lined up and don't stop, just ride it right on to the ferry. I look at Nate wondering if I should bail off the wagon now or wait to get bounced off.

Nate looks over with a grin, "Don't worry, I've done this before, we'll be fine", and with that, he slaps the reins hard against the horse's rumps and with a quick jolt Molly and Bess step onto the ferry. The front wheels lurch down into the mud and pop out thick and covered with gooey muck.

The horses try to dig hard into the planking of the ferry but their hooves are slipping, Nate is slapping the reins, Rusty is barking and Sam is yelling, "Don't stop, keep 'em moving!"

With all the commotion that is going on, I am just about ready to abandon my seat; instead I grab on tighter just as the back wheels drop down into the mud and then pop up onto the loading ramp. Nate is not yet done, he now has to get the wagon stopped on the slippery deck planks. He stands up on the brake and pulls the reins tight enough to bend the horses' heads almost onto their backs. Sam is standing on the other end of the ferry with his lantern waving in the horses faces.

Sam sets the lantern down and grabs their bridles saying, "Good girls, good girls, ya did a good job, settle down. Nate, get that brake set, Jacob, chock those wheels. We still have the river to cross."

"Sure thing Sam, and thanks for being here."

Sam lets loose with a long blow of the whistle and then adds a couple of short blasts. Rusty barks and runs back and forth along the rail. As we ease off the south bank, Sam points the ferry up river into the current. The ferry shack has a couple of lanterns out front and there's lanterns on the ground showing were the landing is. Sam has Nate and me helping Red's men feel for the shallow river bottom. We are using long poles to reach out in front and push deep to help us avoid hitting any boulders that are hidden by the darkness. Sam steers the ferry back down river letting the current push us towards the north shore.

He gives the whistle a blow and there stands Judith with another lantern. She has it held up high, doing her best to light the way. Sam eases the nose of the ferry towards the north shore ramp area and backs the power off. The back end begins to drift slightly ahead of the front and Sam has to throttle-up the engine a little to bring it straight in. With a couple more drifts and bursts of power, Sam slides the ferry right into its place for an easy off load. He keeps the power up churning the water behind yelling for Nate and I to tie off to the pilings and then get up front to help with the ramp. As the ramp touches the north bank, Rusty jumps off and bounds up to Judith, she pats him on the head and admonishes him to stay down and away from her dress.

Still excited, Rusty runs back to Nate and stands on his hind legs resting his front paws on Nate's chest, "I see ya boy, good to be home."

"How was that storm, Nate?" Sam asks.

Nate begins to tell him, "It was a good one. We'd been watching the clouds gather and change most of the morning, but it banged down hard right on top of us just this side of Prospect. There was a lightning strike right next to us that split a pine tree right in two. We pulled the horses and wagon off the road. We stayed put in a stand of trees til it blew past. Thought the road might be too muddy to travel but we plowed through. 'Ole Molly wasn't too happy with me."

Sam says, "As long as you're alright and you got back safe. Better let Judith give you a hug, she's been worried sick. Jacob, it's good to see you. You, okay?"

I answer, "Yeah, Sam, it's good to be back. Who'd ever thought a simple wood delivery, would be so difficult."

"There's nothing simple, not out here."

I look over to Judith, tipping my hat I say, "Ma'am, good evening and good to see you." There is something in the way the light reflects off her face that reminds me of a face I've seen before.

Judith replies back, "Likewise Mr. Sparks, glad you all made it back safe and sound."

Sam looks to us, "Boys, let's get the team and wagon off the ferry. Let's get it secured for the night, we can hear more about the trip soon enough."

"Yes sir, sounds good." Nate says.

Sam shakes hands and thanks the two men that stayed to help, he tells them that there's no need for them to stay, we'll take care of the ferry and to be safe getting back to Red's.

Chapter 9

Nate and I scurry around the wagon pulling the tarps off and setting the supplies down on the back porch. Sam stays with the ferry to make sure it's secure and shut down for the night. He grabs his lantern and takes his usual walk around the area checking to make sure everything is the way it should be. Most of the folks that had been camped out have moved on. Some of those folks, traded with Judith earlier in the day for some fresh milk and eggs, Judith ended up with fresh caught steelhead. Apparently this is another one of those gestures that the Harris's are known for. They share what they have and others share back. Word has gotten around and that's why mostly good folks stop by here and stay awhile before they move on. Some folks just come to stay by the river and spend some time in this peaceful setting.

We set the dry goods in the house for Judith to go through, we set the perishables and bulk items in the root cellar. This is all done with lanterns burning and not much conversation. Nate and I are road weary and we still need to get the horses unhitched and put up for the night. I am following Nate's lead at every step as he has a system and could probably unload the wagon blindfolded.

I didn't even know where the root cellar was until tonight. Like everything else that Sam has, it's in the perfect spot, well hidden, cut into a small slope of a hill, with a firm, dry, dirt floor. It has plenty of shelves and lot's of stored food. Judith has laid up canned fruits and vegetables, some in jars, some dried. There are potatoes, apples and dried beef, along with smoked fish. These people may not be farmers, but they have plenty of stored food all put up by themselves, bartered or traded for with others. In return, the farmer's trade or barter for the firewood that Nate cuts, splits and hauls. This leaves the farmers more time to tend to their fields and cattle. Sam tends to the ferry and makes sure Nate knows what wood to haul when and where, neither of them having the time or desire to farm. It seems to have worked out well for them.

With the wagon unloaded, I sling the covered deer carcass over my shoulder and haul it up to the barn to hang and dry. I ask Nate if Judith would like me to carve off a roast for tomorrow's dinner. He says we'll have to ask her. I'll need to know so I can butcher the meat accordingly. Nate lets me know he understands and when he heads to the house he'll find out what Judith thinks.

I roll the hide out and get it stretched and hung up to dry. I'll scrape the hide down in the morning light, hopefully in a month or so I'll have a dried and tanned deer hide to make some buckskin moccasins and gloves. The hide isn't big enough to do much else with it. The average doe usually dresses out around 100 pounds, this one isn't much different. Fresh meat and a new skin, it was worth the minor delay.

I wash up at the pump and head towards the house. Nate is telling Judith about the fresh venison we brought back. "So Judith, Jake brought back a fresh doe from this morning. Would you like a roast?"

Judith turns towards me as I enter the kitchen and says, "Fresh venison would be a treat. Mr. Sparks a hindquarter roast would be wonderful. I'll get it cooking in the morning. We'll have venison for a day or two."

"Ok, anything else? How about a back strap?"

Answering, Judith says, "That will be fine." Judith then turns to Nate and asks, "I thought Mr. Kimble might send us our monthly balance sheet."

"He said he would prepare it and send it next time. How was the order? Did everything you asked for make it on the wagon?"

"Yes, it seems to be all here. I'll check the root cellar in the morning." Judith continues, "Thank you Nate, you men must be hungry. I have some stew left over, it's still warm."

Nate and I answer in unison, "Sure, that would be great."

"You go on and get washed up and I'll have it on the table shortly."

Nate and I head up to the barn to get the wagon unhitched from Molly and Bess and get them in the stalls for the night. We'll take them up to the meadow in the morning. I lay my bedroll and pack down. Nate and I both let out heavy sighs as we are finally finished and head to the water pump to get washed up.

The kitchen smells great and Sam is sitting having a hot cup of coffee. Judith says she has some hot water for tea if either of us would rather have tea instead of coffee. She ladles out hot stew into our bowls, brings out a loaf of fresh baked bread, still warm and smelling ever so good. Judith asks Sam if he would like a bowl of stew. He shrugs his shoulders and reminds her he already ate supper. She gives him a look with raised eyebrows and sits down just as Sam says, "Well, I suppose I could have a small bowl, need something to go with that bread."

Judith says, "Now that I'm sat down, you can get your own bowl."

Nate jumps up, "I'll get it."

Sam puts up a hand and says, "No, Nate, you sit. I'll get it. I'm the one that couldn't make up his mind. I guess I was just surprised I got asked. It's not often we get second supper around here."

With a sigh Judith says, "Now Sam, you know as well as anybody, you can have second, third or fourth suppers if you want."

With a half smile Sam answers, "Well, it's because of your cooking, that I'm not as skinny as a cane fishing pole. I ain't complaining mind you."

"Well, thank you dear, I know when to keep quiet. In fact, you men catch up with the trip. If you don't mind, I'll be heading to bed. Can I get anyone anything before I say goodnight?"

We all just shake our heads "no" as I grab another piece of bread.

As we are sitting there, Nate asks Sam about the order of logs that we need to get started on in the morning. Sam and Nate talk back and forth for a bit, Sam telling Nate that he made out a list of logs to get separated and pulled down to the loading area. Mr. Winkler will have his crew and wagons up at the staging area the day after next. Nate lets Sam know that the Johnson's signaled him that they need a cord of wood next trip to town. Sam says okay and tells Nate to bring back a load of hay in exchange. The winter was long and the hay is getting low.

I decide to excuse myself. It's late, my belly is full, and morning will be here before I know it. I grab my bowl and cup and head for the sink. Judith speaks out from the bedroom, "You men just set those dishes on the counter, I'll tend to them in the morning. Mr. Sparks, I set your clothes on the chair by the fireplace."

"Thank you, ma'am." I grab up my clothes and head towards the front porch. Before I step off and make my way up to the barn, I decide to sit for a minute to enjoy the moonlight on the river. While sitting there I can't help but overhear Nate and Sam as they continue to discuss the next day's work.

"So are you gonna tend to the ferry tonight?" Nate asks Sam.

"No, not tonight, things are quiet around here. All the families pulled out the past couple of days. Not much action on the river. I just shut the ferry down and checked all the equipment. Think I'll lie down, I'll be rested and able to help you tomorrow."

"There's no need for that. I mean helping and all; Jake and me can handle it."

Sam says, "I know you can, but I just want to be up during the day and be in the woods. The place is alright for tonight, and there's no ferry in the morning."

"Sounds good, I know you'll do what you want anyway. Besides, it will be great to have you work Gus. How's his shin?"

Sam answers, "It's good, I checked it this morning and it looks to be healed. He didn't even flinch when I rubbed it down. He'll be fine. He's probably chomping at the bit to get to work. Knowing Gus, he's jealous that Molly and Bess have been working and he hasn't."

"Yeah, they're like a bunch of kids."

Sam asks, "How'd Mr. Sparks do in town? Give you any trouble, cause any trouble?"

"No, he didn't. He's a good hand, not like others that have come through here. He worked right alongside me the whole time. He helped with the camp, is good with the horses. He drove the team a spell. He seems okay."

With a raised eyebrow Sam says, "Well, we'll see. Time will tell. You know we've seen men like him before. They are eager to work for a meal or two and then they get lazy or lonesome or just restless and they move on."

Nate starts to say, "He's different, he's..."

Sam interrupts, "Remember that one guy that came through here, stayed for a couple of weeks and then tried to make off with Gus in the middle of the night? He didn't know that Gus doesn't let nobody but you and me ride him. That guy ended up pitched over the fence head over heels into that old briar patch and poison ivy, damn near scratched himself to death."

Laughing Nate says, "Yeah, I remember. We nearly died laughing when we found him. His face was puffed up so bad, he couldn't see and his lips were as fat as a couple of sausages. I remember it took us half the morning to cut him out of them briars."

Sam continues, "He high-tailed it outta here and never came back as far as I can tell."

Nate is quiet for a minute and then says, "Mr. Sparks is different, he didn't go into any saloons, he didn't stop to play cards or go visit any of the women's places. He told me he doesn't drink, he doesn't smoke and I never seen him take a chew. He works hard and is respectful to folks, and treats 'em right. I think he wants to stick around a while."

Sam says, "We'll see Nate, we'll see. We best be getting to bed, you've had a long day."

Before Nate gets up he says, "Hey Sam, did Judith tell you Jake bagged a deer. We're gonna be eating on fresh venison for a couple of days."

"No, no she didn't; first a couple of rabbits and now venison. Maybe he is different. Not too many drifters share."

Hearing the two of them say goodnight, I step off the porch and head up towards the barn. With the light from the moon dancing through the trees, I am reassured that mutual feelings seem to be shared by all.

....

Chapter 10

Breakfast the following morning is as good and hearty as before. It seems as if I am now automatically included, invited and expected. There is no hesitation on holding hands as Judith says a brief blessing over the food and the upcoming day. As we eat, the conversation is light and unrestrained. This morning is a bit different as Sam is going to be joining us in the woods working side by side.

My mind is pondering the reasons behind this change in routine and so I ask, "So, Sam, today you are joining us in the woods? Does this log order have a special demand on it?"

He answers, "No, not really, I don't have a lot going on right now, the ferry is in good shape and Red and his crew are going to spend the day at his place."

I say questioning, "Sorry Sam, I guess I don't understand, what place? I thought Red ran the ferry?"

"He does, but he doesn't run it every day, and he doesn't live here. We have a schedule we try to keep so most folks around here can count on knowing when they can cross or when they can't. We try and run every other day and on Saturdays. Sunday is mostly a quiet day. Red has a horse ranch up river that he tends to; his boy and a hired hand help him run that. He needs to take care of his horses and he tries to grow his own hay for winter feed."

"How big a place does he have?"

"It's not a big ranch. I'd say it's about 160 acres and he free ranges his horses if he needs to."

"How many horses does he have?"

Sam thinks for a second and says, "Oh, I don't know, sometimes he has upwards of 40 head, then he rounds 'em up and takes about half to auction. The numbers change year to year."

Nate interrupts with, " 'S'cuse me, Sam, I'm going to head up and milk Bonnie first thing and take Molly and Bess up to the meadow, let them take the day off."

Sam answers, "Okay, we won't be long, just want another cup. Judith, do you mind?"

Nate heads out the door and Rusty bounds after him.

Getting up from the table Judith says, "Not at all dear, be my pleasure. Mr. Sparks, would you like another cup?"

I answer, "Thank you, ma'am, that'd be nice. This was another great meal, thank you kindly."

"Thank you, Mr. Sparks, and that fresh venison will be a real treat."

Turning back to Sam, I change the subject from Red to, "That reminds me. I noticed smoke coming out of the smoke house, I'd like to get that deer butchered up and get the meat smoking. Is there wood piled up that I can use?"

Sam answers, "Yeah, there should be some apple wood chopped and stacked behind the smoke house. Judith has some steelhead being smoked so the coals should be hot and ready to be added to."

"Well, if you don't mind, can I ask if there are any special cuts of meat you want, or should I just cut it into strips for jerky?"

Judith suggests that I take the back strap and the remaining shoulders for roasts and then cut the rest for jerky.

Shaking my head with approval I say, "Sounds good, I'll do that. Sam, I'd like to take care of that first thing if you don't mind?"

"That'll be fine Jake."

Pushing my chair away from the table, "I'll excuse myself then, leave you two. Thanks again ma'am."

"You're welcome Mr. Sparks, and you can call me Judith if you wish."

Being surprised but not embarrassed I say, "Only if you'll call me Jake, if that's alright with you Sam?"

"After a week of feeding you and my wife washing your clothes, I suppose it's time to be less formal. Besides, I get the feeling you're not leaving anytime soon."

With a nod I say, "I'll head on out now, thank you both."

I get to the barn just as Nate is bringing Bonnie into the stall to milk. I pull my wet stone out of my pack and run my knife across the smooth face a few times. I mention to Nate that I am going to butcher the deer up and get the meat smoking. He reminds me that there is some stacked apple wood behind the smoke house. I ask him how Molly and Bess are and he tells me they are just fine. After a quick brush down, they sauntered out into the middle of the meadow and the early morning sun.

I then ask, "So, the ferry doesn't run each day?"

"No, like Sam said, every other day, and Saturdays. Some days no one needs to cross."

"What happens if someone needs to cross and gets here on the off day?"

"That's how the camp area got started. Folks would show

up and want to take the ferry across the river but it takes time to fire up the boiler and build steam. It also takes time to get Red and his crew here so Sam lets them stay. Red and Sam came up with a schedule and they try to stick to it. Some folks still show up on off days but local folks seem to know the schedule. It's the traveling folks who get here and have to wait if it's an off day."

"And on the off days, Sam comes up, helps you cut and chop wood, right?"

"Yeah, some days he does, some days he doesn't."

"And Red, he works his horse ranch and comes just to run the ferry ever other day?"

Nate answers, "Yeah, Sam and him have it worked out. They've been running the ferry for a long time now and it seems to work out for them. Folks need to have safe crossing; up river there are steep narrow gorges with stretches of dangerous white water, down river from us is the set of rapids and then the swimming hole. Further down, the river gets real wide. Mr. Winkler has his mill pond there and he floats logs across to the other side when he needs to."

"Humph, figures things wouldn't be as simple as they seemed. I guess having a schedule makes sense."

Nate finishes up with Bonnie and takes the bucket of milk to Judith. I finish up with one side of the deer and take what I have butchered over to the smoke house. I lay up some split wood on the coals and place a couple of roasts and strips of meat on the drying racks. The aroma is sweet and the smoke is thick inside the smoke house. There appears to be half dozen steelhead fillets laid out, won't be much longer until they're dried and ready to eat.

I head up towards the barn just as Sam, Nate and Rusty are heading up to the meadow. I let them know that I have half of the deer to butcher and I'll join up soon. I mention to Sam that I had Nate get me a couple pounds of roofing nails. I tell him that I have noticed some missing shingles and if he wouldn't mind I could get them fixed.

He stops and looks up. Then he nods okay saying, "I guess you know what you are doing?"

Reassuringly I say, "Yeah, I do. I'm a pretty fair carpenter. I've worked on a lot of new structures and made a lot of repairs to others as I have traveled around. That's pretty much how I've made my living along the way. I just don't have any of my own tools that I am able to travel with. I have found that most folks have the tools I need and they let me use them."

"Where'd ya learn the skills?" he asks.

"When I first left Ash Fork and started traveling, I was headed north and stopped in Craver's Pass for awhile. I was young and didn't know anybody or how to make a living on my own. While I was there I met a man that taught me the trade. It's a long story Sam, and some of it ain't worth telling."

Sam says, "Suit yourself. The roof needs fixin', you're offering, have at it. Just don't fall off and break nothing, it's a long ride into town."

"All I need is a ladder and some cedar bolts big enough to shave some shingles off. If you don't mind, I'll take the liberty to poke around and find the tools I need."

"Yeah sure, help yourself to what you need. We got some cedar, don't we Nate?"

"Sure thing, Sam, dried and ready anytime."

With the deer butchered and the venison being smoked, I make my way to the meadow.

Molly and Bess look up and whinny their greetings. They both come over to the gate, ears perked and snorting, not aggressively, just saying hello. They both are flipping their tails and shaking their heads. It's a beautiful morning; the air is clear and fresh after yesterday's rainstorm. The sweet smell of damp grass fills the air along with the chirps and calls of sparrows and finches as they hop from bush to bush and tree branch to tree branch. The squirrels are squawking their warnings and alerting every living creature that man is near. An owl takes flight low over the meadow gliding from one fence line to the other. A hawk nervously screeches from far above the tree tops, its mate answering back. I watch as they catch an updraft and float over the hill side deciding to hunt the next ridge over. The bull, as usual, is in the back of the meadow, all by himself. He seems uninterested to all that is happening around him except the grass he is chewing. He lets out a beller, apparently just to let me know that if nothing else, he is aware of me.

Looking past him and the meadow, my eye catches the grove of aspen, with their white trunks and light green leaves shimmering in the early morning sunlight. I am reminded of the many times I have spent walking through groves of aspen. I am always fascinated with their beauty and the serenity that exists each and every time I'm able to stop and enjoy the experience. I tell myself that I'll have to walk up there and check the grove out when I get some free time.

Startling me out of my thoughts and memories, I hear Sam

as he yells, "Hey, Jake, you coming?"

Both Sam and Nate are riding on Gus's back and are far enough ahead to almost take them out of eye sight. I wave back letting them know I heard them and that I'll be there shortly. I won't mind the walk; it is a beautiful morning for doing just that very thing. I watch Gus's back side and twitching tail as the three of them saunter around the bend of the worn wagon path that leads to the day's area of work.

By the time I make it to the clearing, Sam and Nate have Gus harnessed up and Sam is driving Gus up the hillside towards some downed timbers. There is a stack of fifty de-limbed doug fir logs, a stack of about half that many cedar logs and another stack of ponderosa pine logs next to that. Nate catches up to Sam and Gus and sets a choker chain around a couple doug firs. Sam gives a yell and snaps the reins hard as Gus arches his back and drags the logs down the hill to a flat cleared area.

Sam sees me and yells, "Get over there and undo the choker chain. Stay put there, Nate will stay up top and set the choker."

With a nod and a wave, I let him know I understand. It doesn't take long to settle into a nice rhythm as the logs are staged into position for Mr. Winkler's crew to load up onto his wagons and haul them back to his sawmill.

Sometime around mid day, Sam reins in Gus and tells us to take a break. We all gather up by the now shrinking piles of logs and have some jerky and water. The morning coolness has turned into hot. Nate has striped out of his shirt, Sam and I have taken off our cover shirts but are still wearing our long sleeved underwear. I guess I am finally convinced that winter is not going to return, I excuse myself and do the same as Nate.

Stripping out of my long underwear, I go shirtless the rest of the day. The hot sun feels good on my skin. I am certainly going to have a tender back tonight, but feeling sun on skin is sometimes worth the future discomfort.

Time has passed quickly and with shadows beginning to lengthen, Sam tells us that the order is filled and staged. There is no need to skid anymore dried logs down to the flat area. While we are here, Sam tells us he would like to go ahead and drop some fresh timbers, get them limbed up and stacked for drying.

Nate points us in the direction of the area that he has been clearing and leads the way. I gather up the cross cut saw and follow the trail which is up and to the west of the clearing we've been working in. It's not much of a walk to the new area. Sam and Nate walk amongst the tall doug fir and select the trees that Sam wants to bring down. The underbrush is thick at the base of these trees so I start clearing it away so we can have the room needed to swing axes and man the crosscut saw. They also discuss the sequence and direction they want the trees to fall. You just don't walk up and start cutting trees down. You have to plan the work and then work the plan. Trees can twist on the stump, change direction of their intended fall or get caught in each other's branches causing the tree trunks to slide in scattered directions. Cutting this tall virgin timber can be very dangerous and Sam makes sure Nate and I understand what the plan is and who the boss is, today.

As the sun continues to make its purposeful arc across the afternoon sky, it is amazing to watch these two men work as a team. They say little to each other and seem to know and anticipate each other's next move.

I sometimes feel that I'm in the way; Sam seems to sense this and lets me know where he wants me to be. I do most of the limb removal of the logs as they fall. Sam handles the skidding of the logs and works Gus as if the horse is an extension of Sam's arms, legs and mind. Gus is proud and works harder than the three of us. He is sure footed and knows the direction of the stock pile to skid the logs down to. He is always eager to head back up the hill to the newly fallen logs. He pulls Sam up the hill without the encouragement of the reins snapping on his back and flanks.

Sam finally calls it a day, but before we leave the area he tells us that tomorrow, when we bring the wagon to load it with more firewood, we can gather the limbs and stack them in an open area for fall burning. He also reminds us that Mr. Winkler and his men will be here for the logs he ordered. I speak up and remind them both that I will need to take about four cedar bolts back so I can repair the barn roof. Sam gives me a nod and leads Gus over to the shed area to release him from the tack, harness and multiple sets of chains that were used to skid the logs around. Rusty lets us all know he is eager to be done for the day, he runs around barking and getting a rub of the ears from each of us. He then runs up to Gus as if to say, let's get going and head to the house.

With three of us and only one horse, I will be the one walking back. I don't mind, it'll give me a chance to enjoy the late afternoon shadows and the cool breeze that drifts through the trees and gently cools my skin. Rusty runs up ahead keeping pace with Gus, occasionally running back, urgently trying to get me to pick up my pace and join the others.

Instead of walking past the meadow and returning to the barn, I turn left at the meadow and head up the incline towards the aspen grove. It's a slight detour, but I already know it will be well worth it. The meadow is bigger than I thought and the incline is steeper than it looks. Reaching the far north fence line, I turn to the south and take in the view of the meadow and the homestead. The tops of the barn and house are visible from this vantage point and I can see a slight bend in the river just before the rapids to the west. There is a steady plume of smoke rising from the smoke house that fills the air with a fantastic aroma of apple wood, slow cooked meat and fish.

In the late afternoon sunlight, the aspen grove is just as beautiful and inviting as it had been this morning. The trees, with their black scars over white bark are straight and tall. The larger, older trees are surrounded and protected by the younger, new growth trees. Judging by the thickness of the older trees, this grove has some age to it. Some of the trees are at least eight to ten inches around at the base. The outer bands of younger trees are a mixture of different heights and smaller thicknesses; the average being about one inch in diameter. The cascading light shimmers through the branches creating shadows that dance on the ground. The lime green leaves are paper thin and are moved gently as a gentle breeze passes through them. The tranquil sound of the leaves is as faint as angels whispering.

I sit down in the middle of the grove and begin to feel a peace that I haven't felt for...well, maybe never. This is not my land, but somehow I feel I belong here, that maybe, just maybe

I have found a place to call home.

I stretch out and lay down flat in the grass that takes shelter amongst the aspens from the direct sun light. This grove sits atop a hidden spring that eventually comes gurgling out on the east side of the meadow. The ground is soft and slightly damp as I press into it, but not damp enough to soak through my pants.

The view, as I look skyward, is a giant moving puzzle of leaves, limbs and blue. As I lay in the middle of the grove, I feel that I am surrounded by peace. I close my eyes, breathe deeply and ponder how it is that I have come to be in this place at this exact moment, hoping I never have to leave.

I startle myself awake. Not knowing how long I dozed, I stretch and can now feel the dampness of the moist ground through my pants and shirt. In fact I am a bit chilly. I look out across the meadow; the shadows are now stretched to their limit as the sun is below the tree line. My stomach rumbles letting me know that it must be close to supper. How is it that within a week of steady meals, my stomach is now a clock? I stand with a full body stretch and try not to beat myself up about taking a little snooze. I just hope I'm not too late for supper.

I decide to take a short cut through the meadow and climb through the fence forgetting about the bull. I stop, look around and don't see him anywhere close by. The horses are down on the south end and the two cows are over in the shade on the west side, there is no bull in sight. I continue to cut through the meadow until a nervous feeling comes over me. I suddenly turn around to see the bull standing tall and staring in my direction. Where exactly he came from I do not know, but he seems to be paying close attention to me. He is bigger than he looked this morning and he has a very impressive set of horns sitting atop his head. I don't know what his intentions are, but his body language is telling me I better get ready to run.

I am still a bit fuzzy headed from my brief nap. Trying to grasp the importance of getting my feet to move faster, I stumble in a small hole and fall to my knees. Evidently, the bull likens this sudden disappearing act of mine as a threatening gesture towards him and his territory. I quickly gather myself. Standing, I see the bull moving quickly in my direction. His head is up and his ears are perked forward. I instinctively pick up my pace; change my line of direction to the east heading for the nearest fence line.

The bull is now definitely in pursuit. I try to tell myself not to run but I see no other option as the bull is gaining on me. He is close enough to me that I can hear a swooshing sound as his hooves slide through the tall grass. Unfortunately for me the tall grass has the opposite effect. As I try to run faster, the grass seems to grab at my ankles. I don't know how I can out run this bastard. Sacrificing my hat, I fling it into the air as far as I can; hopefully it will distract him long enough for me to put a greater distance between us. The bull takes the bait and he veers off to my right. As he reaches the hat he lowers his head and tries to stab it with his horns. This of course infuriates him even more and continues his angry pursuit.

Thankfully, I did gain some distance between us. I now see myself making it to the fence line ahead of him. I reach out both my arms to grab the top rail of the wooden fence, at the same time I stretch out my right leg hoping to land it on the bottom rail. As my right foot lands on the bottom rail I hear a loud crack as the dried out wood breaks. All my momentum is stopped as my foot and leg stab into the ground and my knee slams into the middle rail. Luckily, I have enough hand and arm strength to throw myself over the top rail. The bull sets all four hooves firmly into the dirt stopping only a few feet away from me and the fence. He lets out a panting beller and an angry snort. He shakes his head slinging snot and dust into the air.

I am in a breathless, jumbled heap rubbing the dust out of my eyes and cussing up a storm. The fence is broke and my hat is gone. The horses are standing at attention wondering what all the commotion is about and of course, here comes Rusty. When he gets to me he starts licking my face. I feel lucky to be alive. I honestly think that bull would have gored me if he'd caught me. Standing up I stare the bull straight in the face and realize this broken fence is all that is keeping us separated. I turn and hasten my pace towards the barn.

I am soaking wet with sweat and shaking from the rush of adrenaline. Rusty is running all excited from what he assumed was a great game. I wish it had been a game, but the bull meant business and now I know who the boss of the meadow is. I stop to catch my breath and turn to take another look back; the bull is sauntering over to the north end of the meadow, seemingly unconcerned.

The cloud of dust we created has drifted away. My eye catches the last bit of sunlight touching the tops of the aspen grove. I close my eyes, take a deep breath and realize that angels had indeed been whispering.

broken fence

Chapter 11

Arriving back at the barn, adrenaline is still pumping through my body, my dust covered face and neck are streaked by sweat. After a hard day's work in the woods, then out running a charging bull, I decide I need a swim and a bath more than I need a meal. Knowing I have enough daylight left, I grab soap, towel, and clean clothes. I skirt past the house on my way to the river.

Nate yells out from the front porch, "What took ya, supper is ready." I stop and walk over to the porch and begin to apologize that I won't be joining them for supper. Rusty is still hanging by my side and Nate can see by his excitement and my disheveled appearance that something is not normal. He leans on the porch railing, shakes his head and asks, "What the heck happened to you? Where's your hat?"

I look up, point back towards the meadow and tell him I had a run in with the bull. "You met Brutus huh?" Nate asks.

"Yeah, that's a hell of a name, Brutus. He's a brute alright. He's a mean sucker. Would've tore me in two if he'd a caught me."

With half a smile Nate says, "Yeah, he's been ornery since he was a calf. Been head butted by him more than once. I don't even go near him. We just let him do his breeding thing and leave him alone."

"Well, I'll be walking around that meadow from now on, can't run as fast as I used to. Oh, by the way, tell Sam I broke the bottom rail of the fence, I'll fix that in the morning before we head up to load the wagon."

"Broke the fence? How'd ya do that?"

"Well, like I was saying, I was cutting through the meadow, didn't see the bull and before I knew it, he came running at me. My feet got tangled up in some tall grass and I tripped. I threw my hat to distract him and high-tailed it to the nearest fence. I went to leap over the fence and when I stepped on the bottom rail, it snapped. I had to flip myself over the top rail, ended up ass-over-tea-kettles, cussing and swearing. Rusty came up barking and helped me calm down some."

"So, where's your hat?"

"Still out in the meadow, 'bout time for a new one anyways."

"Ahh, I'll help ya get it in the morning."

From inside the house, Judith yells out, "Come on you two, supper is ready; Sam doesn't like to wait, now hurry up!"

I look up at Nate and tell him, "I can't sit at the table like this. I'm going down to the river to wash up real good, give my apologies to Judith." He nods and goes in the house. As I turn towards the river I can hear him laughing as he tells Sam that I finally met Brutus.

Down at the river's edge, I strip out of my clothes and jump in the cold, clear water. It takes my breath away at first, but once I get moving around a bit, it feels really refreshing. I am glad I'm missing supper and having this time to myself. Rusty followed along and is running up and down the bank barking. He can't make up his mind if he wants to jump in with me or not. I try and coax him in but he just can't relax enough to decide. I soap up and rinse off and then grab my pants, shirt and long underwear to give them a good soaping up.

As I rinse my clothes out I notice Rusty running up the path that leads back to the house. He comes bounding back, Nate and Sam in tow. Looks like I wasn't the only one that wanted a bath, 'course, they could wait til after supper, having missed out on a fifty yard dash with Brutus.

Sam and Nate strip down and jump in, laughing and splashing each other, Rusty jumps in after them, not being able to resist the frolicking of these two. I ring my clothes out, dry off and get dressed. Sam tells me that Nate shared my story with Judith and him over supper; half laughing, he apologizes for not warning me about his breeding bull.

He tells me, "Don't take it personal, that damn bull doesn't like anyone. If he wasn't such a good breeder, I'd butcher him up, 'course, as ornery as he is, the meat would probably be as tough as shoe leather."

"Yeah, you'd probably have to boil it for a month just to make it chewable," I continue, "Oh, by the way, did Nate tell you I broke the fence?"

"Yep, he did. I know you'll make it right. Judith set out a plate if you're hungry when you get back."

I say my thanks, explain I'm really not hungry, and I'd rather head back, hang up my clothes and sit a bit. Rusty runs after me, shaking the water out of his coat. I tell him to go back and I hear Nate call for him. He perks his ears and trots on back towards Nate and Sam.

The barn is quiet and I hang up my pants, shirt and underwear. I climb up in the loft and take a really good look at the shakes on the roof. From what it looks like, I'll need a square or two of new shakes to patch the holes and replace any rotten ones.

I suddenly grab my side realizing that with the wild escape from Brutus, then swimming and washing out my clothes, I hadn't thought to check for my coin. I slide down the ladder and grab my long underwear and frantically rustle through them. I can't feel my coin at first and begin to sweat all over again. I can't recall if I put it anyplace else. Whenever I wear my long underwear I always keep it in a special pocket that's sown into the waistband area. I can't feel it and I start to shake out all my wet clothes. The coin suddenly flips out and flies into the air, landing on the barn floor with a clank, twirling on its rim 'til it stops, "Lady Liberty" staring up at me.

Out loud I say, "There you are, can't lose you, you're all I have left. Thank God I didn't lose you in the river, how stupid of me." Two disasters have been averted in the same day. Maybe things have turned around. With a smile on my face I lie down in the straw and pull out my harmonica.

Rusty comes bouncing into the barn and lies down next to me. After I scratch his favorite spots and he gets done rolling back to belly and belly to back, I decide to walk down to the house before I turn in for the night. I walk up to the front porch where I find Nate, Judith and Sam sitting and looking out at the river. I apologize for interrupting them on this fine evening and get a resounding, "No apologies needed."

Judith extends an invitation, "Please sit down, Mr. Spar... Jacob."

"Thank you Judith, don't mind if I do, too nice of an

evening to be by myself. Lord knows I have spent too many days and nights alone."

I mention that I have noticed that there are folks gathered on both sides of the river waiting for tomorrow's ferry crossing.

Sam says, "Yeah, it will be a full day for Red and his boys. I'll get up early and get the ferry steamed up and ready. He should be here at first light."

I ask if he needs any help and Sam says, "Nah, been doing this along time. You and Nate need to head up to the lumber piles to get ready for Mr. Winkler and get the wagon loaded for another trip to town. It will be a busy day for everyone."

I ask, "When do you think I'll be able to fix the fence and the barn roof?"

"Well, the fence won't be a problem; Nate has some split rails already stacked up by the meadow, just a matter of taking the old rail out and sliding the new rail in. The barn roof can wait 'til you and Nate get back from town. Promise, I'll let you have some time to fix the roof."

I answer, "Sounds good, Sam, that'll work."

Judith tells me that she'll tend to the smoke house and ready the meat for storing. With a yawn and a stretch I stand and excuse myself. For some reason I am suddenly exhausted.

"Goodnight all, sleep well."

All three respond with a goodnight. Nate calls Rusty back as I head up to the barn and my bed of straw.

•

My eyes come awake before the rest of me. Laying there in

the quietness of the pre-dawn morning, I hear the faint hiss of the ferry's steam engine building steam. Sam has probably been up a good hour. I throw on my clothes, minus my long underwear, and decide to hide "Lady Liberty" deep in my pack. The barn is a safe place that no one but the Harris's and myself come into. On second thought, I can't risk losing it. I tuck it in one of my small, leather pouches and strap it next to my bowie knife. With a sigh of relief, I walk out of the barn to the washing post to get my head and face wet.

The house lamps are already lit. I see Judith moving about the kitchen and smoke is coming out the stove chimney. Nate and Rusty come bounding out the back door headed up to get Bonnie for milking. Rusty notices me and comes over for a morning pat on the head. With a soft bark he seems to be asking me to come along. I give a good morning wave to Nate and he lets me know that Judith will have breakfast ready shortly. I wave again and head back to the barn.

The clothes I washed out yesterday are still damp so I move them out to a fence and hang them in the morning air knowing they'll dry faster hanging outside. Resting alongside the barn is a long ladder I will be able to use when I do the roof repairs. I stand it up and lean it against the roof overhang. It is a bit short at the front side of the barn, so I walk it to the back side and stand it up. It stands about two feet above the overhang of the roof which will work out just fine. Leaning there at this angle and with two rungs above the overhang, I will have plenty of ladder to grab onto when I need to get off the roof. The rungs look sturdy enough to hold my weight. All I need now is to find a good rope so I can tie it around my waist while

I'm working up top. I could probably jump from twenty feet if I had to and not get hurt, but working and falling from twenty feet when you don't expect it can lead to a completely different outcome. I fell once from only eight feet shattering my left ankle. To this day I walk with a limp; don't need to fall again. I lay the ladder down alongside the barn and hear Nate putting Bonnie into the stall to milk her.

I ask Nate if there is anything I can do to help, expecting him to say no, he surprises me saying, "Yeah, I need some fresh hay forked down from the loft. Need some for Bonnie and need the hay trough filled for Molly and Bess this morning."

"Sure 'nough, I'll take care of it."

We both hear Judith yell out the back of the house that breakfast is in ten minutes. Nate mutters an apology to Bonnie as he picks up his pace and increases the pressure on her tits. I move a little faster as I flip hay down from the loft above. Once I get enough hay thrown down, I give Bonnie a pitchfork full and start loading the hay trough next to where we'll hitch Molly and Bess to the wagon. Nate and I finish almost at the same time. He leaves Bonnie in the stall while we head to the house.

Judith has us all trained up pretty well, as Nate and I are walking through the back door, Sam is coming through the front door. Men being men, we gather at the table only to hear Judith suggest that we better have washed up before we sit down. Men being boys, we sheepishly saunter over to the sink and wash our hands, each one of us mumbling something under our breath.

Judith is sitting in her place at the table as we pull our

chairs out and finally settle down to another fine breakfast.

With each of us holding hands, Judith blesses the food and the day. As she ends the blessing, she looks up and says, "Now, aren't you glad you all washed your hands."

No reply is needed as we begin to pass the food around. With little conversation we quickly eat. Today there is no time for an extra cup or two of coffee. Nate and I excuse ourselves and take our dishes to the sink. Sam stands and gathers up Judith's and his dishes and brings back the coffee pot. He pours her another cup, kisses her on the forehead and thanks her for the fine meal. She grabs his hand, gives it a gentle kiss and tells him to be safe today.

As he heads out the door he says, "I will. I'm a lucky man, Judith Harris."

The morning sky is beginning to lighten and transform to a rose colored glow. The air is still. The tree tops are motionless. Nate leads Bonnie from the barn and we head up to the meadow. Molly and Bess are standing at the gate, snorting their impatience and bobbing their heads in unison. Gus prances over to the gate as well, eager and ready for whatever the day might have in store for these three work mates. I nervously keep an eye out for Brutus, as we snap the leads on Molly's and Bess's halters. Nate looks up asking which part of the fence got broke. I point up to the northeast corner of the meadow.

He asks, "What were you doing up there anyway?"

"I walked up to that aspen grove to take a look at it."

"Why?"

"I just love aspen groves. I have seen that one every day

we've come up here and yesterday morning with the sun on it, I just told myself that the first time I was able to, I'd walk up to it."

"So, what's so special about aspen groves?"

As we walk the horses down to the barn I begin to explain to Nate what I have come to know and feel about the aspen.

"Well, each aspen has beautiful white bark and soft green leaves that shimmer and float with the wind. Then, in the fall, they ignite the hillsides with their yellow and golden leaves. I have spent a lot of time admiring them from afar and up close. I have walked forest floors that are seemingly carpeted with gold. I wish I had an artist's gift of painting to be able to capture and share with others what I've seen. They also have a unique story about them. Besides their beauty, did you know that if you ever need to find water, aspen usually grow atop a spring, and it doesn't take much digging to get down to the water?"

Nate answers, "No, I didn't know that. Well, I kinda thought about that, because I have cut down aspen and I have always noticed that the ground is damp and moist in the same area as the trees, but I just never put it all together before." He then asks, "So that little stream of water that runs down through the east side of the meadow towards the river, it comes from the aspen grove?"

"Yeah, I'd say so."

Nate continues to ask, "Well, towards the end of summer the surface water dries up. The ground on top is dry, why doesn't the aspen grove dry up?"

"I'm no scientist, but the root system of the grove goes much deeper than the surface of the ground. During the spring and early summer as the snow melts, the ground is full of water and it runs to the lowest point of any area; here it is actually the river. The water above and below the ground will always keep seeping towards the river. In the hot, dry part of the summer, with the snow pack melted away, the surface water dries up, but the underground spring water keeps moving towards that lowest point. That's the reason you dig a well deep, the water isn't always up top, it's deep in the ground. The aspen's root system is spread out and covers a large area. The roots are all connected and gather the moisture from as big of an area as possible, deep and wide."

Once at the barn we work together tending the horses and getting them hitched up to the wagon. Sam is letting the whistle blow on the ferry. Red and his crew prepare the ferry for the first load of wagons crossing from the north shore to south shore. It'll be a busy morning down at the river shuttling folks from one side to the other. Don't know what it is, but it seems that more and more people are being busy traveling from place to place. Maybe we are getting restless as the country moves closer to the turn of the century. There is news of things being invented all the time that will make our lives easier. That will mean more jobs in the cities, maybe that's what is happening, the future is on the horizon and people are sensing it. They are anxious to be in the right place at the right time hoping to be first in line.

I look out as the first ferry of the day gets under way. I ponder the thought and wonder how long it will be before the state decides to build another bridge someplace. Hell, it might even be here at Fletchers Crossing. I dismiss my thoughts with the hope that if that day ever comes, it will be a long time coming. Change is good, but changing this place and this way of life would almost be a sin.

Nate snaps the reins and with a whistle through his teeth the wagon jolts to life. My thoughts return back to Nate's and my previous conversation. It must have done the same to Nate, he asks, "You said that the aspen have a unique story behind them?"

"Yeah, I did. I learned this from a man that is way smarter than me in these things. I spent a week or two working on this man's house. It turned out he was a professor at the university up in Portland. He taught science and biology; all that kind of stuff. I told him I really loved working with wood. I felt like I had a special bond with trees. I was amazed that trees would grow up from seedlings; we could chop them down, cut them up and build things out of them. I have always been convinced that God created each type of tree for us to be able to use in specific ways. The whole process seemed to make me feel like I was part of the life cycle of trees and the earth. He listened for a long time as I told him how I came to learn carpentry. He was envious that I could take a pile of wood and turn it into something that was useful, whether it was a house, a barn or a simple piece of furniture. I told him that in some ways I was envious of him because he knew how trees grew. I mean, he really knew the process and understood it. I just wasn't that smart."

When we get to the meadow, Nate stops and sets the brake; we jump down and Nate ties Gus to the wagon. I tell him I'm going to replace the broken rail. Gus seems excited to be going to work alongside Molly and Bess. Being tied to the back of the wagon doesn't stop him from prancing and shaking his head. As the four of them head out, Nate yells, "Don't take too long, and keep a watch out for Brutus."

I find the extra split rails and hoist one up onto my shoulder. I look up to the aspen. Once again, their tops are lit up by the morning sun. Even though I am on the outside of the fence, I keep one eye on the lookout for Brutus. I fully realize it wouldn't take much effort from him to bust through these old, split rails of cedar.

I get to the broken section of fence and take one more look around the area, no Brutus. I pull the two broken halves of the rail out from the two posts and inter-weave the new rail back into place. I suddenly have the strongest urge to look for my hat. Against my better judgment, I put one foot on the center rail and raise up to scan this end of the meadow. No Brutus close by, he's over on the west side, minding his own business. I jump over the fence and run to where I thought I last saw my hat. In the tall grass I just can't seem to spot it and come to the decision that it really is time to buy a new one. Brutus makes a loud beller, that's enough for me to quicken my pace and get the heck out of his meadow. Being on the right side of the fence brings a sigh of relief; I head back down to the south end and turn to the west, hoping the wagon isn't too far ahead.

It doesn't take me too long to catch up to the slow moving wagon. As we ride along through the calmness of the morning, Nate asks me to continue my story.

"So, as me and the professor spent more time together, he

eventually asked me what my favorite trees were. Well, I couldn't give him one type of favorite tree answer. I explained to him that the Douglas fir is a strong and excellent tree for posts and beams and floor joists, plus it makes great firewood once dried and split. I love the cedar tree because of the perfume it lets off and it is excellent wood for exterior use, such as roof shakes, siding and decks. It also makes good kindling for starting fires. Another favorite tree is the tamarack or Western larch as some folks call it. It is the only conifer tree to shed its needles in the fall. It accents the forest with its golden tops just before the needles let loose as winter approaches. It is especially good to use when building close to damp ground because it is resistant to moisture and dry rot. It also is excellent for firewood. It splits easy and burns clean and long."

Describing the tamarack and the shedding of its golden needles brings me back to the aspen. Continuing I say, "Remember I told you that the aspen tree is unique to all other trees? Well, the professor explained it to me like this. The aspen trees root system is all connected."

"What does that mean, all connected?"

"It means exactly that, the root system of one tree is connected to all the other trees in the grove. In fact, all the trees in the grove are all the same tree. They're all one tree."

"How can that be?" Nate asks in disbelief.

"I don't know, but if you ever cut one down and dig up the root, you will find that the root of one is part of the tree next to it and that trees roots are connected to the next and the next and so on. The professor told me the folks that study these things say that there are some aspen groves that are the oldest living organisms on earth. I can't prove it, but that's what he said."

Nate lifts his hat and lets out a sigh, "It's hard to believe that a grove of trees are all part of one tree."

"Yeah, I know, but it's the truth as I know it. The longer I thought about it, the more my mind could accept it and it made me appreciate the aspen tree even more. It's like a family tree, if you can connect your ancestors from one to another, you realize that you all share the same blood, it makes you all the same family, all connected by blood."

With that, Nate is scratching his head and muttering out loud to himself, "Too much, you're making my head hurt. I thought we were talking about trees."

"We were, just something to think about. Sorry."

As Nate sets the brake he says, "Let's get to work."

Chapter 12

It's not too long into the morning when the horses start to move around anxiously.

They smell the other horses before we can hear Mr. Winkler and his crew coming up the trail to the staged piles of logs. Even though the horses are tied up to trees, Nate goes over to them and calms them down. Mr. Winkler is the first to come into the clearing. With a wave of his hat towards our direction, he turns in his saddle, and gives a forward wave to the drivers of the three teams of horses and trailers behind him. Nate and I leave the horses and walk down to greet Mr. Winkler. This could be a good opportunity to meet Mr. Winkler; it never hurts to get to know anybody that works in the lumber industry. Operators of mills usually know where the work is, especially since cutting timber into buildable lumber starts at the mill. If you can get on the good side of these men, you can find out who ordered the lumber and if they'll be in need of a good carpenter.

Before the wagons can pull up into position for loading, the crew sets up two large tripods alongside and at both ends of the log pile they want to load first. They attach block and tackle to the tops of the tripods. One end of the block and tackle has the free end of the rope; the other end has a sling attached. Two crew members roll a log under the tripods and onto the slings. Once that is completed, a couple of men start to hoist the logs into the air by pulling on the free end of the block and tackle ropes. Once the log is at the correct height, they tie the rope off, suspending the log in midair. While that has been going on, others separate the first wagon into two halves. One half has the fifth-wheel attached to it for turning purposes and the second half is a fixed set of wheels on a axle with a tongue stretched out. The driver guides the first half of wagon wheels under the log. He then pulls the back set of wheels under the back end of the log that is still resting in the slings and hanging in midair. Once they have the two sets of wheels in position under the suspended log, they untie the ropes slowly lowering the log into place. The crew repeats the process until they have three logs stacked on the two sets of wagon wheels. The entire assembly is now one long wagon lashed together by chains; turning wheels up front and a fixed set of wheels in back. The wagons are pulled by teams of four horses each, two men per wagon, three logs per load, this is quite the operation.

During that process, Nate and I stacked the limbs from the day before and loaded the cord wood onto the wagon. Nate used Gus to pull stacks of limbs down to an open area for burning during the wet fall and early winter season.

Before Mr. Winkler starts the wagons headed down the road, Nate and I walk over to make sure everything is okay. Mr. Winkler says it is and he will be back tomorrow to get the rest of the logs.

Before he turns his horse to leave, I approach him asking, "Mr. Winkler, if you don't mind, whose logs are these and where are they going to?"

He says that these logs aren't for any one just yet. These

are replacement logs and will need to be peeled and dried some more before they are cut and used for anything.

He asks why am I asking and I tell him, "Cause I'm a carpenter, and a pretty good one at that; just wondering if there might be any carpentry work around."

Mr. Winkler asks, "I thought you were working here for Mr. Harris?"

"Well, I am, but carpentry is what I do best."

Mr. Winkler then says, "There are a couple of brothers with young families that have got a place about three miles upriver. They've started an apple farm and ordered lumber for a barn of some sort. Once the lumber is cut to order, these here logs will replace the logs used for their barn. Their kids don't seem to be old enough to be of much help yet; they might be able to use a hand."

"If you don't mind me asking, what are their names?"

"They're not from around here, they've got a heavy accent, and one goes by Conrad Meijer, they're Dutch."

"Meijer?"

"Yeah, Conrad, Conrad Meijer, their place is about three miles up the north side of the river. I've never been there, but Mr. Meijer told me that their turn off is marked Holland Road."

With that, Mr. Winkler gives his horse a kick in the ribs and yells for the wagons to move out.

Nate and I tie Gus up to the back of the wagon and head back to the meadow as well. Molly and Bess notice that the wagon is heavier with the extra cord of wood for the Johnsons and the added five bolts of cedar for the roof repair. The going is slow as we follow Winkler's three wagons of logs down the well-grooved road.

I ask Nate, "So why does Mr. Winkler go to all this trouble getting logs from Sam? Doesn't he have his own logs?"

Nate explains, "Sam and Mr. Winkler are old friends; Sam's pa and Mr. Winkler's pa were in this part of the country together from early on. In fact, the lumber for the ferry came from Mr. Winkler's mill. With them knowing each other for so long they trade timber and sometimes labor back and forth. Sometimes Mr. Winkler needs to get his wagons across the river, Sam and Red help Mr. Winkler out with that. Once in awhile the mill will run short of certain types of timber and Mr. Winkler knows that Sam always has good logs."

After dropping Gus off at the meadow, brushing him down, giving him some oats and a little fresh hay, Nate pulls the wagon down to the back of the barn. We get busy unhitching Molly and Bess and make sure they have fresh hay and oats as well. With the horses tended to I jump up and roll the five Cedar bolts off the back of the wagon. I roll them over to where Nate does his splitting of firewood. I ask him if he has a froe and mallet for making shakes. He says he does, he thinks they are in the barn mixed with the rest of Sam's tools.

I meander into the barn and start poking around the clutter of tools. Some are a bit rusted up. The tools that Sam uses more regularly are clean and set out for quick finding. I rummage through an assortment of saws, chisels and hammers. Down amongst the tools at the bottom of a barrel I find the froe. I still need a mallet but I can make one of those if I need to. I can't imagine that Sam wouldn't have a mallet or two laying around. Sure enough, hanging by some twine on a post, are two mallets tied together looking like a couple of bells. I now have everything I need to repair the barn roof and according to Sam, I'll be able to do that when Nate and I get back from town.

Even though we have the wagon loaded and the horses turned in for the night, the work is not completely finished. I help Nate haul wood to the house and down to the ferry shack.

The ferry is on the south side of the river getting ready to make the last crossing of the day before darkness makes navigating dangerous. Not everyone was able to cross the river today and because Nate and I are heading to town tomorrow it looks like the ferry will make a special run in the morning. Sam is explaining this to a fella that appears to be in charge of two wagons traveling together with four men in each wagon. Sam points towards the area that they can pull their wagons to and spend the night. The men are grumbling amongst themselves while Sam and the lead man continue to discuss the situation. The man is explaining that they need to get to the coast. They all have jobs on fishing boats. It is the start of the season and they need to get there before the boats head out. Sam reassures them that they will get an early start first thing in the morning. There's good firewood and fresh water up at the camp area and a nice swimming area down river a short ways if they'd like. There isn't much anyone can do about getting across the river this late in the day, especially with the sun beginning to set.

The head man settles for Sam's reasoning and he tells Sam that they will be ready at first light. Red lets out a cloud of steam and a sharp whistle. The ferry pulls away from the south bank cutting up river before it turns and docks at the north bank. It's only a ten to fifteen minute crossing, but the loading and unloading, along with keeping the steam up adds to the number of trips Red and his crew can make. It'll be a short night for Sam making sure the ferry is ready to go at first light.

Sam looks to me and Nate saying, "I sure hope Red will be able to be back here at sunrise. He don't know it yet, but I agreed to run the ferry on an off day to help those fellers out."

Nate tells him, "Don't worry, if Red can't make it back, the three of us could handle it."

Sam gives him a shrug and says, "I know we could handle it, I just feel better when Red and his crew are working the ferry. The rivers up and it is fast this time of year, that's all."

Agreeing Nate says, "Yap, you're right Sam."

Red eased the ferry into place and the crew secured it and lowered the ramp. There is a wagon with a family of four, all blonde with rosy red cheeks and full smiles ready to come off the ferry. The horses are skittish and strain as the weight of the wagon is to its max. The wagon is filled with all kinds of goods. Even with the load wrapped in tarps, I can tell that this wagon is full of building supplies. I wonder if this is the family that has started the apple farm and ordered the lumber for the barn. The man pulls the wagon up the road, out of the way of the ferry and comes back to talk to Sam. He hands Sam what appears to be two dollars currency. Sam has a few words with the man but all I can make out is something about coins, no paper money.

The man looks around and turns his pants pockets inside

out, Sam tells him, "Next time coins, no paper."

The man says something to Sam, walking away nodding his head. Hearing what few words I could, I was fairly sure he wasn't a local; he had a different accent. He turns and walks quickly towards his wagon.

Just before he gets there, I catch up to him saying, "'S'cuse me, sir, don't mean to bother you. Can I have a word with you?"

Climbing onto his wagon he says, "I am sorry, we are in a hurry."

I continue, "This will only take a minute, please, I just want to ask you a question."

He replies impatiently, "What kind of a question?"

"Are you Mr. Meijer?" I ask.

"Yaw, yaw I am, why do you ask my name?"

"Well, I am a carpenter and word has come my way that if you are Mr. Meijer, then you might be needing some help building a barn?"

The man looks at his wife and climbs back down off the wagon asking, "And who are you?"

"I'm Jacob Sparks, sir, and I'm a carpenter, a darn good one and judging by the size of those youngins, you look like you might be in need of some help; that is if you're the man that ordered lumber from Winkler's mill?"

Thick with a Dutch accent he answers, "Yaw, yaw, I've ordered lumber."

I ask, "Maybe I could come by your place sometime and we could talk. Would that be okay?"

With exasperation he says, "I must be on my way, please

Mr. Sparks, not today. My wife and children are tired; we've had a long trip into town and must get back home. Please let us be on our way."

"Sure, sure thing. You have a safe trip." I reach up to tip my hat to the misses and realize I don't have a hat, "Good day, ma'am, Mr. Meijer."

At that, Mr. Meijer releases the brake and snaps the reins; the wagon lurches forward, leaving me scratching my head, wondering what the heck just happened.

Judith comes out onto the porch and yells towards the river that supper is just about ready. Sam and Red have discussed the situation for tomorrow. With at least three wagons to ferry across, Red assures Sam that he and his crew will be back at sun up. Before the three of us turn to head up to the house, I lean down at the water's edge, wash my hands together and splash water on my face and head. I don't have a towel, but I know I will dry off enough for supper by the time we have to sit. I look over and Nate does the same. Rusty laps up some water and then grabs a stick of driftwood wanting anyone of us to play. Nate and I both take a turn tossing the water soaked stick. We just might have to wash our hands again... maybe Judith wasn't watching.

As we enter from the front porch, Judith says, "I apologize for serving leftovers, but that is what we have tonight. I hope you men are hungry. Mr. Sparks, you'll have to have seconds to make up for what you missed last night."

"Sorry, Judith, but I was just too dang dusty and dirty to be around any one last night."

"Not to worry, Mr. Sparks. Let's sit and Nate, will you

bless the food tonight?"

He nods answering, "Yes, ma'am".

As we all hold hands, I realize that I had better brush up on my praying; it is one thing to hold hands while someone else says prayers; it's another to hold hands while you're the one doing the praying.

Nate prays, "Lord, please bless this food to our bodies and bless the hands that have provided it. Amen."

As Judith straightens her napkins she says, "Thank you, Nate. Pass your bowls around and I'll dish you all up."

Sam lets Judith know what to expect tomorrow. He reminds her that if she needs anything from town, to write it down so Nate and I can bring it back with us. She says we got everything last trip, but she reminds Nate to make sure Mr. Kimble sends the balance statement.

I ask Sam about the man in the last wagon and that there seemed to be a money problem, "Why is it you only take coins?"

Sam says, "I don't know that fella very well. He's only used the ferry a couple of times. He wanted to use paper money and it ain't worth the paper it's written on. Ever since the war, you can't trust printed money."

"But Sam, the war has been over for close to twenty years. The country is doing pretty good. The government seems strong enough to back paper money."

"That might be so, but Red and me don't like paper money, our ferry, our rules."

Judith looks up at Sam and asks him, "Is everything is alright? You seem a little bit out of sorts."

He looks at her and says, "It was a long day and I'll probably be up late watching the ferry and making sure those men settle down. Not much sleep tonight for me and I'll be up before anyone else getting the steam up for Red. Sorry for being tired."

Judith replies, "Now, Sam, no need to apologize for being tired, but no one at this table took the day off you know."

Softening his voice Sam says, "I know, Judith, you're right. Excuse me, I'm going to go sit on the porch for a bit, come on Rusty."

The three of us sit in silence and I apologize, hoping I hadn't brought up a touchy subject.

Judith explains, "Sam gets like that once in awhile. He loves living here, loves working with the ferry and working in the woods, but sometimes he feels like life is closing in on him. As you know Sam's pa homesteaded this land and now things are changing; sometimes change is unsettling."

"Yeah, well, sometimes change can be good." With that I excuse myself and take my dishes to the sink.

It's too early to lie down and sleep, so I walk around to the front porch to see if Sam is there. As I turn past the back corner I see Sam and Rusty headed down to the ferry. He has a lantern and is smoking his pipe. I can smell the aroma as it floats through the air. I never minded the smell of a good blend of tobacco, whether it was a pipe or a cigar, I just never acquired a taste for the habit. Lord knows I picked up enough other habits that weren't good for me.

I approach Sam and ask, "Everything all right? I sure hope

I didn't offend you at the dinner table."

He answers, "Nah, you didn't. Like I said, I'm just tired."

"Yeah, me too, can I help you do anything?"

"No, not really, I got to drain the tank on the boiler, need to check the prop and rudder. I guess you could grab that broom and sweep the deck off. The wagons leave clumps of mud and there's always horse crap to get rid of."

"Sure, no problem, just sweep it all into the river?"

I get a nod that says yes and then Sam says, "Not the horse turds, just the mud. There is a shovel in the shack, throw the turds on the bank towards them weeds."

With a loud hiss, Sam lets the steam off the tank and turns the wheel back and forth aggressively checking the linkage on the steering. Rusty thinks the broom is something to bite and growl at. Sam says, "Rusty does the same thing every time someone sweeps."

I ask him, "How do you intend to check the prop and rudder tonight?"

"Once in a while I get in the water and feel that everything is good, but tonight I'll just shine a lantern to check and make sure the rudder linkage is all connected. I'll make sure the cotter pins aren't working their way out, especially the one holding the prop on. Everything should be okay, Red didn't say anything about having any problems today, and I just did maintenance on the rudder and prop last week."

It doesn't take us very long to finish up with what Sam needed to do. I help stack some wood next to the boiler for morning. With that done, we both rest our elbows on the top railing and lean out over the water. The moon is just over the hill tops and its reflection shimmers in a straight line across this wide part of the river.

Sam asks me, "So, did you happen to know that man that was in the last wagon?"

"No, I just happened to be standing there as he pulled his wagon off. Yesterday, Mr. Winkler told me about this farmer that had ordered the lumber for a new barn, mentioned his name and that he spoke with a different accent, possibly Dutch. So, listening to you and him talk, I assumed that this was the man Mr. Winkler had described. Even though most of his load was covered by tarps, I could tell that the wagon was filled with building supplies. It was a coincidence that this was the man that Mr. Winkler had told me about."

Sam knocks the burnt ash out of his pipe and reaches for his pouch to refill it. With a strike of a match and a couple of deep drags, Sam blows out a large puff of smoke. He asks out the side of his mouth, "Did Winkler offer up the man's name or did you ask him?"

"No, I asked Mr. Winkler who ordered the lumber. Why?"

"No reason. Just curious that's all. You looking for work or something?"

Looking at Sam I say, "Well, yeah, I am kinda. I mean I love being here and helping you all out, but I don't know what tomorrow will bring. I am a carpenter and I love building things. I have learned enough along the way that when the mill is cutting lumber, men at the mill know who's doing the building and that they just might need a good carpenter. I may be a drifter to you Sam, but I like to make money, I told you before that I don't take handouts."

Sam looks my way and says, "I understand, Jake. I know that you landed here to rest up a spell. I've seen a lot of men like you come through here. Helped many out and ran a lot off. In the short time you've been here you have helped out and earned your keep. Sometimes life ain't about the money, ya know."

"Yeah, Sam, I do know, but, the facts are, I do need money." Trying to ease things with a smile I continue, "I got needs and there are just some things my good looks and easygoing disposition can't pay for."

Not taking the bait Sam says, "Like what, what do you need?"

"Well for one thing, I need a new hat. That dam old bull gored it and stomped on it, hell, I couldn't even find it this morning when I went to fix the fence. He might've eaten it for all I know. Do cattle eat hats?"

With a slight smile Sam says, "Oh yeah, that's right. Good 'ole Brutus got after it pretty good. From what Nate said he almost got a hold of you!"

Standing straight I say, "He sure did, came close enough to damn near tear my britches right off me."

Losing the smile Sam asks, "So, did you talk to that new feller?"

"I tried, but he seemed to be in an awful hurry and he just didn't want to talk. I told him I might stop by sometime."

Sam takes a drag off his pipe and says, "What'd he say to that?"

"He didn't, he just drove the wagon away."

Sam and I stand at the ferry's railing staring out at the

moving water. Sam has finished his pipe and puts it away. He motions for us to move off the deck; instead of walking to the house, we walk towards the two wagons and the men camped for the night. The glow from a large campfire casts the groups' silhouette through the forest as they sit talking and laughing to each other.

As we continue making our way towards the group of men, Sam says, "Look Jake, I don't really want you to leave, not just yet anyways. You have really helped out around here and Nate has really taken a liking to you. He has never been much of a talker, until lately that is."

"Like what, what's he been talking about?"

"Nothing in particular, he just seems to be talking more."

"That's good to hear. You and Judith have treated me something special. Nate is a great kid and I have really enjoyed working with him. I figured he was quiet because of me being a stranger and all. But, I agree, he does seem to talk more once you get him started. Hell, he even asked me some questions about that aspen grove that's up above the meadow."

Surprised Sam asks, "Aspen grove? Why did he ask about that?"

"He didn't just ask me about the aspens out of the blue; he asked me what I was doing in the meadow when Brutus took after me. Once I explained what I had been doing, he then asked me about the aspens and why I was interested in them."

Lowering his voice Sam says, "That's what I mean, cause you have talked to him about things that matter to you, he's seems to be talking more. Judith has mentioned that she has seen a change in Nate too. Ahh, about those aspen's, you'll have to tell me about them, later."

We approach the men gathered around the campfire. They've been drinking and are starting to get louder. Sam tells them that the ferry will be ready at morning's first light. The lead man that talked to Sam earlier thanks him and tells the others to keep it down. Sam tips his hat and lets him know that it will be appreciated. A group of men sitting around a campfire and drinking is not as predictable as having a family or two camped out. As we turn to leave, Sam whispers to me that he'll keep his eye on them and his shotgun is always at the ready.

Walking back towards the house, Sam continues our talk from earlier, saying, "I planned on paying you for your work. I can't pay you much, but how's fifty cents a day plus room and board?"

I don't say anything right off, then I say, "Fifty cents a day is not much, some places, I earn double that doing carpentry work, plus room and board."

"I'm sure you do, but I don't need a carpenter. You are already getting fed and have a dry place to sleep, how 'bout I tell Mr. Kimble to put five dollars credit at the general store in your name?"

"Five dollars a week?"

"Five dollars for this week and last week, then two dollars every week after that. I'll let you clear out a space in the loft and build yourself a bed to sleep on. Right now, that's the best I can do."

Not wasting anytime I reply, "Plus the fifty cents a day, paid at the end of each week, deal?"

Sam turns and says, "Deal." With that we stop and shake hands.

Part Three

Foundations

Chapter 13

Sam and I walk back to the house and see Nate and Judith sitting out on the front porch. Sam asks, "Have you been out here long?"

Nate answers, "Nah, we just got out here. I helped Judith with some chores. We washed up the dishes, and then I filled the wood boxes. We got a few things from the root cellar and smoke house."

"Like what? What did you get from the smoke house at this time of night?"

Judith answers this time, "We got some of the jerked venison and dried steelhead. We prepared what we could for their trip into town. We have more time to get things prepared tonight rather than wait until morning."

The men waiting to cross the river in the morning are still whooping it up and have gotten even louder. We all turn our head towards them, and Sam mutters half to himself, "It could be a long night if they keep this up."

Judith asks, "How was your walk? Is everything alright?" and then comments, "I hope those men settle down soon."

Sam tells her that he talked with them and they should settle down shortly. Reassuring her he says, "I'll stay up and make sure they do."

Nate asks if he should stay up in case Sam needs some help and Sam tells him, "Nah, they'll be fine. They're just blowing off a little steam; they'll quiet down. You all head to bed, I'll be alright."

Judith gets up and tells Sam that she just made a fresh pot of coffee and asks if he would like a cup right now. Sam tells her, "I'll wait a few minutes. Why don't you go on and get ready for bed. I'll come in and check on ya and get a cup then."

I say my goodnights and as I head up to the barn, I say, "Hey Sam, I'm close by if you need me."

"Thanks Jake, I'll be fine. I got good 'ol Rusty, he'll let them know who the boss is, won't ya boy."

As I walk up to the barn, I can see the glow of the campfire through the trees. Rusty followed me until I had to tell him to go back to the house. He stopped where he was and sat down until he heard Nate give him a whistle, that's all he needed; Rusty turned and headed to the front of the house.

The pile of straw that has been my bed for the past week is a welcome relief. I strip off my pants and shirt deciding that it is warm enough to sleep in my underwear. Before I climb into my bedroll, I make sure my bowie knife is handy and in arms reach. I settle into the straw and let my eyes stare up at the hole in the roof.

The brightness of the moon shining through the missing shakes confirms that it is near to being full. It suddenly dawns on me why those men could be restless.

My mind begins to drift back to some of the antics that I got involved in that where fueled up by booze and full moons. I tell myself that it will sure feel good in the morning when I wake up with a clear head, clear memory and clear conscience. I chuckle half out loud remembering that I sure had some fun. Reluctantly, I tell myself that I am glad those days are behind me.

•

I must have slept hard, 'cause I don't wake until I hear Nate and Rusty walking past the barn. I sit up and yell out, "Is it late? Did I oversleep?"

Nate yells back, "Nah, well maybe a little, but we've got time, we won't be the first wagon on the ferry today."

I put my clothes on and head out to throw some water on my face and head. There is smoke coming from the house and I give a good morning wave to Judith as she is standing at the window. Once again, there is a hint of a distant memory that is clouded in haze and blurred by miles of dusty roads. My mind is muddled, I've always been good at remembering faces; I'm just not very good at remembering names. I tell myself to let it go, her face is just one of the many that I have encountered during my wanderings.

To my surprise, I find that I am back at the barn just as Nate and Rusty return with Bonnie in tow for her milking. I ask Nate if it is too soon to get Molly and Bess harnessed and hitched to the wagon. He gives me a shrug and a nod that tells me sure.

Then he says, "They need to be brushed and fed a little grain. They might need some fresh hay and water. Just don't overdo it."

It's my turn to shrug and nod, okay. We finish up just about the same time. He leads Bonnie back to the pasture, but doesn't come back right away. He is probably taking time to check on Gus and Daisy since he will be gone for a couple days. I decide to head down to the house, hoping Judith will have the coffee brewed.

"Good morning, Judith. It sure is another nice morning."

"Yes it is, Jacob. Would you like a cup of coffee?"

"Yes please." I then ask, "Is Sam down at the ferry?"

"Yes he is."

"Can I take him a cup?"

"Please, I think he'd like that."

"Did he have any trouble with those men, or did they settle down in due time?"

"Oh, they settled down in good time. It wasn't very long until the fire burned down, soon after, so did the loud laughter. Sam was able to get some sleep before he got up to tend to the ferry."

"That's good. I sure slept hard. I woke up thinking I overslept and missed the ferry."

"I don't imagine Nate or Sam would have allowed that," she says with a slight grin.

Turning towards the door I say, "No, me neither. Thanks for the coffee."

"You're welcome, and please let Sam know that breakfast will be ready about the same time he gets that cup of coffee drank up."

With the screen door shutting behind me I say, "I better get it to him before it cools. Thanks again, ma'am, sure smells fine in here."

Sam has the ferry all fired up and ready to go. He gives a couple of long blasts of the whistle and looks up towards the two wagons; no movement is visible from the camp. I ask him how the night went and he says he had no problems. The men settled down fairly quick.

"Judith told me to tell you that breakfast will be ready about the same time that your coffee is gone."

"Well good, I'm done here anyway. Thanks for bringing me a cup. Sure hope Red gets here soon. I'd like to get those fellers on their way."

"Anything I can do?"

"No, we'll wait 'til Red shows and then I'll go see if they're ready. They should be up and moving around any minute. Maybe I'll give the whistle a couple more blasts."

We head up towards the house just as Red and his men come down the road. Sam waves Red over and they confer about getting the ferry ready for the crossing. Red is wondering where the wagons are and sends one of his men up to the camp. Sam and I head into the house. Judith has breakfast on the table. Nate is already sitting as Judith pours us each a fresh cup. We hold hands as Judith nods towards Sam, apparently it's his turn to bless the food. Without hesitation, Sam keeps the blessing short and to the point.

Half way through breakfast, we hear Rusty barking and hear men yelling. Through the front windows we see a couple of Red's men running from the ferry towards the camp. Red is on his horse headed the same way with Rusty running alongside.

Sam jumps up and runs to the window. Spinning back towards us he yells, "Nate! Get the shotgun. There's trouble, let's go! Judith you stay down, stay away from the windows!"

The three of us run out the back door and up towards the wagons and a large cloud of dust. Men are wrestling with each other and punches are being thrown. Sam grabs the shot gun from Nate and jacks a shell into the chamber. He fires a shot in the air. The men stop, but remain paired up. Red and his men were outnumbered but with the three of us, the numbers even out.

We run up to the group and Sam shouts, "What the hell is going on here."

The lead man points at one of Red's men and tells Sam that he poked him in the ass with a stick. He then told him and his men to get up; if they didn't, they'd miss the ferry.

Sam says, "That's it, so what?"

"Well, I don't take kindly to getting poked with a stick, specially poked in the ass."

Sam says, "You men should have been up an hour ago. Now, get your asses going, the ferry leaves in a half hour. If you're not on it you're gonna turn your wagons around and take the long way to Ash Fork."

A guy in the back says, "Who the hell do you think you are mister?"

Red walks up to him and says, "That's the Watchman and I'm the Ferryman. We own that ferry. If you want to cross here, you best do what this man says. If not, drive those wagons back the way you came. While you're at it, get this place cleaned up and get those wagons down to the ferry."

As Red turns away from the guy, Red gets hit alongside his back with an ax handle, more punches start to get thrown. Nate grabs a guy and locks him in a bear hug. The guy's face turns red and he starts gasping for air. Rusty is trying to bite the guy's ankles and gets kicked. Another guy takes a swing at me and falls off balance. I pull my knife quicker than he can recover; I put my knee in his chest and my knife to his throat. Sam jacks another shell in the chamber and lets loose with another blast.

He reloads again and points it right into the lead man's cheek, "Get these wagons and your men down to the ferry... NOW!"

"Yes, sir. Boys, do as the man says. Let's get our things gathered, we best be moving."

We stay with the wagons while Red and his men head back down to the ferry. It doesn't take long for the dust to settle and we head down towards the ferry together. Sam and Rusty stay close to the front wagon. Sam keeps the shot gun cocked and pointed at the lead driver. Nate and I walk along the side of the second wagon, my hand on the hilt of my knife watching every move. Even though we have the shotgun, it wouldn't take much for things to turn ugly again, especially now that Red and his men are at the ferry. We're out numbered and these men are hung over, hungry, and have been handed their asses. It'll take awhile for them to settle down and sober up, we just need to get them across the river and let them be on their way.

Red has the ferry ready to go when we get to the ferry shack. The ramp is lowered and his men are ready to get the wagons on board. Sam stops them and steps up on the wheel of the lead wagon. Sam puts out his hand and tells the guy, "That'll be two dollars a wagon and ten cents per man."

Loudly protesting the leader answers, "What? That's not what we planned on. It says two dollars a wagon, nothing about how many is on the wagon."

"Well, mister, you can either pay or you can turn your wagons around and take the extra two days to Ash Fork. It's another two or three days to the coast or where ever it is you're headed. Now, that'll be four dollars and eighty cents for the two wagons and the eight men. What'll it be?"

The man pulls out some money, paper money and Nate and I look at each other anxiously.

Sam stops him and says, "No paper; coins only, silver or gold."

Again he loudly protests, "What kinda outfit you running here? This is nothing but strong armed robbery!"

"No it ain't. It's posted right on our signs, both sides of the river, NO Paper Money! That's the rules. You don't like it, turn those wagons around. I'm not telling you again."

The lead man turns towards the others in the wagons and tells them that they either give Sam coins, silver or gold or turn around. They all mumble but know they have to get to the coast as quickly as possible. The boats won't wait and the jobs will be handed out to whoever is there first. One of the men in the second wagon gets down and flexes at me as he walks towards the first wagon. He jumps back as I pull my knife and have it at his throat before he can blink.

He's the same guy as before; my knife blade is still imprinted on his neck from earlier. I get real close to him and whisper, "Go ahead, I'd just as soon slit your throat as smell your breath another second. From what I can see, I'd be doing you a favor. Your call, make your best move."

Nate walks up and lays his hand over mine that holds the

knife still pressed at the man's throat, "Jake, please lower your knife."

Not blinking I say, "Nate, back off, it's his move."

Sam and his shotgun are once again at the leader's cheek. With his voice quivering, Sam says, "Mister, I've had just about enough of you and your boys today. Tell him to back off or someone won't be making the trip to the coast or where ever you all came from."

With a big gulp the lead man slowly turns his head and tells the one with the knife at his throat, "Back off, NOW!"

He puts one hand in the air and with the other reaches for a pouch that is tied to his belt. He reaches in and takes out a handful of coins and counts out five silver dollars. I press my knife into his back as I walk with him to where Sam is. Sam stretches his palm out flat as the guy lays the money in it.

Sam takes the five dollars and says, "No change today fellas. We'll call it even on account of the trouble you've caused."

I walk the man back to his wagon with him yelling, "You owe me! You all owe me!"

The leader tells him, "We'll settle up later, sit down and stay in the wagon."

Sam gives Red a wave and Red whistles the crew to let the wagons on the ferry. He motions for the drivers to bring them onto the ramp slowly. We all get on the ferry without saying a word. There's no way we were going to let Red take these men across by himself and his crew.

Tensions remain high but the crossing is uneventful, most of the men in the wagons have their heads hanging down in their chests.

Before Red lowers the ramp to let the wagons off the ferry, Sam climbs up on the front wheel of the front wagon, puts his shotgun in the man's cheek for the third time and tells him, "Don't ever come this way again. You'll not cross this river on my ferry ever. You go around, is that clear?"

The man doesn't say anything, he just looks straight ahead and as Sam lowers the barrel of the shot gun, the guy lets loose with a spit of chew, wipes his mouth with his sleeve and says, "Clear."

While we are crossing back to the north bank, Sam tells Nate to take Molly and Bess back to the meadow, we won't be going to town for a day or two. Sam's afraid that these men will take their time and he doesn't want Nate and I to run into them somewhere down the road. In protest, Nate tells him that we'll be fine, but Sam reminds him that it would be eight against two. Sam doesn't believe those to be very good odds. I agree.

Judith watches from the ferry shack as we all get busy securing the ferry; it is shut down for the day. She is beside herself with worry and questions. Sam tells her it's all over, he'll tell her all about it and will answer all her questions up at the house. Sam offers Red and his crew to come up to the house for some coffee before they head back to his place. Before anyone can refuse, Judith extends the offer with fresh biscuits and preserves to go along with the coffee. She will need a few minutes but that will give us all enough time to wash up. Red and his crew walk over to check on their horses as Judith, Sam and Nate walk arm in arm up to the house.

We are all sitting on the porch telling each other's version of what happened; who hit who and how hard. Judith comes out with a big tray of cups and a pot of steaming coffee. Sam takes the tray and passes out the cups. Handing me the coffee pot, he follows Judith back into the house. Sam comes back by himself with a bottle of whiskey and pours some into whoever holds their cup out to him. He hesitates when he gets to Nate; with a quick look over his shoulder he tips the bottle and pours the amber colored liquid into Nate's cup. Sam puts his finger over his lips and then drags his thumb across his throat.

One of Red's men says, "It's time, Nate's all grown up. He held his own this morning."

Sam brings the bottle over to me; with my hand over my cup I simply nod, thanks, but no thanks. Once Sam completes the circle, he says, "We did good, thanks for standing together."

We all lift our cups and say, "Hear, Hear."

Judith walks out with another tray stacked with fresh biscuits and preserves asking, "What'd I miss?" She then sees the bottle, mutters something under her breath about men and it still being morning; she excuses herself and closes the screen door behind her.

We each help ourselves to the biscuits and continue to talk about the dust up. Even Rusty seems to know what is going on. He is sitting in the middle of everyone, waiting for a biscuit to come his way. Sam asks Red how his back is; he says it's okay, sore, but okay. It hurts no worse than getting kicked by a mule. Someone makes a comment that they were sure glad we came running and evened the odds. Another was glad to see that Sam had a shotgun and wasn't shy about using it.

Red looks at me saying, "You're pretty handy with that knife of yours. No doubt you would have used it on that feller?"

I tell him, "I wouldn't have hesitated for a second if he hadn't backed down. He meant to hurt someone bad. Sometimes there's just no reasoning when a man is crazed and fueled up on liquor."

With that, Red gives me a wink, tips his cup and says to Sam, "Just one more shot and we'll be on our way."

Sam is obliging to whoever holds their cup out. Nate takes his last gulp and this time waves Sam off.

Red and his men ride out to the east and the three of us gather up the cups and coffee pot, taking them into the house. Judith is in her rocking chair and has her sewing out. She tells Sam and Nate that if they have any clothes with holes in them now would be the time to bring them to her. She only wants their clean clothes, she doesn't want to be sewing on dirty laundry. They both mutter no and Sam says he is going to go lay down.

I look at Nate and point with my thumb towards the back, he nods okay and we excuse ourselves and head out the back door.

Being curious I ask, "So Nate, what are you going to do the rest of the day? I guess we aren't headed to town for a day or two."

"No, guess not." Then he lets out a big yawn and with a stretch he tells me, "I wouldn't mind laying down."

Looking at him I say, "What's stopping you?"

"I don't know, I just never feel like this, at least not this early in the day."

"You ever have a drink before?"

"One other time, it was at Thanksgiving last year. Sam let me have a drink from a jug of homemade whiskey that a friend brought to the house. I had more than one drink and felt dizzy afterward. I woke up with a headache the next day. Judith was upset with Sam for the next day or two. She said that I was too young to drink. Sam told her he felt that I was old enough, that I worked as hard as any man and I should be able to have a drink like any man. Judith argued back that I had the rest of my life to find out if I wanted to drink or not. Sam told her it was best that I learn it at home, rather than learn it in some saloon someplace."

I asked him what happened, he said, "Well, after a couple of days of silence, Judith decided that one drink once in awhile would be okay."

"Like today?"

"Yeah, like today, but you could tell she wasn't happy about it."

"I know and most women aren't either. They have a fear that drinking is gonna change a man, make him mean, make him do things that he won't normally do. It scares 'em. Most women have a sad story about a man that drank too much. When they get around men that are drinking, that sadness comes bubbling up."

Nate asks, "Is that why you don't drink?"

"No, Nate, that's not why I don't drink, I used to drink; I used to love to drink. I was good at it, I loved it."

"Did drinking make your Beth sad?"

"No, not very often; you see, she was one of those women that liked to take a drink also. She didn't like to see me get stupid drunk, but my drinking didn't make her sad."

"So why don't you take a drink now?"

"Let's just say, one's too many and a hundred's not enough." With that I decide it would be a good time to do that roof repair.

Chapter 14

With the ladder standing up at the back corner eave, I grab a rope from inside the barn. Before I tie it to a fence post on the other side of the barn, I give the post a shake hoping that it is not rotten at the bottom. I need it to hold my weight if I should slip and slide off the roof. It appears to be good and solid so I tie a strong knot and toss the rope up onto the roof. The rope doesn't quite make it over the ridgeline, so naturally it comes sliding back down. I look for anything that will add some weight to the rope. I take a piece of wood from one of the many stacks of chopped wood and tie it onto the end of the rope. I give the weighted rope a couple of twirls over my head and let it fly. Rusty thinks this is the best game ever! He is running from one side of the barn to the other waiting and watching for the wood or rope to hit the ground. Rusty is staring up in the air as I walk to the other side of the barn. I climb the ladder, untie the piece of wood and give it a heave back towards the stacked up piles. Standing there, I get a chuckle out of Rusty as he runs from pile to pile trying to sniff out the exact piece that I threw. He didn't see where it landed; he only heard it as it clanked around. He puts his nose to the ground running back and forth checking every pile.

I pull the rope tight and give it a good yank; it is as secure as it is going to be. Tying the rope around my waist and before I climb down the ladder, I check out the rotten shakes that will need to be replaced. The area looks like it will be almost ten feet by four feet once all the rotten shakes are removed.

I estimate that this shouldn't take me more than a couple of hours. I make my way off the roof, gather up the tools I will need and pack the tools up to the roof.

With the rope tied around my waist, I get started removing the rotten shakes and pulling out old, rusted nails. It doesn't take me long to work my way to the edges of the good shakes. I wonder to myself why this area of the roof is damaged. Maybe these shakes had been green and they rotted out quicker than normal. There could be a lot of reasons, none of which matter to me at the moment. I am just glad to have the removal complete. I can now start splitting new shakes and laying them back into place.

When I get down off the roof, Rusty is at the bottom of the ladder; his nose is covered with dust from sniffing along the ground and the many wood piles. He is quite proud of himself as he has dropped a piece of wood right where my foot settles from stepping off the last rung of the ladder. The piece looks to be smaller than the one I used, but I don't tell Rusty that. I pick it up and give it a toss sending Rusty running down the hill towards the house.

I roll a cedar bolt over to the stump that Nate uses when he splits firewood. With the growth rings facing up, I have a urge to count them. About half way to the center I stop at thirty-seven and tell myself the tree was close to eighty years old. I grab the froe and one of the wooden mallets. I set the froe on the line of grain where I want to make my first split and give the froe a whack with the mallet. The blade of the froe slides through the cedar with little resistance. My nose is filled with the fresh aroma of cedar as the pale reddish color of the grain is now fully exposed. This one shake is the first of many. It will probably take close to a hundred shakes to completely cover the hole in the roof. I suddenly realize five bolts probably won't be enough. What looked to be a couple of small holes to be repaired, has now turned into one large hole.

I get the first bolt split as Nate walks over and asks if he can help. I tell him that I need to split the four remaining bolts up and will probably need more than I first estimated. He tells me he has split shakes before. He could split and haul them to the roof while I start getting them nailed down. As much as I love to be splitting and smelling, I would rather be nailing the new shakes in place. I surrender the froe and mallet. Gathering up the shakes that I have already split, I carry them up the ladder, and stack them close to the hole. I begin to fit them one to another and nail them down.

Nate gets busy splitting the other four bolts, hauls the newly split shakes up the ladder and stacks them up so they won't slide off the roof. The hole is closing in quickly especially with two of us working at it. With the hole over half way filled in, it is obvious that we won't have enough shakes to finish. I yell down to Nate to give him the news. He says he'll grab Gus and go get a couple of bolts.

Before I can suggest that we make sure of how many we will need to finish, Nate and Rusty go racing up the hill to the meadow. Apparently, he has recovered from his drowsiness after the morning drink. It doesn't take me long to use up the shakes that Nate had split. This would be a good time to get a drink and let my knees and ankles straighten out for a minute or two.

I give the pump handle a couple of good ups and downs. The water comes up the pipe, gushing out of the spigot. I hold a cup under the spout trying to catch all the water I can. There is more water than the cup will hold so I lower my head under the spigot and let the flowing water give my head a good drenching.

I raise up and notice Sam walking from the back porch up to where I am, he is looking up at the barn and says, "No rest for the wicked I see."

"No, not today anyways. With our trip to town held up, I decided that now would be a good time to patch that roof."

"Yeah, where's Nate?" Sam asks.

"I ended up being a couple of shakes short so he jumped on Gus to go get me a couple more bolts. He shouldn't be too much longer."

Scratching his head, Sam asks, "So he's helping you, not wasting the afternoon away?"

"Sam, you know better than that, Nate is a working fool, he'd just as soon be busy working as doing anything else. Hell if he wasn't working out here with me, he'd be chopping wood or filling wood boxes or something."

Sam turns towards the barn asking, "Yeah, you're right. Mind if I take a look at your patch job?"

"No, not at all, it's your roof."

Nate returns with two cedar bolts strapped down to Gus's hind quarters. Rusty is running alongside and jumps up to let me know they have returned.

Sam is walking back from being up on the roof and is nodding his approval saying at the same time, "Well, Jake you were right, you are a pretty fair carpenter. You got a nice pattern to the shake layout and it looks like you got rid of all the bad ones, thank you."

He slaps his hands and calls Rusty over. He gives him a rub and a pat on the head and starts to walk up the hill towards the meadow. He stops and tells Nate that he'll take Gus up if he's done with him. Nate hands him the reins. Sam hoists himself up on Gus's back, throws his leg over and digs in his heels. Gus rears, spins and leaps forward leaving Nate and I watching the dust swirl with Rusty chasing after them.

"It's nice to see Sam relax a bit," I say to Nate.

Nate doesn't say anything; he just stands there smiling as he hoists one of the cedar bolts up onto the stump for splitting.

It doesn't take me long to feed in the last shake and get it nailed in place. Before I leave the roof I look over the repair. I am pleased and thankful for this opportunity to once again be here at this very moment. I take in a big breath filling my lungs with fresh air while taking in this view from the peak of the roof. Maybe there's time to slip down to the river and take a bath.

With the ladder and tools returned to where I got them from, I gather up my things to head down to the river. I no sooner set out from the barn when Sam rides up on Gus with Molly and Bess in tow. He asks if I ride bareback, I tell him I do. He asks were Nate is and I tell him I really don't know, the last I saw him he was headed to the house.

Sam flips Bess's reins to me saying, "Let's go."

I jump up onto Bess's back and pat her on the neck as we head down towards the house. Sam lets out a whistle and Nate lifts open the upstairs window. He leans out asking, "What's up, are we taken the horses for a ride?"

Sam shakes his head yes and tells him to grab his things, we're headed down to the river to take a swim and a bath, "Hurry up, lights a wasting."

Rusty comes leaping off the porch spinning circles and barking. Nate is right behind Rusty and all in one motion he jumps from the porch right onto Molly's back, he grabs the reins from Sam and gives Molly a kick. With a "YEEAHH", they leave Bess and me standing there. Bess's hooves are seemingly stuck to the ground, Sam and Nate have taken off, the unannounced race is on.

It's been awhile since I was last on a horse, so I take my time letting Bess get into a gallop. She naturally wants to run with the other two, but I am holding her back being glad that she isn't a thoroughbred. Rusty is having a hell of a time deciding who to run with, the ones in front or the ones in the back.

Bess and I show up at the swimming hole just in time to watch Nate swing into the water from the rope. Sam is on the bank and grabs the rope as it swings back towards him. He takes a step back and swings out to his right and with a loud "whoopee" he lets the rope go, splashing down into the cold, deep water. I tie Bess off next to Gus and Molly, strip down to my underwear and walk to the river bank. Sam and Nate yell at me to grab the rope. I tell them I will but want to get used to the cold water first. They have their fun making sissy remarks at my expense, at the same time splashing water on me until I just dive in head first. I come up yelling that it is awful cold but it sure feels good.

Rusty is running up and down the bank barking and wanting someone to call him in. With all three of us in the water, he can't stand it another minute and leaps off the shore. He has no place to go but straight at us. He gets so close his paws are close enough to scratch us, so Sam reaches out and pushes him away telling him to go back.

Sam and Nate won't stop pestering me about swinging from the rope, so I swim over to the bank. Nate floats over to the rope and heaves the loose end up to me. I climb up the bank to the highest point the rope will allow, and with a big push I swing out over the river. Just before the rope gets to its fullest arc, I let go. Flinging my arms over my tucked in legs, I manage to do a flip and dive head first into the clear water below. As my head pops up, twenty feet from where I entered the water, Sam and Nate are on the shore giving me a standing ovation.

Sam yells out, "You're full of surprises Jacob Sparks. Where did you learn to do that?"

I yell back, "I was once a kid too, you know."

After swimming awhile, all three of us scrub up, rinse off and then try to find a place to sit that isn't wet and muddy caused by Rusty's continued running back and forth through the shallow water. We end up sitting on a beached piece of driftwood that is barely long enough to hold all three of us.

Enjoying the late afternoon sun as it warms our refreshed skin, I tell Sam, "It sure is nice to have a little time to relax and the two of you have some fun."

Sam says, "It's not all work and no play. Course, Nate might not agree."

Nate gives Sam a snort, rolls his eyes and says, "Like I explained to Jake, sometimes work is fun. Watching you Sam, all these years, work, fun or whatever you call it, has been just living. If what I have learned is fun, then I like it. If it's been work, then I like that too."

Sam says, "Yeah, I know Nate, I know, I'm just joshing with you. I know how you feel. All I've tried to do is keep it simple. Nate, be a simple man and you'll be a happy man. That's what my pa believed, that's what I've tried to do, live a simple life."

I nod my head and say, "Sam, you've done a hell of a job. You've kept life simple here and you've been blessed because of it. I agree with Nate, sometimes it's hard to tell the difference between fun and work when all you're really doing is just simply living."

It doesn't take long for us to get a chill. As we start to get dressed, Sam looks my way and asks me about the tattoo that is on my upper right arm, "That tattoo, does it have a special meaning?"

With a brief hesitation I answer, "Yeah, Sam it does. I used to run with a pretty rough crowd up in Portland. Some of them had a lot of tattoos that seemed to be mostly for decoration; random names, images of women, animals, birds and things like that. I never wanted a tattoo unless it really meant something."

"So why a cross with a wreath around it?" he asks.

"You're right it is a cross, but it's not a wreath. It's a crown of thorns. It's hard to see but the thorns are blood tipped and there's five drops of blood dripping from the thorns."

"What's the meaning?"

We gather our clothes up and walk over to the horses. Once mounted, we don't run them, we let them walk back. Bess and I are sandwiched between Nate and Sam, Molly and Gus.

No one is saying anything until Nate speaks up and asks, "So what's the meaning?"

I answer, "It's a reminder of the sacrifice and the saving blood that was shed by Jesus Christ when he was hung on a cross and died for all of us."

Sam asks, "So you're a religious type?"

With a chuckle I answer, "No, far from it. I'd say I was more your spiritual type than religious type. Religion has too many man-made rules. You know, do this, don't do that, if you do that you'll go to hell. All that stuff just gets in the way of the Spirit."

Nate asks, "Do you believe in the Good Book?"

"I do, but I don't know it front to back like some. I have a basic knowledge and belief from the Bible, and that works for me."

Then I say, "Look fellas, I don't want to get all religious here. It's not good to talk politics or religion; each man has a right to his own beliefs. I've seen some of the best friendships be ruined after discussing religion or politics."

Sam says, "It's okay Jake; I just want to know about your tattoo. We don't need a religious lesson from you; Judith keeps us in line good enough."

"I'll try and keep it simple then. Jesus Christ was put to death on a cross and shed His Blood as a final sacrifice to God the Father for all of mankind's sins. Jesus had a crown of thorns jammed into His head and I can't imagine what that must have felt like. I was working on a house one time and we had to clear a space for it before we could get started on the foundation. The building lot was covered with briars, blackberry bushes and Canadian thistles. Anything that could grow a thorn on it seemed to grow on this piece of ground. Anyway, it took us a week to clear all those thorny bushes away. At the end of each day my hands and arms would be covered with scratches and cuts. I spent most of every night picking out thorns from my skin. Well, one day I just thought to myself, Lord, You suffered that Crown of Thorns for me! That night I thanked Jesus for His sacrifice and His blood that He shed for me and my sins. Hopefully, when that day comes for me to be called home, God looks down at me and sees me covered by Jesus' Blood and not my sins. That's what my tattoo means."

We let the horses loose in the meadow and start walking back down to the house. Judging by the light left on the western horizon, we are sure Judith will have supper ready when we get to the house. I stop at the barn and hang my wet things over the milking stall rails.

As Sam and Nate walk past the barn, I over hear Nate say to Sam, "I told you he was different than the others that pass through. Have you ever heard anyone talk like that before?"

"Nope, can't say that I have, not even a preacher."

tattoo

Chapter 15

As I walk through the back door, Judith's voice comes from the back bedroom. She asks Nate to empty the bathtub for her. Evidently, while we were at the swimming hole Judith had taken a bath. She comes out from the bedroom, her hair is down and she's wearing a different style of blouse, not her usual high neck with long sleeves. This blouse is low on her shoulders, exposing her neck line and a beauty mark on her right collar bone between her shoulder and neck.

Sam tells her she looks nice, as she thanks him, she replies back, "The day off seemed to do us all good. Supper will be ready shortly, why don't you all go sit on the porch. I'll call you in a few minutes. Coffee for anyone before you go out?"

I pick up a cup off the table and hold it out, "Thank you Judith, don't mind if I do." Then I ask, "Sam, how 'bout you, Nate?"

Sam nods yes and Nate waves his hand no. The three of us head out to the porch, Nate throws a pine cone for Rusty and Sam and I stand at the railing looking out over the river and the last bit of bright light as the sun lowers itself over the southwest horizon.

There are tall, white, thunder heads boiling up in the distance. Their crowns are showing the full shine of the setting sun, their lower halves have turned to a dark, ashen grey. The tallest pines are gently stirring at their very tops making the lower branches start to creak. A few of the trees are shedding loose, dry, pine needles that spiral to the ground.

Sam points with his coffee cup at the building clouds and says, "Looks like we could get a little rain tonight."

Agreeing I add, "The farmers will be glad to get it. Rain this late in the spring is always helpful."

Judith comes out the front screen door, moves over to Sam and puts her arm through his. She tells us supper is simmering on the stove while fresh biscuits are browning up. She reminds Nate to wash up after playing with Rusty. Just as Judith turns to go back in the house, we hear the first deep rumblings of thunder still miles away.

Sam turns before following Judith in, looks back up to the southwest, "Yep, storms headed this way."

We sit down at the table, which tonight is covered with a table cloth and has a vase of fresh cut wildflowers in the center. Sam asks, "So, Judith what's the occasion?"

She just smiles and says, "It's still the month of May. Spring hasn't given way to summer yet."

She tries to set down a large serving bowl, with lid and ladle, in the center of the table. Nate notices, reaches out and slides the vase of flowers over to one side to make room. She returns to the kitchen and comes back with a plate full of biscuits so warm that there is a whisper of steam rising up as she sets them down in front of Sam.

Once Judith is seated we reach out to each other and hold hands, Nate and Sam fidget just a bit in the ensuing silence, Judith looks to me and says, "Jacob, will you bless the food tonight?"

After a split second of thinking "why me", a calm comes over me as I recall telling Sam and Nate about my tattoo on our ride back from the swimming hole.

Clearing my throat I say, "I'd be honored. Heavenly Father, we thank you for this food, we thank you for your blessings that you have bestowed upon us. Bless this food and the hands that have provided it. It is in the name of Jesus that we pray. Amen."

Judith thanks me and reaches out for Sam's bowl. She dishes each of us a full helping of venison stew and asks Sam to pass the biscuits. The conversation is light and simple as we eat. Sam mentions to Judith that we heard thunder just as we were coming in. She remarks that she thought she had heard it also, but it was so far away, she wasn't sure. She thanks me for repairing the barn roof and that if we should get rain tonight, it will be a good test. Thankfully, the repair was done just in time. She likes the look of the fresh shakes and asks if Nate was a big help. I tell her he was. The job was made easier having him split the shakes, bring them up the ladder and set them on the roof. It had saved me many trips up and down the ladder.

Nate and Judith clear the table. Nate returns with smaller bowls in hand.

Sam asks, "What's this, dessert?"

Judith comes from the kitchen with a steaming Dutch oven and sets it down in the middle of the table.

Nate has a huge smile on his face and with my mouth watering I say, "From the smell of things I'd say it is blackberry and dumplings."

Judith answers with a smile, "Yes it is. I hope the berries were ripe enough. It might be a touch early for picking, so I tried to sweeten them up with a little more sugar than usual.

Hope you enjoy."

Sam doesn't wait for Judith to dish up his bowl; he reaches out for the ladle and asks Judith again, "So what's the occasion, this is a fine meal. Is this Sunday or something? Did I miss a birthday?"

"No Sam, it's just been a good day. It started bad and ended good. We are all safe and together."

As I hold my bowl out for a second helping I look up and say, "This has surely been one fine day."

Nate helps Judith clean up the dishes and Sam and I head out to the front porch. There are now flashes of lightning and the rumblings of thunder are louder. The lightning strikes are noticeably closer; each strike rips the black sky with its jagged edges of brilliant light, followed by its own deep rumble of thunder.

Nate gets busy filling wood boxes and yells to Sam asking, "Does the wood pile at the ferry need to be stocked?"

Sam yells back to him, "No, I hauled some wood earlier, there's enough for now."

Nate goes up to the meadow to check the horses and returns just as Judith settles down next to Sam. Nate lets Sam know that the horses are restless and from the looks of Daisy, she could be dropping her calf any day now. Sam tells Nate that he'll keep a close eye on her. We all remark on the fine meal and thank Judith one more time.

She nods her thanks and simply says, "My pleasure."

Sam has his pipe going and Nate asks, "If this rain hits hard, what will we do in the morning? If it should blow over, can we head into Ash Fork?"

Sam pulls his pipe out of his mouth, points with it to the sky and the swirling tree tops and says, "Even if it doesn't rain through the night or into the day, you still won't be going to Ash Fork. Those men from this morning will only be one day ahead of you if you leave tomorrow. I don't want to take any chances that you and Jake could catch them on the road."

In protest Nate says, "But Sam, they probably took up a quick pace. We have to drop a cord of wood off at the Johnson's before we ever get to Ash Fork. They'll be ahead of us the whole way."

Sam says, "Nate, not tomorrow, you'll wait one more day, storm or no storm."

Without hesitation, Judith says, "I like that plan. I agree with Sam, wait one more day."

Nate answers, "Alright, so it looks like I'll be chopping some wood."

I pull out my harmonica, gently put it to my lips and lightly push air out over the holes. My mind is fluttering with a flick of a memory that I can't sort through. I felt it this morning and again while eating supper, there is something trying to let itself come forth inside me.

Sam relights his pipe, looks at Nate and says, "Maybe in the morning we could head up to the north ridge and see if we can scout a bear or two for the fall hunt; see if any survived the winter. With a fresh rain, it'll be easy to track 'em."

Nate shifts in his seat, looks at me and says, "That'd be great. Jake, do you want to come with us?"

I hold the harmonica still, look at Sam, then Nate and then back to Sam saying, "We'll see. Let's get through the night, and then we'll see."

My harmonica sounds sweet in the crisp night air. The first rain drops start to hit the ground which makes Judith wrap up tighter in her shawl and snuggle into Sam's side.

Sam looks over my way asking, "Do you know any songs? Play one if you do."

"I'll tell you the same thing I told Nate, I don't really play songs so to speak. I play what I feel; put notes together that fit my mood. I guess you could call it freestyle."

Judith says, "Whatever it's called it's nice to hear."

"Nate told me that you play a violin or fiddle."

Blushing she says, "I used to play in my youth. Later, I tried playing an old fiddle that Sam's pa had, but no, I don't really play."

Nate speaks up, "Not true Judith. You played me a song or two when I was younger."

Judith replies, "Nate they probably sounded like songs to a little one's ears, but they weren't really songs and I wasn't very good."

"Well I thought they sounded good. I always liked it when you played."

"Thank you Nate, but really Mr. Sparks, I don't play."

Nate looks at me and says, "Jake, you told me you wrote a song once, play that."

"Nah, not now, no one wants to hear a simple old song that no one knows but me."

All three at once say, "Yes we do."

And then Sam says, "Go ahead Jake, play us a song."

Judith smiles and says, "Please Jacob, let us hear it?"

I realize that they won't let me off the porch without either hearing a song or having a very good reason why I can't play one. For the life of me I can't think of a reason why I can't, so I reluctantly clear my throat and say, *"I'll Stop the Roam"*.

I play the first verse and then sing the words,
All that I do; I do for you.
I work all day; for little pay.
My body's so tired; I wish I'd get fired.
If she leaves me now; I'll truly head south.

I play the chorus and then sing the chorus,
This life is too short to end up alone; this life is too short not to share a home.

I play the notes for the second verse and sing again,
I should have lived right and put up a fight.
As I dreamt to roam; I wasted my home.
I can't blame her now; I've hurt her somehow.
If she'd give me a chance; I know we could dance.

Once again I play the chorus and then sing the chorus.
This life is too short to end up alone; this life is too short not to share a home.

I play the third verse and sing,
I hope and pray; I don't waste away.
Lord hear me now; please save me somehow.
I'll stop the roam and build her that home.

I play the chorus for the third time and sing,
This life is too short to end up alone; this life is too short not to share a Home.

I play the chorus one more time and pull the harmonica away from my mouth.

The only sound that I hear is the wind through the trees and scattered drops of rain hitting the ground.

I look over at Sam and Judith. Judith is looking down into her hands and is the first to speak, "That's beautiful, Jacob. Is it for someone special?"

Sam interrupts and says, "Of course it is, and if it isn't it should be."

I look at Nate and then I look out towards the river and say, "Yeah it is. I wrote it for someone special."

Nate looks up, nods and tells me that it is a nice song. He asks me to play and sing it again. I shake my head saying, "Maybe later, Nate, not now, maybe later."

He says, "Sure Jake."

I put the harmonica back to my lips and begin playing random notes, hoping I didn't ruin this fine day.

Judith says her goodnights and heads into the house. As the screen door shuts behind her she stops and asks Sam if he'll be long. He nods his head no and answers that he'll be in shortly. The lightning and thunder has made its way into the river valley. Counting the seconds between flashes of lightning and each boom of thunder, the storm is within a mile or two before it will be right on top of us.

With the rain beginning to pick up, I ask Sam, "Will the ferry run tomorrow according to the every-other-day schedule?"

He shakes his head and answers, "Probably not. With this rain, no one will be on the roads much and if someone does show up, I'll tell them they'll have to wait for the next day. No ferry tomorrow."

Then I ask, "So you think you and Nate will go scout out

some bear?"

Sam replies, "Only if the rain lets up through the night, soft ground and a little mud won't be too bad, but if it's still raining, we probably won't go. Maybe we'll stay and do a little fishing. Sometimes the fish seem to bite more during or just after a rain."

Nate perks up, "I like that idea. I haven't been fishing for awhile."

I say my goodnights and step off the porch.

Sam asks after me, "What about you Jake, what do you think you'll do?"

Standing under the overhang I turn and answer, "I need to build myself a bed up in that loft. Maybe tomorrow will be a good day for that. Goodnight."

Both reply back, "Goodnight, Jake."

By the time I make it to the barn I am wishing I had looked harder for my hat, even if it had holes in it, it still would have kept some of the rain off my head. As I am drying my head and taking off my wet shirt it occurs to me that I should have asked Sam if he had an extra hat I could borrow for a day or two. Oh well, I'll be getting a new one in a couple of days, but it sure couldn't hurt to ask him. I could use something on my head for the ride into town.

I lie back on the pile of straw and stay on the outside of my bedroll. I look up and see the underneath side of the freshly nailed shakes. The area that is repaired stands out and will probably take a few years before they blend in with the surrounding shakes. I am glad the holes are repaired but I already know that I will miss the openings that have allowed me to peer into the night sky. I should be able to build my bed so that I have a view of the outside. That way, I'll be able to look at something beside four wooden walls, a bunch of rafters and the underside of a cedar shake roof.

I turn down the lantern and blow out the flame. I lay my head down and try to calm my thoughts from today's happenings. For starting out to be a typical day it sure got jam-packed in a hurry. Nate and I should be at Unger's Creek resting for the night, but instead we're still here at Fletcher's Crossing. We survived a fight, repaired a roof, rode horses, and went swimming. We shared a great meal and played some music; it has been a fine day.

I can feel my head begin to relax and my breathing becomes rhythmic. The lightning's intensity comes and goes as the storm moves further up the river valley. My thoughts continue to drift back and forth between the morning fight, the roof repair and swinging out over the water. My thoughts begin to swirl together, they stop making sense, and nothing stays in the correct sequence of time.

Without willing it, my mind's eye begins to see traces of Beth and she starts to be included in the events of the day. I can hear her laughing, I can feel her hand in mine and I see her smiling face. She is at the swimming hole with me and then suddenly we are riding on the back of Bess. I look down but we're not on Bess anymore, we're on Gus and he is galloping at full stride through the meadow. I look to my right and Brutus is running alongside us matching Gus stride for stride. Beth is not hanging on to me or Gus; she has both arms over her head waving them in the air. She starts laughing hysterically and points at Brutus. He is wearing my hat and sticking his tongue out at me. Suddenly I hear my Mom yelling, "Time for supper! Don't be late! And wash your hands!" Gus suddenly jumps the fence making Beth and me fall off his back tumbling into a tall field of wheat. As Gus stops, he turns to look at me and winks with one eye. Gus's face morphs into my pa. He is walking towards us with one hand holding a lantern; the other hand is outstretched to help us stand up. He says laughingly, "Do as your Mother says, wash your hands and don't be late. Oh! And one more thing, tell her I'll be late for breakfast." As my pa is walking away shrouded by fog, I yell after him, "Wait, don't go; we haven't eaten supper yet."

I wake myself drenched in sweat just as a loud bang of thunder shakes the barn. With that, the rain bursts out of the sky and is pounding on the roof. Trying not to wake up completely, I shake my head to clear my mind and hope the beating of my heart slows down. I realize I still have my pants on. They are damp from walking to the barn in the rain. The dampness has given me a chill, or could the dampness be from sweat? Either way, I decide to pull them off and climb into my bedroll.

It doesn't take me long to relax my breathing and slowly quiet my mind. In the past when I have had a nightmare that startles me awake, I tell myself to relax and think of a place I have been to that was peaceful. My mind begins to revisit different places where I have witnessed sunrises and sunsets. I let myself remember the expansive views I observed while trekking high above the tree line. I take myself back to one of the mornings I spent walking through the redwoods.

My breathing begins to slow. I feel myself begin to relax and drift off. Without notice, my mind's eye begins to go fuzzy again and I see myself sitting in the aspen grove above the meadow. The sun is fading fast and panic comes over me as I know there is no way I can make it home in time for supper. I turn and reach out my hand towards Beth, but it's not Beth's face, it's a girl's face I can't recognize and she is crying, "Help me, please help me up!" I turn from her and start running as fast as I can; I am now frantic because I know I won't be home in time for supper. No matter how fast I move my legs, I don't go anywhere. I turn to see how far I have run, only to see I haven't moved an inch, I'm still in the aspen grove. With a bright flash of lighting and a loud clap of thunder, I bolt straight up to my feet and yell, "Carolynn!"

Chapter 16

Morning can't arrive fast enough. I press my memory trying to recall the dreams that kept me from sleeping all night. There is light coming through the barn doors and I can hear Bonnie being walked down to the barn. It must be Nate and I have overslept again. I shake my head as I climb out of my disheveled bedroll. I grab my pants just as Judith walks through the barn door with Bonnie in tow.

"Excuse me Mr. Sparks. Please forgive me; I thought you were gone with Sam and Nate. I am so sorry. Please forgive me!"

"Judith, it's okay. I'm the one that should be apologizing to you. I should have yelled out but I thought it was Nate bringing Bonnie down to get milked. Sorry."

We both stand there red faced and laughing. I grab my shirt and start pulling on my boots before I head over to the washing post. I pump the handle a couple of times and shove my head under the spout. Washing the sleep from my eyes will be easier than clearing the cobwebs from my foggy mind.

Walking towards the house, I notice for as hard as it seemed to rain, the area around the house is not a gooey, sloppy mess. I hear Judith yell from the barn that there is hot coffee on the stove and to help myself. I yell back a thank you.

I jump the steps and hit the top of the porch, almost forgetting to scrape my boots before I walk into the house. It is an eerie feeling being in the Harris's home by myself. Instantly my mind is not in a good place. I start moving my eyes from place to place, shelf to shelf. I ask myself where I would stash my valuables if I lived here. I admonish myself for having these thoughts and head out the front door as quickly as I can. It's not the first time I've had old vices pull on me. The ghosts that I've known come back to haunt me every so often; thanking God and all that is good, I take my hot cup of coffee and head towards the river's edge.

Seeing the moving water is a welcome relief from the restless night and unnerving morning. Standing at the water's edge, I swallow the last sip of coffee muttering, "How can one day be so good, then suddenly out of nowhere, nightmares and temptations reach out, trying to grab hold and steal my peace."

I make an attempt to skip a few rocks, but the water is moving too fast for flat stones to skip across. My mind races to sort out the dreams from last night. I am fearful they meant more than I want to acknowledge. I am still haunted by the faces and worried about the truths they tried to expose. Shaking my head to free my thoughts, I notice the usually clear green water is muddied and full of debris. Out loud I say, "There goes the fishing for a day or two."

The sky is clear blue, and the air is cool and crisp. With the empty cup in hand I turn and head back up towards the house. I stop at the front porch not wanting to enter without permission. I sit down on the top step letting the warmth of the sun erase the morning coolness from my skin. I hear Judith walk in as the back screen doors shuts.

She calls out, "Mr. Sparks are you still in the house?"

I reply, "No, I'm out here, on the front porch."

Judith comes to the front screen door, seeing the empty

coffee cup she asks, "Would you like another cup? Did you have something to eat?"

I tell her, "Another cup of coffee would be great. No I didn't eat and please don't bother fixing anything."

She returns with the pot of coffee and a cup for herself. After filling my cup she sits down in the double chair that she and Sam usually sit in.

With a heavy sigh she says, "What a lovely morning. The air is so clear and crisp, the sky so blue. Did you sleep well, Jacob?"

I shrug my shoulders and say, "Actually, I didn't. I slept very restless for some reason. It could have been the storm, I don't know."

"That's too bad; do you feel alright this morning? Maybe you need to eat something?"

"I'm fine, thank you but I'm not hungry. I'm still full from last night's supper and dessert. Did Sam and Nate go scouting for bear?"

"Yes, they did. They got up before first light. After Sam went down to check on the ferry, he took one look at the river and knew it would be too muddy to fish. So, he stuck with his plan to head up into the mountains. With a packed lunch, off they went, Rusty leading the way. I thought you might have joined them from the barn. Did you want to go with them?"

"No, no I don't need to go scout for bear that may or may not be there in the fall. I am sure Sam has his favorite spots that he likes to hunt. It makes sense for him to scout for bear. I need a bed more than I need a bear right now."

"Perfectly understandable, Jacob, now about that bed,

you'll need some type of mattress or something besides straw to sleep on. Any thoughts in mind for that?"

"Well, I hadn't really got that far, but you're right, I'll need something besides loose straw on boards. I don't have anything to make a mattress out of, and I don't sew very good. I mean I can mend a hole and such, but stitching together a bag to sleep on, I'm not too sure about that."

"Don't worry about the mattress bag. You get the bed frame built, let me know how big it will be and I'll sew together a mattress bag. You can fill it with straw and corn husks and whatnot. Just let me know."

I look up at her as I down the last sip of the coffee in my cup and tell her, "Once again, much obliged Judith, thank you." She stands, holds the pot of coffee out towards me. I wave her off saying, "No thanks, I'm good."

She turns and starts to go through the screen door, stopping she looks at me asking, "Are you sure you are alright? You seem kind of out of sorts this morning."

I look up at her, turn away and glance out towards the river. I turn back and hand her my empty cup saying, "A friend once told me, 'The ghost's of the past will dissolve like fog.' But you know Judith, there are just some days the fog doesn't dissolve, it only lifts just high enough to linger amongst the tree tops."

From inside the screen door Judith says, "I hope you feel better, Jacob. Please let me know about that mattress bag."

Chapter 17

Rummaging around the barn and the other out buildings, I am able to gather enough sawn wood and old posts that should make a decent bed. It won't be anything fancy, but it will get me up off the floor and will be strong enough to hold my weight.

Before I lash and nail anything together, I determine the size of mattress that I'll need. I walk down to the house to let Judith know the size that I think will work. If everything works out, I might be sleeping on a real bed tonight. I don't want to startle her so I walk by the kitchen window to see if she is there. I don't see her so I continue to walk towards the front, looking in the windows as I go.

I turn at the corner of the porch and she is sitting in the sun facing the river. "Judith, 'scuse me, don't want to startle you."

Turning towards my voice she says, "Oh, it's you Jacob, welcome, how goes the bed building?"

"Well, I have the material gathered and I know how big I need the bag for the mattress."

"Good, how big do you need it?" Judith asks.

"I work in feet and inches so I need it at least six-foot six inches by four feet."

Judith looks at me, chuckles and says, "I understand feet and inches, but it might be easier to have you come in the house. We know the mattress needs to be bigger than your body, so, I'll hold the linen up to you and mark it out. I think that will be just as easy as trying to measure it out."

"That'll be fine, whatever is easy. I just don't want to be a bother."

"Please Jacob, it's no bother. Come on in," she says as she holds the screen door open.

I follow her into the front room and she tells me to stand next to the window with the sun coming through. She has a couple of linen sheets lying out on the dining table. She brings one of the sheets over and holds it up to my back. She leaves some of the sheet rumpled up on the floor and then stretches the top higher than my head.

She drops her arms and says, "These will work just fine, they are almost the right length just as they are. Now we just have to get them the right width. You said four feet, correct?"

"Yes, four feet," I answer.

She takes the sheet over to the table saying, "We know the table is five feet square, so if I make the bag that wide it might over hang a bit, but it should be just about right once you stuff it and it puffs up."

I look at her and say, "Sounds right to me. That's why you're the seamstress."

Judith gathers up the two linens and a sewing basket and takes them over to her rocking chair that is in front of the window. She pulls needle and thread out and squints as she threads the eye of the needle. I am left standing in the middle of the room next to the dinner table staring at her side profile, wondering why my stomach is doing cart wheels.

She looks up at me and asks, "Is something wrong Jacob? Do you need something else?"

"No, ah, no Judith, I'll be heading back up to the barn

now."

She turns back to her work saying, "I'll have this sewn together shortly."

I don't know whether to run or walk, I just know I need to get my mind busy. For all the comfortableness I have felt these past days, I am now suddenly scared, haunted by a memory that I cannot grab hold of nor chase from my mind.

Just before I head into the barn and my pile of wood, Rusty comes running down the hill from the meadow. He jumps up with his paws at my chest. I grab his head in my hands and tell him I am happy to see him. He drops down to the ground and runs back up the hill towards the meadow only to have Sam and Nate come walking down towards the barn and house.

With a wave I yell, "You are back early, I thought you'd be gone most of the day."

Sam says, "We couldn't get up very high due to the thick mud and low fog." Then he asks, "How are things going here?"

"Just fine. I've started working on a bed."

"Is Judith is in the house?"

"Yeah, yeah, she's in the house, why?"

Sam turns to walk down to the house. Nate is standing next to me with his rifle resting across his neck and shoulders. He asks, "Jake, are you all right? You don't look so well."

"Yeah Nate, I'm fine. I just need to get the bed built. I'll be fine, I mean, I'm fine. Why?"

"'Cause you look like you just seen a ghost."

Before I head up to the loft, I look around for a broom and pitch fork. I need to clear a work area to assemble the bed. Besides, it won't hurt to tidy up the loft; it's going to become my bedroom. The south end of the loft has the bigger of two openings. It has double swinging doors that when open, allow you to push whatever you have right off the floor onto the ground. It has an excellent view of the house and river below.

The north end of the loft has a smaller opening. It's basically a window without glass. The decision of where to set my bed is an easy one to make. I can't set my bed in front of the double door opening so under the smaller opening it will be. It might end up being a bit drafty without a piece of glass in the opening, but there is a small wooden panel that will close over the opening to keep the rain and winter weather out when needed.

I stand over by the opening and look out to see the view. I am pleased to be able to see a big area of the meadow, and to my surprise, I can see about half of the aspen grove. I will be able to keep my eye on the aspens as the changing color of their leaves announces the arrival of the seasons.

Naturally, the corner I have chosen has the majority of hay piled up in it. I tie my handkerchief to cover my nose and mouth and begin to reposition the stock pile of hay. It is dusty as I get down to the dry older straw and broken stems. I grab the broom and sweep the dusty tailings out the double door opening. As the fine, floating dust drifts through the air and then out both ends of the loft, I am thankful for the draft that moves the air freely through my new sleeping quarters.

There is a wheel and rope attached to the top of the double door opening that I can use to hoist the wood up to the loft. I go down and position the pile of wood under the wheel and rope. I realize I should have untied the rope and lowered the free end down to the ground before I stacked the wood, so back up to the loft I go. This time I take some of the tools up with me. The man that taught me carpentry always told me, "If you're going, take something with you, if you're coming back, bring something back, don't waste a trip." It is burned in my brain and even during the times that I'm not working as a carpenter; his advice has served me well.

I tie the loose wood into a bundle that I can hoist up. There are not a lot of pieces of wood needed to make the bed so the pile isn't very big, but it is heavier than I thought. I run up to the opening and as I tug on the rope, Nate comes out of the house asking if I need some help. I shrug my shoulders and this is enough for him to come running. With both of us on the rope the pile comes up to the opening in one easy pull. We swing the pile into the loft and untie it.

Nate looks around and notices the clean loft and says, "Wow, I haven't seen the floor boards for a couple of years, thanks."

I shrug and say, "Well, I didn't need to be sleeping and moving around in old hay tailings and the dust that comes with them."

Nate tells me, "Judith has the mattress bag just about finished."

"That's great. I'd better get to measuring and cutting some boards if I want to sleep in a bed tonight."

Nate asks, "Can I do anything to help?"

Reluctantly I ask, "Do you know how to use a handsaw?"

He says he does so I tell him, "I'll mark the boards to length and you can start cutting them if you want."

"Sure. Hey Jake, did you see the saw horses stacked over in the corner of the barn? It would be a lot easier cutting the boards to length if we used a set of saw horses."

"No, I didn't. And yes, I agree."

He runs down to get them. He has them up to the loft in no time and I am glad he is helping me. I had thought that I wanted to do this by myself, be alone for awhile, but now having Nate here with me, I feel energized for the first time all day. It's more than just his youthful energy that perks up my mood, there seems to be something intangible about his personality that makes me feel not so troubled.

With both of us working it doesn't take long to have the bed parts cut out and ready to assemble. We nail together the box that will hold the mattress bag and stand the posts up in the corners that the box has formed. With some of the scrap, we stack up some blocks to hold the frame steady and at a good height. Once in position I have Nate brace his knee against the posts as I nail the box in place. Not trusting to just use nails, I grab some small lengths of rope and lash the posts and box together. We then lay a dozen slats across the bottom of the open box frame. The bed is ready for a straw mattress.

I ask Nate to go see if Judith has the mattress bag sewn while I sweep up the saw dust and get rid of the leftover pieces of wood. While he is gone I notice there is a long board left over that we didn't use. I look at the wall above the bed and decide a shelf would be nice. I nail a couple of blocks on the studs of the wall and set the board on the blocks and nail it in place.

Nate returns with the bag and says, "It's done, we can stuff it, hey, nice shelf."

"It's not much, just something to put a few things on and get them out of my pockets. Let's get that bag stuffed. We can put some clean straw in and Judith mentioned that there were some cornhusks left over from last fall. Between the two, that should make a nice mattress, don't you think?"

Nate replies, "Anything is better than what you got, but yeah, straw and husks should work. I'll go get some husks."

I stop him saying, "Wait, wouldn't it be easier if we take the bag to the husks?"

"Yeah, yeah it would, good thinking."

I continue with, "Sometimes you just have to work smarter, not harder."

"Okay, okay," Nate says with a laugh.

We have the mattress bag fully stuffed. It is now too big to get up the ladder and through the loft opening. We need to tie it up and hoist it with the wheel and rope. Before we do, we need to sew up the one end Judith had left open so we could fill it.

Judith must have been watching from the window because she comes out on the back porch waving her arm saying, "Here, you might need this needle and thread to sew up that end."

I look up and before I can answer, Nate runs down to Judith and brings back the needle and thread. He asks me if I know how to sew and I tell him, "Yes, I can sew. How 'bout you? Can you sew?"

He says, "I can a little bit."

"Go ahead then and get it sown up."

While he is doing that I get the tools down out of the loft

and sweep up one more time. He sits down on the ground and it isn't very long before I hear the first, "Ouch, dang it," followed by another, "Ouch."

Standing in the loft looking down at Nate, I chuckle and ask, "Do you need a bandage?"

Nate doesn't bother to look up, he is pushing and pulling needle and thread through the linen fabric, occasionally sucking the tip of his thumb and index finger.

Chapter 18

With the bed and mattress complete, Nate leaves to bring Molly and Bess down to the barn so we can harness and hitch them to the wagon first thing in the morning. I am once again left with my own thoughts and feelings. I continue to have a feeling of melancholy that I just cannot seem to shake. My mind is a constant blur of the dreams and quick glances of Judith that don't make sense. I have to get this figured out before my emotions affect my actions which could become obvious to the others. As much as I hate to admit it to myself, I believe I know the answer to this sudden riddle of emotions. I have a very strong suspicion that I know the truth that has been staring me in the face all this time. I now have to decide if I am ready to face what can only be confirmed by meeting these suspicions head on and facing the truths that await me in Ash Fork.

I hear Judith yell out to Nate that supper is ready and to get washed up. For the first time since I have been staying here, I am wishing I could avoid this meal. Everything inside of me wishes I was on the road headed to Ash Fork. Never have I felt so certain that the answers to what is beginning to haunt me lie in the one town I fled from so many years ago.

I finish getting my bedroll, pack and other possessions up into the loft, I then wash and head to supper. As I take my seat at the table, my thoughts are scrambled and I hope no one senses my uneasiness. It is Judith's turn to say grace, after which she starts to dish up. Sam and Judith start to speak at the same time. Sam is asking her if she has the note ready for Mr. Kimble with the instructions to give me five dollars credit while she is asking Nate if he has his things set out for the trip. They both wait for the other to finish, only to start at the same time again. This awkwardness only increases my anxiety and makes me want to excuse myself. Sam tells Judith to say what she wants to say, he'll wait. Judith starts over and asks Nate again if he has everything he needs. Nate lets Judith know that he is ready to go and reminds her he has made this trip many times.

She looks directly at me in a way that almost freezes my blood and says, "Jacob, leave your soiled clothes on the back step and I'll have them clean when you return."

Politely I answer, "I have made enough trips to the river so I have been able to keep my clothes washed, but thanks anyway."

Sam then asks again about the note for Mr. Kimble and Judith says she has it ready. She will get it after the table is cleared. We finish our meal in silence which adds to my uneasiness.

I know Judith senses this also as she asks, "Jacob, you didn't eat much, are you sure you are feeling alright?"

With all eyes on me I look down at my plate and she is right, I have barely touched anything on my plate. Naturally, I can't sit there and ignore her comment, I respond with, "Sorry, ma'am, I can assure you it's not the cooking. I've just been out of sorts all day and I'm just not feeling myself. In fact, I think I'm going to take a short walk and then I'm going to turn in. Morning is going to come early and I'm just as anxious as Nate to get on the road."

Sam stops me and holds out his hand saying, "Here's the two dollars as agreed on. Judith, please get his note for Mr. Kimble, if you would."

She gets up and goes to a writing desk in the corner of the room and brings back a folded paper.

She gives it to Sam and Sam hands it to me, saying, "This should settle us for this week, as promised. Just hand this to Mr. Kimble, he'll honor it."

I unfold the paper and it instructs Mr. Kimble to give me five dollars in credit at his store. I stand up and excuse myself. I shake Sam's hand, "Thank you, looks like we are square."

I turn to head out the front, stopping before I push open the screen door I look at the three of them still sitting at the table and say, "Thank you all for everything. Sam, I don't feel right with you paying me. You and yours have given me more than I deserve or can ever repay. Thank you again. Nate, I'll be ready at first light. Goodnight."

As the screen door shuts, I head down towards the river bank noticing that the moon is beginning to wane. I think to myself, should be nice weather for tomorrow.

Turning down the lantern flame I settle in for what hopes to be the best night sleep I've had in a long time. I begin to think back on how long it has actually been since I have slept in anything that resembled a bed. It feels like months ago and it probably was.

Hoping that I will fall asleep is much easier than actually doing it. With the creaking of the wood and the crunching of the cornhusks, I toss, turn, and just can't get settled. I hear Molly and Bess shuffle themselves back and forth and hear one of them drink out of the trough. Rusty comes into the barn and I can hear him sniffing around the pile of straw, that until tonight had been my bed. He then pads over to the ladder, puts his paws up on the rungs and begins to whimper.

I speak out, "I'm okay Rusty, go back to the house."

With Rusty gone the barn is quiet again and now I am suddenly thirsty. I get my canteen and take a drink. I tell myself to dump this water out and fill it with fresh before we leave. I wonder what else I need to remind myself to do before we leave in the morning. I answer that question by telling myself to bring it all. With that, I try and relax knowing that the only way to fall asleep is to push the faces from the past out of my mind.

As good as the mattress of straw and cornhusks feel, I occasionally wake up needing to reposition myself. Every time I roll over I try not to let my mind's voice speak for fear that I will wake up and not be able to go back to sleep. I doze off and on through the night. Each time I stir to almost wakefulness, I tell myself to relax and know that I am at least resting.

•

I am awakened by Rusty barking and Nate is saying good morning to Molly and Bess. Hearing the commotion, I jump out of bed, nervous and excited to get this day started. I am relieved to know that I was able to relax enough to be able to actually sleep.

Looking out of the loft opening, I see Nate below me positioning Molly so he can put the harness on her. I tell Nate that I'll be right down. Rusty is looking up and jumping around in circles trying to figure out why I am up in the air leaning out of the opening.

Before I can get down the ladder Rusty is at the bottom rung to greet me. I walk over to the water pump to get my head and face wet and then dry off with a small towel that is hanging nearby. It is still damp; Nate must have already used it. I think to myself how comfortable we have become in just these short couple of weeks.

I walk around to the back of the barn to give Nate a hand finishing up harnessing Molly and Bess. We back them into the tongue of the wagon and finish up straightening the reins. Nate tells me he'll bring the wagon around and get it positioned to load onto the ferry. I tell him I'm going to grab my things and I'll meet him there. He reminds me that Sam still has to get the ferry steamed up and Red isn't here yet. We have plenty of time and we still need to eat breakfast.

He looks at me as he climbs up on to the wagon and says, "Looks like you are back to your old self, that new bed must've done the trick."

I just shake my head, "I'm gonna go help Sam.

It's not too long before the sky begins to lighten the eastern horizon. Sam has got the steam engine going and lets the whistle blow a couple of times. He releases some steam with a loud hiss and says, "It's ready anytime Red gets here."

"Can we get the wagon loaded on to the ferry?"

"Nah, no need to rush, we'll eat first and give Red a little more time to get here. After that we'll see about loading the wagon."

As we walk up to the house, he says the same thing Nate had said, that the new bed must've done me some good 'cause it seems like I'm feeling better. This confirms what I had thought the day before. My actions had been obvious. I never have been good at hiding my emotions, they seem to be ever present on my shirtsleeves, exposed for all to see.

After sitting down with grace said and breakfast being passed around, I listen to the three of them chatter back and forth about the upcoming day. Sam is going to chop some wood and get it stacked. Judith would like his help in butchering a couple of chickens and they need to keep their eyes on Daisy. She might need help with that calf of hers when she delivers it.

Rusty jumps off the front porch signaling that Red and his men have arrived. I finish up my last few bites of food, down the last sip of coffee, and excuse myself thanking Judith for the breakfast. I tell Nate I'll be down at the ferry.

Red and his men are on the ferry by the time Nate comes out of the house. Red yells to Nate that he can load the wagon anytime. Once settled in his seat, Nate coaxes the horses as they pull the wagon on slow as usual. With the wagon on board, Nate sets the brake and jumps down to give Judith a hug goodbye.

I shake Sam's hand and tell him thanks for everything, he looks at me asking, "Are you sure you are coming back? You seem to be in an awful big hurry to get out of here."

I look at him and tell him, "Sam, I've got to...hell, with me

I never know. Today I'm here, tomorrow I'll be there. I'm not saying goodbye for good, I'm just anxious that's all. You take care now and thanks again."

At that I turn to walk onto the ferry only to hear Judith say, "What, not even a goodbye, Jacob?"

I stop myself, turning to look at her I say, "Sorry, ma'am, course I'll say goodbye. Can't thank you enough Judith for all you've done for me. It's been a pleasure for sure."

Sam says, "C'mon Jake, your damn near part of the family, give Judith a hug."

All I want to do is get on the ferry and put the river between us. I hesitate just enough that Judith raises both her hands and says, "That's okay. You go, Jacob Sparks, be on your way."

Before I can take a step towards her, she has turned her back and started to walk towards the house. Shaking my head I turn and leap onto the ferry deck as Red, blows the whistle and yells out, "Cut her loose boys!" I stand at the corner of the railing watching as Sam and Rusty turn and walk towards the house.

For some reason, I am anxious, scared and worried all at the same time. For the first time in seventeen years I think that I might be finally ready to face all that awaits me in Ash Fork.

Chapter 19

As Nate drives the wagon off the ferry and up the incline of the south bank, Molly and Bess notice the weight of having three cords of wood on the wagon instead of the usual two. Nate has to lay into their backs with the reins and grabs for the whip. He zings the whip past Molly's right ear and gives it a snap. Molly jerks her head towards the left to avoid the stinging tip and shuffles into Bess. Bess has to side step and almost rears up in protest. Their reaction seems unusual to me but because they are so used to working together they settle down quickly. With Nate's abilities and deft hand at handling them; we slowly crest the hill towards the South River Road.

As we turn west towards, Prospect, Unger's Creek and Ash Fork, Nate and I remark to each other that Red will have a full day hauling wagons across the river. We counted four wagons that were staged and waiting on the south side needing to cross to the north side.

It is early, the air is cool and the sky is as blue as I have seen it this spring. As we move along at a pace that Molly and Bess can handle, we are glad that it rained the night before last leaving the road free of dust.

After a bit of small talk, Nate looks my way, "Jake, can I ask you something?"

"Sure, what's on your mind?"

Nate says, "The other day when we were coming back from swimming and you told us about your tattoo, it kinda sounded like you might have been a preacher at one time, were ya?"

"Nah, I've never been a preacher. I just believe what I believe and I try and keep things simple."

"If you don't mind me asking, tell me more about why the Blood of Jesus means so much to you?"

Gathering my thoughts I say, "Nate, it is His Blood and having it spilt for our sins that makes Jesus's death matter. In the Good Book there are a lot of stories, instructions and rules, but to me, there are some very basic truths that we need to pay attention to. One is the understanding of the meaning of the Blood. Do you know the story in the Old Testament about the Angel of Death that was sent by God to kill the first born sons in Egypt? The Egyptians were going to kill the first born sons of the Jews in order to keep the Jews enslaved to the Pharaoh."

"Yeah, I know most of it," he says.

"Well, God sent a message to the Jews that He was sending an Angel of Death that would sweep through the land. If the Jews took the blood of a slaughtered lamb and smeared the blood over the top of the doorway to their houses, the Angel of Death would bypass the marked houses, in other words, Pass Over. The Jews would be passed over from death because they had covered their households with the Blood of the Lamb."

"Okay, so how does that help us?"

"Nate, if you accept the Blood of Jesus and claim His Blood to cover your sins, then it is God's promise that He will see His Son's Blood and not our sins. We will be Passed Over by the Death of Sin and live eternally."

Nate asks, "But Jake, I thought that was what being baptized was supposed to do for us."

"Nate, it is, but as we go through life, we continue to sin

and sin gets in the way of us being able to stay in favor with God. So, I claim the Blood in hopes that God sees Jesus, His Son and not me and my sins."

Shaking his head in approval Nate says, "Oh, I get it."

Without pause I say, "There's something else I think about. Well, two things actually. One is this, you know that there were two thieves that were hung on crosses, next to Jesus, to die right?"

"I think so, why? Why is that important?"

"Well, the thief on the one side, I believe it's the left, he says to Jesus, 'If you are the Son of God then why don't You get Yourself down?' And the thief on the other side says, 'If you are the Son of God, then take me with You.' Jesus tells the thief on the right, 'This day you will join Me in Heaven.' So, I always pray, to have the presence of mind, to be like the thief on the right and ask to be taken with Jesus."

"Yeah, I see that. So, what's the second thing?"

"It's something I heard from someone a long time ago, and never forgot it. It goes like this; 'I'd rather live like there is and find out there isn't; than live like there isn't and find out there is.'"

Nate looks up, pushes his hat back off his head, then looks at me and says, "You'll have to say that again, slower this time."

I repeat it and then explain it to him. We repeat it together about four more times, each time he nods his head with understanding.

We are quiet for a while and then I hear Nate say, "It seems so simple."

"I think that's what God intended all along. His Love is

Simple; it is man that makes it complicated."

Nate looks skyward and replies, "Yeah, I like simple."

The sun is getting intense and my head is heating up. I forgot, again, to ask if Sam had an extra hat, so I take my handkerchief out and tie it over the top of my head. It helps protect my head but I can feel the sun on my ears and face. I hope I don't get sun burned to the point of blisters.

As we pass through Prospect, we get the usual waves and good day wishes from the folks that live there. The kids run alongside the wagon and some of the boys ask if they can climb on up and ride for a while. Nate says no and shoos them away, they are upsetting Molly and Bess. They both have their ears laid back and are snorting more than normal. Nate gives them a snap of the reins and they pick up the pace.

Once through Prospect, Nate feels the need to remind me that we have to stop at the Johnson's place. He says their turn off is just a mile up the road. It seems he is a little anxious. Maybe he is just feeling it's time to take a break and get down off the wagon. I'm sure Molly and Bess won't mind if we stop. I know I'm ready to move around and stretch my legs.

Chapter 20

Not very long after turning down the Johnson's road, we are met by a couple of barking dogs. They don't seem aggressive, they are more curious than anything. Nate whistles at them and tells them it's okay. Up at the house there is a woman waving with a younger child standing next to her. As we draw closer, the woman turns out to be a teenage girl.

With a very pleasant smile she gives a warm, "Good morning, Nate, how's the road this morning?"

Nate answers back, "Great! Good morning to you too, Lizzy. Is your pa around?"

As she points up to the north she says, "He's up in the north field this morning. Do you need him?"

"No, we just have a load of firewood to drop off. Last trip we seen the red flag on your fence. We'll stack the wood in the usual place if that's okay?" Lizzy says it will be just fine and stands there holding on to her brother that looks like he is about six years old.

Nate motions to Lizzy and says, "I'll keep the wagon moving to the back of the house if you don't mind. Is Mrs. Johnson around?"

Out from the front door Mrs. Johnson says, "Yes, Nate, I'm here. Michael, you stay out of the way. Those horses don't need you under foot. Good to see you Nate. How's Judith, she alright?"

"Yes, yes she is and she sends her regards."

Mrs. Johnson continues, "You go on around back, before

you get started help yourself to some fresh water and I have a fresh pot of coffee on the stove if you'd rather that. Lizzy, show them where pa wants the wood put, and watch your brother around them horses."

Lizzy answers with a, "Yes, ma'am, come on, Michael. Nate, follow me please."

I give Nate a nudge in the arm and he looks at me with a look that says, "what and don't say a word", both at the same time.

I give him a wink and give him another nudge saying, "She's cute, no wonder you were anxious to get here."

Nate sets the brake and we jump down off the wagon. Lizzy walks up to Nate and they shake hands, both blushing as they look at each other. Nate introduces me and Lizzy offers us both a fresh dipper of water. Little Michael is already climbing up onto the back wheel of the wagon trying to see what's inside. Lizzy tells him to get down, there's nothing to see, cept firewood. He naturally ignores her and keeps climbing up the side boards until he is sitting side saddle on the top rail smiling like he got away with something he shouldn't have.

Mrs. Johnson comes out the back and gives Nate a half hug. Nate introduces us to each other and then she asks me, "So, how did you come to be with Nate?"

I tell her, "It's a long story, but I have been staying at the Harris's for only a week or two and this is my second trip into Ash Fork with Nate."

She asks, "Can I get you two anything? Coffee or something to eat?"

We both decline and I say, "Thank you, ma'am, but we

better get started unloading this wood. We still have to get to Ash Fork."

She says she understands and tells Lizzy and Michael to leave us to our work. She tells us she'll be inside if we need anything.

Nate motions for me to get up in the wagon and throw the wood down to him, he'll stack it. Once up on the stack of wood, I start throwing the wood down. It doesn't take very long for both of us to work up a sweat. Nate takes his shirt off, much to the pleasure of Lizzy, as she coos some remark about him possibly needing another dipper of water.

Nate tells her, "Thanks but not just yet, we barely got started."

While they are making eyes at each other, Michael is eyeballing my knife and asking me about it. He asks me how big the blade is, so I take it out of the scabbard and show him. He is just as interested in the buckskin scabbard as he is the knife. He extends one finger and gently rubs it across the intricate bead work. I put the knife back into the scabbard and remove it from my belt. I tell him, "If you sit still I will let you hold it for me." With a warning I lay the scabbard across his lap, "Be very careful, don't try to take the knife out it is very sharp." He picks the scabbard up in both hands and naturally tries to pull the knife out. Luckily, the knife is big enough and the scabbard is tight enough, I can trust he won't be able to pull it out and hurt himself.

About half way to getting the cord of wood unloaded and stacked, Mr. Johnson comes riding up from the field. He ties his horse up and after introductions are completed, he looks at the firewood saying it looks good as usual.

Walking into the house Mr. Johnson says, "Sam Harris has the best firewood around."

Lizzy offers us both some water. Before Nate and I resume our unloading and stacking, Mrs. Johnson comes to the back door and asks if she can get us a bite to eat.

She says, "You might as well eat with us. Mr. Johnson is going to take his dinner now before he heads back out into the field. We have plenty, please have something to eat."

Nate and I look at each other and know that it would be impolite to refuse, so we both say thank you and look to where we can wash up. Lizzy motions towards the well pump and says that she'll get us a clean towel to dry off with. I help Michael down off the wagon and tell him I need my knife back. Before he hands it to me he asks to see the blade again. I oblige him and he is fascinated by its profile and shininess. He wants to touch the blade, but I refuse to let him. I reach down to my boot and pull out one of my throwing knives and tell him that this knife is more his size. Before I can even turn the knife over in my hand, he grabs it and runs into the house wanting to show his pa.

All I hear is, "No running in the house and where did you get that knife, boy?"

I look at Nate and roll my eyes knowing I got little Michael in trouble. We follow Lizzy into the house and into the dining room. Mr. Johnson motions for me to sit between him and Michael, which leaves Nate sitting on the other side next to Mrs. Johnson and Lizzy, much to Lizzie's delight.

While Mr. Johnson blesses the food and this year's crops,

there is no effort made to hold each other's hands. The food passes around the table quickly as well as the conversation. The Johnson's don't have many visitors, so they are anxious to hear anything about anybody's health and what have you. Mr. Johnson asks me where I am from and how I got to be staying at the Harris's. I tell him my usual story about being a carpenter, going from town to town looking for odd jobs, being able to make a few bucks before moving on. He doesn't much like that way of life and determines I'm nothing more than a drifter. Having taken my small knife away from Michael, he lets me know that he would appreciate it if I would keep my knives to myself. I apologize for letting Michael play with the knife and it won't happen again.

At that Michael lets out a, "Aw shucks Pa, I'm old enough to have a knife."

Mr. Johnson looks at him saying, "Maybe a pocket knife for whittling, but not a knife for killing. Now, Mr. Sparks, would you be so kind as to take this knife and put it away?"

"Yes sir, my apologies."

Dinner finishes up rather quickly and Nate and I excuse ourselves and head back out to finish the unloading and stacking of the firewood. Lizzy stays to help with the dishes, but the boy is right alongside us and up into the wagon once again. This time he climbs up over the buck board seat. In doing so he spots my bow and arrows that are tucked away with my pack and bedroll.

With a "Wow", he asks, "Hey, mister, is this yours? Is this a real bow and arrow?"

"Yeah, it is, but it's not a toy for young boys to play with.

It will stay right where it is for the time being."

Mr. Johnson comes out of the house and tells Nate thanks for the wood and he'll have a stack of fresh hay ready for him when he gets back from town.

He holds out his hand, saying, "It was a pleasure to meet you Mr. Sparks. In case we don't see you this way again, good luck in your travels."

"My pleasure and thanks for the great meal."

"Well, you've earned it and good luck to you," he says as he mounts his horse and heads back out to the field.

We finish up with the off load, but before we can get to saying our goodbyes, little Michael asks if I can show him how to shoot my bow and arrow. I am reluctant to say yes, but the boy just won't stop asking. Mrs. Johnson comes out to see how much longer we'll be and asks what Michael is going on about. I explain to her that Michael wants to see me shoot my bow and arrow but I'm not so sure Mr. Johnson would be okay with it. She says it should be alright as long as I don't let Michael try and shoot it.

I ask Nate if we have the time to spare and he surprises me with a, "Yeah, how long can it take? Besides we are only going as far as Unger's Creek tonight."

I get out my bow and arrow and once again Michael is fascinated with the buckskin leather work that makes the grip on the bow and the buckskin quiver for the arrows. I hand him one of the arrows to look at and he slides it through his fingers feeling the smoothness of the wood and glides the feathers along his fingers. He notices that the feather is stiff, splitting into gaps when pushed one way and then the gaps close and come together once brushed the other way.

I tell him to pick out a fence post for me to shoot at and he points to the closest one which is about twenty feet away. I tell him that it is a little too close, how about I shoot at one that is twice that far away. He says sure and climbs up into the wagon seat so he can get a better look. I pull back the bow string tight, take a slow deep breath and tell myself, "Focus, exhale, aim small," releasing the arrow, it splits the air and connects with the fence post.

Michael stands up clapping and asks me to do it again. I tell him one more and let him walk to the fence post with me. I let him try to pull it out, but it is sunk in too deep. Reaching up I grab the shaft of the arrow at the connection to the tip and pull straight out. The fence post releases its hold and frees the arrow.

We walk back to the same spot as before and this time I let Michael stand next to me. I go through the same motions as before and Michael is excited as he hears the twang of the bow string and the whoosh of the arrow. He is so excited he runs ahead of me to the fence post and jumps up trying to grab the arrow shaft. He is not tall enough to grab it which is a relief, because if he had, he probably would have snapped the arrow at the tip. With that I tell him that it is time for us to be leaving.

I walk over to Mrs. Johnson and tell her it was nice to meet her and her family and thank her again for the fine midday meal.

She says, "The pleasure is all ours, Mr. Sparks. Will you be coming back this way?"

"Probably so and thanks again." I tell Nate that I'll be at the wagon whenever he's ready.

Chapter 21

We settle in to the rhythm of the road and find ourselves staring directly into the face of the sun. Nate remarks about how Michael had been impressed with my knives and bow and arrow. I shrug his comments off and am more eager to discuss the obvious attraction that Nate and Lizzy had shared. As usual Nate clams up and is embarrassed that I noticed the attention that the two of them had shown each other.

I ask, "So how long have you been interested in her?"

"Sometime in the middle of last summer I noticed that she wasn't a little girl anymore. By late fall, just before winter set in, she began to hang around watching me unload firewood the last couple of deliveries. This spring when it came time to start delivering again, I found myself anxious to make the first delivery. It was a pleasant surprise when Lizzy seemed excited to see me."

"So have you kissed her yet?"

With a blushed face the color of a ripe fall apple he says, "No, but I sure would like to. Whenever her parents aren't around, little Mikey is always pestering us."

"Well, that's what little brothers do. They pester, be patient, one of these days she'll make sure that you get your chance to be alone with her. When that day comes be ready to change your thinking about what's fun and what isn't. I have a feeling that chopping wood won't be number one on your list anymore."

He laughs at the thought, and then says, "I can't wait to

have my mind changed."

Nate changes the subject by asking me where I learned to shoot the bow and arrow. With a heavy sigh I begin to tell him the story of how I came to know one of my best friends that I ever had in this life.

"I called him Chief, his real name was Charlie Tanner. I don't know if Charlie ever minded me calling him Chief, he never said, but I think he knew that I meant it as a sign of respect. I liked him right off."

"How'd you meet?"

"I met Chief up in Portland. He was about eight years older than me, but he had the youth of someone my age or younger. I was a carpenter working on a hotel and Chief came around looking for work. He said he was a carpenter too, but the foreman didn't really believe him. He hadn't had too much luck hiring Indians, said they drank too much and that they were unreliable."

"So did he get the job?"

"Yes, he did. Look Nate, just listen and I'll tell you everything, you don't need to interrupt. Okay?"

"Okay."

I continue, "So, the foreman hires Chief on as a laborer, but Chief doesn't want to dig ditches or haul material around to the carpenters. One night, after we had gotten paid, some of us headed over to the saloon to get a drink and I wanted to get a good steak. Chief was already at the bar and he was starting to think about the fact that he felt men on the crew talked down to him because he was an Indian and a laborer. Voices were starting to get loud and Chief began to get sullen and quiet, which was a bad sign. I knew if he got into a fight, he'd probably get thrown in jail and then get fired. I went over to him and told him that I'd buy him a steak if he left with me right then and there. He didn't like that too well, but I guess he felt like eating more than he felt like fighting, so we left and went over to a café. As I recall, the steak wasn't all that great, but at least neither one of us went to jail that night."

Nate butts in again, "So, what happened next?"

"A few days turned into a month, Chief and I become almost inseparable. I got the foreman to make Chief my helper, my apprentice you might say. By the end of the next month the foreman started paying Chief carpenter's wages. Chief couldn't have been prouder. I think for the first time in his life he felt like he was equal, that he had respect, that he could live free."

"What do you mean free? Indians aren't slaves or nothing like that."

"No, no they aren't slaves, but Chief's tribe had been ordered to live on a reservation, around the Gray's Harbor area in the state of Washington. They were being forced to live with a much larger tribe. Chief didn't want to live on a reservation so he headed south. He was tired of all the rain up there on the Washington Coast anyway; it was time for Chief to move on. One day he just started walking south, when he got to the Columbia River, he crossed over to Portland and stayed. Even though he knew how to live off the land, he wanted to learn other skills. His people were known for their wood working abilities. They were known for crafting wooden canoes out of cedar logs they split and dug out by hand. They built what they called "longhouses" out of cedar planks. They didn't live in teepees. They didn't need to move around hunting for food, they had an abundance of fresh fish and the mountains were full of game."

"It sounds almost perfect."

"Yeah to you and me maybe, but Chief wanted to be free and being told to live on a reservation wasn't free to him. Chief had learned some basic carpentry skills, he knew there was more to learn and knew that if he could make a living in our world, then no one could tell him where he had to live."

I stop with my story there as we pull through Unger's Creek. I know that the camp spot is just up the road and we'll be stopping for the night. I let Nate know that I'll continue Chief's story once we settle in to camp.

"That'll be great; I want to hear more about Chief."

We pull into the same spot we camped at the week before. We unhitch Molly and Bess and get them watered. Nate doesn't want them to gorge on the green grass so we give them some fresh dry hay. Nate is busy getting a fire started while I walk down to the creek. While there, I bend down and soak my face and head in the cool running water. I get shivers as the water makes my face tingle. I am well aware that my face has been pointed right at the sun and now there will be a price to pay dealing with the sunburn, "Damn that Brutus."

Nate walks up behind me asking, "What, what was that you said?"

"I was just thinking about that damn bull of yours and wishing I had my hat."

Nate looks at me trying hard not to laugh and says, "You

don't look too bad, for a ripe tomato."

With Nate still laughing I grab hold of him and wrestle him into the creek. With a huge splash we hit the cold water and laughing I say, "I don't like tomatoes unless I'm eating them."

Once back at camp we build up a larger than normal fire in order to dry out our wet clothes from our impromptu wrestling match. What a sight we must be as we sit around the fire, wrapped in blankets, and rotating our socks, shirts and pants from side to side.

Because we had a large meal only a few hours ago, neither one of us are very hungry. We decide to settle in for the evening and have some of the deer jerky and a apple. We give Molly and Bess a few cups of oats and then slice some apples in half for each of them. They worked hard today and seem to enjoy the attention given to them as we brush each of them down. After making sure the horses are tethered to a nearby tree for the night, we sit back and enjoy the nice fire for the evening. It doesn't take but a minute for Nate to ask me to continue telling him about Chief and our living in Portland.

"Where did I leave off, do you remember?"

Nate says, "Yeah, Chief had crossed the river to Portland. You and him were working together and Chief was getting paid as a carpenter."

"Yeah, that's right. I kinda lost track when I started talking about why he left the res."

Throwing another log on the fire, I begin, "Chief and I rarely disagreed about anything while we were working. Chief had good skills; he was meticulous and refused to nail anything together if it didn't fit just right. On the other hand he wasn't skilled as a layout man, cutting stairs, or figuring rafters, like I was. So, as the days and months linked together, he was eager to learn from me how to do the math it took to figure certain things, and I learned to have patience and be more meticulous from him. We would spend time working and re-working a finish piece of wood before we could nail it in place. I don't want to say Chief was slow, but when I learned carpentry, I learned to be fast, especially during the rough framing of a building. I had to learn to slow down. By the time we got to the fine finish work, Chief had become the teacher without even knowing it."

"So how long did you work on this hotel?"

"Oh, I'd say close to eight or nine months, could've been a year. It was a big hotel in downtown Portland. It was called Hotel LaMonte and it was supposed to be the finest in the city."

"Well, was it?"

"It was at the time, but there were plans to build a couple of more hotels and each one was going to try and out do the other one. But we didn't just work on that one hotel, we worked on other buildings and houses for the better part of five maybe six years or more. Portland was growing fast. It had the Columbia River that was wide enough and deep enough to have cargo ships to load and unload at. With the railroads connecting cities and places up and down the coast and back east, Portland turned into a hub for the entire territory. Anyway, like I said earlier, Chief and I were inseparable. We'd get one day off a week, usually Sunday and we'd head out to the river to a little Indian village that local Indians would gather at."

"Why go there? I thought Chief didn't want to live like that?"

"He didn't mind being with his own kind, he just didn't want to be forced to live on a reservation."

"Oh."

"Besides, I loved spending time there, and I had to keep Chief out of the saloons. See, for as good a man as Chief was, he had a bad drinking problem. It wasn't that he couldn't drink, hell no, he could stay up with me drink for drink. His problem was he'd get to drinking and then he'd want to fight. Sometimes he'd pick a fight just to fight. He didn't even need a reason."

"Why? Why would he do that?"

"You know, I never could figure it out, some men just seem to get crazy in their heads when they drink and that craziness turns to wanting to fight."

"What about you, didn't you want to fight?"

"Who me? I don't like to fight. Don't get me wrong, I'll fight if I have to, I've never backed down from a fight, but I always try to find a more sensible way out of arguments. I was what you'd call a happy drunk. I wanted to be everybody's friend. No, I don't like to fight. Someone always gets hurt and sometimes they get dead."

"Did you ever kill anyone?"

"Not that I know of, but enough about fighting. So, we'd go out to this little Indian village along the river and that's where Chief taught me how to snare rabbits and hunt with a bow and arrow. I learned to tan hides and then let the women do their fine bead work. When the salmon were running we'd sometimes fish from the shore with spears and other times we'd use these big nets. We'd throw them out into the river and pull in huge numbers of salmon. It was great fun. We ate fresh fish all the time. We regretted having to go back into town for the next week of work, but that's how we made our money."

"What did you do with your money?"

I just shake my head and say, "You don't want to know."

"Yes I do!"

"I drank most of it away. See, Chief had his problem and I had mine. I would get to a point that the more I drank, the more I wanted. There were times I thought that there wasn't enough liquor in Portland. Once I got started, I couldn't stop."

Nate is quiet for a minute and then asks, "So what happened? Why'd you keep drinking and living that way?"

"Well, Nate, that's a good question. You see when someone gets to drinking and living the way I was, they begin to think that this is their life and they're living it the way it's meant to be lived. I might have been a drinker with a bigger drinking problem than I realized, but I was able to get up every morning and go to work. I was a law abiding citizen, didn't cause no problems. I just liked to be with people having a good time. Over the years the booze just took over."

"What do you mean? What took over?"

The fire has died down, I roll over and tell Nate, "That's enough for tonight, I'm tired."

•

We wake up to the singing of birds and chirping of squirrels.

We have to shoo the squirrels away, they seem to have overran the wagon looking for an easy meal. There are a couple of blue jays squawking and jumping around looking for anything shiny that they might claim and call their own. Once we get all the little critters chased off, I tell Nate that I'm headed down to the creek to get my head wet hoping it will wake me up. He says he'll make a fresh pot of coffee before we pick up camp.

I acknowledge him with a wave. As I walk down towards the creek, I can't help but look out towards the band of trees where I shot the deer last week. I expect to see a deer or two in the same spot as before, but none are there, not today. I get back to camp and realize I should have walked Molly or Bess or both down to the creek, what was I thinking. I ask Nate if he thinks we should take the horses down to the creeks edge. He says they'll be fine. We can water them good here at camp. Without saying another word I sense that he is anxious to get on the road.

After watering the horses I empty the left over water onto the bed of coals. As they sizzle and steam I jump up onto the wagon. Nate has the reins in hand and releases the brake. It'll be about two maybe three hours to Ash Fork. I tell Nate, that the first thing I'm going to do is buy a new hat. My face is burnt and I'm gonna be sore for the next couple of days because of it. He agrees that buying a hat first thing is a good plan. I know that Nate has more questions about my life in Portland, but he needs to ask, I just don't want to offer up my past if someone isn't that interested.

As we ride along with the rising sun to our backs, we talk about the weather and other things that come to mind. He tells me he wants to take a good hot bath and get another shave. I tell him that those are on my list to do as well. He asks if I'd be interested in meeting up for a meal. I hesitate and try to explain that this trip to Ash Fork is important to me and that I have to meet someone from before. I anticipate the upcoming questions that Nate has for me but he doesn't ask any questions about Ash Fork.

Instead he asks, "So, Jake, what did you mean about drinking and the booze taking over your life?"

"Nate, I didn't realize it at the time, but all the drinking I'd done, ever since I had left Ash Fork, it was starting to kill me from the inside out. I was starting to want a drink earlier in the day. I began to figure out ways to have a drink or two while I was still working, I wouldn't wait 'til quitting time. I started to want a drink just to get up and face the morning. As it turned out, I had a drink in me all the time. My health began to fail me. When I caught a cold I couldn't shake it off. I started to want to drink instead of eat."

"That sounds bad, what'd you end up doing?"

"I ended up being real sick. By this time, Beth and me were together, she and some friends made me go see a doctor. He told me if I didn't stop drinking, I'd die."

"So, that's when you quit."

"Yeah, for about three weeks, but then I started to feel better and thought I could stay in control by having one drink once in a while."

"What happened?"

"After a week or two of that I was right back at it. Only this time I was getting mean when I drank. I was mad, mad at the world, mad all the time, mad I couldn't control it. I started pushing people away from me. I even tried to run Beth off, but she stayed by me."

"So, what happened? Did you get sick again?"

"You might say that. I got arrested for drunk and disorderly and ended up in jail for three days. When I got out I had to pay for the damages to a bar I busted up. I got fired from the job I was on and I ended up just about broke. That's when I decided to head back to Carver's Pass and see if I could get hired building houses. I told Beth if she would stay with me, I'd never take another drink. She stayed with me until she passed. True to my promise I haven't had a drink since. Once I realized that having a clear head was better than being drunk, I looked forward to being sober. To be honest with you Nate, the longer I stayed sober, the more awake I felt. I could truly feel my brain becoming more awake with each passing day."

"That's great Jake. Whatever happened to Chief? Did he ever stop drinking like you?"

"Sadly to say, he died around the same time I had decided to leave Portland."

"Sorry Jake, how'd he die?"

"Chief and I had a falling out. For some reason, Chief's fighting ways turned into always wanting to fight me. After awhile when Chief and I would get to drinking, Chief would get quiet on me; he'd get that look in his eye and decide I was the one he wanted to fight. I couldn't fight him, I loved him. As much as it hurt me to stay away from him I had to. It was the only way I could protect the both of us. Eventually, we just drifted apart. A mutual friend got word to me that he had crashed a wagon up on a mountain road late one night. He laid up there for a day or two 'til someone found him and was able to get him to town and to a doctor. Evidently it had taken too long to get him help. The doctor couldn't do anything for him 'cept to make sure he wasn't feeling any pain. Chief never recovered. He was taken in by a mission house where he died alone in a bed that looked out over the river."

"Did you ever try to find him?"

"No, I never did. I was fighting to save my own life at the same time. We were best of friends, maybe even closer then brothers. He was and always will be Chief; he died free."

Chapter 22

Nate pulls the wagon into the back of Mr. Kimble's General Store. He positions the wagon so it is next to the stacks of wood that we dropped off the week before. Mr. Kimble comes out and exchanges hellos with Nate.

Looking up at me, he says, "Well, Mister, I see you came back. You must be settling in pretty good with the Harris's."

I jump down off the wagon and reach into my side pouch and pull out the note from Sam. Mr. Kimble unfolds the note saying, "What's this?" After reading it, he tells me, "When you get done unloading the wood, come on in and we'll see what it is you need credit for."

"Sure will, Mr. Kimble. I sure hope you have hats for sale."

"I sure do. By the look of your face, it looks like you need a hat and you could use some sunburn ointment. I got 'em both. We'll fix you up."

"Sounds good, I'll be in shortly."

Mr. Kimble then asks Nate if Judith has a list for him to fill, Nate tells him no, not this week but she would like the balance sheet on the account. Mr. Kimble tells him he has it ready and set aside for him to take back. With that Mr. Kimble turns and heads into the store.

We don't take long unloading the wagon, keeping the three types of wood separated and stacked in the correct piles. We unhitch the horses, give them a quick brush down and get them watered. Nate makes sure they have an apple and then some fresh hay. Satisfied that they will be comfortable for awhile, we both have a quick wash from the water trough and head into the store.

I make a beeline to a hat tree that has about a half dozen hats on it. The selection isn't all that great. All the hats are made of straw, for summer use. I am looking for a good felt hat that will last me longer than just one season. Looking around Mr. Kimble's store I decide I could use a pair of pants. I have two pairs of pants now, but one is getting thread bare, especially in the knees. I find a table that has a stack of work pants and shift through the pile. I sort out my size. As I do that, I think that a new shirt wouldn't hurt either. It's been awhile since I could afford to make a purchase or two without worrying about having to ration my money. I pick out a shirt, a pair of socks and a set of summer underwear; God knows I could use them.

My tally leaves me with $1.15 in credit. Mr. Kimble apologizes for not having a felt hat in stock. He tells me he could order one and have it in a week if I didn't mind waiting that long. I tell Mr. Kimble to leave the credit on the books for me. Before I leave, I find Nate and let him know that I'm headed to the barber shop to get a good hot bath and a trim. He says that he'll be along shortly. I leave the store with my purchases wrapped up and shoved into my pack.

Once out of Kimble's, I look up and down the street trying to get my bearings. Even though I was in Ash Fork just a week ago, it takes me a moment to know what direction to walk in. It takes me just a quick glance to spot Bill's Barber Shop; I start walking in that direction. Now that I know where my first stop will be, I take notice of where my second stop will be. I spot Cooper's Dry Goods and hope that they will have felt hats for sale.

Walking in to the barber shop, I get a good morning from Bill and a nod from a customer that is having his hair cut.

Bill stops to ask what I need and after I say a hot bath and a quick trim, Bill takes a second look at me and asks, "Weren't you in here last week, mister?"

"Yes, I was. I'm Jacob Sparks. I am staying with Sam Harris at Fletcher's Crossing."

"Yeah, that's right. Did Nate come into town with you?"

"Yeah, Nate's in town, he'll probably be in soon."

"You know where the tubs and towels are. If the water isn't hot enough, you can use the water in the kettles that are sitting on the stove. You'll have to help yourself."

"Thanks, I will."

"You gotta pretty good sunburn. I got some salve that might help."

"Thanks, but I just picked some up from Kimble's."

As good as the hot water bath feels, the new underwear and socks feel even better. Not wanting to walk in new stiff pants I put on my last pair of clean pants and unfold my new shirt.

After Bill trims my hair and beard, he remarks that I look like a new man with my new shirt and all. As I am headed out the door, Nate is walking up. He asks where I am headed next and I tell him I going to check out hats at Cooper's Dry Goods. He says he doubts that they'll have the kind of hat that I am looking for, but I might get lucky.

I hold the door for him and hear Bill say, "Nate, good to see you. What'll it be today, my boy?"

I cross the street and walk into Cooper's. There are a few customers in the store and the same sales clerk from last week. She is busy at the counter which gives me some time to look around the store. I find a hat rack and just as Nate had predicted, the selection isn't any better than at Kimble's.

The sales clerk finishes with the last customer and comes over asking, "Did you come back for that broom, or are you looking for something else this time?"

With a smile I say, "Good morning ma'am, how are you this fine day?"

"I am just wonderful, you are looking well today. Are you finding what you are looking for?"

"Well, to be honest, no I'm not. As I am sure you can tell by my sunburnt face, I need a hat but I don't want a straw hat. I am looking for a felt hat, something sturdier than a straw hat. Do you have anything like that?"

She surprises me when she says, "Yes we do, we have them in the back. Most men want straw hats in the summer, so we put the felt hats away until fall. Would you like to go to the store room and see for yourself?"

"Sure, as long as it won't be a bother."

She yells to someone that I don't realize is there, "Mr. Cooper, I am taking a customer to the store room, can you watch the floor?"

From a small office comes a reply, "Sure will, Flora."

It doesn't take long to sort through the hats that are in the back store room. I pick a tan colored hat with a nice braided hat band. I look at the price and it costs more than the cash I have. Flora is sympathetic to my situation. She takes the hat from me and I follow her back out to the sales floor. She excuses herself and discusses my money problem with Mr. Cooper.

Returning with a smile she says, "Mr. Cooper says that those hats are on sale since they are out of season and all. He also said he has a broken window and a screen door that need to be repaired. He would trade you the hat for the repairs if you are able to do that sort of thing."

This is not exactly what I wanted to do. I am anxious to be on my way, but getting a hat and keeping some money in my pocket would be well worth delaying the visit with my mom for a little while longer.

I tell Flora to show me the window and door, "Let me take a look at the repairs needed. Do you have the glass?"

She turns and asks Mr. Cooper, "Do we have the glass?"

He nods and says, "Yes, it is in the back on the work bench. It might need to be cut. There is a glass cutter on the shelf above the bench."

Having looked at the window and screen door, I determine that it shouldn't take too long to make both repairs.

As Flora turns to leave she asks, "You know my name, but I don't know yours?"

Reaching out my hand I say, "Jacob Sparks, ma'am, nice to meet you."

Flora puts her hand over her mouth and with a squint in her eyes she says, "You were in here last week asking about Sarah Sparks, weren't you? You said you were a friend."

"Yes, yes I was. I am her son and I need to go and visit her. I planned on visiting her today. I apologize for not being totally truthful, but it is complicated. "

Flora spins and as she leaves she says, "You better get busy then."

The repairs are not difficult. I have made similar repairs before. I repair the window first and putty the piece of glass into the frame. The screen door needs to have the top hinge repositioned because the wood screws have stripped the wood, leaving nothing for the threads of the screws to grab hold of. I could use bigger screws, but there's a risk that the door frame could split and turn into a more difficult repair. Instead, I raise the hinge just enough to sink the hinge screws in to solid wood and rehang the screen door. With both repairs complete, I make my way out to the front of the store.

Flora is behind the counter. As I approach her she says, "You must be finished. Mr. Cooper stepped out for a little while, and he isn't here to inspect the repairs. You are welcome to wait here or you can leave and come back a little later. He shouldn't be gone long."

"Sorry, ma'am, but I need to be on my way. Would it be possible for you to check out the repairs instead of making me wait for Mr. Cooper?"

With reluctance she says, "I would have to leave the sales floor unattended."

"Could you put the Closed sign on the door? It will only take a minute or two to check out the repairs."

Flora takes a look around the store. With no other customers around, she cautiously walks towards the door and says, "I guess it won't hurt."

I follow her into the back of the store and as she inspects the repairs I ask, "Would you happen to know where Mrs.

Sparks lives? Is there a house number and a street name?"

Reluctantly she says, "I don't know her house number. I am not sure I would be comfortable giving it to you even if I did know it."

"Please, Flora. It is very important that I talk to her. I don't have a lot of time to go up and down the streets hoping to find someone that knows her or where she lives. I apologize again for not being totally honest with you last week. My reasons are personal and it's complicated. I'd like to see her, make sure she is okay. Please, any information would help. Please?"

Flora looks at the broken window and then tests the screen door. She looks at me, bites her lip and says, "Mrs. Sparks lives in a small house a few blocks away. I'll write down the directions when we get back up front."

As she hands me the hat, she tells me, "Mr. Cooper will be pleased to have the window and especially the screen door repaired. He cussed at that door every time he had gone in and out of it lately."

"Flora, thanks for everything; for this new hat and especially for understanding and giving me the directions to my ma's house."

Flora asks, "Where have you been all these years?" And then says, "Your mother, Sarah, turned so sad with each passing year. I think she finally gave up waiting."

My voice is strained as I say, "I tried to write her over the years. Did she say if she ever got any of my letters?"

"If she did, she never mentioned them. I sure hope you know what you are doing."

Without turning around I say, "Me too."

Chapter 23

Orienting myself to the handwritten directions and the street, I walk west down Main Street. I pass a couple of saloons, one of which is the one I walked past last time I was in town. The same smells and sounds linger out the front door. Without any yearnings to go inside, I continue walking west.

At the corner of Main and 4th St., I turn right. This street feels somewhat familiar. Up ahead at the far end of the block, there is a large house with a wrought iron fence around the yard. I suddenly get nervous. My stomach does a roll and a flop, it's Doc Hodges's house. It looks run down. In fact, the windows and doors are all shuttered. The place looks vacant. The yard has weeds growing up all around and the shrubs are overgrown. It is not the show place it used to be. I think to myself, what time, weather and neglect will do to a place? I grew up on this same street, only on the opposite side and down one more block.

According to Flora's directions, I'm supposed to turn left at the corner of Doc Hodges' old house. In the middle of the next block, there should be a small green house with white trim and a blue spruce tree in the front yard. The closer I get the more I want to run. Turning the corner and walking past the side of the doctor's old house, I can't resist the urge to look up at the second story window. The fateful day that would forever change me comes flooding back into my memory. Standing there I almost heave my guts and hope my legs don't buckle. I slowly turn my body and force myself to move forward. I take a step towards the little green house that is in the middle of the block hoping my legs will stop shaking.

There is no fence or gate at the front yard, just an old tilted walk way that leads to a couple of wooden steps going up to a wooden porch. There's a big picture window in front which has lacy curtains that cover the window. The front door has an etched window in it and it too has a lacy curtain over it. There is a brass knocker at the center of the door. I hesitate before I put the brass stirrup between my fingers. With a deep breath, I put my hands on either side of my face and press them against the glass. Not seeing any movement, I slide my fingers over the knocker and tap it against the face plate. I give it three firm raps and again I put my face to the glass. All I can hear is my own breathing. I give the knocker another three quick raps. There is still no sound or movement. As I put my face to the glass one more time, I wonder if this is such a good idea after all. I have myself half convinced that I could come back on my next trip into Ash Fork, but on second thought, I realize that with my life of wandering, there might not be a next trip.

I tell myself, I've come this far, I might as well see it through. I grab the knocker one more time and I tap the brass stirrup and plate together harder and longer this time. I then bang on the solid wooden door yelling, "Ma, Mrs. Sparks, anybody, are you home?"

I look through the glass again and there is still no movement. I repeat my knocking and yell again. This time, I hear the thumb latch of the lock click open. The door opens about one inch to a frail little voice asking, "Who's there?"

"Mrs. Sarah Sparks, is that you?"

The frail voice answers back, "Yes, I'm Mrs. Sarah Sparks. Who wants to know?"

As I gulp for more air I say, "Ma it's me, it's Jacob, your son."

She opens the door, squinting into the brightness of the late afternoon sun. Her thin frail lips quiver as she says, "Jacob, is that really you? How can it be, after all these years?"

I realize that the odds are against her being able to recognize me and recall that Flora had told me that her eyes had gone bad. I tell her, "Ma, it's me Jacob, after all these years I finally made it back here; I want to see you. Can I come in?"

She grabs at the neckline of her house coat and pulls it tight to her neck. With hesitation and bewilderment she says trembling, "Jacob, Jacob is that really you?"

"Yes, Ma it's really me. I am sorry it has taken me all these years to get back here, but it's me and I really want to come in and talk to you if you'll let me?"

As she opens the door half way, she holds up her hand and gently touches my face. With tears streaming down her cheeks she opens the door the rest of the way and says, "Jacob, it is you, my Jacob's come home."

The inside of the house is sparsely furnished. She doesn't appear to be living in poverty, but she doesn't have an abundance of furniture. She puts her arm in mine and asks me to walk her to a table that is separate from the little front room. The table makes for a small dining area before leading to an archway and into the kitchen.

As she sits down, she is muttering to herself that she just can't believe it. Once she is seated she says, "I must look a mess and I don't have any fresh cookies like the ones I used to bake when you were a young boy. You always loved my cookies."

"It's alright, Ma. You look just fine and I'm not hungry."

I can tell that she doesn't believe me, but she doesn't press it further.

She tells me, "There is a kettle of hot water on the stove and a tin of tea in the cupboard. I am sorry, I don't have coffee."

"It's okay. I'll get us both a cup of hot tea.

I set my pack down by the front door before I go into the kitchen, noticing this she says, "So you're not staying?"

With a loud sigh I answer, "I'm afraid not, Ma. I am staying with a family at Fletcher's Crossing and I have to head back in the morning."

"You have to stay the night."

"Ma, I'm sorry, I just can't. I have to help with a wagon and the team and we are going to get started back at first light. I'll be back in a week or so and then I'll stay, but not tonight. In fact, if you need anything done around the house, I'll stay long enough to take care of it. I'll fix it all. I'm a really good carpenter and can fix anything with wood. Today I just want to visit. I just want to hear how you've been doing, where's Pa and what's he been up to?"

She doesn't say anything while I'm in the kitchen pouring the tea. She is staring out the side window as I set a cup of tea in front of her. As I sit down, she reaches out and takes my hand in hers, trembling she says, "It's been so long Jacob, what happened? Why did you run off? Why?"

I look at her and say, "Ma, does it really matter right now, can you tell me how you've been?"

She takes her hand away and wipes her eyes with a napkin saying, "What does it matter? No one cares about me."

"Ma, I care, I'm asking about you. I want to know how you've gotten along all these years. What happened to you and Pa? Where is Pa?"

She takes a sip of tea and almost misses the saucer as she sets the cup back down. She turns her head back towards me and grabs my face between both her hands saying, "What happened to you, why'd you run off the way you did. You didn't even say goodbye."

"I know Ma, and I'm sorry. I just couldn't. At the time I felt I had to run. At the time, with what was about to happen, I didn't have a choice."

She takes her hands away and says, "That's not what I heard. You know, people talk and what people were saying, it was bad and it was embarrassing. Your pa, he started coming home less and less. He wasn't around much anyway, always on that damned railroad or at least that's what he told me. After you left, well, I guess he just didn't have any reason to be here."

"Ma, that's not true, Pa had you."

"No he didn't, all he wanted was to work. If he had loved me half as much as he loved that railroad, he would've spent the other half of his time here with me."

I realize that this is not going very well. She is bitter and if I don't want to get into an argument, I had better watch what I say. It is selfish of me, but I came here needing to get reacquainted and some answers.

"So, what happened Ma, what did Pa do, where is he?"

Again she turns and looks out the window. "Last I heard

he was someplace over by the coast. The railroad was building a new line that would connect some of the fishing towns with the logging towns, and join up to the main line north to Portland."

"Did you ever hear from him much? In fact, did you ever get any of my letters I sent you?"

She turns her head back towards me and says, "Yes dear, I got your letters. It was always good to know that you were still alive. I appreciated you sending me money every so often. You're father too. He'd send money every other month or so. He was good about that."

This brings me to ask, "How you doing for money now, Ma? Is Pa still alive, is he still sending you money?"

"Oh, I guess he is still alive. I get an envelope once in awhile, not regular like he used to send. The envelopes don't have post marks on them so I don't know where they're from or where he is. I don't need much. I still have a little left over from selling the old house; you know the one you grew up in. I worked at Mr. Cooper's up until a year ago. I did a lot of his book work. He always told me that because I helped him so much, that if he could and business stayed good, he would help me out. Good to his word, he sends a boy around once a month with a couple of dollars for me. He doesn't have to you know, I'm no charity case, but if he wants to, who am I to say no. I worked at his store when his daddy owned it, I've earned it."

"Yes you have, Ma, yes you have."

Chapter 24

Ma asks if I am hungry yet. This time I know she won't take no for an answer so I tell her I could eat. She tells me she can fix us some soup to go along with some bread she baked yesterday. As she gets the soup started, I wander around the house. It is just right for her, not much to keep up and she has a small vegetable garden out back. Before I mosey out to take a better look, I notice there is a wood box that sits next to the stove and it needs to be filled. I go out back and bring in a couple armfuls of wood. I then go back out and look over her vegetable garden. Her vegetables have their tops up out of the ground about four inches. I'm no gardener, but I can tell the difference between veggie tops and weeds. It's not my favorite thing to do, but I bend over and pick a few weeds hoping anything I do will help her in some way.

There is a small fence separating both of the neighbors' yards from hers. One of the neighbors has chickens that wander around free. Once back inside I say, "You have a start to a great garden. I notice your neighbor has some chickens. Do you have any of your own?"

She tells me, "No, but there is a hole in the fence and the chickens are sometimes in my yard."

I ask, "Would you like me to mend the fence?"

"No, I like the chickens to eat the bugs. Occasionally, my neighbor gives me fresh eggs."

"How do you get your groceries?"

"I walk to the store with a friend that lives a few houses

down. Sometimes a neighbor boy comes by and takes a list for me. He also fills up the wood box for me."

"It seems like you are getting by fairly well."

She agrees, saying, "I don't do too bad for an old lady."

"Ma, you're not old, you're not even sixty yet."

With that she says, "How would you know?"

We sit down to fresh hot soup and warmed up bread. My mouth starts to water and my mind returns to my childhood as I remember how good of a baker she once was. Her apple pie was the best around. No one could match her crust or how she seasoned the apples. We hold hands as she blesses the food. She starts to cry as she thanks God for bringing me home and hopes that Pa is someplace safe.

I start to ask her about Doc Hodges' place and she stops me mid sentence and says, "Not another word until you tell me what happened that day. What made you run off the way you did. You owe your mother that much."

Knowing that she is right, I relent saying, "Ma, you're right. I guess I should start at the beginning. I had been friends with Doc Hodges's daughter, Carolynn. She and I had gotten together a few times down by the river."

With sternness to her voice she asks, "What does that mean, gotten together?"

"It means exactly what you think it means. We had gotten together in a man and woman type of way."

"You mean you had relations out of marriage?"

"Yes, Ma, that is what I mean. One day Doc Hodges had gotten word to me that he wanted to talk to me. He wanted my help with fixing something at his house and he wanted me to come over this one particular afternoon. He was very specific and not to be late."

"What day, when did this happen?"

"Ma, I don't remember the exact day, it was too many years ago. All I know is that I showed up at Doc's house and he was mad as hell at me. He started yelling about getting his daughter pregnant. Carolynn and her two sisters, the three of them were all crying and there was another man there in the room. The Doc called him a preacher, but he wasn't a preacher that I ever saw before."

Ma, is holding her handkerchief with both hands, covering her mouth and with a muffled sound she says, "He was gonna get you two kids married, wasn't he?"

"Yeah, Ma, that's what he had planned. Carolynn and me, we didn't even get a chance to talk about nothing. Hell, sorry Ma, I didn't even know if she was really pregnant. We didn't even do it but a couple of times and the first time I wasn't even sure what the heck happened. Sorry again, Ma, I don't mean to embarrass you."

She reaches out and touches my hand and says, "It's alright dear, just go on. What happened next?"

"Doc told me to go up stairs, get myself washed up. He'd come up and get me once the girls had calmed down some. So, I went upstairs and I must have turned into the Doc's bedroom by accident. There was a highboy dresser next to the window, I ran over to the window and opened it up. I had made up my mind that I was gonna run, I couldn't get married, I was only seventeen and Carolynn was only sixteen herself. I was scared and Doc, he was spitting mad and yelling. Carolynn looked like she'd been slapped a couple of times."

"So, you jumped out the window and ran?"

"Yeah, yeah I did, but not before taking three $10.00 dollar gold pieces from top of his dresser. They were just laying there and I didn't have a penny on me. If I was running, I knew I'd need some money. I knew it was wrong, Ma, but I just couldn't be forced to get married. Maybe if Carolynn and I had been able to talk about it first or maybe been able to talk to you and Pa, maybe then I could've done it, but I just couldn't be forced. Once I grabbed the coins and jumped out the window, I knew there'd be no coming back. Besides, I didn't know if she was even pregnant, old Doc could've been making it all up."

Ma sits there real quiet for a few moments. I get up and get another cup of tea and when I return she is dabbing her eyes with her handkerchief again. She is trembling as she says, "You should have stayed; we would have worked it out. You running off the way you did, changed things for two families and even around town. It wasn't too long after you ran off that your Pa started staying away for longer times. The doctor, he spread rumors about you saying that you raped his daughter and robbed him at gunpoint."

"That's a lie, Ma, all of it, it's a lie. I never raped Carolynn! We were young and maybe thought we were in love, but, how could we have been? I don't even think either one of us knew what real love was. I took some money, yes I did do that, but not at gunpoint. I didn't even have a gun, 'cept the .22 I had for hunting rabbits and it was in my bedroom. I didn't have time to grab that or anything else. I left with the clothes on my back. What else were people saying?"

"Folks said that the doctor had gotten the sheriff to go look for you, but they came back saying they couldn't find you. Where'd you run to?"

"I ran most that day and into the night. I headed east at first and crossed the river up at Fletcher's Crossing. I made my way north to Carver's Pass. I met a man that took me in. He was a woodsman and a carpenter. He gave me a place to stay and I worked as a laborer. After awhile he took a liking to me and he taught me carpentry and I got really good at it. I stayed at Carver's Pass for close to three years and then I got restless and headed further north to Portland. I stayed up there most of the time working on hotels and other buildings."

"You never thought to come back home all that time?"

"It wasn't that easy, Ma. I got into a way of life that wasn't a good one. I got to drinking, gambling and all sorts of things. I kinda lost my way, my way home and my way through life."

"So, what made you come back, why now?"

"Ma, I just knew it was time. Something got me traveling this way and the more I walked south the more it just felt like it was time."

We sit in silence for what seems a long time, I look out the window and notice the sky is losing its light and the shadows of the trees have lengthened across the yard. My thoughts turn to Nate and I get the feeling that he won't understand what's keeping me. I still haven't gotten any answers from Ma. I need to be going, but my need to find out what happened after I ran away is just too strong of a pull on my mind.

"So, Ma, what happened to Carolynn? Do you know if she

ever was pregnant? I am sure you heard talk. You must have seen her around the neighborhood or out shopping?"

Ma looks at me with a blank look on her face and she says, "You know, it is a funny thing. Up until now, I hadn't given much thought to her."

"But Ma, you had to hear something, for as mad as Doc Hodges was, she didn't just stop living."

Ma continues almost in a whisper, "Like I told you, the rumors were mean and rampant at first. As time went on a few folks would share what they heard, but you couldn't trust anything. The stories were so outlandish, they were almost unbelievable."

"Like what Ma, what was being said? What happened?"

Ma doesn't look real well, she stares at the wall and then looks back at me, but doesn't focus on me, it's like she is looking right through me. After a moment she continues, "We heard that the girl ran off with you. No one saw her for a couple years and then we heard that maybe she had never left. People were fairly sure that she had been pregnant. There was a rumor that she had given birth to a baby boy, but no one ever saw a baby, let alone a baby boy. Every once in awhile someone would think they would see the girl out in the yard or out on the porch but no one could confirm it."

"What about Doc Hodges, didn't anybody ever ask him what happened? Where did his daughter go or was there ever a baby or not? What about the sisters, didn't anybody ever run into them and ask them what the heck had gone on?"

Ma whispers, "People say that terrible things happened in that house. Folks came to be afraid of the doctor and they quit going to see him. They say he just went crazy."

In disbelief I say, "Ma, that doesn't make any sense, Doc Hodges was one of the best doctors in town. Are you telling me that Doc went crazy because I didn't marry his daughter?"

"It was more than that. There were rumors that, when his girls were younger and before his wife died, that he had mistreated the oldest girl. It broke his wife's heart when she found out about it. That very next winter she went to her bed one day and just never took to her feet again. She had lost her will to live. They say she died because of a broken heart and shame."

"Ma, what does that have to do with Carolynn and me?"

Ma looks up at me and says, "Everything, Doc Hodges got accused of abusing the oldest daughter, lost his wife and then you pulled your shenanigans and ran off. His life fell apart; folks stopped going to see him as their doctor and worse yet, his daughter Carolynn must have ran off. It seems there was a new rumor that would spring up every other year or so. One winter, news spread that someone had fallen through the ice on the river and drowned. The sheriff and his deputies never reported that they found a body. It was presumed that whoever it was could have very well been the Doctor's daughter. He just couldn't take it. With his reputation shattered; people say he just went crazy. He finally died about eight years ago. His life and family were surrounded by rumors and mysteries. Some folks in town think the place is haunted. No one wants to go near it, not even to tear it down."

I shake my head in disbelief, some of the things Ma has told me just don't add up. I try and make Ma start over from the beginning but her memory abandons her. Even though the story I have just heard, is based on rumors, it is more than I had before I came to visit. I sit in silence letting the sequence of those lost days sink in.

Sitting in silence, I repeat what I have just heard to myself. Apparently, Carolynn was pregnant. After I ran, Carolynn was either sent away to have the baby or she was kept in secret at Doc's house. If there had been a baby, no one ever saw it. Maybe Doc gave the baby away, but whatever happened, it could have made Carolynn desperate enough to run away. Hopefully she was trying to find her baby. Maybe she got away from the house and while trying to cross the frozen river she fell through the ice and drowned. No one could prove it, no body was recovered. The Doc just couldn't handle all the tragedies, he went crazy and died. The house sits vacant; some folks think it is haunted by the ghosts of the shamed wife, the baby and Carolynn.

That's the best I could get out of my ma. I could tell she was extremely tired and I needed to join back up with Nate. I reach out and hold Ma's hands and tell her that I'll be back soon. She looks up, starts to cry and begs me not to leave her again. I tell her I have to go, I can't stay.

She slowly walks me to the door. I put my pack on my back, she grabs my hands and falls to her knees crying, "Don't leave me Jacob, not again. Please don't go."

"Ma, I have to, please don't do this. I'll be back, I promise."

Suddenly she stands up, straightens her housecoat and starts screaming, "Go! Just go, you're just like your father. Men, you're all alike, promises, promises, that's all you're good for. Now GO! Don't bother coming back!"

Stopping before I close the door; I look at her and say, "Ma, you don't mean that. I'll be back, I promise."

I close the door, as I walk off the porch and down the tilted sidewalk I can hear her sobbing, "Don't go, Jacob, please don't leave me. I'm sorry, I'm sorry."

Doc Hodges' house

Chapter 25

My mind is swirling with each step I take away from Ma's house. I can't make my mind focus on what or where I am until I see old Doc's house on the corner. I look up at the second story window again and suddenly I break out in a run. I can't stop running until I get to Main Street. As I slow to a walk, my breathing returns to normal. I have no concept of time; I just know that it is late. Nate is a big boy and is capable of taking care of himself but I have a sense of unexplained urgency. My feelings are mixed with the emotions of seeing my mother and hearing the revelations of the past seventeen years.

As I walk along Main Street towards Mr. Kimble's, I pass by the same saloons that I had passed earlier in the day. Early evening hours yield to more activity. The loud music, talking and laughter makes my head turn to look and my heart begins to race. Once again I allow myself to look in the smoke filled windows; the patrons are frolicking with no regard for time or concerns for daily routines.

At the last window, my eye catches a glimpse of a couple of men that seem familiar, men I have recently had contact with. I stop for a better look and it dawns on me that these men look like they were with the group that came through the ferry crossing and gave us trouble. My stomach goes into knots. To make sure I am seeing what I think I am seeing, I back up and put my nose to the glass one more time. It sure looks like the same men, but I only count six, I thought there were eight in all. I take a walk around to the back of the saloon and I see two wagons pushed up alongside the back of the building. There are no horses in sight; they must be stabled for the night. Judging by the way the six where acting, these men have been drinking for awhile and are in no hurry to be moving on.

I instinctively start to run down the alley towards Mr. Kimble's. It dawns on me that I left my bow and arrows at the wagon. I wish I had them with me just in case there is trouble. Before I get to the fenced in area behind Mr. Kimble's, I slow my pace in order to quiet my breathing. The back of Kimble's is dimly lit with light coming from a window at the back of the store. As I walk up to the fence, I hear someone moaning and then I see what looks like a body lying on the ground. Dear God, don't let it be Nate. I slide through the fence rails and set my pack on the ground ever so quietly.

On the other side of the wagon I can hear the angry voice of a man and he is threatening someone, "You're gonna pay now, boy. You're not so tough out here all by yourself are you, boy?"

I crouch down and pull one of my throwing knives out of my left boot, and I have my bowie knife in my other hand. I crawl up to the body of the man that is lying on the ground. I check his throat for a pulse; he is alive but barely conscious. Looks like Nate was able to fight at least one of them off.

I crawl under the wagon and weigh my options; at least there is only one of them. It looks like the same guy that I had put my knife to twice before. He's got Nate tied to the wagon wheel. Nate's shirt is ripped off his back and the guy has the horse whip out. Nate's face is busted up pretty bad with a broken nose and a black eye already starting to show.

I have to act quickly. I grab the wagon wheel for leverage and swing out from under the wagon with my legs hitting the man's legs just behind his knees. He tries to back up quickly but I have enough force to knock him off balance. From the position I am in, I am able to throw my small knife and it sticks in his thigh.

He lets out a half scream and yells, "It's you. You're that bastard from the ferry that almost slit my throat!"

Jumping to my feet, I say "I should have done it too, you no good piece of shit, real tough guy, picking on a boy."

"He ain't no boy, he already took out my partner."

I look to Nate, "Nate, are you OKAY?"

Mumbling he says, "Yeah, I think so."

I say to the attacker, "And now I finish it. You and your friends should have kept on moving."

He takes the whip and lunges it at my face, I slide out of the way. Grabbing his outstretched arm I am able to swing him around, twist his arm backwards and shove it flat between his shoulder blades. With my bowie knife in hand, I pull it up against his throat. This time, I have the blade positioned from the center of his throat to the base of his ear. I walk him away from the wagon towards the alley and into the dark.

With his one hand pulled up tight between his shoulder blades, he is not able to do anything but wave his free hand around trying to grab the knife at his throat. I tell him to calm down and open the gate to the alley. His eyes are as big as saucers and he is starting to beg me to let him go. I can hear Nate telling me to stop and asking me to let him be.

As I walk him down the dark unlit alley, I say, "I suggest that you make your peace with God, 'cause you are about thirty seconds from coming face to face with Him."

The man is begging me for his life, he wets himself in fear. Trembling, he drops to his knees and says, "Look mister, I didn't mean to hurt the kid. We just wanted to get our money back. I was just gonna scare him a bit."

"Bullshit! Men like you are just plain mean. You think you can treat people any way you want and get them to do whatever it is you want them to do. You think life owes you something. It doesn't work that way. I've had enough of your type. Tonight, is your end."

I increase the pressure on my knife and a trickle of blood begins to run down his neck.

Suddenly there is a shotgun blast from the back of Mr. Kimble's. I turn to look and standing next to the wagon is Mr. Kimble with a lantern, he has Nate untied. Nate is standing but is bent over at the waist. The other man that had been passed out is sitting up but not moving.

Mr. Kimble yells out to me, "Mr. Sparks, bring that other feller back here, don't do what you intend to do. It stops here tonight. Bring him back, Mr. Sparks. I'm not asking you again. I've already sent for the sheriff."

I turn the man around, I reach down, pull my throwing knife out of his thigh and wipe the bloody blade on his pants. He lets out a yell in anguish.

I tell him, "Shut up! It's a long way from your heart." Just for good measure, I bust him upside his head with the butt of my bowie knife, "You'll live to see tomorrow. It'll be from inside a jail cell, but you'll live. Now get walking."

It doesn't take very long for the sheriff to get to Mr. Kimble's yard. He sorts out the events of the night and takes the two away in handcuffs. Mr. Kimble tells me that Mrs. Kimble has some hot water on the stove, and she'll get Nate cleaned up. We help Nate into the back of the store and sit him down at a table. Mrs. Kimble brings over a wash basin filled with hot steaming water and stirs in a couple scoops of Epsom salts. She takes a wash cloth and starts dabbing it on Nate's eyes and forehead. His hands are swollen and he winces with every breathe he takes.

Mr. Kimble looks at me and says, "They busted him up pretty good. He's probably got a couple of broken ribs. I don't think he should travel. He needs to rest."

I motion with my head for Mr. Kimble to follow me outside. I tell him about the dust up at Fletcher's Crossing two days earlier and that there are six more down at the saloon getting pretty tanked up. I think we need to get out of town and headed back to the ferry before the others get wise to what's happened and come looking for Nate and me. Mr. Kimble doesn't agree, but I tell him I can get Nate into the back of the wagon and he'll be able to lie down. I'll get him back to the ferry crossing in one piece. We'll be back by tomorrow night and then Judith can tend to him. Mr. Kimble finally relents and says he'll give me a hand with the horses and getting Nate comfortable.

Mrs. Kimble cleans up Nate's face, has put a wrap around his ribs, and has gotten him a new shirt while Mr. Kimble and I ready the wagon. We get Nate into the back of the wagon and lying down on a pile of blankets. I grab the rifle from under the seat and load a round into the chamber and set it next to me. I pull the team and wagon out of the yard. Mr. Kimble gives me a wave as I tip my new hat.

Chapter 26

With an empty wagon, we are able to make good time even in the weak light of the waning moon. Nate seems to be comfortable and sleeps most of the night. As the sky begins to lighten in the east, I pull the wagon off to the side of the road. Grabbing my canteen, I jump in back and shake Nate awake. He stirs and groans as he tries to sit up. I grab his head and hold the canteen to his lips. He takes a couple of gulps and winces as he swallows. I lay his head back down and pat him on his shoulder.

He reaches out, grabs my hand and says, "Thanks for saving me. Thanks for coming back."

I don't know what to say. I look down at him and fighting back my emotions I say, "Nate, get some rest." Before I release the brake, I take a look back and Nate is fast asleep.

Through the night we passed through Unger's Creek. With the sun up to mid morning height we are not too far from the Johnson's turn off. Nate is stirring in the back of the wagon and is awake enough to ask, "Where are we?"

I tell him, "We are almost to the Johnson's turn off. I think it would be best not to stop there today. I'm going to get you home and then I'll come back and get the load of hay."

Nate thinks he feels good enough to sit up. Moaning and grabbing his side; he manages to rise up and lean his back and head against the front boards of the wagon. He then decides he is capable to sit up in the seat. I try to tell him to lay back down, that it is too soon to sit up, but he is young and stubborn and insists that he is able to sit up front. I slow Molly and Bess to a stop and set the brake. I tell him, "If you're gonna sit up front than at least let me help you."

Once settled and sitting up he looks over at me and says, "I want to stop at the Johnson's today. I'm feeling good enough to get the hay. There's no need for you to have to make a second trip back. We are here now."

I realize it won't do any good to argue with him. When we get to the Johnson's turn off, I turn in, but not before telling him that he looks terrible.

We pull up to the Johnson's house, the dogs are barking, and Lizzy and Michael are waving. Mrs. Johnson is scratching around in her flower beds.

Lizzy comes up to Nate's side of the wagon and with a squeal she asks, "What happened? You're hurt!"

She jumps up on the wagon wheel and is holding Nate's face in her hands even before I can set the brake. Mrs. Johnson is telling her to get down but Lizzy ignores her.

Little Michael is on my side of the wagon as Mr. Johnson comes out of the house yelling at the dogs to stop barking. He looks at Lizzy and tells her to listen to her Mother and get down from there.

I tip my hat to Mrs. Johnson as Mr. Johnson says, "So, you're back. I see you got yourself in a bit of trouble. How bad is he?"

Before I can answer, Nate says, "I'm fine. A couple of men jumped us last night. Jake saved me from getting whipped."

Lizzy has her hand over her mouth and jumps down from the side of the wagon. Mrs. Johnson directs me, "Help me get

Nate down and into the house. I want to take a look at his side."

Mr. Johnson tells me, "Once we get Nate in the house, pull the wagon up to the barn and we'll get the hay loaded."

With Nate being looked after, I return to the wagon to find Michael sitting up in the wagon seat. I tell him to sit still as I pull the wagon around to the back and alongside the barn. I roll up the blankets that where spread out for Nate. Mr. Johnson and I start pitching the loose hay into the open back.

Michael is straddling the top rail of the wagon once again and Mr. Johnson asks me, "So what really happened? You took him into a bar and got yourselves into a bar fight didn't you?"

"No sir, that's not what happened. Nate was jumped, just like he said. I came along just about the time he was gonna get whipped."

Mr. Johnson stops and looks at me saying, "That doesn't make any sense. Who'd want to jump Nate?"

I tell him the entire story starting from what happened at the ferry to how Nate got jumped while I was visiting my ma. I finish with the fact that Mr. Kimble called for the Sheriff and the men that jumped Nate got put in jail.

All Mr. Johnson says to that is, "Well, I'll be. That's some story." Then he says, "I see you got yourself a new hat."

I don't bother to respond. All I can do is shake my head and keep forking hay into the back of the wagon.

Mrs. Johnson insists on feeding us lunch again. Nate looks like he'll survive and has a bit of an appetite. Lizzy won't leave his side. Surprisingly, Mr. Johnson doesn't seem to be anxious having them sit so close together. Both parents seem to sense that these two have feelings for each other.

After our meal, I tend to Molly and Bess and make sure they are ready for the rest of the trip. Nate insists on riding up front. I don't blame him; riding in the back on a pile of loose hay wouldn't be that comfortable.

Once we are back on the road I explain to Nate where I was all afternoon and into the evening. He says he understands that I wanted to see my mother, but doesn't understand why I didn't try to visit her the first time I was back in Ash Fork.

I tell him, "I am still putting the pieces together. When I get some answers and am able to make sense of it, I'll explain it to you. Right now, I'm trying to sort it out myself."

The rest of the afternoon, as we make our way to the ferry, Nate and I replay yesterday's events and string them together. We both agree that the men from the ferry must have seen Nate walking around town, maybe even while they were in the saloon. Once they started drinking, they let their anger fester and decided to find Nate. They probably spotted the wagon and waited til dark to get to him. They must have thought that Nate was by himself and would be an easy mark sense they hadn't seen me.

Nate asks me about my mother, "How old is she and where does she live? Did you see your pa, is he still alive?"

I try to answer each question saying, "Ma is not quite sixty years old. She lives by herself about a block off Main Street and a few blocks west of Shorty's Saloon. I don't know the house number, I was following directions."

"Directions, where did you get directions?"

"I got directions from Flora, the sales clerk at Cooper's Dry

Goods, which by the way, is where I bought my new hat."

Nate looks at me and says, "Oh yeah, nice hat. I hadn't even noticed, sorry Jake."

"Ma used to work at Cooper's for many years until her eye's started going bad. Last time, when we were in town, I walked past Cooper's a couple of times to see if she might still work there. I wasn't ready to go see Ma yet, but knew I would eventually. This trip I decided I had to go see her and got directions to her house from Flora, plus look for a hat."

"So what about your pa, did you find out anything about him?"

"Not much, Ma's not sure exactly where he is. He sends her a letter every other month or so, but lately, there hasn't been a post mark so she lost track of his whereabouts. All she knows is he still works for the railroad."

"How old is he?"

"I'm not sure, I think he was a couple of years older than Ma, so he might be sixty or sixty-one, somewhere in there I suppose. It doesn't much matter. I don't really remember much of him. Even growing up, he was gone all the time."

With a heavy sigh, Nate looks out over the horizon and says in a muffled voice, "Yeah, I've had feelings like that before."

"What do you mean?

"The feelings like you don't really have a pa."

"Not true Nate, you have always had Sam."

Swallowing hard Nate says, "I told you once before, Sam's not my real pa. It's not the same being raised by just anyone, instead of being raised by the pa that brought you into this life. It's just not the same. Don't get me wrong, I love Sam and

I know he loves me, but I kinda picked him. He gave me a safe place to live and has always been there watching out for me."

I look over at Nate and he is staring out, straight ahead. I ask, "So how did you come to get together with Sam? How'd that happen?"

Nate looks at me and says, "I was real young. I don't even know how old exactly. My memory is real foggy. All I really remember is that I was afraid all the time. All I knew was fear and pain. I never knew my ma or my pa. I never got to go outside or nothing. There was an old man and he would feed me just enough to keep me alive and he kept me down in a dark damp cellar. I could hear voices once in awhile and hear footsteps from upstairs, but I never saw anybody else. The old man would bring me food, and he would talk to me and make me repeat words to him."

I interrupt and say, "That was probably so you would be able to at least talk. Sorry Nate, go on."

"He didn't beat me every day or nothing like that, only when I would cry and ask to go outside or when I would complain that I was cold and needed another blanket or something. He always called me Little Bastard. In fact, I thought that was my name. When I got with Sam and he asked me my name, all I could say was something like, Lilastir. I remember Sam asking me over and over again to repeat it. I think he got so tired of me saying the same thing that, he just finally started calling me Nate and that was that."

I can hardly believe what I am hearing, "Nate, I am so sorry that you had to go through that. I just can't imagine. Did you ever know your ma or have any contact with a female?"

Nate looks at me and says, "You know, Jake, I do remember having a woman come down the stairs one time. I don't know if she was my ma or not. She brought me some hot soup and a jacket. The jacket was too big for me, but it was warm. She had a knitted stocking hat and she told me to eat my soup and put the hat on my head. She gave me a hug and told me that once I was done with my soup, to climb the cellar stairs that went to the outside. She said that the cellar door would be heavy but if I pushed real hard it would open and I would be outside. She told me, once outside, that she wanted me to run, run as fast as I could and as soon as I found someone to talk to, I was supposed to tell them that I needed help."

"I can hardly believe what I am hearing. Obviously, you did what she told you to do, right?"

"Like I said, I was really young, but yeah, I did as she told me. I ate my soup and climbed the cellar stairs. I remember that at first, I couldn't make the cellar door budge. I tried and tried until I realized that I was pushing on the side that had the hinges on it. Once I pushed on the middle I was able to get the door to move upwards. I remember the light being so bright that when it first hit my eyes it gave me a pain that felt like someone had poked my eyes with a stick. I let the door shut and I sat there rubbing my eyes. I remember being so excited that I just knew if I tried again I could get the door open enough for me to get out. I tried again, but this time I only opened it just enough to let a little light in and my eyes didn't hurt as bad that time. I pushed again, but I couldn't lift it up high enough from the step I was on, so I held it and kneeled down on the next step up. Once I got my weight under me, I pushed again and the door opened a little wider. My heart was pounding so hard that I thought my ears where going to beat right off the side of my head. I thought for sure that's why the lady had given me that stocking hat to wear."

I let out a laugh at that. What else would a little kid that hadn't been taught anything think?

"What, what's so funny?"

"Nothing Nate, I just love the logic, that's all, please go on. What happened next?"

Nate goes on saying, "I never did get the cellar door completely open, but I did manage to get it open enough to wiggle my body out between the steps and the door. Once outside, I did exactly like the lady told me. I ran and ran, but I didn't know where I was running to. I ended up running down the alleys. I was so scared I didn't want to stop to talk to anyone. I ran until I got to what turned out to be Sam's wagon. It was in the alley behind the old general store and it had a tarp over the back of it. I hid behind a fence and didn't see anyone moving around. I remember being so scared I just knew I had to ran to that wagon and climb up under the tarp. Sam didn't know I was there until he got back to Fletcher's Crossing."

Shaking my head I ask, "What did Sam do then?"

"When he pulled the tarp back he just looked at me and said, "Well, well, what do we have here? What's your name boy? Like I said, all I could say was Lilastir. He could tell that I was scared and hadn't been treated right. He picked me up and took me in. I've been with him ever since, even before Judith came to be with us."

Nate finishes his story just before we turn down to the road that leads to the ferry crossing. I am in shock and can hardly breathe. With what I have just heard and what my ma told me, I am sick to my stomach. My head is swimming with thoughts and my mind is screaming out, could this be? It can't be.

As we roll down the hill towards the river's edge, I look to Nate and tell him, "Nate, I am truly sorry for your pain and all the suffering you had to go through. Our Good Lord must have looked down on you with favor and taken care of you. I do believe that Sam was, has been, a guardian angel sent to watch over you."

Nate looks over at me and says, "I don't know about that, Jake. I just know that I was glad to be out of that cellar. I guess that's why I like being outdoors so much." We look out over the river and say to each other, "Looks like Red is just about ready to make a crossing."

Chapter 27

Before the ferry leaves the north side of the river, Red or one of his men must have yelled to Sam and Judith that we where back and on the south bank waiting to cross. Rusty ran down and jumped on the ferry just before Red had the ramp raised and gave the order to push off.

Nate mutters half out loud, "Judith will be fussing over me something awful. She probably won't let me do any work for a few days."

"It would be best for you to take it easy. You gotta let those ribs heal. You'll be sore for awhile, besides, it's not a bad thing to have a woman fuss over you every once in a while."

Nate answers me with a "humph" and mutters something like, "We'll see."

Red pulls the ferry up to the south bank and lowers the ramp. Rusty is the first off, running past the wagon and folks that just came across. He runs between Molly and Bess's legs barking and wagging his tail. Knowing the unloading of one wagon and loading our wagon will take awhile, I jump down and give Rusty a rub and a pat. He is confused when Nate doesn't get down off the wagon to say hello. He whimpers and whines so I give him a boost up into the seat. Rusty is all over Nate in an instant. He is too excited for Nate to control. In between groans of pain and weak attempts of laughter, Nate is only able to tell Rusty to calm down.

We finally get Rusty settled down and he is sitting between

us as I acknowledge Red's order to bring the wagon on board. I release the brake and give a gentle snap of the reins along with a sharp whistle. The horses respond and pull the wagon slowly onto the ramp. There is a bit of an uneven transition between dirt road, to ramp, to ferry deck, but I keep the reins tight and my right foot resting on the brake just in case something should spook the horses.

With the wagon squarely on the deck and after a long sigh, Nate says, "Nice job, Jake. Not bad for the first time loading this big old wagon."

I look at him and say, "Thanks, Nate."

Red gives the order to chock the wheels and comes over to the side of the wagon. He inquires about Nate, asking, "You don't look so good, Nate, what the heck happened? Get into a little bar fight this time in town?"

We both start to talk at the same time, but I stop and let Nate answer, "No, Red. It wasn't a bar fight. Remember those men that came through here a few days back?"

"Sure do, don't tell me you boys ran into them on the road?"

Nate shakes his head and says, "No, not on the road, in town. These two guys came to where I was at behind Mr. Kimble's and jumped me. Jake came just in time to save me from getting horse whipped by one of them."

Red looks up at me and shakes his head with a stern look on his face and says, "Mister, you better not have been drinking and leaving Nate to fend for himself."

Before I can answer, Nate tells Red that I had been to visit my ma and I got back just in time to save him. Red gives the order to shove off from the ramp area. Before he goes to the wheel he looks up at me and says, "If I find out different from what Nate says, I'll come and horse whip you myself."

Nate says as Red turns away, "It's true, Red. Jake got back just in time and those fellers got put in jail, honest."

Red releases some steam and blows the whistle as the ferry pulls from shore headed up river, against the current.

The ferry eases into the north shore ramp area and Red's crew goes through the process of securing the ferry to the pylons. Once tied off, Red gives the order to drop the ramp. Molly and Bess are anxious to move off the ferry and get up the hill to the barn. We've had a long trip and I pushed them hard. The hay doesn't weigh as much as the cord wood, but I didn't stop much and they didn't get an overnight rest.

As the team pulls the wagon off the ferry, I don't let them slow down or even come to a stop; I just tip my hat to Judith and Sam and snap the reins hard as I work them up the hill to the barn. Judith notices Nate's black eye and swollen nose. She tries to make me pull up and yells at Sam to make me stop. I act like I don't hear either one of them and keep the team moving.

Nate looks back and then says, "Judith is going to be as mad as a hornet in August at you for not stopping."

"She'll get over it once she hears the whole story. I want to get Molly and Bess unhitched from this wagon. They have pulled enough. Judith can wait."

As we pass by the back of the house, it dawns on me that if I don't stop here, Nate will have to walk back. So I ask, "Nate, you want me to stop here? If not, you'll have to walk back from the barn."

"No, I'm alright, I can walk. Thanks for asking."

I pull the wagon up to the front of the barn door and give the reins a tug. Molly and Bess stop and shake with approval. Rusty jumps off the seat with a little coaxing from Nate. Before Nate can swing his legs down over the front wheel, Judith is at the side of the wagon. With her arms extended up to Nate, she grabs at him only to hit his sore ribs.

Nate lets out a yell, "Hold on, Judith. Let me get down myself."

Well, he can't get his legs to cooperate and Judith doesn't know how to grab him, so I walk around the wagon and let Nate put his arm around my neck. I grab him by his lower waist and ease him down to the ground.

Sam comes up to the wagon just as Judith lays into me for allowing Nate to get hurt. Sam stops her and says, "There will be plenty of time for all that later. We need to get Nate in the house and get him comfortable. Besides, I think you might owe Jake an apology, maybe even a thank you. Nate explained to Red what happened and Red passed it on to me. He says Jake actually might have saved Nate's life."

Judith turns as she is holding onto Nate and walks him towards the back the house saying, "We'll see about that."

Sam looks at me, shrugs his shoulders and says, "Sorry about that, Jake. You'll have to forgive Judith, she don't mean nothing. She just goes off once in awhile, especially when it comes to Nate. She's been acting strange these past couple of days. I can't figure her out...Women!"

I look at Sam and tell him, "It's okay, I understand. How

about we get this wagon unloaded?"

"Sure thing."

Chapter 28

We use a canvas sling to get the loose hay up into the barn loft. Once that is done, I take my pack filled with my new clothes and my bow and arrows up to the loft and set them on my bed. I then take Nate's belongings and rifle to the back porch. After that, I pull the wagon up to the back of the barn where I am finally able to unhitch Molly and Bess. I let them drink at the trough while I grab the brushes. While brushing them down, I give them both a nice helping of oats. I check their hooves and grab three apples from the root cellar before I lead them up to the meadow.

Once we are at the meadow's gate, I stop and cut two of the apples in half giving each of them one half at a time. Before they even get finished with chewing, Gus comes up with ears perked, knowing that he will be next. I lead Molly and Bess through the gate and then cut the third apple in half. Gus is not as comfortable with me as Molly and Bess have become. I have to coax him closer with a gentle, "Come here boy. It's okay. Come on."

I reach out my hand letting him get a good whiff of my scent. He stops short, jerks his head back, bobbing it up and down a couple of times and then steps back even further. He stands there with drool leaking out his muzzle wanting to take the apple from my hand. I just stand there and tell him, "It's your move. I won't hurt you."

He stomps his front hoof and paws some dirt. He drops his head a bit, and then stretches his neck out to my hand. With his nimble lips he grabs the half apple and jerks his head up. As he is munching on that I reach out and let him smell me again. He doesn't shy away this time. He lets me rub the back of my hand up and down his forehead. He steps closer and nudges his nose into my other hand. I don't want him to think I am teasing him, so I give him the second half of the apple.

From behind me I hear Sam's voice, "Looks like 'ol Gus has taken a liking to you. He doesn't let anyone but me and Nate get close to him. In fact, my whole family has taken a liking to you, Jacob Sparks. You've worked your way in here pretty damn good."

I turn and look at Sam as he walks towards me. I am trying to read his mood. I can't tell if what he just said was a compliment or if he just threatened me. Before I am able to say anything, Daisy comes up to the fence with her calf bouncing alongside of her. As soon as she stops, the little guy nestles up under her crying and poking around looking for a tit to suckle.

With a smile I turn to Sam and say, "Looks like you had your hands full while we were gone. Congratulations on the new little calf. I take it everything went well?"

Sam pushes his hat back on his head and says, "Yeah, we sure did. Daisy did real good. Judith and I got her into the barn just after you and Nate left for town and by night fall she had dropped her calf."

"Did you name him yet?"

"Yeah, we did. We thought we'd call the little guy Sparky, kinda after you and your run in with Brutus."

Laughing, I say, "Yeah, rub it in. Sparky the Bull, maybe he won't be as mean as Brutus."

I stand there asking myself if I should pursue Sam's earlier comment or not. Before I can stop myself, I fumble for the right words and say, "You know Sam, my life's been a topsy-turvy mess for most of it. I done a lot of things I'm not proud of and I've hurt a lot of folks that have been close to me along the way."

Sam stops me and says, "Look, Jake, you seem like you've got something on your mind. If this is about what happened in town, Judith and I can't thank you enough for being there. You may have saved Nate's life. No need to go on about it. Those men were trouble from the start."

"No, Sam, let me finish."

Sam backs off and says, "Alright, Jake, alright."

"Like I was saying, I've hurt some folks and done some bad things. I've tried to make amends with those I've hurt and I've tried to make sure I always paid restitution for anything I did that cost money to fix. I'm sure there are things I didn't make completely right and I'll probably pay the price for those mistakes once my days here on earth are finished, but I tell you this, I have not meant any harm or had any unhealthy thoughts for you and your family. I am sorry Nate got jumped. You say I saved Nate, but Sam, if anything, being here has saved me. I stumbled into your life..., what was it, two weeks ago..., and you have done nothing but treat me like family. I only hope I haven't done anything but return your kindness with the same. I'm not trying to work my way into anything."

Sam looks at me and says, "Let's take a walk you and me. I think it's time you and I had a heart to heart."

We walk along the fence line and turn up towards the

aspens. I let Sam say what's on his mind, "Jake, I've been living here a long time and seen a lot of men come through here. Some are just passing through knowing where they've come from and where they're headed to next. Some men have been trouble makers, some have been thieves, some have tried to push their way in hoping to get a piece of this place, hell, some have had eyes for Judith. Through it all, I've managed to run 'em all off..., and then you come along. You have a way about you, Jake, that seems to put folks at ease. You never seem to struggle with the truth. You seem to have a good heart and you want to share the good that is in your heart. To be honest, I've never met a man like you."

Brutus gives us a snort and scuffs dirt up into the air as we walk past him. Once again, I am thankful for the fence that keeps us separated.

"I appreciate you saying all that Sam, but I can say the same about you. You are kind, you share and you are honest. But Sam, you are settled, you have this place and you know your place in this life and you just live. You have kept your life simple."

"Jake, this life was given to me. I've just continued what my pa and ma started. Most of this was all here, it was all set up for me. Sure I've grown it some, I guess you could say I'm successful. I've got some money, the land here at the crossing is paid for, the ferry is paid for, we've got everything we need, but Jake, you have something I'll never have."

"What's that?"

"Freedom Jake, you've got your freedom."

"Freedom, what the hell does that mean? Good God man,

you're free!"

As we get to the aspen grove, Sam says, "I know I have freedom, but not like you. You can come and go as you please; you traveled and met folks from other parts of this country. Sometimes that way of life can be appealing to folks and cause confusion, make 'em question the way they've been living."

"Sam, it seems like we both have things on our minds. What are you trying to say?"

We walk up to the top of the aspen grove, Sam remarks, "I've always liked the view from up here. It's been a good while since I was up here last."

I tell him, "I agree; it is a view that a man might never get tired of seeing." Then I ask, "What is it Sam, tell me what's eating at you?"

He looks at me and says, "It's you, Jake. I think Judith cares for you more than a married woman should."

I walk under the canopy of the aspen and sit down trying to catch my breath. Once again my mind is racing and I can't believe what Sam has just told me. I realize he is not saying Judith is in love with me, he is merely thinking she has strong feelings for me.

"Sam! What are you saying? Do you even know what you are saying? Where is this coming from? I can't believe this. Here I am trying to sort out my own life and you come at me with this. I don't understand."

Sam comes over to where I am sitting and says, "What, don't you feel the same way?"

"No, no I don't. How could you even think like that? She is so committed to you and Nate. Having you think anything other than that is ridiculous."

"It's obvious that she feels something for you. The day before you and Nate were leaving for town and you were not acting yourself, well she wasn't either. She hasn't had a good night sleep for almost a week. She wakes up tossing and turning. Jake, you've been upset and so has she. What am I supposed to think?"

I sit there in disbelief trying to calm myself and gather my thoughts. "Look Sam, you're right, I haven't been myself these past few days. I haven't been sleeping very good either, but I don't think, in fact, I know that not being able to sleep has anything to do with Judith. I have some things I have to sort out from my life before I left Ash Fork. Those things are what have been making me feel out of sorts, not Judith."

"Are you sure, Jake? Judith and Nate are all I have. I love this land, I surely do, but if I ever lost Judith and the boy, my life would cease to exist."

I reach out my hand to Sam, I stand up and say, "You have everything, guard it with your life. Don't ever think of me in that way again, ever. I promise you Sam, I'll do everything I can do to help you protect your life here and your family."

I have only hugged one other man in my life until now, and that was Chief. As Sam and I stood in the aspen grove hugging each other, I prayed to God to help me with my promise to protect Sam's family. In the same breath I ask forgiveness for the lie I just told, the lie that Judith hadn't been part of the reason for me being out of sorts.

Chapter 29

Sam and I walk down away from the aspen grove, past the meadow, and towards the house. I am not one hundred percent sure that Sam is convinced that his suspicions are false. I know in my heart, that I am missing a piece of truth that is needed to help me understand what has been going on. As much as I don't want it to be true, I am afraid that the missing piece I need, does in fact, involve Judith. Deep down inside I know the truth. I just need the courage to face it.

With a sudden flash of fear I know what I need to do. I am too close to this situation, I need to leave. Before we get to the house, I hesitate at the barn and say to Sam, "Sam, I've been giving this some thought lately. I think I am going to ask Mr. Meijer if I can help him build his barn. I could use the steady work."

"You have steady work here."

"It's not carpentry work Sam, I'm a carpenter. Mr. Meijer just might need some steady help."

"Jake, you're just doing this because of what we just talked about, aren't you?"

"No Sam, I'm not. I was going to tell you once we got back from town regardless of what we just talked about. Honest."

"I don't believe you. Sorry, Jake, but hey, if that's what you want to do, who am I to stop you. Like I said earlier, you've got your freedom."

This is not the way I wanted this to go, "Sam, now that Nate is hurt, I'll stay and help until he is on his feet. I'll head up to the stock piles and cut and chop cord wood and haul it down so you have ferry, camp and house wood."

"We don't need your help."

"Sam, don't get mad, look, you know as well I do, that this will be the best for all of us. I'll only be up the road a couple miles or so. I just need to do what I love doing and that's building things."

Sam walks off in a huff, "Suit yourself."

I let him go, I think I know him well enough, he'll go off by himself and once he thinks it through, he'll be fine. I decide to go down to the river for a swim and a bath.

I try to get Rusty to come with me, but Rusty won't come off the back porch, he is vigilant as he waits for Nate's recovery. When I get back from the river, I go through my regular routine of hanging out my washed clothes, but this time I hang them over a rope I tied up.

I decide to wear my new pants and shirt and head down to the house to check on Nate. Rusty is not on the back porch and there isn't any activity as I pass by the kitchen window. I walk around to the front porch and find all three plus Rusty sitting, enjoying the view. No one is talking as I make my way towards the steps. Interrupting the quiet I ask Nate, "How're you feeling?"

"Better."

Judith says, "There is some stew on the stove if you are hungry."

"Thank you, but I'm not hungry this evening."

Judith surprises me by asking, "Sam tells us that you are going to leave us. You're going to go build a barn for that young family up the river?"

"That's what I've been thinking. I haven't really worked out all the details yet. I still need to talk to Mr. Meijer about it, but yes, that's what I would like to do. I miss building."

Judith says, "It's been a pleasure, Mr. Sparks, just let us know when you decide."

Sam stands and says he is going to go check on the ferry. Nate is slow to stand up and says he is going to go lay down. Judith and I are left sitting on the porch by ourselves. She stands and asks if I would like a cup of coffee, I tell her that would be nice if it's no bother. She says she was getting one for herself, it's no bother.

While Judith goes to get the coffee, I move over to the chair that Nate was sitting in. Judith comes out and hands me the steaming cup. Sitting down she looks my way and says, "You sure upset Sam and Nate."

"Yeah, it isn't easy for me either, but if I can be building something, I'd rather spend my time doing that. Besides, like Sam said, he and Nate have been handling the wood operation way before I got here. I am sure they'll be fine. Did Sam tell you that I'll stay until Nate gets back on his feet?"

"Yes he did."

I take a sip of coffee and then Judith says, "I must thank you for being there for Nate. He told us everything that you did and I was wrong to jump to conclusions earlier, I apologize."

"I should have never let it happen. If I hadn't...." I stop mid-sentence, not wanting to finish it.

Judith looks at me and says, "Go on Jake, please finish what you were saying."

I hesitate and then say, "If I hadn't been wandering the streets...I guess I lost track of time. I should've gotten back sooner. It's me that should be apologizing to Nate."

Judith stands up, looks at me, and straightens her dress and apron saying, "Jacob Sparks, you aren't a good liar."

I stand up and reach out trying to grab her arm. Judith goes through the screen door before I can stop her. Turning she says to me, "Don't touch me, don't you dare!"

As she is closing the screen door, I say, "Carolynn, we have to talk!"

I set my half filled cup down on the arm of the chair. I tell myself that I had no right to say that. I admonish myself for calling her Carolynn. I know in my heart that it is true, but I have no proof. I step off the porch into the darkness of the night.

The ground is dimly lit by the slanted light coming from the windows. As I get to the back porch, I turn my head to see that the back door is open, exposing Judith's silhouette. I take my hat off, turn towards her and say, "We need to talk."

"Carolynn is dead; she died a long time ago."

Part Four

Freedoms

Chapter 30

I make my way through the darkness of the waning moonlight, into the barn and up the ladder to the loft. I am exhausted after being up for the past two days. As I kick off my boots and strip off my clothes, I hope I will be able to fall asleep quickly. Out of habit, I search through my pack fumbling around for "Lady Liberty". With relief, I say half out loud, "At least you're still with me." I shove my bowie knife under my makeshift pillow and put one throwing knife on the floor next to my right boot and the other knife on the shelf above my head. There is a slight breeze that helps move the air through the loft which is scented by the fragrance of the fresh hay. The night has the makings for a perfect sleep. My only hope is that I will be able to quiet my mind. Taking in deep breaths, I tell myself to relax and just sleep. There will be plenty of time to sort out these past few days later. I have the rest of my life and I have my freedom. Ha! That's what Sam thinks. I am more bound up right now, at this very moment, than I have ever been. I roll over on my side, telling myself, "Don't do this, not now, just breathe."

I wake up not knowing how long I've been asleep. My hip is numb and I have to pee, must've been that last cup of coffee. I get up and try to climb down the ladder but with my hip still not moving correctly, it forces me to take my time. By the time I am at the bottom rung I decide there is no need to walk all the way to the outhouse. I simply step outside and relieve myself on a nearby cluster of weeds.

With my hip and mind now fully awake, I climb back up the ladder. All I can think about is that last cup of coffee. Why did I call her Carolynn? Even though every fiber of my being knows it to be true, I can't prove it, Judith denied it...or did she?

In angst, I shake my head hoping to dislodge my thoughts. I lay back down, but cannot get comfortable. I toss and turn, trying everything, telling myself anything in hopes that I will be able to calm my mind and fall back to sleep. Could it be that I've been sleeping on the ground for so long that having a bed is a luxury I can do without? This corn husk mattress isn't all that comfortable anyway, so I get up and throw my bedroll on the floor, hoping that something solid is what I need to help me sleep. I begin to drift off only to have my hip start to go numb again. I roll over giving my other side a try, but to no avail, the floor is just too hard. I get up and throw my bedroll back on top of the mattress.

Before I lay back down, I walk over to the loft doors and realize that I hadn't slept that long at all. There is a lamp still burning bright in the one of the downstairs windows. I wonder to myself who is still up at the Harris's and suddenly I begin to feel very sad. I shouldn't have stopped here. Why didn't I just keep on walking, board the ferry, and go to Ash Fork like I had meant to. I seem to be able to cause trouble without even trying. Everything was going so good. If I just hadn't noticed that beauty mark on Judith's lower neck.

Damn! I know I won't be able to sleep now. I throw on my pants, shirt, and boots. I grab my hat and knife, and head towards the ladder. Before I get to the first rung, I turn back, pull my harmonica out of my pack and slide it into my pocket.

I certainly don't want to go anywhere towards the house, so I head up towards the meadow. It is a pleasant evening and I can faintly hear the current of the river as the water moves through the rapids. Before I even get to the fence line at the meadow, Molly and Bess have picked up my scent and are slowly walking over towards the gate. As I get closer, I apologize for not bringing any apples. They both give me a snort and a head bob, how can I refuse a welcome like that? I go over and give them both a good head rub and scratch under their muzzles. With a sigh I say out loud, "If you only knew the trouble I've caused this time, girls."

I slowly turn and walk towards the road that leads to the logging area. Without a lantern it's hard to see exactly where I am walking. I begin to feel a little light headed probably due to the lack of sleep. I question what it is I am doing and decide to turn around and make my way back to the barn.

Remembering my harmonica, I pull it out and gently put it to my mouth. I wet the holes with my tongue and softly play the song I wrote for Beth. I quietly sing the words and before I realize it, I am back at the barn. After climbing up to the loft, I look out the double loft doors and notice the lamp, which was burning earlier, is now out. Feeling more relaxed this time, I get undressed and lay back down on the bed. With a deep breath my head settles in and I feel my mind and body relax.

•

The loft is in full sunlight when I finally open my eyes. I can hear Rusty barking at something down by the river's edge and the air smells like coffee and bacon. I throw my clothes on and grab my hat and knives. Before I head down the ladder, I look out the loft doors and see a whisper of smoke coming out of the house chimney. It looks like Sam and Nate are walking back up from the ferry.

I climb down the ladder and head to the water pump to wet my face and head before I go to the house. Sam and Nate both wave my way as Rusty comes running and stands up on his hind legs. I tussle with him a bit and tell him it's sure good to see him. He does a couple of quick circles and then runs back down to Sam and Nate. As the three of us approach each other, Judith comes out on the front porch and yells to us that lunch is ready.

"Lunch...How long did I sleep?" I ask.

Sam answers, "It's close to half day. You musta been out cold."

Nate says, "We didn't sleep for two days. Well, I guess Jake didn't, he drove the wagon all night while I got some sleep."

I comment, "If you can call lying in the back of the wagon, being all busted up, sleeping, than I guess you slept some."

Sam goes, "Well, whatever you call it, you both deserved to sleep as long as you did."

Turning towards Nate I ask, "So, Nate, does that mean you just got up also?"

Nate answers, "I got up a little bit ahead of you. I missed morning milking and hauling wood."

Then I ask, "Have you seen the new calf?"

With an excited voice Nate says to Sam, "Daisy had her calf? What is it? What's it look like? How's Daisy?"

Sam answers all four questions, "Yeah, Daisy had her calf, a little bull calf, red with a white face and one white sock. Daisy is just fine. Maybe after we eat, if you feel up to it, we can walk up and you can meet Sparky."

"Sparky, is that his name? You named him already?" asks Nate.

"Yeah, Judith named him. She thought it was fitting and hopefully he'll have a little of Brutus's fire." Sam says.

Out of the corner of his eye, Sam looks my way. I ignore the look hoping the mood from yesterday has been diluted. Things seem almost back to normal, I'd like to see them stay that way. Hopefully Judith's mood is back to normal as well.

To my surprise, the table is set special again with a table cloth, a vase of wild flowers, and napkins. Even though it is lunch time, Judith has cooked up a breakfast of fried eggs, bacon and fresh bread.

She tells us, "If you're washed up, you can all sit down."

She looks much like she did the day after the fight we had in the camp area. Her hair is down and she has on the same kind of low fitting blouse. I fight back the thoughts that try to creep into my head. I have to trust that she is just being Judith and is not trying to send me a message of any sort. Why would she? I tell myself that all the emotions I have been feeling have got to be self induced. I have to let it go.

Without even realizing it, we are all holding hands and the three of them are looking at me. Judith is saying, "Jacob, are you listening? Please, can you say grace this morning? You won't be with us much longer. Please, we'd be honored."

With that I clear my throat and begin, "How bout we all say the Lord's Prayer this morning? All of us, together."

The three of them are silent, so I ask, "You do know it, don't you? You know, the Our Father?" Again I get nothing, so I ask, "Do you want me to start it?"

Without wasting another moment I start, "Our Father, who art in Heaven...." By the time I get any further into the prayer, all four of us are saying the Lord's Prayer in unison.

As we finish with the Amen, Nate says, "That was nice, we never pray like that, together I mean, all at once."

We sit through a quiet meal, no one having much to say. I push my chair back from the table saying, "Sorry for sleeping half the day away. I'll head up to the logging area and chop some wood, if that's okay."

Sam tells me, "It won't be necessary today. We have a big enough stock pile."

Nate interrupts with, "If you wait one more day, I'll be able to help."

Sam looks at him and says, "We'll see, those ribs may take a day or two longer."

Judith starts to clear the table but not before offering more coffee. She tells us, "Go out to the porch if you would like, I'll do up these dishes." Naturally, Nate offers to help, but Judith declines telling him, "You will have to wait one more day, even to help with the dishes."

He lets out a groan and says, "I'm fine now, I'm not a baby," to which we all give a chuckle.

Once out on the porch I ask Sam, "Is everything alright?"

He says, "It is. I've had time to think about things and I agree that it is probably best that you move on. Nate and I talked about it before you came down this morning and Nate feels okay about you leaving."

Nate just nods and says, "It's been nice having the company riding back and forth into town, but I understand that you'd rather be doing carpenter work."

I tell him, "Nate, I've enjoyed the riding back and forth as well. I appreciate that you understand my desire to go work on a building." Then I say to both of them, "It's not like I'm going away, I'll just be up the road. I think Mr. Winkler said that the Meijer place is about two to three miles east of here. If you all don't mind, I'd like to come and visit once in awhile?"

At that, Judith comes out the screen door and sits down next to Sam. She reaches for his hand and says, "Jacob, we certainly hope that you do come by and visit every now and again."

Before I get up to leave I ask Sam, "I need a favor. Would it be alright if I rode Bess to the Meijer place so I could make arrangements for work?"

"Yeah, sure. There is a saddle and tack in the barn."

"Well then, I'd like to get going." I tip my hat as I step off the porch and thank Judith again for the delicious meal.

Nate asks if he can ride along and all three of us say at the same time, "NO!"

I walk up through the barn, gather my canteen and get my bow and arrow. I decide not to grab my whole bedroll, knowing that I should be back before dark. I reach down in my pack, grab "Lady Liberty" and my jacket and head up to get Bess. Before leaving the barn, I grab bridal, bit and reins and throw a heavy horse blanket over my shoulder. I decide against putting a saddle on her. I anticipate it to be a fairly easy ride.

I head up to the meadow to get Bess. My emotions seem to be in check. Sam, Judith and Nate seemed to be in much better spirits today, so maybe it's just been me. Is it possible that I was just out of my mind tired and overly sensitive? Could I have misunderstood Sam's concerns? Am I totally wrong with my assumptions about Judith? Have I been reading everyone's emotions incorrectly? I have always felt like I have had a gift to understand the unspoken feelings of others. This gift has served me well at times and other times, not so well. When trying to explain this ability to others I have called it a gift and a curse at the same time.

Maybe that's all that has happened. This has been one of those times that I have misread the situation and I've been wrong about everything.

Seeing Bess in the meadow shakes me from my thoughts. With a heavy sigh I tell myself to clear my head and stop over thinking all that has happened. I need to let it go and just get back to living free. It's all been a big mistake, a big misunderstanding and even a bigger coincidence.

Bess smells the tack and horse blanket and whinnies with approval. I open the gate, grab her by her halter and pull her out, shutting the gate behind me. We have Molly and Gus's attention as they saunter over to the fence rail. I don't know horse talk, but it is evident that these three are not separated from each other very often, especially Molly and Bess. Molly usually gets the attention and she lets me know that I have made a mistake by getting Bess ready for a ride. She is shaking her head back and forth and kicks up dirt behind her. Gus has lost interest and moves away from the fence. Molly studies my every move. I mount Bess and we walk along the outside of the fence going east. Molly follows along until the corner of the meadow stops her. With a head bob and a snort we hear Molly's last attempt to protest. Bess twitches her tail and nickers back as we break into a gentle trot headed towards North River Road.

If I remember correctly, the turn off to the Meijer place is Holland Road. I hope the road is clearly marked. Out here in open country, most of the least traveled roads don't have signs. Most folks give directions by landmarks. The only thing I recall Mr. Winkler saying is Holland Road.

North River Road seems to be well traveled. It is worn and well defined but not deeply rutted by heavy wagons. It is much like the South River Road we take when we go to Ash Fork. It's hard for me to imagine but from what folks say, most of these roads will be used by those horseless carriages someday. I've seen quite a few in my day, not too many in this open country, but one or two in Ash Fork. There were a lot of horseless machines in Portland. Big city that Portland; it has brick and cobble paved streets. Most of the downtown area has brick sidewalks that are lined with gas and candle street lamps. Course, I hear, Portland is small compared to San Francisco. I hear San Francisco has ocean going steamers from all over the world that make port there. I have never been to San Francisco, maybe someday I'll get there. Talking to Bess I say, "How 'bout you Bess, how'd you like to go see San Francisco?" All I get from her is a perk up of her ears as she hears her name.

The road winds up and away from the river basin. Periodically, I catch glimpses of the moving water through scattered stands of heavy timber mixed with open fields of scrub brush. There are farms spread out on both sides of the road that utilize the abundant supply of water and southern exposure to the sun. Some of the fields have been worked, the fresh soil turned and planted, while others lay fallow for this growing season. The thought crosses my mind and I question if I ever would have been happy living in one place, being a farmer or doing what Sam is doing. It doesn't take me long to answer and dismiss that thought with an emphatic no. If I remember right, I think Chief and I discussed that very same topic more than a time or two. The answer always came up the same, "Freedom of the road." I guess Sam was right, I have had a certain kind of freedom. I pull up Bess as I see a weathered sign that has "Holland Road" carved into bleached grey wood. I give Bess a pat on her neck, saying, "Let's go girl, I sure hope I know what I'm doing."

Chapter 31

The road has a slight incline up and away from the river. The land is open, cleared of rocks, scrub and timber. The land rises up to a flat area and then continues terracing up towards a bluff. As Bess and I follow the slow rising road we get to a flattened area and see a large farm house that is nestled in against some large shade trees. Instead of rows of wheat, hay or oats, the land is laid out in rows of apple trees in various heights of growth. At the top ends of the fields, there are three large wind mills that have their blades turned into the breeze and are rotating freely. As Bess and I get closer to the house, there are flower beds growing next to the house and a large vegetable garden that is positioned to take advantage of every minute of sunshine.

Two blonde haired kids are in the front yard. A boy is swinging on a rope that is tied up into one of the trees and a girl, who appears to be the older of the two, stands behind him to give him a push. She notices me and Bess, stops the boy's momentum and yells to her mother. I bring Bess up slowly, tip my hat, telling the girl, "Howdy, my name is Jacob Sparks and I am here to speak to your father." She lifts her brother off the rope and holds his hand as they run into the house.

It doesn't take long, for what I have to assume is Mrs. Meijer, to come to the front door. With her heavy accent, she asks me if she can help me. I introduce myself again and explain to her that I am from Fletcher's Crossing and would like to talk to her husband about possibly finding a job. She wipes her hands on her apron and tells the girl to go out back and ring the bell. I am not sure if she thinks she is in danger or if she just wants her husband to know that there is a stranger at the house. While we are waiting, I ask her if it would be alright for me to climb down off my horse and tie Bess to the nearby fence that surrounds the garden. She nods her head yes and gestures towards the fence.

From what I can tell, the fields, the area around the house, the gardens and even the barn, are as neat and clean as I have ever seen. The house is painted white with green trim and the barn is painted red with white trim. There are smaller out buildings that are painted to match either the house or the barn. The three windmills are built strong and sturdy, with shafts that are attached to pumps that have large outlet pipes running to the top edges of the orchards. Every tool, every wagon and every farm implement is stacked, stored and set in a designated place.

It's only a matter of minutes before a buckboard wagon comes pulling up to the back of the house. There are two men sitting on the wagon, both blonde haired with beards. I recognize the one driving to be Mr. Meijer, the other looks like he is his brother, if not his twin. They both jump down and make their way over to me, neither one removes his hat.

I walk towards them with my outstretched hand and say, "Mr. Meijer, I am Mr. Sparks. I spoke to you the other day at the ferry about possibly getting a job with you. Do you recall?"

"Yaw, Yaw I do. I didn't think you were serious. I remember being in a hurry. You are here now so, what do you think you can do to help me?"

"Well, I was told that you were building a barn, I'm a carpenter and a darn good one. I'm just down the road and if you are in need of a good carpenter, then I can be available to help." Neither one seems to be eager to respond. In fact, the other one hasn't said a word. "What do you think?"

Mr. Meijer turns to the other man and they walk out of listening range. When they return, Mr. Meijer puts out his hand and says, "My name is Conrad Meijer, this is my brother, Walter. He doesn't speak very good English, so I will speak for him. We don't have money to pay you, so I don't think it would work out for you."

I walk towards Walter, extend my hand and introduce myself, not caring if he can't understand me. I know he does though, he shakes my hand and with a big smile he repeats my name in English.

Conrad says, "Mr. Sparks, we don't have money to pay you, we are sorry."

I say, "Look, why don't you show me what you are building and we can talk about it. What do you have to lose? Besides, I am curious why you need another barn. You have a beautiful barn already."

Conrad says, "Apples, we grow apples."

"Yeah, I saw the starting of an orchard coming up the road, but why another barn?"

"We need storage, we want to grow lots and lots of apples and sell them back east. We will need to store them and then get them to Ash Fork. Once we get them there, the railroad will ship them back east."

"Oh, so you will build an open air, cold storage type barn

to be able to store them long enough to ship them through the winter?"

Shaking his head Conrad says, "Yaw, this is correct."

I tell them both that they have a beautiful farm and we begin to walk around the barn and corral area. The Meijer's have the usual assortment of milk cows and horses. They have a small pasture with goats and sheep. There are chickens running around the back of the house. In fact, there are chickens everywhere. Looking up towards the bluff, I notice another farm house further up the road. I point to it and ask, "Who owns that house? Do you have a neighbor?"

Walter says, "My house, my family."

Conrad explains that Walter has two sons, ten and twelve and they are out in a new area getting it ready for new seedlings to be planted.

We continue to walk up past the barn and stop at the leveled out building area. There are stacks of lumber that are separated into piles by size and length. This must have been where the Meijer brothers had been working earlier. There are string lines tied to stakes that are hammered into the ground at the four outside corners of a building. The outside dimensions are stepped off to be, twenty feet by sixty feet. I ask the height the ridge line will be and Mr. Meijer tells me the roof will be at least twenty-five feet at the peak.

As we turn and walk back towards the house and alongside the corral, I notice that there is what looks like a two year old colt standing behind three other horses; two of the three are a matched set of draft horses. The colt is a beautiful silver and grey with a speckled rump, three dark socks and a white spot on his forehead. I walk over to the fence to get a closer look, he doesn't shy away, but he won't come closer to the fence either. He stays huddled next to the other three but remains curious. He holds his head high. His ears are perked and his nostrils are flared.

Before we get to the house, I say to Mr. Meijer, "How bout we make a deal. I know you said you had no money, how about, room and board and that two year old grey?"

Mr. Meijer doesn't say anything. We just continue to walk while he and Walter speak in Dutch to each other.

We get out to the front yard where Bess has been tied, he puts out his hand, and says, "Good. When can you start?"

I shake Conrad's hand and then Walter's hand saying, "I can be back in the morning."

Walter is grinning and shaking his head saying, "Good, this is good."

Before I leave I ask, "Mr. Meijer, where has your family come from and how long have you been living here?"

Mr. Meijer says, "We are from the Pennsylvania Dutch country. This is our fifth year here in this area." He reaches out his hand again and says, "Call me Conrad."

"You've come far in five years." I grab a hold of Bess's mane and swing up onto her back. Tipping my hat to Conrad and Walter, I tell them, "Thank you, I'll see you tomorrow."

Chapter 32

Bess and I head down Holland Road which is actually nothing more than the way to get up to the Meijer's house. I chuckle to myself with the thought of Pennsylvania Dutch living on Holland Road. Maybe Conrad has a sense of humor? Maybe he has plans to have more of his kinfolk move out this way making Holland Road the main turn off to his own little settlement. One thing's for sure, that farm is the tidiest and cleanest farm I have ever seen.

As I turn Bess to the west and down North River Road, it dawns on me that I have over committed myself. I say out loud, "I can't start tomorrow; I told Sam I would work for him until Nate is all healed up. Bess, did you hear me?" Bess perks her ears and I do believe she nodded her head. I pull her up and say, "Sorry 'ol girl, but we have to turn around and head back. I have to make this right. I don't want to get started on the wrong foot." I give her a bit of a kick in the ribs and snap the reins on either side of her mane. She picks up the pace and settles into a nice even paced trot.

It's not long before we are back up to the house and Mrs. Meijer greets us at the front fence.

She asks me, "Did you forget something Mr. Sparks?"

This catches me a little off guard because we actually hadn't been introduced, but I quickly surmise that Conrad had told her what we had discussed and that's how she knew my name.

I tip my hat and jump down off Bess. With the reins in my hand, I lead Bess over to where Mrs. Meijer is standing and say, "Ma'am, we haven't been introduced, my name is Mr. Sparks and I need to explain something to your husband before tomorrow comes along."

She puts out her hand and says, "Yaw Mr. Sparks, I know your name, I am Mrs. Meijer, Margrit Meijer. My husband tells me you will be helping him build the new barn. This is good. He can use the extra help, especially now that growing season is upon us."

"Yes Ma'am, that is correct and that is what I need to discuss with him. I forgot to explain something to him before I can start. I don't want any misunderstanding. Can I leave my horse here again?"

"Yaw, sure, or you can ride on up to the work site, suit yourself, Mr. Sparks."

I tip my hat and jump up onto Bess's back saying, "Thank you, Ma'am."

"You can water your horse at the trough next to the barn."

"Thanks, I'll do that," I say as I gently give Bess the heel of my boots.

We make our way up to the building site and find Conrad and Walter measuring out a string line that runs down one side of the layout stakes. They both lift their heads as I ride up and slide off Bess. Conrad comes over and has a puzzled look on his face. He reaches out to let Bess get his scent, then reaches up under her muzzle and rubs her long jowls asking, "Did you forget something, Mr. Sparks?"

"Conrad, I must tell you, I will not be able to start tomorrow. I was so excited to start working on your new barn that I forgot that I had promised the Harris's to work one more week for them."

Conrad speaks to his brother in Dutch and his brother shakes his head in disapproval. Conrad says, "This is troubling news, Mr. Sparks. My brother thinks that you are not a man of your word."

I explain, "If I wasn't a man of my word, I would not feel obligated to the Harris's. I turned around as soon as I realized the pickle I had gotten myself into."

"Pickle, what is this pickle? I don't understand."

"It means situation or problem."

"Oh, problem, that I understand," he says. Turning to his brother he repeats this and they both have a laugh and repeat, "Pickle" and laugh again.

I continue saying, "Look, I think that my wanting to honor my commitment to the Harris's shows you I am a man of my word, but if this problem gets in the way of our agreement, then I will understand and I won't bother you again. I'm just trying to do the right thing here."

Conrad and Walter confer again. Turning with smiles on their faces, Conrad reaches out to shake my hand asking, "So, when can you start?"

I shake his hand and then Walter's hand saying, "One week from today. I need one week to fulfill my promise to the Harris's, and then I will work for you here until your barn is completed."

"Okay, Mr. Sparks, okay, next week it is."

I swing my leg up over Bess's back but before I turn her to leave, I remind them, "Don't sell my horse."

I ride Bess down towards the barn and corral to let her take a drink before we head back to the Flecther's Crossing. While she drinks, I am watchful of the grey. He is a good looking two year old. He holds his head high and prances when he walks. He won't leave the security of the other three horses, but he is very curious of Bess and me. He is well aware that there is another horse in his area. He would have been a good stallion for breeding, too bad they gelded him. It's probably for the best. He'll be easier to work with and won't be so aggressive when he gets around other horses, especially mares in heat. I bet he's fast.

As I pull Bess away from the trough, the grey whinnies and shifts his position amongst the other three horses. He doesn't seem to be agitated, more curious than anything. I start to mount Bess and notice that the two kids are leaning up against the corral fence. I say hello to them and mention to them that I'm going to help their pa and uncle build a new barn. They don't say anything, but the look in their eyes tells me they are full of questions. Before I jump up on to Bess's back, I crouch down so I am eye to eye with them and say, "My name is Jacob Sparks, what are your names?"

The little boy slides behind his sister, not saying a word. The girl answers, "My name is Abby and his name is Fritz."

"Well, Abby, that is a pretty name, and Fritz, that is a good strong name. I bet you two are a big help to your ma and pa, aren't you?" Neither one replies, they just seem to push in closer to the fence. I look out into the corral and point to the horses and ask, "See that grey there, does he have a name?"

Shaking her head, Abby answers, "One Spot, we call him One Spot."

"One Spot, I bet I know why."

"Why?" Abby asks.

"Because of the white spot on his forehead, right?"

"That's right mister, how'd you know?"

"Well Abby, I've been around a lot of horses and most folks name their horses because of their markings. I just figured that if I'd seen that colt born with that big bright spot on his forehead, then that'd be a darn good name for him."

Neither one of them say anything, Abby grabs Fritz by his shirt sleeve and says something in Dutch to him. They both turn and run towards the house leaving Bess and I at the watering trough. I sling my leg up over Bess's back and tell her, "Time for us to leave, girl."

Passing by the place in the road where I turned Bess around, I regain a sense of confidence that things are going to work out for the best. I reassure myself that I did the right thing by turning around and explaining my situation to the Meijer's. I could feel something was wrong and I knew I had to fix it. I didn't want to come back to an awkward situation. It seems as I get older, or maybe it's being sober, I am learning to listen to that inner voice and heed the little jabs that enter my mind when my judgment is in question. I keep telling myself that decision making is a process. In the past, I just didn't allow myself to be patient enough to let the process transform itself into positive results. In the past, I would react and let my emotions generate the actions that would result in causing more harm than good.

If I can get through this next week with the Harris's, without overreacting to my emotions, maybe, just maybe, the tension that exists between Judith and I will go away. Wishful thinking...I tell myself. I know what I know and with that I give Bess a snap of the reins and put my heels into her ribs as we gallop towards the setting sun.

Chapter 33

As I slow Bess from a gallop, to a trot, to a walk, I realize that if I can work for Sam another week, it will give me another dollar or two credit at Mr. Kimble's plus another fifty cents a day in my pocket. It won't be much, but if I'm not going to make any money at the Meijer's than any money I make will be a good thing.

Before I turn Bess loose in the meadow for the night, I walk her down to the barn so I can get her cooled down, brushed, and give her some grain. It is almost dark when I get finished tending to Bess and return her to her work mates.

While I was grooming Bess, I had noticed that there were a couple of lamps burning in the house, but I hadn't seen any movement. I haven't thought too much about food because of the late meal we had before I left to go to the Meijer's, but now that I'm finished with Bess, I suddenly feel like I could eat something. I swing by the water pump and wash my head and hands just in case the Harris's haven't eaten yet. I have learned it's best to be washed up before Judith calls you to sit down for any meal.

As I pass by the kitchen window and make my way to the front porch, I look inside. Not seeing any one in the house, I expect to see Sam, Judith and Nate sitting on the front porch. Up until now it hadn't dawned on me that I hadn't seen or heard Rusty. I turn the corner of the house and the front porch is empty. My ears pick up a faint bark that comes from the direction of the rapids. Rusty's bark sounds playful, so I relax my mind, not letting it jump to any conclusions that something might be wrong. I decide to wait down by the river's edge for Rusty and the others to return. It is such a nice evening they probably just wanted to take a walk along the river. The only thing missing is the light from the full moon that we had a week ago.

It's not long before I see the reflection of a lit lantern. Rusty's bark is getting closer and louder. Nate must be throwing a stick or playing a game of keep away that keeps him barking. Sam, Judith and Nate slowly emerge from the tree line at the start of exposed river rocks and boulders that eventually turn into the serious set of rapids. Judith has her arm entwined with one of Sam's, while his other holds the lantern. Nate is holding on to one end of a stick, while Rusty tugs on the other end. Releasing his bite, Rusty finally breaks free of the stick. Nate, while holding his side, throws the stick underhanded, much to the delight of Rusty.

Not wanting to disturb their walk, I remain sitting on a stump. They haven't taken notice of me until Rusty stops, puts his nose to the air and catches a whiff of me. He lets out a bark in warning and I call out his name. Reluctantly he starts to make his way towards me, but stops to make sure that the others are close behind.

Nate speaks out, "Is that you, Jake?"

I answer back that it is. Hearing my voice, Rusty relaxes and runs the rest of the way over to where I am seated. I rub and scratch his head. Standing up, I tip my hat to Judith and say, "Good evening."

Sam reaches out his hand to shake mine and asks, "Well,

how'd it go, did you get hired?"

"It went good. I told them I could start next week."

Nate asks, "What are you going to be working on? Is it a barn like Mr. Winkler said?"

"The Meijer's are building up an apple orchard. They are hoping to be able to grow enough apples to store them in an open air barn until they can get them to the railhead in Ash Fork for shipment to other cities. So yeah, I guess you could call it a barn."

Sam points towards the house with his hand that holds the lantern and says, "Let's go on up to the house and you can tell us all about it while we have a cup of coffee and some fresh black berry preserves and dumplings." He then asks, "Did you eat, Jake?"

As we walk towards the house I answer, "No, Sam, I didn't. By the time I got back and brushed Bess down, it was dark and you all were gone. That big meal we had earlier stuck with me, I guess I wasn't real hungry."

Once at the porch, Judith tells us, "Please sit. I'll be back with coffee and some dessert for us all."

Sam tells Nate, "Help Judith if she needs it." He then pulls his pipe out and fills it with sweet smelling tobacco.

Sam gets his pipe lit and says, "It's none of my business, but is this feller, what's his name?"

"Meijer, Conrad Meijer."

"Yeah, Meijer, is this Mr. Meijer gonna be able to pay you?"

"You're right Sam it is none of your business, but I don't mind you asking. Hell, I've never really cared about money. Don't get me wrong, I like having it and I like spending it, but

I have just never worried about having it. I work, I get paid, I get what I need and pay for it. But, to answer your question, he and his brother have invested all their money in getting the orchard started and lumber for the barn, so their money is real tight right now."

"That doesn't sound too promising," Sam says.

Before I can finish telling Sam the deal I made with the Meijer's, Judith and Nate come out with coffee and dessert on a couple of serving trays. I start to get up out of the chair that Nate usually sits in, he stops me, says, "Stay seated, Jake. I'll sit on the steps. I'm feeling better."

Once Judith is sitting next to Sam, we all begin to eat the still warm blackberries and dumplings. Each bite is a savory mouthful, followed by a sip of hot coffee; it is an excellent finish to the day.

Instead of continuing our conversation about what the Meijer's were going to be able to pay me, Sam asks, "So, Jake, you mentioned the Meijer brothers, I take it there's more than one family working this farm? Where'd they come from, any idea?"

I shake my head saying, "Yeah, from what I gathered, there are two families up there. I didn't meet both families, but I did meet both brothers. The family that came through here last week is the Conrad Meijer family. Conrad has a wife, her name is Margrit, with a daughter, Abby and a son named Fritz. Conrad's brother's name is Walter. I haven't met his wife. They have two sons that are both older than Abby. And she is older than Fritz"

Sam asks, "Did you say where they came from?"

"No, I didn't say, but they have been out here for about five years. You've must have seen them use the ferry during that time."

"Well, I've seen a lot of folks. I just don't take much notice anymore."

"Anyway, they are originally from Pennsylvania Dutch Country."

"Amish huh?"

I shake my head and say, "I have no idea, Sam. All I know is that their farm is as neat and clean as I have ever seen. Not a flower or weed or piece of farm equipment out of place. They have got three windmills that pump water up to the top of a rise and that lets them water the orchard by gravity using rows of irrigation ditches. They have a real nice place with southern exposure. Their land butts up against the bluffs and has a nice elevated view of the river. Their place doesn't border on the river, but it does border North River Road. And get this, the sign for their turn off says Holland Road...Dutch folks living on Holland Road."

Sam and Judith do not show any reaction to this light hearted comment, Nate on the other hand says, "I don't get it, what's that mean?"

I look at him and say, "The Meijer's are Dutch, and Holland is the country that the Dutch come from. It's just seems funny to me."

Without saying another word, Judith and Nate gather up the dishes and head to the kitchen leaving Sam and me sitting there. I suddenly get the feeling that I'm the only one with a sense of humor tonight.

Sam relights his pipe and once he has a good glow of embers in the bowl he looks at me and says, "So Jake, if you don't mind me asking again, what kind of arrangement was agreed to?"

Before I answer, I realize that it really isn't any of Sam's business as to what I agreed to work for. I stop from going into details and just say, "I will be duly compensated."

Sam takes a long drag on his pipe. Before he thinks of a comment, I say, "Since we are talking about money and pay, are we still good with our arrangement?"

Sam looks at me through the smoke that drifts up from his pipe and says, "What are you asking that for? You got something else in mind?"

I take a deep breath and continue, "I told the Meijer's I wouldn't be available until next week because I have an obligation to you. I told you I would help out here until Nate gets back on his feet. I was thinking that I would work here and make another run with Nate to Ash Fork this week. If that fits in to your plan for the week and our agreement was still good, then that would give me three dollars in my pocket plus another two dollars credit at Mr. Kimble's. It would help me out for getting a few things I'll need up at the Meijer's. Hopefully, my staying around one more week will help you out as well. What do you think?"

Judith comes out the screen door and says, "Think about what?"

Between the two of us we retrace our conversation and explain it to Judith. As she ponders what I purposed, Sam asks where Nate has got off to and Judith tells him that he took Rusty and a lantern up to check on the animals.

Judith has lost some softness to her voice and her demeanor seems changed. I can sense it and I know Sam is aware of it as well.

Sam takes another deep drag off his pipe and says, "That's what was agreed to. I told you that you were welcome here anytime for as long as you wanted to be here. I will honor my word."

As I sit there, I notice that Judith has been twisting a hankie through her fingers. I decide to let these two be alone. Standing, I excuse myself and say, "Goodnight Sam, goodnight Judith, I hope you both are able to enjoy the rest of your evening."

I step down off the porch and walk towards the barn. I see Nate, with lantern in hand, and with Rusty alongside him, walking down from the meadow towards me. We stop midway between barn and house and I ask, "How are the animals?"

"They are all quiet, and settled in for the night."

I ask him, "If you were able to work tomorrow, what would you start out working on?"

"I would start out splitting some of the cord wood that is down by the house. None has been split for awhile and the stock piles are shrinking, they need to be replenished.

"That is where I will start in the morning then. Enjoy the rest of your evening."

Nate says good night and offers the lantern to me. I decline it. Nate starts to walk to the house, stops, turns and says, "Hey Jake, thanks for being here, thanks for helping out and thanks for the other night at Kimble's."

Choking back tears, I answer, "You are welcome."

Chapter 34

Morning is upon me before I am ready for it. The bed and mattress are starting to feel pretty darn good. There is no time to entertain wishful thoughts, so I pad around in the light of early dawn and get dressed. I make my way to the water pump to wash the sleep from my face and head. I notice there is a lamp burning, casting a dim light through the kitchen window. By the size of the shadow, it appears Sam is up and getting a fire started in the stove. My stomach rumbles as I anticipate a hearty breakfast. I know if I keep busy, the morning and the breakfast will get here quicker than if I stand around waiting for it. I decide to walk on up and get Bonnie for her morning milking.

There is a slight chill in the air this morning. I am glad I threw on a flannel shirt over my undershirt. The warmth on my arms and neck send a warm shiver through me. When I get to the meadow, the sky has lightened enough to allow me to see the animals in the meadow. I call out to Bonnie and give her a whistle. Milk cows are very regular when it comes to getting milked. She eagerly makes her way over to the gate. All the animals have their heads up, curious at the activity. Little Sparky, gives out a bleating cry and runs the few feet that separate him from Daisy. Old Brutus is off by himself not wanting to mingle with the others. He seems to stay up at the north end of the meadow, which doesn't hurt my feelings one bit. Gus, Molly and Bess are standing in a tight group, relaxed but curious none the less. I grab Bonnie by the halter and slide a rope through a ring that makes it easy to lead her down to the barn.

With Bonnie in the milk stall, I grab the stool and bucket and proceed to milk her. I apologize as I fumble around trying to apply enough hand pressure to produce positive results. I am able to avoid a couple non-threatening kicks from her back hoof, but I am not able to dodge her tail as she manages to smack me in the face a few times with it. I tell her, "I get the hint." I finally settle into an acceptable rhythm accomplishing the task at hand. With the bucket three-fourths full, I stand and pat her on her hind flank. She turns her head and lets out a loud beller that sounds to me like she is saying, "It's about time."

I tell her that I'll take her back up to the meadow, but before I do, I need to run and get a couple apples. She gives a twitch of her tail just as Judith enters the barn with a small basket of fresh eggs that she has been busy gathering. We say good morning without making eye contact. She tells me that I didn't have to take the time to milk Bonnie but that it was appreciated. She goes on to let me know that breakfast will be ready shortly and she hopes I don't mind oatmeal. I tell her that a hot bowl of oatmeal will be just fine. I excuse myself and run to get the apples. We both avoid eye contact once again as she is on her way to the house and I'm on my way to walk Bonnie back to the meadow.

As I wash up for breakfast, I hear steam being released from the ferry. I think to myself that this is another typical day here at Fletcher's Crossing. We gather around the table, grace is said, oatmeal is eaten and coffee drank; Nate is the only one talking as he tries to convince Sam that he is ready to do some work. Sam isn't completely convinced. Sam and Judith both remind Nate that he has only had a couple days rest. As soon as we are finished with our meal, Sam tells Nate to stand up and unwrap his side. Nate is reluctant to show off his bruises. Judith leaves and comes back with the coffee pot and pours us refills.

I am just as curious to see Nate's side as Sam and Judith are. He slowly reveals his bruises. Most of the swelling has gone down but the deep purple that is surrounded by yellow suggests that the area is still very tender. Sam reaches out to touch Nate's side, but Nate pushes his hand away. Judith sets the coffee pot down and says, "Here, let me."

Nate protests, but gives in when Sam gives him a raise of his eyebrows and tells him, "You'll not go to work until one of us can see for ourselves how sore those ribs are."

"Yes, sir. Go ahead, Judith."

She lays her hand gently on Nate's discolored skin. Nate does not flinch until she starts to apply firmer pressure with her finger tips. It is the first time since the fight, that any one has been able to touch his side firmly. She pulls her hand away and says, "I think everything is healing nicely. I don't think they broke more than one or two ribs."

Sam says, "Well that's good. From the size of that bruise, it looks like there could be three or four broke.

"I don't think three, one is still very tender, another is so-so, the ribs either side of the two bad ones don't feel broken, they just seem to be bruised." Then she goes and comes back with a jar of menthol rub, she gently applies it to the bruised area and rewraps his side.

Sam looks up and says, "Give it a day or two more."

Nate shakes his head walking towards the front porch. I excuse myself and head out to the back of the house, eager to start splitting wood.

Chapter 35

A hard day of splitting wood deserves a swim and a soak, I tell myself. I grab soap and a towel, but before I head down to the swimming hole, I try to coax Rusty to tag along. He still won't leave Nate. I yell to Nate asking if he would like to go, just to walk some if nothing else. He yells back with a no. Before I get half way to the river, Nate and Rusty are coming up behind me on the trail. I slow my pace to let them catch up to me. Nate tells me the coolness of the water might feel pretty good after all. I tell him I am glad he changed his mind.

The water does feel good and once Nate is completely wet, he is finally able to relax and his mood seems to lighten. As we begin to leave, he has a little more bounce in his step and there is a spark to his voice. On the walk back, he throws a pinecone for Rusty. He is still only able to throw it under hand, but at least he is showing some flexibility and joyful energy.

He tells me, "Sam was right, resting today really helped, but I think I needed to get away from the house. This is the best I've felt in three days."

"That's great, but you still need to take it easy. If you're not careful, you can hurt those ribs again and make the healing process take twice as long.

Rusty drops the pinecone at my feet wanting me to throw it farther than Nate has been able to throw it. I give it a toss and we laugh as Rusty goes bounding after it.

Before we get back to the house, I ask Nate, "Tomorrow, should I haul some blocks of wood down to the house to replace what I chopped today or should I stay up in the woods, sawing blocks for future splitting?"

He tells me, "That's not a bad idea. Stay up in the woods tomorrow and saw up some eighteen inch blocks."

I leave Nate to go to the barn and hang up the wet clothes I washed out. Judith comes to the back porch and yells out that supper will be ready in about fifteen minutes. Once again, my stomach reminds me that I worked up an appetite today.

At supper, I mention to Sam, "Nate and I discussed what I should work on tomorrow and Nate thought it would be good for me to saw up some eighteen inch rounds."

Sam says, "I thought about cutting some wood myself, but I would like to take the day and ride up to the high country. I still need to scout for bear and see how the elk herd fared this winter."

Nate joins in, "I would sure like to go with you."

With hesitation Sam says, "We'll see how you feel in the morning. It'll be a long day in the saddle and a rough ride to the high country. What do you think Judith?"

After a long sigh she answers, "We'll see how tender your side is in the morning."

Trying to strengthen his argument for going, Nate says, "Soaking in the river felt like it did a lot of good. I feel the best I have felt in days."

Sam chuckles and says, "We'll see. Hey Jake, do you want to ride along?"

I decline saying, "I need to work and I've seen high country."

He gets up from the table saying, "Suit yourself," and walks out the front door. I excuse myself and head out the back.

•

Sleep came quickly and the new day begins much like the day before. It is still dark out but the sky to the east is quickly beginning to show the first signs of light. Since the day before seemed to work out well, I decide to follow the same routine.

I go up to the meadow to get Bonnie and milk her first thing. With light coming from the house and smoke coming out of the stove chimney, it means that Sam is probably up. If he hasn't changed his mind, he and possibly Nate will be headed up to the high country to scout bear and elk for the fall hunts.

As I make my way back down to the house from taking Bonnie back to the meadow, Judith is out on the back porch and gives me a motion to come in for breakfast. I wash up before I head to the kitchen.

There is an anxiousness in the air as we sit and hold hands to bless the food and the day. Nate takes the lead saying a simple prayer, asking Our Lord to protect us and keep us all safe. We eat quickly and I decline a third cup of coffee. If I am feeling anxious, I tell myself that it is because I am eager to make the walk to the area of stock piled logs and work in the woods all day away from others.

I excuse myself, but not before Judith asks, "Will you be wanting a midday meal?"

"I'll be fine. I'll take water, apples and jerky with me."

"I am preparing food for Sam and Nate, preparing one more will not be any trouble."

I politely decline, but not before asking, "So Nate, you're

going on the scouting trip? You must be feeling better, that's great."

Nate grabs his side and says, "My side looks a lot worse than it feels. Judith looked at my ribs this morning and she says the swelling went down a lot over night and when she pressed on the worst area it didn't take my breath away."

Sam takes a sip of coffee and says, "It is amazing what a day of rest will do."

Nate comments, "Or it could be that river water. Maybe there is something special about it, right Jake?"

I grin and say, "It's possible. I've heard that the Rogue River can be both healing and mysterious, at times."

Sam pushes his chair away and tells Nate, "If you're going with me, you best be getting your things. I sure hope you can sit in a saddle all day."

Nate heads to the stairs that lead to the loft and his bedroom saying, "I'll be fine Sam, stop worrying."

I head up to the barn to gather a few things that I might need throughout the day. I rinse out my canteen and fill it with fresh water. As I come out of the barn, Sam is striding up to the meadow to get the horses. I catch up to him and we walk together in silence. When we get to the gate, Sam calls to Gus and all three horses come eagerly walking over.

I ask, Sam, "Can you use a hand taking Gus and Molly down to the barn and saddling them?"

"No. Nate should be there by the time I get the horses to the barn."

I turn to start my walk to the logging area but before I go, Sam stops me, grabs my arm and says, "I hope you two are going to be alright here by yourselves."

I pull my arm away and looking him right in the eyes, I say, "Sam, don't embarrass yourself, if you don't trust Judith by now, then shame on you. If you can't trust me, then agreement or no agreement, I'll be gone before you get them two horses saddled. You'll never see me again."

Sam moves back on his heels and says, "Ah Jake, don't get all riled up. I was just stating the obvious."

I move right up on his chest and say, "Go to Hell." I walk away leaving him standing there with nothing to say.

Chapter 36

It takes me the entire walk to cool down. I am talking to myself and with every step I take I ask myself all the same questions that I have been asking for the past few days. I thought I was going to be able to put all this anxiety behind me. At least I thought that is what I've been trying to do. I just can't believe how the past few weeks have led to this.

As I saw round blocks of wood into eighteen inch lengths for cord wood, I just can't shake the disturbance I feel throughout my entire body. I drop the cross cut saw mid stroke and know what I have to do. I grab my canteen, dowse my head with water, pick up my shirt, my small day pack, and start to run.

Before I turn to go down to the house, I take a look up to the aspens and ask Our Lord to answer Nate's prayer to protect us all. I hope what I am about to do is going to set me free. I stop at the barn, pack my belongings, roll up my bedding and head towards the house. I see Judith at the clothesline. She has washed some clothes and is hanging them to dry. I don't want to startle her, but I don't want to sneak up on her either. Luckily for me, Rusty didn't go with Sam and Nate this trip and he stayed at the house. Rusty lets out a short bark and comes my way with his tail wagging. Judith turns towards me with a terrified look on her face.

She starts to run towards the house and screams, "The shotgun is loaded and I'll use it if I have to!"

I drop my pack and run at an angle cutting her off before she can get to the back porch. I grab her by her forearms and yell, "Judith, I'm not going to hurt you! I just need to talk to you."

Judith is hysterical. Her breathing is out of control. She suddenly stops at the back porch step. She slumps to her knees and sits down.

She is sobbing into her hands and says, "I have always dreaded that this day would come. I have hoped and prayed that you were dead or that you were so far away that you would never find me."

I sit down next to her and ask, "Do I call you Judith or Carolynn?"

She looks up at me and says, "I told you, Carolynn is dead."

"Fine...So, when did you know?"

She looks at me dumbfounded and says, "The very moment you told me your name, that very first day. I didn't recognize you at first, but your voice hadn't changed that much and I could see it in your eyes, and I knew." She then asks me, "What took you so long? Have I changed that much?"

Before I start to explain, I ask her if we can either go inside or sit on the front porch so we can be comfortable. She stands up and tells me she'll meet me on the front porch.

I am sitting in Nate's chair as she comes out of the house. To my surprise she is holding the shotgun, pointing it at me she says, "I should shoot you right where you sit, Jacob Sparks, for leaving me the way you did."

"Judith, please, put the gun down, let me explain, please."

She looks at me and says, "I could shoot you and tell people that you attacked me. I'd put this behind me once and for all. Problem solved."

. . . .

"You're wrong, Judith, it would just be another problem, another lie, stacked up on the mountain of problems and lies you have had in your life. Let's talk this out. I promise, I'll leave and never come back. I just need to know what has happened all these years. Please, put the gun down. Please sit down."

She uncocks the shotgun and leans it up against the house, making sure it is in arms reach.

Sitting, she begins to relax her breathing. She looks up at me and says, "What is it you want to know?"

I have hundreds of questions and my mind races to pick out one. Not able to stop myself, I tell her, "I need to start at the beginning. I apologize. So were you pregnant?"

"Yes."

"Was it mine?"

"Of course it was."

"Did you have the baby, did it live and was it a boy or a girl?"

She looks at me and starts crying, saying, "I don't want to do this. I don't want to sit here while you ask me all these questions. Let me get my thoughts together and I'll just tell you what happened, if at the end, you still have questions I'll try to answer them...Alright?"

"Sure, whatever it will take to get to the truth."

"Before I start I have a question for you, Jacob."

"What is it?"

"The same one you asked me when we were out back, "What made you finally recognize me?"

I simply say, "It was your beauty mark. That day you wore your hair down with that open blouse you wore. I noticed the beauty mark and your teenage face came back to me in my sleep. I've been piecing it all back together ever since. But I still don't know the truth as we sit here today."

She says, "Jacob, before I tell you what I'm about to tell, you have to swear on all that is good that this stays between you and me."

I look at her and say, "I swear."

She grabs the shotgun, she is quivering as she points it at me and says, "Swear it, swear to me, Jacob Sparks, that what you hear today, you will not repeat."

"Judith, I swear it, please believe me, what you tell me dies with me."

She looks directly into my eyes and says, "If you are lying, I'll put you in that river. Do you hear me?"

"Yes Judith, I hear you. Now, please put the gun down."

Judith leans the shotgun up against the house again and starts to tell me her story.

She begins, "After you went upstairs and my father realized you had run off, he went crazy. He went looking for you at first and when he couldn't find you he got the sheriff to look for you.

Well, the sheriff didn't have time, but he told my father that he had a couple of deputies riding out looking for you. Pa was so angry. He never was the same after that day. He told me that he hated me and that if word ever got out about me being an unwed mother that his name would be ruined in Ash Fork. As time went on, he turned meaner and meaner. He started keeping the blinds closed and wouldn't let me go outside. Patients started to not show up for their appointments. He would yell at me and my sisters all the time, telling us that it was our fault that Ma had died and we were ungrateful daughters out to ruin him. The more my belly grew, the more he drank and the angrier he got. He started threatening me that he was going to hurt me and do harm to the baby."

"Like what? What was he going to do?"

"I don't know. He just went crazy. He made so many threats. My oldest sister started to make sure that he was never left alone with me. My other sister, the youngest one, she left with her boyfriend, she got out quick. That really set him off. Then the baby came and it was..."

Judith stops there. She starts to sob and needs a minute to compose herself and then she continues, "The baby was a boy and he was healthy and beautiful. But Pa would hardly let me hold him or be near him 'cept to nurse him. My sister would take care of him mostly. My pa just hated me and that little boy."

I stop her and ask, "Did you name him? You had to call him something?"

She catches her breath and goes on, "Me and my sister called him Joseph. We thought it was a good strong name from the Bible and all. Once Pa decided that the boy was old enough to stop nursing, he took him away from me and I never got to hold him again, not for a long, long time. My pa kept me captive and told people that I had run off with you. He would beat my sister if he caught her talking to anyone. He would send her out for groceries, but if she didn't come back right on time she would get a beating. It was terrible. He even took our shoes! We were prisoners!"

"So what happened, how long did this go on?"

She looks at me and starts crying again, through the tears she says, "He treated that little boy something awful from what my sister said. She came to me with a plan to set Joseph free. She was convinced that if the boy didn't get out and find help he wouldn't live to see his seventh birthday. So, she took him some food and a jacket and a stocking hat I had knitted him and one day when Pa was passed out drunk, she told him how to get out of the cellar."

I stop her there and exclaim, "My God, it was Nate! Nate's our son! How could this happen, how could that monster get away with that? My God Judith, I am so sorry. I had no idea that any of that would happen. God forgive me, God forgive us all for the pain and suffering we have caused. I can't imagine what that boy went through. Nate tried to explain some of this to me on our way back from Ash Fork, but some of it didn't make sense. I thought maybe he was in so much pain from the fight, that he was delirious, but it's true. Nate's our son Judith, he needs to know."

At that she leaps out of the chair like a cat on fire and jumps on me with her hands around my throat, screaming hysterically, "Don't you dare, I'll kill you first, do you hear me, I'll kill you! You promised! You promised!" She slumps to the floor sobbing, "You promised, you promised."

I sit down next to her, put my arm around her and through my tears I tell her, "Your story is safe with me. I have caused enough pain."

We sit there for a long while gently rocking back and forth. My arm is around her and she has her head buried into my chest. She finally stirs and asks, "So, where did you go, Jacob?" What happened to you?"

With a heavy sigh I tell her, "I ran and ran. I have been running my whole life."

I help her up to her feet and set her down in her chair. I ask her if I can get her a drink of water, she says that would be nice. I go into the house and pump a pitcher of water from the sink spigot and grab two glasses.

Returning, I pour us both a full glass of water and say, "Once I jumped out the window, I ran most of the way here to Fletcher's Crossing, took the old ferry across the river and headed north. I got as far as Carver's Pass and stayed there for a few years. I learned to be a carpenter while at Carver's Pass and after a few years I made my way to Portland and lived there mostly."

Judith stops me and asks, "Did you ever marry?"

"I never married but I loved a gal named Beth. I had a drinking and gambling problem and after awhile I just got tired of being sick and tired all the time. I had made a promise to stop drinking and that promise got me to sober up. Once sober, I needed to stop running and find my ma and pa. I felt the need to start repairing some of the hurt I had caused. Little did I know that any of this was going to happen."

We sit quietly for a bit and then I ask, "So does Sam know any of this? Does he know that you are Nate's mother?"

She looks at me with shameful eyes and says, "Sam is a really good man. He saved Nate first and then he saved me. He didn't even know he was doing it. He just let us live. The way he took Nate in is the closest thing to a miracle that I've ever seen. He loves that boy and has watched over him as if Nate was his own. He probably loves him even more than he loves me. I wouldn't blame him if he did, after what my pa did to that boy."

"So, Judith," I ask, "How'd you get out of there? How much longer did it take for you to escape?"

She looks far away, there is a look in her eyes that makes her see past the river. Not focusing on any one object she says, "I waited until winter. I thought that if I could get to the river, I could fall in under the ice and just float away. Die slow but quiet. I waited until Pa was passed out real good. My sister had made sure that he was out cold. I waited until it was real late and dark out. She came up and unlocked the door and let me out. I walked straight to the river from the house and walked out onto the ice. I walked and walked but couldn't find any thin ice until I was east of town. By then I was so cold I was probably close to freezing to death without even falling in. I eventually found a soft spot and jumped and jumped on the ice. A hole finally began to open up but by that time, something had come over me and I wanted to live. I started fighting from inside myself to live. I couldn't get off the ice and to the river's edge quick enough. Because I had been jumping on the ice, the water had splashed up and made what looked like a really big hole. It looked like someone had fallen in. I walked up the bank and found the North River Road and started walking east. I got so tired I crawled into some bushes and got down real close to the ground. I didn't freeze that night or the next or the next. Each morning I would just get up and start walking. By the time Sam found me, I was so cold and hungry that he thought I was going to die before another morning."

"Where did he find you?"

"I guess I made it about a mile west of where the road from the ferry meets up with the North River Road. He was out looking to shoot some snowshoe rabbit and stumbled upon me laying in some wagon tracks. He carried me down to the house and he and Nate got a wash tub, filled it with water, started a fire under it and set me in. He saved my life. When I came to, he said I told him my name was Judith."

Judith continues, "Sam and I didn't talk much for a long time. Between Nate not talking at all and me not wanting anybody to find me, it was awful quiet around here. Sam is the most patient man I know, he just waited us out. I knew Nate was my son from the start, but I was so ashamed that I couldn't tell anyone, not Sam, not even Nate. I lived in fear of being found out and punished. By spring time I had to tell Sam something that he could believe and live with. I told him I had been traveling with an abusive man and jumped off the train in Ash Fork. I walked until Sam had found me. I never admitted to being Nate's mother until a few years back."

"My God Judith, what made you be able to tell so many lies and keep so many secrets for so many years?"

She looks at me with the coldest eyes I've ever seen and says, "Do you know how it feels to give birth to a child and find out that your child has been so badly mistreated that it makes him, at age six, be so driven to escape on his own, just to survive? He was only six years old. I was his mother and couldn't protect him. I still live in fear, that if he ever found out, that I was the cause of all that pain and suffering, he'd turn his back on me.

And what kind of a woman does that make me. How would a man like Sam ever want to be with me? No, Carolynn died that winter night and Judith survived."

"Didn't any one ever come looking for Carolynn?"

"Not that I know of, because my pa had needed to keep my being pregnant a secret, he started the rumor that I had run off with you. When the Sheriff's posse couldn't find you and because he had kept Nate and me hidden for all those years, he couldn't tell anyone that I had run off at the time I actually did. By that time, the town was convinced that he was insane and it didn't matter much to anyone what happened to him or his three daughters. I don't think anyone would have listened to him anyway. We were pretty much forgotten. I think Sam had it figured out before I told him but he never brought it up. Like I said, Sam is a patient and good man. We had fallen in love and he was so fond of Nate that he was not going to let anybody interfere."

"How long before you got married?"

"By midsummer I had moved into Sam's bed. He didn't want anyone talking bad about me, so as luck would have it, a preacher came traveling through and Sam talked him into marrying us."

"How'd he do that, I mean did Sam have a marriage license and all?"

"I think he paid the preacher off to make up a hand written paper saying all the legal words. You know out here, the law doesn't say too much. We've been together so long; folks just know that I'm Sam Harris's wife. I wouldn't go to Ash Fork for a long time. I still don't go but maybe once a year. I don't socialize with any others unless it is with folks from right around here close by. I have all I need right here. I heard my pa passed and I lost track of my sisters. Like I said, Carolynn died, so did her life before Fletcher's Crossing."

I pour us both another glass of water, "I am real happy that you found this life."

She doesn't thank me, instead she says, "My life is sure not what I thought it would be, but it has been a nice peaceful living."

"Why didn't you and Sam have any more kids?"

"When Sam was a young boy, he had gotten kicked by a mule in the groin area. The doctor told his pa that Sam's testicles were so mangled, he'd probably never be able to get a woman pregnant."

I realize that this is none of my business but I can't stop myself from apologizing to her for Sam and his condition.

"No need to apologize Sam functions just fine, he just can't have kids. And truthfully, Nate has been the only child either one of us needed."

I look at her, fighting back my tears I say, "He is one hell of a kid, and turning into a man's man. I am so thankful that I have gotten to know him just the little bit that I have. Spending time with him has been a blessing."

She looks at me and says, "Nate has taken a liking to you, Jacob. When we are alone, you are all he talks about. Sometimes I feel bad for Sam, but Sam knows how much Nate loves him. Sam will be fine."

"So, you never did tell Sam the truth?"

"Truth about what?"

"The truth about you being Nate's mother?"

"You don't let up do you? A few years back, once I heard that my pa had passed, it made me not so scared and as far as I could tell, no one had ever asked about me, so I sat Sam down and told him my whole story. He said he wasn't surprised and that he was proud of me for doing what I had to do to protect my son. I told him I didn't see it that way, but Sam made me understand it through his eyes. He told me I had done the best I could at the time. I had survived to find my son and be with him."

"Sam is absolutely correct. I am proud of you Judith and I am sorry for running away. I was a scared, weak young boy. I need to ask for your forgiveness."

She reaches out and touches my hand and tells me, "There is nothing to forgive. Our lives took a turn that neither one of us could have predicted. My pa was an evil man and almost destroyed three lives while destroying his own." She continues, "My pa was pure evil, he didn't deserve to live and I am glad he is dead."

We are both exhausted, but before we move I say, "So, I have to ask, Nate has never asked about his real father or mother?"

Judith looks out over the river and says, "I truly think that he was so traumatized at such a young age that his feelings about wanting to know the truth are buried so deep, even God Himself can't resurrect them."

"But don't you want him to know that he has had his mother's love all these years?"

She looks at me and says, "I have to believe he knows."

Swallowing hard I say, "You're right, he does know. He knows he is Judith and Sam Harris's son. Judith, rest assured. Your secret is safe with me."

I stand up and can't believe that the afternoon sky has clouded over. Judith realizes how late it is and stands to start supper. She turns and as she opens the screen door she asks, "So what now, Jacob Sparks?"

I tip my hat and say, "I'll be leaving as soon as I can say my goodbyes to Sam and Nate." Before the door swings closed, I reach down and hand her the shotgun, "Here, you won't be needing this, put it back in the house."

I walk around to the back of the house to gather up my belongings that had been scattered during our earlier confrontation. I make my way to the barn and with the sunlight that is remaining, I decide to walk up to the aspen grove one last time.

Chapter 37

Realizing that by the time Sam and Nate return it will be dark, I will spend one more night here and leave in the morning. I take my bedroll, pack, bow and quiver of arrows back up to the loft. As I head out of the barn, I grab a lantern just in case it is dark when I walk back from the aspen grove.

Passing the meadow, the only animal that seems to notice me is Bess. She didn't get to go with Sam and Nate and is probably wondering if I am going to call her over to say hi or take her for a ride.

With my heart heavy and my mind whirling, I am only able to say half out loud, "Not today Bess, sorry." I don't know if she has heard me or not, after I walk past her, I look back and already she has her head down and is content to linger in the tall meadow grass.

As I climb higher up towards the aspens, the breeze lets itself be felt. I can hear the wind swirl through the tops of the pines and I can see the aspen leaves shimmering obediently. I climb to the top edge of the aspens and turn to take a look behind me. Because I am not yet above the aspens, all I see is the white, scarred tree trunks and lime green leaves. I decide to climb higher up the hill to take in the view looking down and over the tops of the aspens.

Looking up I notice an outcropping of rock about fifty yards above the grove and make my way up to these rocks. Once there, I climb up on to the outer edge of a large boulder and am pleasantly surprised with the view.

As I look down onto the tops of the aspens, I tell myself the same thing I have told myself hundreds of times before, "Don't forget to turn around once in awhile, the best view you see could be the view behind you."

I chuckle to myself and then begin to be overwhelmed by emotion. I sit on this outcropping of rocks overlooking this beautiful draw that I have just walked up and through. The aspens are shimmering, the meadow grass is gently waving, the barn, house and river look to be close enough to reach out and grab them. I have been able to touch this place, but this place isn't mine to grab hold of. Evidently, my place is farther down the road. I wonder if I will settle down in Ash Fork? It is doubtful; there are not enough joyful memories of Ash Fork that will overcome all the pain that seems to be lurking around every corner. I've been up north and I've been to the coast; maybe I'll make my way back to the coast and then head south. I hear the weather is warm all year round once you get to southern California.

The weather is beginning to change from breezy to gusts of wind. High clouds are now transforming into low grey clouds. It is apparent we are in for some rain. I hear very faint rumblings of thunder off to the west and north. Not knowing exactly where Sam and Nate where headed on their scouting trip, I have to hope that they are headed back here before night fall. I hear the whistling sounds the wind makes as it gusts through the tree tops and I decide to pull out my harmonica and play along.

Once again I am overcome with emotion. It seems my mind is dead set on playing back the events that have gotten me to this moment of time. I had set out to find answers to questions and found answers that now I cannot embrace. Is it possible to claim a child, a son, that you had no part in his upbringing? Is it fair to him to know the truth? As I lay back and look to the threatening sky, I slide my harmonica through my lips, playing a melody that is not part of any song that I have ever heard until this very moment.

I know the promise I have made to Judith is a promise I must keep. The time I have spent with Nate has been the greatest joy of my life, but now I am bound to the greatest secret and sacrifice of my life. I know that I absolutely must leave this place and take with me Judith's secret that I have sworn to keep.

As I stand to climb down off the boulder, I am dizzy with grief. My heart feels broken beyond repair, but I have a love inside me, for Nate, that I now must protect. I must begin to replace my feelings of guilt and shame with this new found love. I must trust that God chose Judith and me, to be the ones to bring forth Nate into this life. Nate isn't the result of a mistake. God doesn't make mistakes, man does. God took Nate and placed him in this loving environment under the guardianship and watchful eye of Sam. I tell myself that this is how I will have to live; to try and be joyful, knowing that God stepped in and corrected my mistake and took care of Nate for me.

I know in my heart that I must apologize to Sam for my earlier remarks I made to him. Hopefully this will be another step in replacing the shame that floods my heart.

The afternoon has passed quickly. As I walk back down

through the aspen's one last time, I find my mood matches the sky and weather; heavy and dark. My steps are quiet as I walk through the damp, spongy center of the grove. I reach out trying to touch each tree, believing that if I touch one, they will all feel my presence because they are all connected. Walking past one of the larger aspen, I catch my sleeve on an old, dried out stub of a branch. It almost feels like the tree reached out and pinched my arm. I stop and look at this tree and walk a circle around it. l put my back up against its trunk and tilt my head back as far as I can looking up through the canopy that is made by its branches and leaves. I calm my breath and whisper a thank you to God's Spirit and His earth. The first drops of rain begin to land on the leaves as I pull out my knife and carve JS into the white, thin skinned bark of aspen.

By the time I emerge from the companionship of this family of trees, the gentle falling drops of rain have turned into a steady drizzle. I am glad I am half way down the east fence line headed towards the barn. I pick up my pace not wanting to have the clothes I am wearing get too wet. I don't want to start out traveling in wet clothes, and I certainly don't want to pack clothes that are damp.

As I get to the end of the meadow and to the south gate, I decide not to light the lantern. All I have to do is stay on the well worn wagon path because it goes right to the barn, and I've walked this same way on darker nights than this. Looking past the barn, I see that Judith has a couple of lamps burning bright and there is smoke coming from the fireplace chimney as well as the kitchen stove chimney. I will by-pass supper tonight and get some jerky and apples from the root cellar.

I stop at the barn, grab my canteen and pause to finally light the lantern. I fill my canteen as I pass the water pump and walk to the root cellar. I grab what I need plus a little extra for my walk tomorrow. I am sure Judith will serve a large breakfast and insist on sending half of it with me.

I head back to the barn and settle in for the night, hoping that Sam and Nate are not caught in any weather worse than this. Higher elevations can be unpredictable, even with summer just around the corner. I leave the lantern burning as I lie on the bed and wonder if Sam will want me to dismantle it. Maybe he'll just throw a tarp over it and stack hay on top. Oh well, it is built now, it never hurts to have a spare bed. Like he says, you never know who'll will be next to come down that road.

I must have dozed off because I am suddenly awakened from the sound of the rain hitting the roof. The storm has intensified, and there is still no sign of Sam and Nate. Ordinarily I would head down to the house and check on Judith, but I am reluctant because of the reality that now exists between us. This feeling to go see how she is doing continues to linger. I don't believe it is very late, and I am sure this is not the first time she has had to wait for their return. I don't know why I am compelled to see how Judith is doing. I can't seem to end this emotional argument, so I pull out my rain poncho and decide to see what Judith thinks is taking them so long.

Just as I step off the last rung of the ladder, Judith comes through the barn door with Rusty by her side. She has a worried look on her face and a lantern in her hand.

I explain, "I was just going to come down and see if you where alright."

She says, "With Nate's sore ribs and now this storm, I thought the two of them would be back by now."

I tell her, "I bet they are close."

"Jacob, could you saddle Bess and go look for them?"

Shaking my head no I say, "Judith, I wouldn't have a clue as to where they went. I am sure they are fine. Sam knows this country like the back of his hand and I don't. I wouldn't know where to even start. There is no need to worry."

"You are probably right."

"Why don't you head back down to the house and I'll keep an eye out for them up by the meadow. Leave Rusty with me and when they get hear I'll have Nate and Rusty come right down."

"I suppose you are correct. Please, as soon as you see them, send them to the house."

Judith turns and heads back towards the house. Rusty wants to go with her, but after a quick game of tug-a-war, he is distracted and stays with me. It is no more than a few minutes when Rusty's ears perk up and with a bark he runs to the barn door. I grab the lantern and as I open the door Rusty bolts through it, headed up towards the meadow. It is not long before I hear the horses and see Sam and Nate riding towards the barn. They are wet and cold, but otherwise seem to be okay. I open the large barn door so they can bring Gus and Molly in and get them unsaddled.

Sam says, "I'd like the horses to stay in the barn tonight, they have worked hard today."

I tell Nate, "Judith was just up here checking to see if you had returned and I told her I would send you and Rusty down to the house first thing. Nate you need to let Judith know that everyone is safe. I'll help Sam with the horses."

He looks at Sam and gets a "yes" shake of the head.

Once Nate is out of the barn, Sam stops and says, "What's on your mind Jake? I know you got something to say, that's why you ran Nate off."

I look at him and keep Molly positioned between us. I don't need another confrontation, not tonight.

It takes me a moment to gather my words, and then I say, "First off Sam, I owe you an apology for what I said this morning. I had no right to tell you to go to hell. Secondly, I didn't get much wood cut today. I have come to the conclusion that it is time for me to be moving on down the road. I have worn out my welcome. I will be leaving first thing in the morning or whenever the first ferry crosses."

Sam comes around the back side of Molly and extends his hand saying, "Jake, apology accepted, as long as you accept mine. I was an ass this morning. You were right to be angry at me. What you said to me about trusting Judith is a reflection of what kind of a man I am. I spent a long day in the saddle with nothing to think about but the words you said to me and I am ashamed to have lashed out at you. Jake, you seem to be a real good man, I don't know much about your past, but I feel you have been looking for something your whole life. I hope and pray that you find whatever it is you are looking for."

I clear my throat and say, "Sam, you're the good man here, and you are right, I have been searching for something for a long, long time and I believe I have been able to find it, right here at Fletcher's Crossing."

"What...what on earth have you found here?"

"It's something that I can't fully explain to you. There is a verse in good book that says it best, 'And the Truth will set you Free.'"

Sam looks at me puzzled and says, "I am not sure I understand. To be honest, I'm not sure I want to understand. Your business is your business, but if you found something here and you can move on with a better feeling about yourself, than I am happy for you." We shake hands again with Sam saying, "Let's go down to the house, get something hot to eat and get warm by the fire."

I shake my head and say, "Thanks Sam, but I'm going to stay up here, you go on down and enjoy your family."

•

The rain seemed to continue through the night. It never came down hard, it just came down steady. I am hoping Red decides to run the ferry, if not, it will be a long day of waiting. Morning is a long time coming when you are anxious to be someplace else. I'd like to blame the straw and corn husk mattress on my lack of sleep, but I can't as I realize that I have already had a few good nights' sleep on this simple bed. It is probably my internal restlessness.

Sometime during the long sleepless hours I realize that I will have to ask Nate to do me a favor. I will need him to get word to the Meijer brothers and let them know that I won't be helping them with their barn. I feel bad that I made a promise to them, I hope they understand.

•

The rain subsided sometime before daylight. While getting dressed, I go through my pack and sort some things out and reposition some things making sure to put "Lady Liberty" in my pants front pocket for traveling. Once I run my knives across my sharpening stone, giving them a fresh edge, I take everything out of the loft and set it by the door. I walk over to Molly and Gus and run my hands along their backs. Gus seems to tolerate me but doesn't let himself relax. Molly however, knows my scent and knows my voice as I give her a good rub up and down her muzzle. I reach up to her forehead and whisper in her ear, "I have enjoyed spending these past few weeks with you and Bess." She nods her head up and down; I'd like to think she agrees.

Chapter 38

The ground is muddy and sloppy from the rain that fell through the night. It makes me think that Red may not run the ferry today. If the ferry doesn't operate today then my options would be to head north and then west walking to Ash Fork on North River Road or I could stay one more day. I could chop some wood and earn another dollar for road money.

Before heading towards the house, I wash the long night from my head and face and walk down to the river's edge. The fast moving river is silted brown with small scattered debris. Across the river there is a wagon that is staged at the loading area anticipating the ferry to be running today. The river appears to be crossable. Hopefully the roads aren't too muddy and are passable.

The smell of fresh coffee drifts through the early morning air so I turn looking to see if there is any movement in the house. There is the usual lamp burning in the kitchen area and smoke coming from the kitchen stove chimney. I notice a shadow moving about the kitchen but cannot determine whose shadow it is.

I know I must be hungry, but cannot decide if my stomach is rumbling from lack of food or knowing that saying goodbye is inevitably hanging over my head.

I decide to head up towards the house and wait on the front porch. Just as I begin to sit on the top step, Sam comes out the front door. We exchange good mornings and ask how each had slept.

Sam asks, "Have you been down to the water? How's the river look after the rain?"

"Yeah, I have been down to the water's edge. You can tell from here that the water is muddy this morning. There doesn't appear to be too much large debris flowing downstream."

He makes a comment saying, "That's good, guess I'll take a look for myself."

I stand and walk down to the ferry with him. Once at the ferry shack, he opens the door and grabs his gloves and oil can. He looks across the river and notices the wagon that is staged at the ramp area.

He turns to me and says, "I sure hope Red decides to run the ferry today. Those folks will have another days wait on their hands if he doesn't think the river is safe."

"Will Red show up to check the river out or will he not even bother, thinking the roads are too muddy and want to wait one more day."

"We'll just have to see won't we? Regardless if he shows or not, I'm gonna get the ferry ready, build some steam up and be ready for what happens."

"Sounds good, I'll give you a hand."

I help out by hauling some wood and buckets of water for the boiler. Sam watches the gauges as the temperature and pressure slowly begin to rise. Sam must be aware that I am feeling anxious because he asks, "Jake, are you alright? You seem a little nervous this morning?"

Leaning on the railing and looking out over the river, I say, "I wouldn't call it being nervous, I'm just not looking forward to saying goodbye to Nate."

"Jake, living the life you have, this isn't the first time you've had to say goodbye to someone."

"I've never had to say goodbye like this before."

"What's that mean? You'll forget about us and this place before the next full moon. Besides, I thought you were going to go help the Meijer fella build his new barn? You'll just be up the road and you can come by and visit anytime."

Choking back my emotion I say, "Not this time Sam, I'm afraid everything has changed. I'm gonna head to Ash Fork to see my ma and then head south." My voice drifts off to a whisper as I say, "I can never come back here."

Sam says, " 'S'cuse me, I didn't quite catch that?"

I walk down to the other end of the ferry shaking my head and wiping my eyes. The folks at the south ramp give me a wave just as Sam releases some steam and gives the whistle a short blast. He stands up and says, "I'm headed to the house to wait for breakfast. Jake, you coming?"

"Yeah, I'll be up in a minute."

Looking to the sky, as I walk from the ferry to the house, there is still a heavy cloud cover. It looks like it could start to rain at any time, but I am hopeful that the heavy rain clouds have moved on up the river valley and into the mountains beyond.

I sit down on the top step waiting to be called to breakfast. Nate comes out and sits down next to me.

"Good morning Nate, how's your side?"

"I feel much better today. My ribs are still sore but I think I have gotten past the worst of it. I know one thing, I'm about to go stir crazy, I need to do some real work."

Judith calls us in to breakfast and we sit down to pancakes, eggs, syrup and of course fresh coffee. We reach out for each other's hands and Judith begins saying grace. She blesses the food and then asks a special blessing for me during my travels. Before we can get the Amen out Nate is looking up at me with disbelief written all over his face.

He blurts out, "Travels, what travels, where are you going and when? I thought you were going to stay the week and then go work on that barn for that man up the road?"

I look at Judith, then at Sam and say to Nate, "Things have changed. I really feel the need to go stay with my ma, in Ash Fork for awhile. The longer I stay here the more my feelings seem to be telling me that it is time that I go spend time with her and help take care of her."

Nate looks at me and says, "What about the carpenter job you were going to start?"

I take a sip of coffee and say, "Well, like I said, things change. I might be able to pick up some odd jobs in Ash Fork and take care of my ma too. There's always someone around that is in need of a carpenter. Speaking of that, Nate could you do me a favor? When the Meijer's come through here next time will you explain to them that I moved on to Ash Fork."

"Sure Jake, but aren't they counting on you?"

"I am sure they will get on just fine without me. Worst of it is, they'll think of me as another unreliable drifter. I don't like it, but I was just passing through the day I stopped here."

Nate seems accepting of this explanation. The questions have stopped as we continue to eat our fill of pancakes.

Breaking the silence, I ask. "How did yesterday go? Did

you see any bear or elk?"

Nate answers, "We didn't see any bear, but we did come across some tracks and other signs letting us know that there is bear in the area. The elk herd has moved up to the high country for the summer. We came across a large number of tracks, which means a decent size herd survived the winter. The fall hunt should be a good one." Then he says looking intently at me, "Maybe you can come hunting with us. Maybe, we'll get you close enough to a bear that you could finally shoot one with your bow and arrow."

I nod my head and say, "Yeah, maybe."

Judith begins to pick up the dishes and brings the pot of coffee back with her. I decline a refill. For as good as those pancakes tasted, my stomach is suddenly not cooperating this morning. I excuse myself and head to the outhouse.

Stepping out of the privy, I look up to see Nate sitting on the back porch with Rusty. They both jump up and start walking my way. Nate asks, "Do you feel ok?"

"Yeah, my stomach is just a little upset this morning."

"Me and Rusty are headed up to give Gus and Molly a brush down and then walk them up to the meadow."

"I'll go with you and give you a hand if you don't mind. I wonder if Red is coming, I haven't seen any sign of him yet."

"Maybe he just is running a little behind today. He'll most likely be here. I've seen the river worse than this morning and he still ran the ferry."

We give the horses a good brushing and make sure they have been fed some grain. Nate grabs a feed bag of oats for Bess. We then lead Gus and Molly up the road to the meadow.

Seeing us, Bess makes her way over to the gate quickly. The horses are all nickering back and forth to each other. Nate slips the feed bag over Bess's head and she munches away eagerly.

Nate releases Gus and Molly into the meadow. Shutting the gate he turns towards the house and barn, but I stop him saying, "Nate, can we stop before we head back down? I just want to visit a bit."

"Sure."

We walk away from the horses and I point up to the aspen grove and say, "Nate, if you ever need to find a place to be by yourself, up there amongst the aspens is a great place."

Nate looks at me and says, "Yeah, I've been up there a time or two. I appreciate you telling me about the aspens and what that professor told you."

"Have you ever walked above the aspens and seen that out cropping of rocks? There is a big boulder that faces out towards the south and the river. It's a great view if you climb out on it. It's a real peaceful place to sit and calm yourself down if you ever feel the need."

"I've been up there a couple of times when I was younger. I climbed around those rocks, but I wasn't much interested in the view. I was just climbing around, you know, just exploring."

"Yeah, I know what you mean...to be a kid again."

Due to the recent rain, the little seepage of ground water that normally runs from the aspen grove down through the meadow is now a small creek. We both comment on the fact that the water will continue to flow out of the hills for a day or two, maybe for as long as a week, giving the animals good water while it does.

There is some awkward silence between us and Nate says, "You about ready to head back?"

"No, not just yet, it'll put me closer to leaving."

Nate turns and says, "Jake, I don't understand. If you don't want to leave, then don't leave."

"It's not that easy. It is very complicated, there might be a day that comes along and then you'll understand, right now there is nothing I can say that will change things and the way they are. Before I go I want to leave you with two things, one is advice." I pause and then say, "Nate, just be a simple man, don't make your life complicated. Will you do that for me? Keep your life simple, follow the example that Sam has shown you. Don't become bitter over things that you had no control over. Keep God and His Peace in your heart. Will you do that for me Nate?"

"Sure Jake, I'll protect what we have here. This is about as simple as it gets."

With a sigh I say, "Yeah, this life is simple, you'll not find much better than this. The second thing is, I want to give you something, well actually two things, both have been with me a long time and helped me through most of my experiences."

I reach in my back pocket and pull out my harmonica. I tap it into my hand and give it to Nate.

He protests saying, "I don't know how to play this."

"I know, I didn't either, but maybe it will bring you some comfort if you ever find yourself wanting to let the song that is inside of you, out." I reach into my front pocket and roll "Lady Liberty" through my fingers. I tell Nate to hold out his hand, pressing the coin into his palm, I close his fingers over the top making a fist and say, "I came across this coin about seventeen years ago and it has been with me every day since. I thought I lost her a couple of times but always managed to hang on to her. It's a ten dollar gold piece. I call her "Lady Liberty" because of the lady's head and circle of stars that is depicted on the front of the coin. As long as you hang on to her and don't spend her, you'll never be broke. I might have been a wanderer, but I've never been a broke wanderer. I've never had to beg for nothing. I want you to have her; it's all I have to give you Nate. Keep your life simple, keep a song in your heart, and keep "Lady Liberty" in your pocket."

Nate looks at me saying, "I don't know what to say Jake. I, I..."

"There's no need to say anything."

Nate rolls the coin around in his hand and says, "It feels good," then gives the harmonica a quick blow and a run up and down the scale, "Sounds great, Thank you, Jake. I'll take real good care of these, promise."

We turn to head back to the house just as the ferry whistle blows. I lay my arm across Nate's shoulders and neck, saying, "We better get going, I can't miss my ride."

Lady Liberty

Chapter 39

By the time Nate and I make it down to the barn and I pick up my belongings, Red has blown the whistle a couple more times and has left the ramp area headed for the south side to ferry the waiting wagon across.

Sam is at the ferry shack as I walk up to him asking, "Will Red make another crossing if it is only me that needs to cross?"

"That'll be up to Red. We'll see when he gets back."

Turning towards the house I notice Judith sitting on the front porch. It looks like she has her knitting basket next to her. I decide I'd better go say goodbye just in case I can talk Red into taking me back across the river.

Walking across the front area, I look up and the sky has not made any effort to clear, it is still full of low clouds and they seem to be heavy with rain. Just as I get to the porch, I hear a wagon approaching from North River Road. It looks like Red will have to make one more crossing after all. How lucky can I get?

At the porch, I set my things down, remove my hat, and say, "Judith, looks like I'll be leaving as soon as Red gets that wagon loaded on to the ferry. I can't thank you enough for all you've done for me. I know we have said it before, but I just want to..."

She stops me there and says, "No need to say anymore Mr. Sparks. We appreciate you being here and all that you have done for us. Sam wanted me to give you this."

"What is it?"

She holds out an envelope and says, "A weeks pay and credit slip as agreed to."

I tell her, "But I didn't do a full weeks work, I can't accept it."

In turn she says, "Sam won't take no for an answer. He says you earned it and Jacob, you have done more for Nate than words can ever explain. I mean it. You have done a lot. We will be forever indebted to you."

I take the envelope from her and tip my hat saying, "Thank you, Judith. I am sorry, and grateful. There is just nothing left to say, but thank you."

She stands up and walks over to me, she opens her arms and says, "Come over here and give me a hug." As we embrace Judith says, "Jacob, I hope you live a peace filled life."

Just then, Nate comes out of the front door, saying, "Judith, look what..." stops and is surprised to see us hugging, he than says, "Excuse me." Judith and I separate and then Nate says, "Look what Jake gave me; his harmonica and this ten dollar gold piece."

Judith stifles a gasp and with raised eyebrows she says, "How nice, may I see the coin?" Nate gives it to her and she looks at me and says, "Jacob will you walk with me? Nate, go help Sam. See if that wagon is here to cross on the next ferry and tell Red that Mr. Sparks will be crossing as well, so please hold the ferry for him."

Nate answers, "I will, but I think Jake has time, the ferry hasn't even left the other side yet."

Judith says sharply, "Nathan, do as I say. Now go."

Judith motions for me to grab my things and follow her.

She is walking so briskly I don't stop to grab my things; I can hardly keep up with her as it is.

As we walk towards the river's edge and in the direction of the rapids, I am talking to her back side saying, "What is it Judith, what is wrong?"

Once she stops, the roar from the rapids makes it difficult to hear. With her hand open she turns to me yelling, "Where did this coin come from, tell me the truth Jacob."

I look at her in disbelief and say, "What do you mean? What does it matter where it came from? I wanted to give Nate something and thought a ten dollar gold piece would be perfect."

"Yeah, what seventeen year old kid wouldn't love to have a ten dollar gold piece? Isn't that the age you where when you got this one?"

I look at her and say, "How would you know?"

"My pa told me and the sheriff that you made off with three of his ten dollar gold pieces. If this is one of them then I will not have it become a part of my life as a reminder of his brutality. Did you tell Nate where it came from? Did you?"

"No," as my shoulders slump forward I say, "No, I didn't. Once again, I apologize, I didn't even think about the coin being one of your pa's."

She screams, "So, it is one of his! How could you bring this evil thing into my house?" Judith suddenly turns towards the water and tosses the coin as far as she can into the middle of the raging water.

I stand there looking out into the turbulence. Judith turns to me and says, "You have a ferry to catch, kindly be on it."

I am void of words and feelings. I know she was absolutely justified in what she has done. As Judith makes her way back to the house ahead of me, I stay back, not wanting to infringe on her feelings another moment. I wait for her to go inside the house before I walk over and pick up my belongings. I yell out as I turn to head down to the ferry, "My intentions were good, Judith, my intentions were good."

Making my way to the ferry, my attention is suddenly jolted by the realization that the wagon that is going to be loaded onto the ferry is the wagon that belongs to the Meijer's. Setting my things down next to the ferry shack, Sam asks, "What was all that about between Judith and you?"

"You'll have to ask her, Sam." I suddenly wish I had just gotten up and left in the middle of the night. It seems the longer I am here, the more trouble it is causing.

I excuse myself and walk over to Conrad and his family. He reaches out his hand and with a smile says, "Good to see you, Jacob. By the looks of that pack, it looks like you are going someplace?"

I shake his hand, tip my hat to his wife and say, "Yes, yes I am going someplace. I need to go to Ash Fork to check on my mother."

Conrad says, "That is good. We are headed into Ash Fork for supplies. Can we give you a ride?"

Without a second thought and say, "Yes, it would be greatly appreciated."

I walk back over to where I left Sam and tell him, "Judith gave me the envelope, thank you." Shaking his hand I say, "Thanks for everything, Sam."

He says the same thing back to me as Red begins to maneuver the ferry into the pylons and loading area.

Red and his crew have the unloading and loading process completed quickly, I lift my pack and bedroll up into the back of Conrad's buckboard and notice that Fritz is holding what looks like a six month old puppy. I say hello and ask what the pup's name is.

Fritz doesn't answer, but Abby speaks up saying, "Ringer. His name is Ringer." Then she asks, "Can you guess why his name is Ringer?"

I look at the pup and can see a white circle on the tip of his black tail, but I just shake my head and say, "No, why did you call him Ringer."

Fritz lifts the pup up and says, "He has a ring on his tail."

I look at both of them and say, "Yes he does. That is a good name."

As the first wagon is unloaded, Red starts barking orders to get the Meijer's wagon onboard. He says he is anxious to get the wagon on and off before the sky opens up; it looks like a downpour is coming. I walk over to where Nate and Rusty are. I tap my pant leg and Rusty walks over to me with his head down and his tail tucked between his legs. I kneel down on one knee and tell Rusty, "Thank you for being my friend and making me laugh. You're a good dog Rusty."

Standing I reach out and give Nate a big hug. He doesn't resist but he is not comfortable either. As we separate, he looks at me and says, "I get the feeling that you won't be coming back here, will you, Jake?"

"In all honesty, no, I won't be coming back this way. I am

going to stay in Ash Fork for awhile and then I'll probably head south were it is warm all year round."

"Can I visit you in Ash Fork?"

"Sure Nate, you can visit me anytime. You'll have to get directions to my ma's house from Mr. Cooper or Flora. She is the clerk that works there. I don't know ma's house number."

"Okay Jake, I'll check with Flora at Cooper's."

Before Red gives the order to cut the ferry loose, I grab Nate by the back of the head, pull his forehead to me and give him a kiss just above and between the eyes, asking God to keep him safe.

The ferry makes its way up against the current, the water is moving faster out in the middle and is full of larger size debris then it looked like from shore. I am leaning up against the railing and watching the north shore slowly drift away. Abby and Fritz are standing up in the back of the wagon. Fritz hands Ringer to Abby and then starts to climb down to stand on the deck of the ferry.

All of a sudden there is a flash of lighting that hits almost on top of us. Without warning there is an ear splitting boom of thunder. Even though the wheels have been chocked, the team of horses is spooked and rear up jolting the wagon wheels up and over the wedges that were used to brace the wheels.

Mrs. Meijer and Abby both scream and without warning, Abby is thrown out of the wagon and over the side of the ferry. She hits the water and is sucked under by the current. Mrs. Meijer is out of her mind with hysteria and Conrad grabs her trying to control her. Fritz has climbed back up into the back of the wagon and is safe.

Most of Red's crew are trying to settle the horses. I have only one choice; I climb the railing and dive in after Abby. My only hope is that she has come out of the current and is floating on top of the water. I come up and out of my dive, spinning in circles looking for her blonde head. I look back at the ferry and see Conrad pointing to my right towards the north bank. By swimming with the current and letting it take me in the same path as it took Abby, I am hopeful that I am gaining on her position. It is close to impossible to be in this water while dodging debris, sticks, and branches. They bounce off of me as I try to focus and swim in what I hope is Abby's direction.

I am able to catch a glimpse of the shore and see that the ferry landing is quickly approaching. The speed of the water should begin to slow before it picks back up as it makes its way to the entrance of the rapids. Looking towards the shore, I notice both Sam and Nate running along the river's edge and Sam has a rope in his hands. He is screaming and pointing just ahead of me. I lift my head out of the water as far as I can. Suddenly I see a flash of blonde hair against the foaming, muddy, brown water. I yell out Abby's name and swim as hard as I can; continuing to hold my head up and keeping my eyes on Abby's blonde hair. I have closed the gap between us and am within twenty feet from her, I scream out Abby's name again and she is able to turn towards me.

I raise my one arm and she screams out, "Help me, help me!"

I yell back, "I'm almost there. I'm coming, hang on!"

With all my strength I swim over to the left side of her. I think that I will have a better chance to grab her from the side than if I continue to chase her from behind. I only need a few more firm strokes and I am suddenly even with her. She has not taken her eyes off me since our eyes met. I am within a few feet of her and she flails her arms towards me. I kick with all the strength that I have in my legs and am finally able to grab her with a firm grip. She clings on to me with what little strength she has left. She begins to cry and begs me not to leave her. I promise that I will not let go of her.

She is clinging to me so tight that I can't move my arms in a swimming motion. I need to be able to keep swimming towards shore or we'll head into the raging rapids that are getting alarmingly close. I look to the shore and see that Sam and Nate have ran ahead of us, but at this rate I don't think I can get close enough to shore to be able to catch a rope. If I am going to make it to the shallow water before the rapids, I am going to need both my arms. I try to explain to Abby that I need her to slide around and lay on my back keeping her arms tight around my neck. It takes me a few seconds to convince her but once I start maneuvering her from my front to my back, she seems to understand and stops fighting. Once she is on my back there is only one problem left, I can't breathe because of the strangle hold her arms have around my neck. I reach up and put one of her hands on my chin leaving the other secured on my neck.

Sam is pointing to a boulder that is jutting out of the water. If I can stop and secure Abby there, Sam will be able to throw the rope to me. I start kicking in that direction. It is rapidly approaching, and we are moving so fast that I am not even sure I will be able to grab hold of the rock and stop us there. I keep kicking and this time I decide to position us directly in line with the boulder. With any luck, we'll run into the rock as opposed to trying to grab it on the way by.

Sam is on the shore. He has the rope swinging over his head ready to throw it at the first possible moment. We are lined up to squarely hit the boulder. I stop paddling and get my legs and feet out in front of me to brace for the collision that is inevitably about to take place. I tell Abby to hang on tight. I will not let her go no matter if we hit the rock or end up sliding by it. At the very last moment I cry out to our Lord to help me hold fast to this rock. As my feet and legs slam into the unwavering boulder, I feel my right leg snap just below the knee cap. I let out a loud moan. I manage to reach out with both arms and hug the jagged rock.

The water pressure is so extreme that the current is actually keeping me plastered against the face of the boulder. I yell to Abby, "I need you to climb off my back and sit on top of this boulder." She is too scared to even hear me, I know that my leg is broke and with the pressure from the fast moving water, I am frozen in place. I decide to try and pull us up to the top of the rock so Abby will be able to stay on my back.

I feel around the sides of the boulder and there are a couple of sharp edges that I can latch onto with my fingers. I am able to pull us from the current enough to get my waist and Abby's legs out of the water. With my left leg and foot I feel a little ledge that is just under the water line. I think I can use it for leverage and give myself a boost upwards. Before I do that,

I feel around the side of the boulder for another hand hold higher up. The right side has a sharp edge that goes up to the top of the rock. There is sharp edge on the left side but it stops short and will be of no use. I decide to push with my left foot and leg and pull with my right hand.

I tell Abby, "Hang on one more time, don't let go no matter what."

She says with a sobbing and shivering voice, "Okay, please don't leave me."

"I won't, just hang on. I'm going to count to three and then I am going to pull us on top of this rock. Ready? One, Two, Three...!" With all the strength I have left in my arms and one good leg, I push and pull and dig my fingers into the rocks solid granite face. We are suddenly lying on top of the boulder but the top is not big enough or flat enough for both us to sit or stand together.

I tell Abby to stay calm; I need a minute to gain my strength. I can hear Sam and Nate yelling to be ready to catch the rope. I turn my head towards them and wave my right hand in their direction. I look down at my right leg. Getting a glimpse at it for the first time, I can see bone sticking out of my pant leg. I need to reposition Abby and myself on the top of this rock, but I can't do anything while I am lying face down with her on my back. I explain to her that I need her to climb up off my back. If she does, there is enough room for her to sit on the top of the pointed rock. She shakes her head no and is too scared to respond in words.

I look over to Sam and Nate and they are ready to throw the rope. I motion with my hand to let Sam know I am ready.

He twirls the rope and lets it fly only to have it land about five feet short of the rock. He pulls the rope back in but this time he walks into the river up to his waist and lets the looped end fly towards the boulder. The looped end lands on the downstream side and floats away from us and the rock. On his third attempt he walks upstream a few yards and starts to twirl the rope over his head. He steps out into the river and lets the rope fly out over the fast moving water. The loop at the end of the rope is out farther than the boulder and the current carries the rope so it straddles the rock face.

I reach down the side of the rock with my left foot and am able to pinch the rope against the granite face. I start rolling the rope up the face of the rock with my boot until I can reach down with my left finger tips and grab the rope. Sam and Nate are screaming with relief that I finally have the rope in my hand.

I turn to look towards the shore and see Judith hugging Nate. Sam takes his end of the rope and ties it to his waist and starts motioning for me to do the same. I explain to Abby that I want her to take the rope and put it over her head and pull it tight around her chest up under her arms. She is too afraid to answer me so I keep talking to her and finally get her to calm down enough to understand what I am telling her to do. I make her repeat my instructions step by step and we count them off together. Before she realizes it, she has the rope tied around her just like I told her to do and is sitting on my back looking back up river towards the ferry landing. She is pointing and crying for her mother. Red has managed to get the ferry stopped and is returning it to the north landing.

Sam is yelling for me to grab a hold of Abby and he and Nate will pull us both into shore. I am shaking my head no. I want to get Abby safely on land. Sam keeps gesturing that he wants to start pulling on the rope. I tell Abby that I am going to lower her into the water and those two men on shore are going to pull her to safety. She keeps saying, "No, no, I don't want to go in the water. Please no."

I realize that Nate and Judith are screaming and pointing up river. They are trying to get Sam's and my attention. Nate runs to where Sam has been standing waist deep in the water and he turns Sam to make him look upriver.

Sam turns back towards me and yells, "Now Jake, now!" Pointing up river he yells at me, "Get off the rock, now!"

I lift my head and look over my right shoulder. I see what looks like the root ball of a tree coming in direct line with the boulder that Abby and I are perched on. Without hesitation I roll and buck Abby off my back and into the water. As her head bobs up above the foamy brown water, Sam is pulling her in towards shore. Nate and Judith are screaming at me to jump. I look up just as the tree stump, roots and all engulf me and the boulder.

I am knocked off the rock and have become entangled in the root system. I am underwater and do not know which way is up or down. The water is so turbulent I cannot make out any direction. My arms and legs are locked in tight with the root ball, making us one and the same. We are floating and crashing into rocks. With each crash at each rock, more and more branches of the root system break off. The root ball spins and rolls, allowing me to inhale a breath of air.

The roots and I are tossed violently as the current has pushed us into the heart of the rapids. The sound is ferociously loud and I begin to notice extreme pain coming from my left shoulder, stomach and left thigh. As the entire root ball turns, I find myself looking skyward and inhale the deepest breath possible while feeling large raindrops hit my face. The stump has spun so that the trunk of the tree is now facing downstream. I am now hopeful that the worst is over because I am able to see calmer water at the end of the violent rapids. The ball of roots slowly rotates to the left as the current begins pushing my entrapped body into the direct path of a massive boulder. There is nothing I can do but tense my body and fill my lungs with as much air as possible. With only a second before we crash, I hear myself say, "Lord, take me home with You this day." Darkness and quiet surround me.

start of rapids

Chapter 40

I awaken not knowing how long I've been out or where I am. I try to concentrate on my body, I don't know if I am numb or in extreme pain. The first thing I hear is, "Ma, Ma, Jake is awake, Hurry!" Nate reaches over and grabs my hand saying, "Jake, don't move, you're busted up something awful." Then he turns and yells again, "Ma, Jake's awake!"

Judith comes over to the bed and puts her hand on my forehead. She puts her finger to her mouth and softly says, "Be still, don't try and speak."

I move my eyes around the room and recognize that I am in the Harris's front room; I don't remember a bed being in this room. I make a whisper with my voice asking, "How's the girl, how's Abby?"

Nate says, "You saved her Jake. She's okay. You saved her life."

Judith tells Nate to shush; there will be plenty of time for that later. I try to lift my right hand, but it doesn't move. With all my concentration I try to move each of my legs and arms, nothing cooperates, I'm not even able to move my head from side to side. I look up at Judith and she simply puts her hand on my shoulder, and pats it up and down before turning away.

Fighting back her tears, she walks away and from the other room I hear her tell Nate, "Go get Sam. Be quick, tell him Jake is awake and tell him to hurry."

Nate runs out the front door. Judith comes back and sits in the chair that Nate was sitting in. She has a handkerchief in her hands and is squeezing it so tight that her knuckles are white.

I look up at her, with a whisper I ask, "How bad am I?"

She just looks at me through her tears and says, "Oh Jacob, it's not good. You are broken. Your body is broken."

"How long have I been out?" She tries to shush me but my eyes seem to say, "Please answer me."

"About twenty four hours."

"Where am I, whose bed is this?"

She shakes her head and says, "You are in the front room, in Nate's bed. We brought it down here so we could keep an eye on you." I start to ask about Nate and Judith answers, "We thought Nate would sleep in the barn, but he hasn't left your side. He and Rusty slept right here on the floor last night. It's okay."

It's not long after, that Sam walks into the room. He kneels down next to me getting as close to my head as he can and says, "That was the most heroic thing I've ever witnessed, Jacob. Thank you for saving that girl's life." He wipes his eyes and says, "Now you just lay here and be still. We sent for the doctor, but it's going to take another day for him to get here. You need to be still."

He starts to get up to leave but he sees something in my eyes that stops him. I manage to whisper again, "Sam, the truth, how bad am I?"

Sam tells Nate and Judith to leave us alone, Nate says no, Judith turns and leaves. Sam puts my right hand in his and says, "I'm no doctor, but as far as I can tell, you damn near broke every bone in your body. You lost a lot of blood because of that broken leg, but to be honest Jake, your stomach is so busted up inside, I don't know how you're still here. All we could do was keep putting towels and sheets on you to help soak up the blood and hope to keep it stopped."

I look at Nate, barely hearing my own voice I ask, "What happened after I hit that last rock?"

Sam starts and then stops, letting Nate explain. Nate says, "After the tree stump hit the boulder, it split into a million pieces. That freed you from it. You must have been out cold, cause, you didn't move. You floated face up almost clear down to the swimming hole till we could get to you and fish you out."

Sam stops him and says, "It was Nate that swam across the river and got to you, Jake. A couple of Red's boys got into one of the skiffs and floated down to where you and Nate were. With you being on the other side of the river and Nate still having those sore ribs, they put you in the skiff and brought you back across the river. The Meijer's came down with their buck board and we hauled you up here to the house. You've been out this whole time. Once we seen how bad you were, one of Red's men hightailed it to town hoping to get a doctor back out here."

I try to raise my right arm but can only squeeze my fingers making a fist which is still cradled in Sam hands. Sam tells me, "Relax, Jake. Try and get some more sleep." Standing he says, "I'll check on you later."

Before he lets my fist go I say, "Will someone get word to my ma. My ma needs to know I'm not coming to visit."

Sam helps me unfold my fingers and says, "Sure Jake, we'll get word to her, don't you worry. Get some rest."

As Sam walks out of the room, he tells Nate to follow him to where Judith is. I can't make out everything Sam says, but what I do hear lets me know that even if the doctor was here right now, it wouldn't really matter.

I hear Judith say, "Sam, I need to check Jake's bandages again. Nate, please stack up some firewood by the stove; it could be another long night."

Sam says, "I'll be down at the ferry if you need me."

Judith comes to my side and pulls the blanket off me. I look up at her and twitch my fingers for her to come close. She puts her face close to mine and I say, "Judith, I kept your promise. I didn't tell."

"I know, Jacob, I know."

Then I say, "He needs to know the truth, Judith. Promise me he will learn the truth. Promise me."

She pulls her head away and yells, "Nate, bring those bandages, be quick." Nate comes into the room, and he hands her a stack of white cloth strips and squares.

Nate looks at me and says, "He's bleeding again. How do we stop it, Ma? You got to stop it."

Judith says, "I can't Nate."

Nate tells her through his tears, "Then tell me how, I'll stop it. Just show me how. We got to stop it. We got to save him, Ma. Please!"

Judith puts some of the squares on my stomach and chest and pulls the blanket over my body. She says to Nate, "I'll get some fresh water, you stay here next to him, keep him warm and safe."

I blink a couple of times and get Nate to move in close to

me. With whatever breath I have left in me I whisper up to him, "Forgive us, we didn't know. I'm proud to have known, the watchman's son."

Epilogue

We buried Jake two days later. He never spoke another word, he never woke up. The doctor arrived just in time to make it official and pronounce Jake dead. I never left his side the entire time and was with him as his Spirit was lifted up. Word spread fast through the area and on the day we laid Jake's body to rest up above his beloved aspen grove, Mr. Winkler arrived with a cedar lined, pine casket that he had one of his men build. Red and his crew showed up, along with Lizzy and her family. Both Meijer families came and gave us the two year old grey that was to be payment for the work that Jake was supposed to do for them. Sam tried to refuse the gift, but Mr. Meijer was so overcome with grief and gratitude, that Sam finally relented.

I changed the horse's name to Ace, because of the shape of the white mark on his forehead. Jake was right, the grey was fast. We retired old Brutus once Sparky figured out he was a bull. He remained as gentle as could be, but we renamed him Spartacus once he became the best breeding bull in the county. Gus, Molly and Bess are still with us, but they are retired from their hard working days. Every so often, I hitch them up, let them pull the wagon around and let Gus skid a log or two just to let them know they still have purpose.

Sam and I made good on our promise to visit Jake's mother. On the next delivery to Mr. Kimble's, Sam went to town with me and we went to Cooper's Dry Goods and talked to Flora. She was shocked to hear about Jacob's death and did not hesitate to give us directions. She said she would check in on Mrs. Sparks every so often. She said that Mrs. Sparks had not been herself lately and she hoped this news would not cause her more harm.

We followed Flora's directions. Little did I know, the directions Flora had given us would lead us into the very neighborhood I had fled in my youth. I was able to resist the urge to run and remained focused on the promise I had made. Sam and I walked together to Mrs. Sparks' house. She wouldn't open the door at first, but we kept telling her we had a message from her son Jacob. She finally relented and opened the door. She did not invite us in. All we could do was explain to her what had led up to Jake's death. We told her he was a hero and saved a little girl's life. We thought she would be proud but all she would say was, "I knew he wasn't coming back. Men and their promises, there is no honor." We left but it wasn't until years later that I realized that I had met my grandma. Mrs. Sparks was institutionalized not to long after our visit. She died before I could visit her again.

Sam passed away five years after Jake. He went down to fire up the boiler on the ferry like he always had. When he didn't come up for breakfast, I went down to check on him. He was sitting slumped over on his stool. We think he died of a heart attack, but we don't know for sure. Once again, people came from all around the area to pay their respects. We placed Sam in a grave next to where he buried his ma and pa. At least Sam got to meet his grandsons before he passed. Lizzy and I were married the summer after Jake died and we had twin boys the next year after. We named them Sam and Jacob. Grandpa Sam was able to enjoy bouncing a couple of two year olds on his lap. They are the joy of their Grandma Judith's life.

We added a bedroom onto the house to match the growth of our family. Once Sam passed, Judith honored Jake's request and she was finally able to explain everything to me. I was never angry at her for all the lies and forcing Jake into silence, it just made me extremely sad; sad that we all lived with so much pain, so deep inside of us, that if the truth could have been shared sooner, we could have comforted each other and experienced the joy that comes with knowing the true meaning of unconditional Love.

Red gave up his half of the ferry for me to run, but that didn't last long. The State decided to build a bridge across a narrow section of the river just upstream from Fletcher's Crossing. I sold the ferry to the construction company that built the bridge and gave Red his half of the profits. The contractors used the ferry to shuttle equipment and material back and forth. Then they turned it into a pile driving barge to set the pylons that support the bridge.

I still cut cord wood and sell it, but most people come to Fletcher's Crossing and haul it themselves. I spend most my time cutting big timber and sell it to Mr. Winkler for his mill. I fall the trees and trim the limbs off and he comes in with large crews and they do all the skidding and loading just like before. I'll keep buying or leasing land and making a living off the trees.

It's been seven years since that spring day that Jacob Sparks walked down the road looking to cross the Rogue River on the ferry, instead he ended up stopping at our front porch. Occasionally, I go sit amongst the aspens and play his harmonica. I became good enough to bring down a bear with his bow and arrows.

For the brief time he shared with us, Jacob Sparks reshaped the way I look at life. I like to think that I have made him proud.

I am a Simple Man, I am the Watchman's Son and just like the Aspen Grove, our family is connected by our Roots.

The End

A note by the author

This book is inspired by many events that I have encountered throughout my life. The names of places are fictitious as are the locations. All the names of people used in this book are fictitious. I apologize if anyone that reads this book and feels that a name or a characterization of a person; refers to or resembles the reader. The reference is used strictly by accident.

I feel I would be remiss if I did not explain the title and motivation that prompted me to write this book. Singer songwriters, Mumford and Sons have a song "Babel". In that song there is a lyric that says, "I'll explain it all to the watchman's son." From the very moment I heard that lyric, I started formulating the concept for this book. It took me another two years to nurture the story. I would like to think that Mumford and Sons would not mind that a lyric from one of their songs gave me inspiration.

Throughout the writing process, I connected too many other songs by various other artists as well. As the book was written chapter by chapter a list of songs that seemed to enhance the visuals in my mind followed along. I compiled a list of those songs and reference them hoping that if listened to, they might help to explain some of the emotions surrounding the events that took place during the three weeks that Jake, Nate, Judith and Sam spent together.

The list is as follows:
- *Babel* by Mumford & Sons
- *I am a Man of Constant Sorrow* (as sung by Sawyer Fredricks)
- *Ghosts that We Knew* by Mumford & Sons
- *Roll Away Your Stone* by Mumford & Sons
- *Awake My Soul* by Mumford & Sons
- *Four & Twenty Years Ago* by Crosby Stills & Nash
- *Holland Road* by Mumford & Sons
- *Hero* by David Crosby
- *Simple Man* (As sung by Sawyer Fredricks)
- *Old Man* (As sung by Sawyer Fredricks)
- *I've Got a Name* by Jim Croce

Note: Words and Lyrics to the song, "I'll Stop the Roam" written by R.J. Stachofsky, July 26, 2010, while on a construction project in Tyler, TX.

About the author

I was born and raised in Spokane, Washington. I grew up in a house with five siblings and a father that worked on the railroad and a mother that was able to stay at home. Our house was surrounded by the Gonzaga University campus. At the time of my youth, the university campus was bounded by the Spokane River on its southern border. The Spokane River became my playground.

As the campus grew and the university expanded, the area that bordered the river changed and today is almost unrecognizable from the area that was the wonderful playground that provided me and a few of my friends countless hours of imaginary fun and games.

I made my living as a carpenter, first framing houses and then due to the economic downturn in the late seventies I gravitated to the commercial side of the industry. Eventually I settled in as a superintendent for various construction companies and ended my career as an Owners Representative for a national retail department store. The retail department store gave me the opportunity to travel and work in almost every state in the Union, including Alaska and Hawaii. I have had the unique experience to travel out of country working in Mexico City and working multiple times in the Middle East, specifically the United Arab Emirates and Saudi Arabia, where I constantly asked myself, in wonderment, "How did a carpenter from Spokane, Washington, end up working half way around the world?"

I presently reside in Phoenix, Arizona, with my wife of 34 years.